For Mary Lynn Vassar, whose encouragement kept me going even when things were impossible,

and for Diane Davis, Penny Richards, and Terri Herrington, who patiently bore with my beginner enthusiasm and taught me the craft of writing.

HeartStorm

ELIZABETH STUART

ST. MARTIN'S PRESS/NEW YORK

HEARTSTORM

Copyright © 1989 by Elizabeth Stuart.

ISBN: 0-312-91527-6   Can. ISBN: 0-312-91528-4

Printed in the United States of America

First St. Martin's Press mass market edition/May 1989

10 9 8 7 6 5 4 3 2 1

PROLOGUE

A crackling fire burned warmly behind the grate, its flickering fingers casting a crimson glow over the opulent richness of oak-paneled walls and furniture upholstered in costly velvet and brocade. A dozen tall candles burned brightly on the polished oak table, illuminating the tear-streaked countenance of a slight, trembling child, cowering against the silk skirts of a slender young woman at her back.

"But she's only a child, Robert," the woman pleaded. "She meant no harm." She half lifted an arm in supplication to the lean, impassive man standing stiffly erect a few feet across the floor.

"Eight is old enough to understand the meaning of my words!" the man snapped. "You've coddled the girl far too long, Mary. It's high time she learned to accept the consequences of her actions."

He gazed down in disgust at the squirming spaniel puppy he held firmly beneath one arm. "Anne was told not to bring this animal above stairs, yet she deliberately disobeyed me. Now the beast's ruined my best boots. Had she done as she was bid, this interview need never have taken place."

The child took one faltering step out from the protection of her mother's skirts, raising wide, tear-filled blue eyes to the man's dispassionate face. "Please, Father, Flurry didn't mean to ruin your boots. H . . . he didn't understand. I'll take him back to the stable now, and I p . . . promise not to bring him up again." Her lower lip trembled as her thin arms reached up beseechingly. "I'm s . . . sorry, Father. I promise it'll not happen again. Please let me take him down."

"I'm afraid your penitence isn't enough, Anne," he stated softly, a grim smile curling his thin lips. "You must learn I mean what I say. Your disobedience will cost the life of your pet. Perhaps that will teach you to respect my words."

With a strangled cry, the child launched herself across the floor, but the man neatly sidestepped her clumsy attack. She stumbled to the floor to lie in a sobbing heap, her inarticulate cries muffled against the luxurious pile of the carpet.

The small, furry dog wriggled impatiently in the man's tightening grip. It gave one frightened yelp and then was still. The shrill cry tore a shuddering gasp from the woman. Her eyes dilated in fear, heightening the haunted look on her too-pale face as she moved across the floor. Kneeling, she drew the child into her arms. "It's all right, darling," she whispered in a choked voice. "Everything will be all right."

The limp head of the lifeless puppy hung at an awkward tilt against the man's velvet-clad arm. He moved wordlessly toward the door. One powerful hand on the knob, he paused, turning to study the woman as she clutched the sobbing child protectively in her arms. "You know full well the cost of disobedience, Mary," he reminded her, a flicker of impatience in his cold, gray eyes. "You'd best see your daughter learns it as well. Oh, and Mary, be sure you keep her out of my way the remainder of this visit. I might decide the loss of her pet insufficient punishment for the girl."

The door closed with a resounding clap, and the room

was still save for the sound of the child's muffled sobbing. The woman gently stroked the child's golden curls back from her heaving shoulders, her own silent tears slipping down her cheek to mingle with those of her daughter in a bitter pool upon the floor.

CHAPTER ONE

*A*nne Randall clung wearily to the saddle, too tired even to be frightened as she gazed across the desolate expanse of Scottish moor in the yellowish light before the storm. She had been in the saddle more than eight hours already, and that long ride, coming on the heels of her storm-tossed voyage from London, was almost more than she could stand. At least the prospect of her future no longer filled her with dread, she thought darkly. Enduring the present was her only immediate concern.

Long strands of honey-gold hair snarled about the pale oval of her face in the biting April wind. She raised one gloved hand and shoved ineffectually at the mass, squinting in the dim light to see if her English escort showed any sign of halting for the night. Pray God they stopped soon. She doubted she could go on much longer.

Her narrowed gaze focused on Captain Kincaid's bearded face, and she studied the man her father had trusted to fetch her from Leith harbor to Ranleigh. Lord Randall had written that he hadn't the time to come himself. She smiled bitterly. Was time really the problem, or was it inclination? Was he as loath to see her as she was him?

As if in answer to her prayer, Captain Kincaid turned the party off the rocky trail into the dubious protection of a narrow tree-shadowed glen. Gnarled oaks and white-barked birches grew thick and tangled along the sides of the sheer granite cliffs, their gaunt branches twisting in wind-whipped torment, slapping at the riders as if to prevent their passage into the cleft. Anne's fingers tightened uneasily on the reins. In the early twilight, the gloomy valley was distinctly menacing.

The party came to a stop just as the first scattered, icy raindrops fell from the lowering heavens. Anne swung down from her lathered mare, shivering uncontrollably. All about her, bedraggled soldiers scurried about, some to picket the horses, others to gather dry wood for cooking fires. In a few minutes she would be warm, Anne promised herself. Just another few minutes . . .

Beside her, a fumbling soldier struggled in vain to light a fire in the gusty wind. She watched in numbed exhaustion, wishing he would hurry. The man glanced up, a curse of frustration dying half spoken on his lips as he froze to immobility beside the pile of sticks at his feet.

Following the direction of his gaze, Anne forgot her own misery. Some twenty mounted men ringed the camp, gleaming lances and pistols held threateningly. They had appeared from nowhere, men and horses seemingly sprung full-blown from the tangle of trees and dark granite around them. "Dear God!" she breathed, blinking in disbelief.

She turned, searching frantically for Kincaid. He had been standing by the horses when the men appeared. Now he grabbed for his sword, halting mid-reach as the point of a Highland lance caressed his chest.

"I'd do no so foolish a thing as to waste me life with a reckless gesture," a rough voice suggested from out of the gloaming.

A stocky figure swathed in a dingy Highland plaid nudged his mount from the circle of raiders. The lower half of the outlaw's face was obscured by a heavy beard, and a filthy cap sat low on his brow shadowing his eyes. "You be fair trapped—you and your lads here," he continued, "but there'll be no blood shed if you do as I say."

Kincaid's hand moved slowly away from his sword, his taut face a study in impotent rage.

"There's a good lad," the man said softly. "We'll be relieving you of your horseflesh, though God knows the nags don't look fit to steal. Mayhap we'll find better sport with the lass, there." He jerked his head toward Anne.

"Are you a fool, man?" Kincaid gasped. "Don't you know who we are?"

Ignoring Kincaid's protest, the man walked his horse deliberately toward Anne, while two savage-looking clansmen covered the English captain with their pistols.

Anne stared at the approaching man, her weary mind refusing to make sense of the situation. This whole scene was ridiculous. In a few minutes she would awaken from this nightmare back in her own warm bed in Lincolnshire. Just then a large and piercingly cold raindrop struck her face. God in Heaven, she was awake and this was real!

Ignoring the underbrush snarling about her ankles, she stumbled backward a few steps, an unyielding slab of granite finally blocking her flight. Wide-eyed with fear, she stared up at the stark figure on horseback. Silhouetted against the storm-heavy sky, he was a frightening apparition indeed.

Her lips moved dryly, but the words wouldn't form. No! This couldn't be happening. She had not survived so long only to be murdered in this godforsaken country!

"Come lass, would you see the lives of fifteen men shed for your stubbornness?" the outlaw asked boldly. Leaning toward her, he spoke in a voice barely above a whisper. "I promise you'll come to no harm with us, lass. You'll be safe as any bairn in its mother's arms."

Ignoring his words, Anne cast wildly about in the underbrush for a weapon. A stubby branch lay half concealed in the heather. Bending quickly, she caught it up and swung it at the man with all her strength.

He dodged the club effortlessly. "Nay, lass, that I'll not take." Catching her arms, he dragged her up across his saddle bow, and her struggle ended almost before it had begun. Holding her easily with one powerful arm, the man kicked his horse toward the murky depths of the trees. "Our compliments to Lord Robert of Glenkennon," he flung over his shoulder. "He'll be hearin' from us."

The Highlanders moved quickly, cutting the ropes corralling the horses and stampeding the animals out of the clearing into the dark, misty woodlands. Horses and riders melted into the forest as quickly as they had appeared, and the storm, which had held off all afternoon, suddenly broke with a raging fury.

There was no time for questions as the horses plunged through the dripping gloom of the forest, racing confidently over the rocky ground into the deepening night. Wet branches slapped at Anne's sides and tore her sensitive skin as the band made its way at a dangerous pace through the wild countryside.

Cold rain streamed in torrents down her face and trickled in an icy rivulet down her back beneath her sodden cloak. Fear clutched at her heart. It chilled her blood and cowed her spirits far more effectively than the penetrating rain.

She had ceased to struggle immediately after her abduction, recognizing at once that it would be useless against the armed might of her captors. Staring down at the gauntleted hands capably holding the reins before her, she shivered. Who were these raiders and what harm did they mean?

The rain settled to a steady drone and the wind finally dropped as the horses struggled to the summit of a rock-strewn hill. The men drew rein in the dubious shelter of a dense stand of shivering Scots pines, allowing their mounts the first breather in over an hour of hard travel. Without a word, Anne's captor shifted his arms about her. He drew her closer, tugging at her wet cloak.

At that provocation Anne struggled to life. She disliked

the feel of his doublet against her back, of his sinewy arms pressing tightly about her shoulders. Heart pounding, she choked back the scream that sprang to her lips. She'd not have him laugh at her fear.

"Hold, lass. I mean you no harm," the man said softly, his surprisingly courteous voice softened by the lilting burr of the North. "This plaid of mine'll turn some of the rain. Mayhap it'll keep you from perishing o' the damp."

Trying to fling herself from the saddle, she twisted in his arms. She had heard tales enough of these wild Highlanders!

"Hold, lass," the outlaw hissed again, crushing her against his chest. "I'll no' be drenched because you've no' the wit to keep still!"

His words finally penetrated her fear. Trembling, she forced herself to sit quietly while the man carefully wrapped his plaid about them both.

The shadowy figures of the raiders clustered silently about them in the falling rain. Anne stared at them, a feeling of utter helplessness sweeping over her. "W . . . what do you plan to do with me?" she asked, disgusted with the quavering of her own voice.

"There's no time to discuss the matter now, and I'm no' your man. Be assured you stand in no danger, though. My name is Donald, mistress, at your service."

A tiny spark of hope flamed to life in her breast. "Then take me back to my father's men. See me safe to Ranleigh and you'll be richly rewarded," she promised eagerly.

There was a slight pause, then the man chuckled softly. "That I canna' do, lass, though I'll try to please you in all else."

He nudged his horse forward through the dripping trees, his clansmen following slowly, saving their animals. With a sinking heart, Anne wondered at her fate. Despite his assurances, it must be none so pleasant.

The journey continued through the night with the men alternately walking and cantering their horses through the increasingly rough countryside. The rain stopped, and an occasional star peeked briefly through the thinning clouds. The men rode single file now, following a tortuous path that snaked among huge, scattered boulders and scrubby trees, climbing ever deeper into the brooding mountains.

Hours passed, and though Anne could not trust her voice, she longed to know if they intended to ride all night. Her head throbbed, and she felt permanently stuck to the hard leather of the saddle. Fortunately, the cold had numbed her so, she no longer felt the ache in her back and legs. She wanted to rest but was terrified of what might happen when they stopped.

"Here we be," Donald finally whispered. "Pluck up now, lass."

Anne straightened, straining her eyes to see into the darkness ahead. Where were they? She could see naught save the blackness of towering granite walls.

The trail suddenly twisted to the left, and they plunged unexpectedly into the midst of a large, armed camp. The horses surged forward into the clearing, which was little more than a narrow cleft in the mountain protected from the sides by rising cliffs. No fires could have been seen by pursuing English soldiers, even if they were hot on her trail, which she doubted.

Anne stared about bemusedly as the flickering light of the campfires threw weird, dancing shadows over the walls. Men and horses milled about the narrow glen in confusion, while outside the circle of firelight, a darker-than-night form moved in the shadows. Donald nudged his mount forward toward that hint of movement.

A large black horse stepped nervously into the light, half rearing at the sudden noise and bustle about the fire. Anne glanced at him in admiration, her attention sliding quickly past his powerful, flailing forelegs to the stiff figure on his back. The man curbed his mount easily, his harsh expression unchanging as he turned his stern gaze upon her.

The meeting of their eyes was like a physical jolt, Anne's own widening in awe as she caught her first good look at the man. He was dressed in midnight black, his heavy cloak swirling about him in the wind, making him appear, for a moment, like some winged apparition from hell. Renewed fear tensed the muscles of her fatigue-relaxed body. The devil himself had come to claim her! Would this nightmare never end?

Indicating she was to dismount, Donald swung her from the saddle, but even her own body now conspired to betray her. The cold, wet, fear and long hours in the saddle had taken an incredible toll, and to Anne's dismay, her numb legs buckled, sending her sprawling ignominiously in the mud at the Highlander's feet.

She sat limply where she'd fallen, in a muddy puddle left by the spring storm. Icy water soaked the velvet seat of her skirt, wetting her in the only place that had been reasonably dry. Shivering uncontrollably, she lifted her head, more cold, wet, and utterly miserable than she had ever before been in her entire life.

A restless moonbeam suddenly lit the drenched clearing, gleaming silver against the glittering blade at the Highlander's belt. He flung back his cloak, unconsciously revealing his powerful frame as, hands on hips, he grinned down at her in amusement. "Good evening, mistress. I'd ask you to sit down, but I can see you've already decided to make yourself comfortable."

At his humorous sally, a coarse guffaw of laughter rippled from the men, twisting Anne's humiliation even deeper. She stared at him in resentment. Light from the moon and the campfires played over his strongly sculpted features, touching the sharp angles of his face with burnished bronze. His cold blue eyes gazed haughtily out at her from beneath dark, mobile brows.

As she watched, his mouth curled up in a mocking grin, revealing the flash of even, white teeth. "And have you looked your fill, mistress?" he asked. "God's body, gentlemen! Should I not be flattered the daughter of an English earl finds a MacLean so intriguing?"

Furiously, Anne tore her eyes from his. Fear and shame struggled for supremacy in her breast as she realized she had been caught staring at the man in admiration. Her face burned, and she kept her eyes focused on the muddy forelegs of his mount. She'd not answer him. Hadn't her mother told her often enough it was a man's world? Silent endurance meant survival for a woman.

"What? Have you nothing to say?" he mocked. "Perhaps it's because we've not been properly introduced." He bent forward in a half bow. "Sir Francis MacLean, chief of Clan MacLean," he grinned, "and chief annoyance of Robert of Glenkennon, at your service, mistress."

So the Highlander was her father's enemy! Now at least she knew why she had been taken. Slowly she raised her eyes to his. The man was laughing at her.

Lashed by the knowledge of his contempt, a saving surge of anger washed through her. "I've no interest in knowing your name, sir!" she snapped. "My father will hang you soon enough."

The amused smile faded from MacLean's hard face. Eyes narrowing grimly, he rested one arm on his sword hilt and leaned insolently toward her. "You'd best remember where you are and to whom you speak, mistress," he warned softly. "If you wish to see me hang, you'll mind your tongue . . . else you'll not be around to enjoy the sight."

The sustaining anger seeped away. How ridiculous she must have appeared, sitting in a muddy puddle spitting like a bedraggled kitten. Highlanders were a cruel and ruthless lot if even half the tales she had heard were true. And doubtless her father would care little if she came to grief at their hands, despite her earlier boast.

Fear and misery surged in her and with them a powerful urge to weep. Her fate now rested solely in the hands of the arrogant outlaw glaring down at her. Sinking back dejectedly into the mud, she raised her chin a notch, fighting to hold the humiliating tears at bay.

"For Christ's sake, Francis, don't frighten the wits out of the poor lass," Donald said sharply. He slipped from his mount, slapping his numb hands together to restore their circulation.

No flicker of feeling crossed MacLean's impassive face. Anne stared at him, her own tenuous composure dangerously near the breaking point. "I'm not afraid of him," she put in quickly, dashing the wet hair out of her eyes.

MacLean threw back his head and laughed, the rich sound echoing back from the granite walls of the glen. "Well, I'm glad to hear it, mistress." His words broke the breathless tension among the gathered men. They chuckled and nudged one another in obvious relief.

Throwing one long leg over his saddle bow, MacLean slid from the back of his sidling stallion. He tossed his reins to a waiting clansman and strode to Anne's side.

Anne shrank back instinctively, the Highlander's towering frame alone enough to inspire her fear. Dear God, would she never learn to govern her tongue? He was going to strike her now for her insolence. She only hoped she would have the strength not to cry out.

MacLean gazed at her in silence. In the uncertain light, the harsh lines of his face seemed to soften somehow. "Let's get you to the fire," he said brusquely. Taking her arm in a bruising grip, he dragged her to her feet.

In spite of her determination to walk unaided, Anne was shaking so hard from exhaustion and cold she could scarcely stand. Before she realized his intentions, MacLean scooped her up in his arms and strode across the clearing toward the fire.

She tried to struggle but quickly realized the futility of the effort as his steel arms tightened their hold. She had thought Donald strong, but this man seemed carved of the same dark stone as these mountains.

Depositing her on a log beside the blazing fire, MacLean

gazed down at her, his cold blue eyes missing nothing. "Walter..." he snapped, jerking his head toward a young clansman standing nearby. The lad nodded, disappearing immediately into the shadows. "You're soaked through," MacLean said harshly. "Off with those wet things."

Anne stared up at him knowing a sudden fear so elemental and overpowering it made all that had gone before it seem like naught. She clutched the sodden folds of her cloak tightly about her, struggling desperately to steady her breathing. So now it would begin...

The tall Highlander read her thoughts easily. "Just your cloak and gloves, lass," he said more gently, turning at once as the young clansman returned with a length of red and green tartan.

Taking the cloth, MacLean dropped it over her shoulders. He smiled slightly as she jerked away, shamed by the weakness of her own shaking limbs and the paralyzing fear that must be so evident to her enemy.

"Don't be too hard on yourself," he said softly. "You've been in the saddle the better part of a day, and have held up well for a lass... far better than I expected." He studied her in silence, then flashed a mocking smile. "It's that good Scots blood in your veins. You're half MacDonnell, lass, and I've yet to see one that wasn't pluck to the backbone."

Anne glanced up at him in amazement. Few people knew her mother hailed from the MacDonnell clan. Before she could question him, MacLean reached into his doublet and drew out a metal flask. Removing the top, he held it out. "Drink," he commanded, "it'll warm you."

Anne shook her head. She would take nothing from this man. Did he think to make her drunk?

"I'll not have you die of the ague," he informed her. "Will you take it like a good lass, or shall I force it down your throat?" He bent his dark head so close she could see the flames reflected in the pupils of his eyes. "Believe me, I'm quite capable of doing so."

The intensity of his gaze stopped her breath. "I've no doubt," she snapped, holding out a hand for the flask. Her eyes meeting his defiantly, she lifted it to her lips for one small swallow. She'd not give him the satisfaction of humiliating her in such a manner.

The liquid fire took her completely by surprise. She coughed and gasped for air as the raw whiskey burned its way down her throat and into her stomach. She glared at MacLean from watering eyes. Had he poisoned her?

A look of unholy amusement danced in MacLean's eyes as if he took a perverse delight in her discomfiture. "Take a deep breath, lass," he commanded. Taking the flask from her unresisting hand, he raised it to his lips and took a long pull. He wiped his mouth on the back of his sleeve and tossed the flask to a nearby clansman. "Pass it about among the men as far as it'll go. It'll keep us warm till we've food to line our bellies." Without another look at Anne, he sauntered off into the night.

Anne's trembling soon ceased as the heat of the flames and the whiskey-fire within combined to warm her body and chase away the dampness. As the worst of the misery left her, a sharp hunger reminded her of the long hours of travel and the dearth of nourishment she had endured. The smell of roasting meat was agonizing, and by the time MacLean returned, she felt faint from lack of food.

MacLean bowed with an assumption of humility, holding out two pieces of meat spitted neatly and cooked to a turn. "I beg you share our humble fare, m'lady. I'm sure it's not the kind of dinner an earl's daughter is accustomed to, but for tonight I'm afraid it'll have to do."

Mouth watering, Anne gazed at the food longingly, wishing she had the strength of purpose to fling it at his feet in disdain. "I thank you, sir, but I've no taste for poached game."

MacLean ignored her insult. Sitting down on the log, he stretched out his long, booted legs beside her. She was uncomfortably aware of the breadth of his shoulders, of his muscular thighs only inches from hers. An uncontrollable shiver fluttered along her spine, and she wished she had never listened to a servant's tale of one hapless lass caught by a band of Northern raiders. Gathering her muddy skirts away from him, she swallowed hard, staring resolutely into the darkness in silence.

"Come lass, let's call a truce," he remarked. "You'd like to throw this in my face, I know, but it'd be a useless gesture. We both know you've little enough strength left. You'll never make the journey if you take no nourishment now."

His cold statement of fact demolished all her proud pretense. She glanced up. His eyes were sharp and hard, seeing more than she cared to reveal. He wordlessly offered her one of the sticks, sinking his teeth into his own share.

She hated to barter her pride for the mere prize of a meal, yet the aroma of cooked food made her sick with hunger. The man was right; she needed to eat. She'd had nothing substantial since leaving ship that morning, and she was certainly no match for him at that moment. She must eat, else she'd not find the strength for whatever was to come. Reaching for the offering, she carefully avoided any contact with the long, tapering fingers holding the stick.

The Highlander's eyes warmed slightly, but his lips preserved their sober lines. "There's more," he said, leaning back comfortably against a rock and licking the savory meat juices from the tips of his fingers. "You'll hurt Donald's vanity if you eat but one piece. He considers himself an expert in the cooking of venison."

Her pride soothed, Anne ate heartily beside the outlaw, sure she'd never eaten tastier fare. She even helped herself to another piece of meat, washing it down with wine shared from a common flask Donald carried. At last, glutted with wine and warmth, she nodded, fighting the uncontrollable desire to surrender herself to sleep.

A warm, contented languor began spreading through

her body. As if from a distance, she heard the voices of the men and the soothing crackle of the flames. At that moment she cared nothing for her eventual fate, if only she might have a few precious moments of sleep.

A strong hand shook her arm. Out of the oblivion, a deep, strangely familiar voice spoke. "Come, mistress, we must ride."

"Ride? But it's still night," Anne protested faintly.

MacLean chuckled. "The best time for Highlanders to ride."

Her eyes widened, and she was suddenly fully awake. The man must have been insane to expect her to get back on a horse!

Two new mounts were being led forward, a big chestnut gelding and a delicate bay mare with a mane and tail as dark as the Scottish night. The chestnut pawed the earth impatiently as MacLean swung up. He curbed the animal, waiting for Anne to mount.

She stared in dismay at the horse, every muscle and bone in her body screaming in protest at the idea of another moment in the saddle. Though her life might depend on it, she did not have the strength to pull herself onto the mare.

Sensing her predicament, MacLean caught her under the shoulder and swung her up before him. She struggled against the intimacy of his hands, but succeeded only in upsetting the restive horse.

"Hold still," MacLean warned, "else I'll tie your hands and feet and carry you across my saddle like a bag of oats."

Anne choked down the retort that sprang to her lips. She was not such a fool that she would tempt him to carry out his threat.

"Lancer isn't used to carrying off struggling damsels," he said lightly. He adjusted the reins, his hands riding casually along her waist.

The easy familiarity of his hands goaded her beyond her fear. "Don't tell me you've not kidnapped a lady before," she snapped. "You're much too practiced for me to believe it."

"Never yet a reluctant one.'"

The man was impossible, Anne decided. She'd not let him provoke her into further speech.

A moment later Donald appeared, riding a tall, leggy gray. He took the reins of Anne's mount tightly in one hand. At that, the three horses struck out once again into the chill, star-frosted night.

The damp smell of peat mingled with the fresh scent of rain-washed heather as they rode silently through the sleeping countryside. MacLean wrapped his plaid around them both, and despite all concentration to the contrary, Anne's body slumped from time to time against his broad chest. The easy rocking gait of the chestnut soothed her and the strong arms around her were warm and secure. She had no idea where they were and even less of their destination, but those concerns seemed trivial as her body surrendered to sleep.

CHAPTER TWO

$\mathcal{A}$nne struggled slowly from the unconscious realm of sleep. Aware at first only of a general aching in every part of her body, she gradually became mindful of the hard dampness of earth against her back. Groaning, she attempted to uncurl her cramped limbs.

Across the clearing, Donald tended a tiny fire and stirred something in a small iron pot. He looked up from his work and sent her a sympathetic grin.

She sat up slowly, carefully, trying to make a movement so small it wouldn't bring pain. "I never knew I'd so many muscles that could ache," she murmured. "And to think —I used to enjoy riding a horse!"

Donald poured something from the pot and moved toward her, carrying a mug of the steaming liquid. "You'd a rough day yesterday, lass, and an even worse night, thanks to us." He gave her a heartening smile. "The world'll look ever so much brighter with a spot of somethin' to warm ye."

She stared at him suspiciously a moment, then accepted the mug of hot spiced wine, gratefully cupping her hands around its radiating warmth. Taking one delicious sip, she lifted her eyes to his. In the bright light of morning there was nothing threatening about the man. His beard was scraggly and unkempt, to be sure, but his gray eyes glowed with an honest, friendly light, and the smile on his face was fatherly. Her fears lulled, she smiled back at him. "Thank you," she said simply.

He nodded, returning to his breakfast preparations.

Sipping the hearty brew, Anne watched the morning mist drift in swirling trails over the dewy grass of the small glen. The sun sifted through the haze, its rays offering little warmth, but giving promise of a beautiful day to come.

It seemed the whole world had been washed clean by the storm of the night before. The song of a linnet came to her from a short distance away, and a strange contentment filled her soul. At that moment she felt more at peace with herself and the world than she had since the death of her mother six months earlier.

That six months had been a season of such loneliness and hell as she hoped never to experience again in the course of her lifetime. Mary Randall had been her life and her joy—her mother and her dearest friend in one. Her death was a staggering blow, a tragedy Anne was only beginning to accept a few weeks later when Philippa, her dear old nurse, was struck down with the same fever that had taken Anne's mother. Still reeling from the shock of that first bereavement, Anne had watched helplessly while the life slowly slipped from Philippa's shriveled form.

She'd had no one to comfort her then, no one to care. She'd lost her last friend in a large and uncaring world, and life, at eighteen, seemed too great a burden to bear.

Her father hadn't been with her during that time. He'd not even come when her mother lay dying, though she'd sent him word at the first sign. The King's business in the North kept him too busy for personal affairs—or so his letter said.

But Robert Randall, earl of Glenkennon, representative of King James's government in Scotland, was an extremely busy man and had never made any pretense of caring for her mother or her. Still, he could have come, Anne thought darkly, clenching her fists in well-remembered anger. For once, he could have come!

Unbidden, her father's stark image swam before her: dark auburn hair, thin-pressed, scornful lips and eyes as dark and cold as winter rain on the stormy North Sea. She remembered his eyes readily enough though she'd not seen him in more than three years. She recalled the disconcerting way he could look through her and the icy edge to his soft, melodious voice . . . and the way her mother's laughter had always ended whenever Lord Robert was home.

Anne shook her head slightly to dispel her father's disturbing image, ignoring the despair twisting her insides at the thought of living under his hand. He had sent for her and she'd had no choice but to come. Now that her mother and Philippa lay cradled in the damp earth, there was no place else to go, and she knew she might as well stop haunting herself with hateful memories. She had no choice but to make the best of her life in this new land with a father and brother she scarcely knew. That was, if she ever reached Ranleigh!

A sudden sound brought Anne back to the present with a start. She turned. Donald was regarding her thoughtfully.

"I asked if you were feeling better, lass, but by yer troubled look, I can guess my answer."

Anne stretched carefully and put down her empty mug. "I'm feeling much better now, thank you. At least my insides are warm." She gazed around her curiously. "I must have been tired last night. I don't remember making camp."

"That's because you were sound asleep," he said with a chuckle. "Francis tucked you in with his own plaid . . . without even waking you."

She frowned, her pride pricked that she should have slept so trustingly in the outlaw's arms. She pushed back the warm wrap with ill-concealed disgust.

As if conjured out of the mist by the sound of his name, the tall Highlander appeared, striding boldly up the trail toward them. His thick black hair tumbled in disarray across his tanned forehead, curling damply about the base of his neck. Though he still wore the dark leather breeks of the night before, a fresh shirt clung damply to the broad expanse of his shoulders. Its sleeves were pushed back to reveal his muscular arms and the shapely, aristocratic hands Anne had noticed the night before.

Anne's eyes traveled slowly over him. She had forgotten how straight he stood, how arrogantly he held himself. Reluctantly she met his eyes—eyes an unusually deep shade of blue that gleamed in vivid contrast to the dark bronze of his skin. She took a deep breath; this powerful stranger was her father's sworn enemy.

MacLean appraised her briefly before moving to take the steaming mug Donald held out. "There's nothing like a cold bath in a mountain burn to wake a man and get the blood stirrin'," he remarked. "And how's Mistress Randall this morning?" He gazed at her critically. "You look a wee bit the worse for wear, lass, if you'll pardon my saying so."

Beneath his gaze, Anne was suddenly aware how disheveled she must have appeared. She rubbed ineffectually at a patch of dried mud on the back of her hand, knowing it ought not matter how she looked. "Make sport of me as you will, sir," she said stiffly, "but keep your criticisms for those who might value them."

MacLean's lips twitched into a grin. He turned to Donald. "Haven't you something for the girl?"

"Aye, that I do," Donald replied, giving her a conspiratorial wink. He moved away to fetch a mysterious bundle wrapped in a length of old plaid.

Removing the tartan, Anne gazed in amazement at the collection of clothing she had packed days earlier: her brush and combs, her blue moreen riding habit, even the undergarments she had carefully slipped into the bundle.

"There's a stream just down the hill where you might wash off a bit of the mud. The water's cold, but bearable," MacLean said innocently. "I'd be happy to offer my services to keep a lookout for marauders. We can't be too careful of your safety with so many lawless men about."

So that was his game. "Thank you, but I'm comfortable as I am," Anne stated coldly. "I don't care to trust myself to any lawless men we might encounter."

"Give over teasing the child, Francis," Donald said in exasperation. "You've given her the devil's own time since last night."

MacLean grinned, a warm glow in his eyes as his gaze traveled over her. "The thought of acting maid to you is tempting, lass, but I'll play the gentleman this morning. If you give your word as a MacDonnell you'll not try to escape, I'll give mine as a MacLean I'll keep my back turned till you call."

"My name is Randall," she reminded him, "and your word means nothing to me. From what I've seen of the MacLeans, I doubt they've honor enough—"

"I suggest you hold your tongue, mistress," MacLean warned softly. "And I further suggest you take me at my word. I'm an ill man to provoke."

Anne bit back the retort that rose to her lips. "Why can't Donald go with me?" she countered, glancing toward the older man.

"Because Donald has a soft spot in his heart for every lass with blue eyes. And I'd not have you wheedle your way around him and get the poor man into mischief." MacLean handed his empty mug to Donald, then turned back to her, one eyebrow raised impatiently. "Either you come with me now, or we ride. Which will it be, lass?"

Anne studied the tall MacLean chief. He was obviously accustomed to having the upper hand. She thought with longing of the stream and her desire to wash finally overcame her fear of him. Had he meant her personal violence, he'd certainly had the opportunity before now to complete it. She stood up with decision and moved off down the hill before she could change her mind.

Accommodating his long-legged stride to hers, MacLean

walked beside her in silence until they reached the stream. There he matter-of-factly pointed out where she might kneel beside the stream to wash and where the water was deep enough to bathe.

"I'll be there behind those trees when you're done," he finished. "Call if anything frightens you."

She stared uncomfortably at the ground, unconsciously twisting the folds of her ruined habit. Now that the time had come, she could not imagine disrobing with him not twenty feet away—yet she dared not protest again.

Sensing her unease, MacLean took pity on the girl. Reaching out a strong, brown hand, he lifted her chin, his touch so gentle it was almost a caress.

Blue eyes bored into blue as the two carefully studied each other. There was no trace of mockery or amusement in MacLean's face, just an expression of understanding Anne found unusual in a man.

"Imagine yourself in the privacy of your own chamber in England, lass," he said gently. "I promise no rude Scotsman will invade your bath." His fingers lingered on her cheek for the space of a heartbeat, then he was gone, striding away across the dew-drenched grass to disappear into a nearby grove of young birches.

She stood hesitantly for a moment watching him disappear, then turned her attention to the water. Kneeling in the bracken at the water's edge, she gazed in dismay at the vision reflected in the still waters. Her unruly hair tumbled down her back in a cascade of tangles and caked mud, and her velvet habit was torn and heavily stained. Even her face was spattered with grime.

No wonder he isn't tempted to join me, she told herself wryly. What man would be? She drew a deep breath, then resolutely began unfastening her habit, wondering as she did what MacLean's opinion of her was. It'd be a misfortune to take his fancy, she reminded herself firmly, chiding herself for the wayward bent of her thoughts.

Anne purposefully slipped out of the habit and petticoat, then removed her boots and warm, worsted stockings before she could think better of the whole idea. She glanced nervously over her shoulder toward the trees. She could see no sign of MacLean, but that meant nothing. Pushing one inquisitive foot into the pool, she gasped at the coldness and removed the offended member from the icy water with a jerk. Quickly revising her idea of stepping into the pool, she cast about for another way to bathe.

Keeping her back turned squarely in MacLean's direction, she slipped out of her shift and dipped it in the water, then used it to wash her body. Working quickly lest she freeze before she was done—or the Highlander lose patience—she scrubbed ruthlessly until her pale skin tingled and gleamed a rosy pink. Hastily donning the clean shift from her bundle, she turned her attention to the mess of her hair.

With a deep breath, she thrust her face and hair into the icy water, determined at all costs to wash her unkempt mane. She worked furiously to remove the mud and tangles before her fingers grew numb with the cold.

Her ablutions finished, Anne squeezed the excess water from her hair and sat up, drawing the fresh habit over her head and tugging it into place. Hands trembling, she struggled with the tiny buttons, but two in the very center of her back eluded all her efforts to manage them. Why in heaven's name had she packed the thing? She had always had trouble closing it without Philippa, and with stiff fingers, it was impossible.

Finally giving up, Anne stepped into the sunshine. She nervously held the edges of the habit together behind her as she called to MacLean. He strolled out from the stand of trees, his knowing eyes taking in the situation at a glance.

"I'm afraid I can't . . . ," she began, but she broke off in consternation.

"If you'll allow me, mistress." MacLean calmly caught

her arm, turning her around. "I've done this often enough for my, ah . . . sister."

Anne was overwhelmingly aware of his hands at her back, of the warm feel of his fingers through the thin cloth of her shift. When the job was done, she drew away, glancing up warily to see if he meant mischief.

"How is it the daughter of the earl of Glenkennon travels without a maid? Not that I'm complaining at the duty, mind you," MacLean said lightly.

"The woman who tended me from childhood died within three weeks of my mother." Anne forced the words out calmly enough, though the bleak look in her eyes gave the lie to her even tone. "The new girl took fright at London harbor . . ."

She faltered, remembering the awesomeness of the ocean and the storm-churned swells shaking the ship the day of her departure. "I didn't blame her. There was a storm brewing, and I'd have refused myself had it been possible."

MacLean's narrowed eyes gently probed her own, reading there the terror of a young girl alone on her first sea voyage. "I'm sorry, lass," he said softly. "Was there no time to find you another companion?"

She shook her head. "My father left orders for the day we were to sail."

His lips tightened grimly and the understanding warmth in his eyes chilled. "And Glenkennon's used to being obeyed, I know. Well, he'll have a long wait to see his orders carried out this time." Taking her arm, he turned toward camp. "You're shaking with cold. Let's get you back to the fire."

At sight of the two returning, Donald began ladling up a thick gruel. "How did you manage to prepare breakfast out here?" Anne asked, sniffing the delicious aroma and settling herself before the warmth of the fire.

"Never ask Donald how he does a thing—just enjoy it," MacLean stated with an appreciative smile directed toward the other man. "Whether it's for food, spirits, or a clean shirt, Donald's never at a loss." He shrugged his broad shoulders. "I gave up years ago trying to figure out his secrets, but I suspect he's in league with the faeries."

Anne reached for her cup, suddenly feeling amazingly lighthearted. "Are you magical, Donald? That would provide a group of English soldiers I know with a convenient excuse when they try to explain last night's happenings to my father."

"Nay, mistress," he explained with a grin, "there's no magic. But 'tis easier to face the ups and downs o' life with a full belly and a clean shirt, and I do my best to keep m'lord here in both."

Anne gazed covertly at the powerful figure of Sir Francis MacLean as he breakfasted. His hard manner was unexpectedly gentled that morning, and the slow smile that warmed his face tamed Anne's fear.

She looked him over curiously. In spite of their rugged surroundings, the man was immaculate. His carefully stitched shirt of fine linen and well-cut leather breeks bespoke a fastidious attention to dress without a showiness out of place in this wilderness. A narrow band of lace edging the cuff of his shirt and a black onyx ring set with a single diamond were the only adornments he wore. His dress and aristocratic bearing sat poorly with her idea of him as an outlaw, yet he seemed nothing like the foppish gentlemen she was used to seeing in England.

If Anne was puzzled about Sir Francis, the man was certainly in a quandary over her. He had expected beauty— Mary MacDonnell had reputedly been one of the greatest beauties to come out of the clans—but he'd been ill-prepared for the reality of her daughter.

The girl sat now before the fire, absently running her comb through the long silken curtain of her drying hair. The gleaming mass tumbled halfway down her back in a cascade of burnished gold touched with shimmering coppery highlights. Her eyes, wideset and heavily fringed with remarkably fine, dark lashes, were the color of a midsummer sky, their expression so luminous and deep a man might forget himself in their depths.

Her wide, full-lipped mouth curled up now in an engaging grin at some quip of Donald's. It was a mouth made for kissing, MacLean noted with a suddenly quickened heartbeat. His eyes slid lower, to the slender white column of her throat, which rose from her demure blue habit to support a gently squared, determined chin. He smiled, recalling the stubborn defiance of that chin as she had sat in the mud the night before.

Without thinking, he caught a silken strand of her hair, staring bemusedly as it slipped between his callused fingers. The girl was too lovely for his own comfort. He wondered if Glenkennon knew what a valuable tool she had become.

At the gentle brush of his hand against her hair, the nerves along the back of Anne's neck tingled, and a strange warmth rippled from his fingers down her neck to her toes. She glanced up in surprise, abruptly forgetting what she had been about to say.

Coming to himself with a start, MacLean dropped the silken strands as if they were burning coals. "If you've dawdled long enough now, we must ride," he snapped.

Anne glanced toward Donald, unsure how she had angered MacLean, but Donald was frowning in puzzlement at his chief. MacLean doused the fire and turned impatiently to the saddling of the horses, leaving Donald to gather the few cooking implements and cover all signs of the camp.

Anne watched the two men nervously, once again frightened and confused. The laughter and easy companionship of a few moments earlier might never have been.

"We've no lady's saddle, lass," Donald apologized, leading her to her mount, "but if you'll tuck yer skirts beneath yer knees here, proper decorum may still be maintained."

"Proper decorum is the least of my worries," she whispered, moving stiffly to accept his assist into the saddle.

"What I need most is a bolster between myself and this brute."

"The soreness will ease after a short while in the saddle. In an hour you'll not even remember it," he said hopefully.

She nodded, then shot a quick glance at MacLean. What had she done to provoke his swift anger, and why, in heaven's name, should she care? He was her father's enemy, and thus her own. His earlier gentleness must have been merely a passing fancy.

MacLean preserved an unyielding silence as they swung out across the grassy moor. He was reminding himself grimly of his many grievances against the wily Robert of Glenkennon. Gazing out over the sun-drenched beauty of the day, he hardened his heart. He'd not be swayed from his purpose by a pair of engaging blue eyes, no matter how lovely they were.

CHAPTER THREE

Anne shifted her weight onto one hip and tried to stretch her aching back as inconspicuously as possible. She glanced resentfully at MacLean. He had pushed the little group at a punishing pace all morning, carefully scanning the distance for any indication of trouble. He had remained grimly silent, his hard face shuttered and remote. No trace remained of the understanding companion Anne had glimpsed earlier. In his present mood she could easily imagine him engaged in any treachery against her father and King James.

With renewed fear, she realized that every mile put her that much further from the hope of rescue, and her spirits, which had been markedly improved by clean clothes and a hot breakfast, plunged to her boots once again. After all, she reasoned, no matter how kind Donald was, he would leave her to her fate if MacLean commanded it.

They paused for a hasty meal in the cover of a small stand of greening trees. The place was well chosen, for the open country around would give sufficient notice of any stirrings of man or beast. Whether by witchcraft or some more orthodox means, Donald produced a hare from his saddlebag, claiming to have snared it beside the stream in the early hours before dawn. In a few moments, he had it neatly spitted and roasting over a tiny, smokeless fire.

While Donald struggled with preparation of the meal, MacLean stared morosely over their back trail, one foot propped on a decaying log. Fidgeting with a broken twig, Anne studied the intimidating expanse of his stiff back, attempting to screw up her courage to approach him. It was now the better part of a day since she had been abducted, yet she still had no clue about her future. During these last hours, she had imagined every hideous fate, and she was determined to have the matter out before they went another step.

She moved to stand a few paces behind MacLean. "My lord. I would speak with you now."

He turned, eyebrows raised in surprise at the interruption.

Taking a deep breath, she lifted her chin and returned his haughty stare. "You've kidnapped me at great peril to yourself and your men, and have now dragged me over a goodly portion of Scotland. I would know to what purpose."

"Have you never wondered at your value to your father?" he asked after a moment of thoughtful silence.

"If you think to harm my father through me, you've been badly misled," she said bluntly. "He's not cared enough to see me in over three years."

"I speak not of affairs of the heart, for Robert of Glenkennon doesn't have one," MacLean scoffed. "I'm talking of value in cold, hard gold. Glenkennon needs an alliance with one of the wealthy Scots clans, for both the increased military strength, and the gold he'd get for offering such a prize. And it's my guess you'll more than answer the need," he added, his knowing gaze appraising her. "I can name a dozen or more lords who'd pay handsomely to have a lass like you warm their beds." His eyes narrowed. "Not to mention their future political advantage in a blood bond with Glenkennon."

Anne's face flushed hotly, and she glanced away, unable to meet the cold contempt in his eyes. She had always known she must marry to please her father but had never thought of it in such bald terms. "And why should that interest you?" she asked, struggling to steady her voice.

"Because that makes you valuable to the earl. He'll pay anything I ask to have you returned safely."

"So you plan to make him buy me back?" She bit her lip, her anger rising as her sense of helplessness and ill-usage grew. "Didn't you take a foolish chance for a few bags of gold... or is that why you sent Donald to do the work while you stayed safely in camp? Were you afraid, m'lord?" she mocked.

She was sure he would have struck her had she been standing closer. The blazing fury in his eyes made her stumble back a step.

"I've no fear of the English, if that's what you mean," he snarled, "and I've nothing but contempt for Glenkennon and his kind. The earl prefers to gain his ends by guile and treachery in the dark of night rather than by honest strength and wit... and Kincaid's nothing but his lackey, and a blundering ass to boot! We were never in any danger. Even you should have realized that!"

Hands on hips, he gazed at her, an arrogant smile curling his lips. "Did you know we followed you from the moment you left ship yesterday morning, just waiting for the best moment to strike? Donald led the raid because we didn't wish the fools to know our identity. He even grew that beard these last weeks on the chance one of them might recognize him as my man.

"You were an easy plum to pluck, and one that will be quite useful. Your capture was no more trouble than that," he added with a snap of his fingers in the air before her.

Anne struggled to keep her temper. He had slandered her father and her countrymen and indicated she was naught but a pawn to be bought and sold for gold. The arrogance of the man! He thought—no, he knew—she could do nothing!

Then a tiny dart of fear tempered her rage. Her father would blame her if MacLean made a fool of him. . . .

MacLean turned abruptly, dismissing her with less concern than he would give a servant. She glared at his back, silently vowing to overset his plans. It would take him down a notch to be outwitted by a woman. And perhaps —just perhaps—her father would be pleased with her for once.

Lunch was a silent and uncomfortable meal with the angry words of the two hanging like a pall over the group. Anne took the food Donald handed her without comment, forcing herself to chew and swallow the gamy meat. After all, she reminded herself, if she could escape, this just might be the last meal she would have for some time.

At the end of the meal Donald doused the fire and covered all signs of the makeshift camp. He led her toward her mount, smiling at her encouragingly. "Francis is in one of his black moods, lass. They seldom last for long, so pay him no mind."

Anne remained silent; in fact, she barely heard the man. Her mind was busy devising and rejecting wild plans of escape. She knew she must take the men by surprise, and even then chances were slim that she could successfully evade recapture. She had no food or water or even the remotest idea where she was, but she vowed she would rather starve in the wilderness than proceed meekly along with MacLean's plans. Surely if she made her way south, she would come across search parties sooner or later. But first, she had to find a way to escape MacLean.

Her chance came shortly after they had traversed a narrow mountain pass that knifed through the rugged barrier of rock rising about them. Donald leaned forward over his mount's right shoulder to study the rocky trail. "My nag's favorin' his right foreleg," he shouted to MacLean. "I think we'd best be takin' a look."

Without so much as a glance in Anne's direction, Mac-

Lean dismounted. The two men knelt in the dirt, absorbed in their inspection of the animal's hoof.

Anne watched them carefully. Neither one paid her any mind as she eased her mount a few steps past them on the trail. Now was the time.

In a flash, she was away. She bent low over the mare's neck, urging her on, and the animal responded with a burst of speed that hurtled them down the narrow trail and onto a short expanse of open moor.

Glancing triumphantly over her shoulder, Anne could just make out the look of astonishment on the faces of the two men. Their surprise bought her a few seconds of valuable time, but it wasn't much. Seconds later, MacLean threw himself into the saddle, and the chase was on.

In spite of her early lead, Anne quickly realized MacLean's big gelding was gaining on her. She lashed the mare with her reins. "Come on, sweetheart, run!" she begged. The animal answered with another surge of speed.

The narrow expanse of heather-covered moor ended abruptly with a steep, rocky slope twisting down to a shallow burn. Anne drew rein and the Highland-bred mare frantically shortened her stride. She plunged down the slope, scrambling and sliding, but miraculously remaining on all four feet.

Breathing heavily, Anne clung desperately to the saddle as the mare took the stream in a flying leap and was away again across the next hillside. Anne whispered a prayer of thanks that she was still in one piece, then settled herself more deeply in the saddle.

Chancing a quick glance over her shoulder, she noted that MacLean had dropped back slightly. He had taken the slope at a more sensible pace than she, but she knew her lead was only temporary. The big chestnut would quickly gain ground on the open hillside where he could stretch his muscles. Her only hope lay in entering rougher terrain where the agility of the nimble mare might lend her some advantage over the speed of MacLean's stronger mount.

She turned the mare up the rock-strewn hillside and onto the rough plateau above, dodging boulders and stubby bushes at a frenzied pace. She knew it was folly traveling in unknown country at such breakneck speed. Just one false step could throw her to her death—but she urged the animal on.

Ahead, a craggy hillside surged up from the barren plain like a scraggly giant, cutting off Anne's route of escape. Behind it, gaunt mountain peaks rose darkly against the sky, marching one after the other into the distance as far as the eye could see. It was a moment of decision. Right or left? She cut to the right, praying her choice was correct.

Without warning, the plain ended. A narrow expanse of uneven, rocky ground sloped steeply on one side to a deep, narrow gorge. On the other side, the sheer granite face of the mountain frowned down at her disapprovingly. Slowing the laboring mare, Anne searched frantically for a way out of the glen. A low cry of frustration escaped her. She was trapped!

In desperation, she kicked the mare across MacLean's path toward the narrow edge of the ravine. Above the labored breathing of the mare, she heard his shout of warning. She ignored it, hoping her mount had the speed to beat the chestnut to the gorge.

The mare was game, but after the morning of hard travel, she could not summon the strength necessary to outdistance the gelding. MacLean pulled alongside her, his face stiff with rage. God in heaven, what would he do to her now?

The Highlander snatched the reins from her hands and swung the horses in a long, slow arch, gradually bringing them to a halt. Anne clung to the saddle, sick with dread. Surely he wouldn't kill her...

As the lathered animals stumbled to a standstill, MacLean slid from his mount. Her jerked her from the saddle with a snarl of rage. "Fool! What in God's name were you trying to do?" His powerful hands crushed her shoulders in a painful grip, and he shook her until she thought her bones would be ripped from their sockets.

She instinctively struck at him, kicking hard with one foot while she shoved against his chest. Caught off guard, MacLean stumbled back in surprise, losing his footing on an unsteady rock and dragging her down with him.

He took the brunt of the fall against his shoulder, holding her carefully away from the rocks. They hit the ground, rolling together down the incline to the grassy expanse below.

A seasoned fighter, MacLean kept his grip on the girl as they tumbled to a halt in the cool, spring grass. He pinned her down with his weight, holding her easily, despite her struggles. Ignoring her useless attempts to free herself, he captured both her wrists in one powerful hand and stared down at her.

The girl lay beneath him, her golden hair spread like a halo around her pale face, her moist lips parted as she panted for breath. Her breasts rose and fell rapidly against him with her shallow breathing, while her terrified eyes gazed up into his own.

His grip on her tightened slowly. He could feel the frightened thud of her heart against his chest—or was it his own that beat so furiously at the feel of her beneath him? He was intimately aware of the soft ripeness of her body, of the velvet smoothness of her skin against his callused palm. His anger slowly faded, a much more powerful emotion taking its place.

In the distance the wind moaned brokenly over the rocks and a nesting grouse cried for its mate. Lost in the fathomless blue of the eyes now raised to his, MacLean heard nothing. With his free hand, he stroked a tangled strand of loose hair back from Anne's face, feeling the pulse in her wrist leap frantically beneath the fingers of his hand. A hint of awareness flickered in her eyes, and she went painfully still beneath him.

Seconds ticked past. He swallowed heavily, ignoring the

unexpected urgings of his body. God's blood, he didn't need this!

Rolling to one side, he dragged her roughly to her feet. "Did you think to kill yourself and my horse as well by that stupid trick? You're lucky you're not broken to pieces riding like that in this country!"

Anne stared at him silently, her chest heaving with fear. He might kill her now with not even Donald to say him nay.

"And just what did you think to gain by that foolish flight?" MacLean continued more gently. "You can't possibly know where you are, lass, or even in which direction to run."

The black rage was gone from his face. Her heart steadied to a more regular beat and she glared up at him, purposely recalling his arrogance back on the trail. "I thought to give you a bit more trouble than that," she said, snapping her fingers beneath his nose.

He stared at her uncomprehendingly at first, then the corners of his lips quirked upward and his eyes began to dance. "So you set out to prove you're no' so easy. I meant naught against you; 'tis Kincaid who's the fool." His eyes teased her as his fingers tightened on her wrist, drawing her toward him. "I doubt any man would have an easy time of it with you, lass."

She looked at him in renewed alarm, the memory of his body pressing hers into the grass still unsettlingly vivid. "You're . . . you're hurting my arm," she stammered, dragging back.

MacLean noted the flash of fear in her eyes. His grip loosened immediately, but he maintained his hold on her. "Let's see to the horses," he said, suddenly matter of fact. "And God help you if you've injured my favorite mare."

She followed him back up to the crest of the slope where the horses stood quietly cropping grass. While Anne held the reins, MacLean ran gentle fingers over the legs and sides of the mare, carefully searching for any sign of injury. After a time he seemed satisfied.

"I ought to beat you for the risk you took," he said, looking up at her candidly, "but since no harm's done, I'll let you off easily this time. If Cassie can forgive you for running her into the ground, I suppose I can too."

He turned and squinted up at the sun. "At least you've succeeded in causing me trouble, lass. These horses are spent. We'll never reach Camereigh tonight. Let's see if we can find our way around that damned ravine and get back to Donald. The poor man will think I've strangled you by now."

He placed a reassuring hand on the sweaty withers of the big chestnut and glanced at Anne over his shoulder. "Come here, lass. Lancer's best able to carry your weight now."

For a moment she didn't move. She had no wish to go near MacLean again.

At her hesitation, MacLean raised one challenging brow. "I said, come here."

His soft command sent a shiver down her spine. She stepped uncertainly up beside him, catching her breath as he reached for her. His powerful hands closed about her waist, lifting her easily onto the chestnut's back. She gave a sigh of relief when he moved away.

MacLean led the animals along the rim of the ravine until they could edge down the rocky slope to a narrow valley below. They skirted the swift-rushing burn, moving slowly over a ragged hillside until a lone rider on a gray horse appeared. At sight of the two of them, Donald broke into an easy canter, reaching them in a flurry of hooves.

"The gray's obviously not lame," MacLean stated in greeting as his friend drew to a halt beside them. "That, at least, is good news."

"Nay, there was but a wee stone wedged in his hoof. I removed it in a trice," Donald remarked, his eyes moving anxiously from the face of his chief to the pale, silent one of the girl.

"Well, no harm done here," MacLean said, "though our

guest wanted to take wing and fly over a deep gorge a ways back. Thank God I was able to cut her off, or we'd be trying to explain to Glenkennon how his daughter got a broken neck while in our tender care."

"Are you afraid my father won't pay for damaged goods?" Anne asked contemptuously. "Don't worry. You'll get your gold."

Donald looked at her strangely, but MacLean only grinned.

They walked the horses until the animals were cool, finally allowing them to drink from the icy mountain burn. Though she tried to ignore MacLean's movements, Anne was acutely aware of the frequent, sidelong glances he gave her. Was he remembering those unsettling moments between them? The thought made her heart beat wildly.

Keeping her eyes downcast and her mouth firmly closed, she belatedly reminded herself that she had best control her unruly tongue. Sick with disappointment at her failure to escape, she was yet aware that she had fared far better than she might have done. She had best not risk MacLean's rage again—especially since the last episode had ended in so disconcerting a manner!

The party continued traveling at an easy pace through the afternoon, finally making camp at dusk in the corner of a sheltered glen. As the chill of evening crept forward with the dying of the day, Donald shared the last of his wine and a few dried meat strips with Anne.

Huddled in MacLean's warm plaid, Anne gazed abstractedly into the fire, wondering if her father and brother knew yet of her kidnapping. The thought of her brother, Charles, brought a sharp ache to her chest.

She remembered him best as the mischievous child she had often rescued from the consequences of childish pranks. Unfortunately, he had been taken to live with their father at the promising age of nine, and she had seen very little of the boy in the last eight years. He had been cold and remote during their visits, far more like her father

than the happy child Anne had known. Now she wondered if she would ever see him again.

She closed her eyes tightly against the threatening sting of tears. Her defiance had been short lived. She was now cold, hungry, and frightened at thought of her helplessness in MacLean's hands.

The distant cry of a hunting wolf sounded from somewhere out in the darkness, and a log collapsed on the blaze, almost smothering the tiny flame. She groped for nearby twigs, feeding them to the greedy fire in an effort to keep her one solace alive.

A slight sound caught her attention. Turning, she found MacLean standing beside her. Damn the man; he was quiet as a cat! Before she could move, he dropped to one knee, catching her wrists and quickly trussing them with a narrow piece of cord.

"Since I can't trust you not to run, I've decided to take precautions tonight," he explained, giving the rope one final tug to make sure it was secure.

She stared at him speechlessly, unable to believe what he had done. Rage washed over her, drowning out her fear. "I hate you!" she hissed, unable to think of anything more scathing to say.

MacLean's expression did not change. "As you please, lass," he said, tying the loose end of the rope around his left wrist. He stretched himself out unconcernedly on the ground not three feet from her. Pulling his cloak around his body for warmth, he closed his eyes. "Wake me if you get cold," he said softly. "Now good night."

She could hear the smothered laughter in his voice. Tears welled in her eyes, and she almost choked on a strangled sob. Huddling miserably before the dying fire, she gazed at his disgusting form in the waning light, wishing she were anywhere in the world besides this desolate Scottish hillside at the end of a short rope held by Sir Francis MacLean.

* * *

Anne was awakened by gentle hands untying the cutting rope from about her wrists. She blinked sleepily as MacLean chafed her numb hands, quickly restoring the circulation to her tingling fingers. Her muscles ached from the cramped position in which she had slept, but MacLean dragged her to her feet, obviously impatient to be off.

While Donald held their mounts, MacLean gave her a boost into the saddle. "We should make Camereigh by midmorning if we push," he stated with a quick look at the spreading dawn.

As he walked across the clearing to collect his plaid, Anne turned to Donald. "What's Camereigh?" she asked, covering a wide yawn.

"Camereigh Castle is the stronghold of the Clan Mac-Lean," he explained simply. "We're almost home now, lass."

She shivered in the chill dawn, longing to snuggle back under the woolen tartan. Though she spoke no complaint, MacLean noticed the movement. He silently untied the cloak from behind his saddle and moved to spread it over her shoulders, tying it firmly beneath her chin.

She longed to throw it off, but its warmth was too welcome. She contented herself with coldly ignoring him.

MacLean gazed quizzically at her. "Do I have your word you'll behave yourself today? If not, I can't allow you the freedom of your mount."

Fully awake now, she glared at him, her pride still rankling from his treatment the night before. "I give you my word on nothing save to cause you as much trouble as I can."

He accepted her challenge, eyes gleaming. "Fair enough, lass. If it's open warfare you want, I feel safe enough predicting the winner."

Swinging into the saddle in one easy movement, he caught the reins of Anne's mount in his left hand. "If you don't mind, I'll lead Cassie today. I consider my horses too valuable to risk foolishly again."

She dug her nails into her palms, wishing it were the Highlander's bare skin instead. Oh, how she hated the man and his mocking smile! For the first time in her life she longed to commit murder.

Since she could do little about her predicament Anne retreated into cold indifference, riding hour after hour without a word to her companions. She doubted now that MacLean would harm her. Hadn't he admitted he needed her in one piece for a ransom? But what a joke it would be on them all if her father refused to pay for her safe return.

The thought was not so far-fetched that she could completely dismiss it. What would become of her if MacLean had no reason to keep her safe? She recalled the hungry way he had reached for her the day before. Closing her eyes, she tried desperately to think of something else.

Before noon the travelers had left the trackless moors and were riding through more hospitable country. Here and there Anne noticed a smudge of gray peat smoke rising lazily against the horizon from the stone huts of numerous crofters. The men and their families frequently ran out to wave and shout words of greeting to their chief, and MacLean would draw rein, calling the people by name, spending a moment with each one as though he had all the time in the world.

The land here was not so barren and rocky as much of the terrain over which they had ridden the past day and a half. Rich grass of a deep, spring green carpeted the wide straths, a delightful profusion of bluebells and forget-me-nots ornamenting the rolling hillsides. The shadowy woodlands teemed with the song of birds, and once, a pair of red deer were startled from a glade in sudden, graceful alarm.

As the group rode on, a cool breeze lifted the curls about Anne's face, teasing her nose with the tang of the sea. Sensing their stable, the horses leaned into their bits, eagerly threading a thin stand of birch.

As Cassie broke through the last of the trees, Anne

caught her first glimpse of Camereigh. Across a wind-stroked carpet of green, its high stone walls rose steeply upward as if climbing to the sun. On the fretted battlements above, the colorful pennants of Scotland and the Clan MacLean rippled gaily in the wind. Two formidable towers guarded the gates, and within the forbidding walls the massive buildings rose in an impressive jumble of dark stone. Riding slowly toward the fortress, Anne wondered if she herself soon would be swallowed up forever within those walls.

They passed through the great arched gateway to the glad shouts of dozens of clansmen, the enormous din stretching Anne's taut nerves almost to the breaking point. She slid stiffly from her mount and was hurried from the courtyard through a sturdy oak door into the cool dimness of a stone-flagged corridor. Great oak beams arched above her head like the bars in a prison, and armed clansmen swarmed from every doorway. There would be no second chance of an escape.

From the corridor, MacLean, Donald, and Anne moved past the door of the great hall up a broad stone staircase. Anne followed Donald silently up the worn stairs, one hand on the heavily carved railing to support herself. She could sense MacLean following closely at her heels, and her breathing quickened in apprehension. Now she knew how a trapped hare felt with the hounds snarling at its back.

They entered a comfortably appointed room where a small fire burned cheerily in a massive stone fireplace, the dancing flames chasing away the remaining chill of the morning. She had a brief impression of the soft gold of Turkish carpets and of richly colored tapestries along the wall before noticing a man lounging at his ease in a sturdy chair beside the fire.

MacLean stopped short, his face breaking into a broad smile. "Ian, you dog! What do you mean invading my house in my absence?" He held out a welcoming hand in obvious delight. The seated man rose, catching MacLean's hand in the strong clasp of friendship.

The intruder was a handsome man, somewhere near his fortieth year, Anne surmised, with the weather-lined face of one who spent his days in the out-of-doors. Tiny smile lines etched themselves around his hard mouth, and his blue eyes twinkled merrily as he surveyed the three newcomers. "Since you were expected last night, 'tis I who's feeling abused, wandering around this infernal barracks without a host," he complained. "Did you have problems with the raid?"

"I'd a bit of trouble convincing our guest here she was expected at Castle Camereigh," MacLean explained lightly. "She had other ideas, it seemed."

The two turned their attention to Anne, the stranger, Ian, walking slowly around her as though inspecting a horse at a fair. She felt an all-too-familiar fear tensing the muscles in her stomach, though she kept her head high and her eyes trained coldly on the crackling fire.

The man completed his survey, obviously pleased at what he saw. "She doesn't look enough to give a braw lad like yourself much trouble," he commented. "Perhaps you're losing your touch, Francis."

MacLean grinned. "Well, I was tempted once to wring her neck back on the trail," he admitted. "But if a Highlander can think of nothing more interesting to do with a troublesome wench than strangle her, he'd best retire to the fire with the old women." His warm gaze slid over Anne suggestively.

She looked quickly away in confusion, struggling to keep her poise in spite of her recollection of those strange moments between them on the moor.

The stranger chuckled as though reading the unspoken conflict readily. "I can see I'm come in good time to protect you, lass." Taking her cold hand, he bowed over it almost reverently. "Allow me to present myself, Anne. My name is Ian MacDonnell. Your mother, Mary, was my sister."

CHAPTER FOUR

$\mathcal{A}$nne stared at the man in stunned surprise, robbed of the power of speech by his unexpected words. Silently, she studied his lean form, from the top of his gray-streaked, russet hair to the stirrup-worn leather of his boots. Ian MacDonnell—she could not believe it!

MacDonnell released her hand, leaning back against the oak lintel with an appearance of nonchalance. Only the intensity of his regard and a slight twitch in the muscle along his tanned cheek betrayed his anxiety as he waited for her to speak.

"I'm . . . I'm pleased to meet you . . . sir," she stammered, still struggling to calm the swirl of unreasoning emotion that engulfed her at the sound of his name. "My mother seldom mentioned Scotland or any family here . . . but she spoke of you with the greatest affection. It was her dearest hope you and I might meet."

The sudden image of her mother's loneliness those last weeks rose to choke off her words. Tears flooded her eyes, but she blinked them back determinedly. "Did you know she died six months ago?" she asked accusingly. "We were alone when it happened. No one came."

"I know, Anne, though I didn't hear of it till near two months ago," MacDonnell replied, his blue eyes narrowing as at some internal pain. "I'd have come if I'd known.

Believe me, lass, I'd give all I own to have seen her one last time." He cleared his throat roughly and looked away, but not before Anne noted the suspicious brilliance of his eyes.

Why, she wanted to ask, why hadn't he come? It would have taken so little. Even an occasional letter would have meant so much. Questions crowded her mind. She longed to ask them, but it wasn't the time. "Mother spoke of you...at...at the last," she said, stumbling. "I think she'd be pleased by our meeting now."

At her words, MacDonnell swiveled back. "Aye, lass, she'd be pleased." He measured her with his eyes. "You've much the look of her, you know. I'd have known you for her daughter anywhere, though I'm afraid I'd have been looking for a wee lass about so high," he admitted, with a hand raised to his waist. "Let's see...you must be a good eighteen or nineteen summers by now."

"Nineteen come July," she replied. "I'm afraid I'm grown quite old."

"Old enough to give Francis a run for his money, I'll be bound," Ian said, with a quick wink. "That's the MacDonnell in you, lass! A hearty set down once in a while is good for the lad, lest he think too much of himself...especially where the lassies are concerned."

Sir Francis MacLean! She had forgotten him in the excitement of meeting her uncle. She turned toward the window where MacLean and Donald had withdrawn. "Oh, really? I can't imagine he should have cause for conceit, especially in that respect."

Ian MacDonnell cackled in delight, and MacLean's eyes gleamed appreciatively as he recognized the rebuke. He swept her a practiced bow, as gracefully correct as if he addressed the royal court. "Now that I have you here safe, mistress, I shall endeavor to show you the hospitality of my house. My MacLeans and I shall see if we can't make you recant your slur upon our honor."

Feeling a great deal braver in the presence of her uncle,

Anne smiled sweetly. "Oh?" She raised an arched brow in polite disbelief. "I didn't know you had any honor to protect."

MacLean rolled his eyes at Ian. "Gad, but she's a sharp-tongued shrew, Ian. I fear those years in proximity to Glenkennon may have made her unreclaimable. You'd not believe the trouble she gave me on the trail."

"Sir Francis is an old friend of mine, Anne," Ian explained with a grin. "Don't provoke him beyond his temper lest I be forced to call him out in your defense. I'd hate to come up against his sword arm now, though I fenced with him often when he was naught but a clumsy lad."

Reminded of the bond between her uncle and her abductor, Anne turned to her uncle. "You're a friend to this man?" Somehow she couldn't blend the shining image she had held of him all these years with this new picture as friend to a rebel chief.

"Aye, lass, I admit I am." Ian looked sharply toward MacLean. "Though what he's done to make you believe he's such a devil, I suppose I'd best be asking."

"Nothing that can't be easily explained once the lady is rested," MacLean put in quickly. "We've a room prepared for you, mistress, and Donald will find you fresh clothing." He nodded toward Donald, and the man obligingly opened the door.

There was little Anne could do; she had obviously been dismissed. She started to protest, but the idea of fresh clothing and some privacy sounded too good. Following Donald to the door, she paused, looking back uncertainly at her uncle. "You'll not be leaving yet? I will see you again?"

His face split into a wide, reassuring smile. "Aye, you'll see me again, Anne; I plan to stay a while. We've years of catching up to do."

MacLean watched the gentle sway of Anne's skirts as she disappeared through the open doorway, unexpectedly recalling the stirring feel of her slender thighs pressed against him. She was a lovely piece, he thought with a grin. A lass like that could lead a man quite a dance.

"Just what in God's name are your plans, lad?" Ian asked, interrupting his pleasant musing. "You're playing with fire to annoy so powerful an enemy as Glenkennon, may God rot his soul."

MacLean's face hardened and all trace of good humor vanished. "Glenkennon needs the girl, not only for the gold she can bring, but for the alliance he can contract with Campbell or Howard should she marry one of those devils. He might feel those concerns more pressing than toying with my kinsmen."

"I see the bent of your thoughts, Francis. A fair exchange that: the girl for MacGregor, Cameron, and the two lads with them. It's the only way we'll spring them from that hellhole in Edinburgh." Ian paused, staring into the dancing flames reflectively. "I hate to see the child given back to that bastard though. Damn, but the sight of her brings back memories! I'd not expected her to be so like Mary."

Francis's eyes narrowed, and the ghost of a smile flickered in their depths. "Aye, she's an engaging lass when she's not trying to stir my temper. She deserves better than what Glenkennon has planned." He shoved a hand through his hair. "Nothing's decided yet, Ian. We'll play this hand as the cards fall."

Upstairs, Anne stared in amazement at the most luxurious bedchamber she had ever seen. Even the rooms at the court of King James couldn't be more richly appointed than this, she thought wildly. Silk tapestries covered the rough stone walls and a carpet of a warm rose color lay upon the floor. The color was repeated in the satin and lace coverlet thrown over the massive tester bed and in the velvet curtains gathered back from the windows with cream-colored satin cords—and everywhere the MacLean crest was vividly embroidered in rich gold thread.

Off to one side of the room, a large brass tub stood behind a woven screen with linen towels laid out in readiness for a bath. Wordlessly Anne looked about, her regard finally resting on the carved stone fireplace where a small fire crackled behind the grate. The bright flames added a welcoming warmth to the elegant room.

"Francis's mother loved beautiful things," Donald said unexpectedly. "It's mostly her taste you'll see in the bedchambers of Camereigh." He shook his head, remembering. "She was a fine one, the last Lady MacLean."

"And what of the present lady of the house?"

"There isn't one."

"Oh . . ." Anne stared at the bed, her finger carefully tracing the MacLean crest embroidered on the cool satin. Her heart lurched unexpectedly and began to pound uncomfortably in her chest. "And where is your chief's chamber, Donald?"

"Down the hall some three or four doors and to the right," he answered in surprise. "Why d'ye ask?"

She moved away from the bed uneasily, refusing to meet his gaze. She could think of no proper way to ask the question that disturbed her. "I see there's no inside bolt . . ."

"You've no need to fear Francis—that's no' his way," Donald answered in immediate understanding. "I won't say the lad doesna have an eye for the lassies, but he'll no' go where he's no' asked—he doesna have to," he added, gray eyes twinkling beneath scraggly brows. "We're more like to bar the gates of Camereigh against too many husband-seeking females for his protection."

He turned and made for the door, his long stride taking him quickly across the floor. "Make yourself easy now, lass. It's food you're needin' to dispel these wild fancies. I'll be back with a good meal. Then we'll see if you're no' feelin' more the thing."

The door closed behind him, and Anne gazed about her luxurious prison with a sigh. In spite of Donald's assurances, she remained unconvinced. The clansman had not seen the look in MacLean's eyes on that lonely moor.

True to his word, Donald returned shortly with a steaming bowl of savory stew and a loaf of freshly baked bread. Balancing a decanter of claret precariously on the tray, he made his way carefully to the polished oak table at one end of the room. Pouring them both a glass of wine, he set one down on the table beside the stew and drew up a velvet cushioned chair for Anne.

The succulent aroma of the food drew her attention immediately. She could barely remember her last meal. There had been no breakfast that morning and little food the night before. Her fear and weariness forgotten, she fell ravenously on the meal.

The stew was delicious, and Anne ate as fast as she could chew and swallow the hot meal. Belatedly recalling Donald's presence, she glanced up to find him regarding her curiously. At his expression, she almost choked on the large chunk of meat she had plopped into her mouth. "Forgive my manners," she mumbled in embarrassment. "I'm afraid I was hungry. Have you eaten yet?"

"Aye, lass, I caught a bite in the kitchen just now." Donald smiled in a preoccupied manner and moved to stand beside the narrow window. Leaning against the wall, he stared out thoughtfully, his half-empty glass forgotten in his hand.

"Did . . . did you have something to discuss with me?"

He turned toward her, scratching his beard in indecision. "Aye, lass, that I do, though I don't know Francis'd wish it."

Her curiosity fully aroused, Anne leaned back, waiting for him to continue.

"I'll not have you thinkin' so ill of the Laird," Donald finally said with a dark scowl. "He doesna traffic in kidnapping and intrigues of this nature. Nor does he plan to ransom you back to your father in spite of his angry words earlier. As you can see, we're in no' so great a need here." He threw out an arm, encompassing the richness of the room.

Anne held her tongue, biting back the words that sprang to her lips. Her pride still suffered from MacLean's treatment the last two days. If Donald had not been so kind, she would have told him what she thought of his precious chief.

"The truth of the matter's this, if you be wantin' to know," Donald growled. "A fortnight ago Francis's brother-in-law, Jamie Cameron, got a message from Glenkennon. It stated records had appeared casting doubt on grants made to the Cameron family near a hundred years ago. Glenkennon insisted Jamie come to Edinburgh to clear the matter up, claiming he wanted no clan warfare over boundary lines.

"Jamie went, the trusting fool, taking his two sons of ten and fourteen years, and a friend, Sir Allan MacGregor, who was visiting at the time. They'd no inkling then of the treachery your father planned."

Donald studied his hands silently for a few moments, then went on. "They'd scarce crossed the border of Cameron lands when Glenkennon's lackeys jumped them. Six of the villains were slain, but Jamie's party was finally overcome by the greater number of English troops.

"Five Cameron clansmen died in the fight," he added, taking an angry turn about the room, "but one escaped, wounded, to carry the sorry tale back to us. MacGregor and the Camerons were marched off to Edinburgh on the false charge they'd ambushed Glenkennon's men. 'Tis a damned lie, but the lads have been in prison ever since."

Donald paused, overcome by his own anger. "Some say Glenkennon plans to execute them . . . others that he simply plans to hold them as surety against Francis's good behavior. The MacLeans have never taken to English orders and of late the tension's grown."

He brought his fist down sharply upon the table, making the dishes rattle on the tray. "Glenkennon dares no' strike at Francis openly, for the lad's too popular a chief in these Highlands. Every clan'd unite and Glenkennon'd have an uprising on his hands that'd make the Catholic risings a few years back look like child's play." He gave a harsh laugh. "He thinks to hold Francis by threatening the Camerons, but we've neatly scotched the bastard's plans now."

Anne stared at Donald in dismay. No wonder her words had provoked such an outburst from MacLean on the trail. If Donald's tale were true, the Highlander had good reason to hate her father. She felt a sudden flush of shame for the name she bore and the treachery in which her father seemed to be involved. She had known him to be a cold, hard man but had never expected villainy such as this.

"So I'm to be exchanged for those men instead of gold," she said softly. "And what happens if my father decides his prisoners are more important?"

Donald's lips formed a mirthless smile. "He won't . . . but in any case, you'll be treated with courtesy here. You're the kinswoman of Ian MacDonnell, and the MacDonnells and MacLeans have been allies near a hundred years."

He finished his wine with a gulp, as though suddenly embarrassed at his wordiness. "I'd best find out what's takin' that wench so long with yer bath." He moved across the floor, hesitating at the door with a sharp look back at her. "I wanted you to know the truth, lass. Now you can judge for yourself what manner of folk we be."

The slamming of the door echoed loudly in the silence, and Anne was suddenly alone with her uncomfortable thoughts. There was always more than one side to a tale, she reminded herself, yet Donald didn't seem the type to spread falsehoods. Perhaps MacLean was not so black as she had suspected. Perhaps her father . . .

Sighing deeply, she closed her eyes, forcing her mind to

emptiness. She was far too tired to think clearly. For the moment, she would reserve judgment.

She had scarcely begun to relax when a knock at the door brought her quickly to her feet. The sound prefaced the arrival of a sturdy, gray-haired woman of indeterminate age carrying clothing of every description in her arms. The woman dropped her burden on the bed while four men filed past her lugging buckets of steaming water for Anne's bath.

Ordering the men about in a tone obviously used to command, the woman supervised the filling of the tub with a sharp scolding for the men and their clumsiness. The grinning men did not seem to mind her harsh words, however. They glanced at Anne curiously, one even smiling and nodding in a friendly manner as the woman herded them out.

"They be great dolts, all of them, but good enough if a body can keep 'em in hand," the woman said, turning at last to scrutinize Anne with her sharp gray eyes. Hands on hips, she looked the girl up and down boldly. "Pur lass, I can guess those lads have no' treated you as they should. I'll speak to Francis about his rough handlin'. You look fit to drop in exhaustion," she added with a shake of her graying head. "And I'd no' be blamin' you if you did, poor child. Now come here to me, and we'll have you in this warm bath where you can forget yer troubles awhile. My name's Kate, child, and I'll see no one abuses you further in this household!"

After the many lonely months without affection, the woman's mothering was like precious water to Anne's thirsty soul. Gratefully, she moved toward Kate, her throat tightening at the memory of just that tone of motherly concern in Philippa's voice for so many years. "My name is Anne," she said, with a tentative smile directed toward the kindly, wrinkled face before her.

"And of course it is, sweeting. I've been hearin' your name for some time," Kate replied, helping Anne quickly out of her dusty garments and into the steaming water. "And half mad with worry we've been too...expectin' you as we did last night and awonderin' what trouble our Francis had gotten himself into."

Her charge safely into the tub, Kate turned her attention to the clothing on the bed, sorting through the stacks of gowns and undergarments, keeping up a stream of comforting chatter all the while.

Anne luxuriated in the heaven of the warm water, the aches of travel slowly easing from her weary body. Even her swirling thoughts began to quiet in response to the slow relaxation of her tense muscles and the flow of conversation from Kate.

Her father would rescue her soon, she assured herself. If Donald's tale were true, Glenkennon would arrange to trade his prisoners for her and she would be on her way to Ranleigh in no time.

But what if MacLean's family were harmed? Her stomach tightened at the thought and she sank deeper into the comforting warmth of the tub. MacLean was not the man to suffer her father's treachery—if such it was—without retaliation. And she was here beneath his hand, an easy tool for revenge.

The dark image of the Highland chief bloomed in her mind, and she remembered the angry set of his face and his bruising grip upon her shoulders. Her hands crept up involuntarily to cover the purplish markings now marring her white skin. He'd not really hurt her, she reminded herself—not even in his anger. She shook her head and reached for the bar of soap Kate had brought.

She dropped the soap into the water. The heady fragrance of flowers wafted to her, and her thoughts immediately took another course. So Sir Francis MacLean had plenty of women eager for his attentions. . . .

She retrieved the costly bar and rubbed it over her body, indolently watching the water slide from her silken limbs.

Sniffing the scent suspiciously, she wondered if it, too, had been a favorite of the last Lady MacLean, or if there had been some more recent female who had voiced a preference for that very seductive scent.

CHAPTER FIVE

𝓘t did Anne little good to wonder about MacLean, for it was three days before she spoke with him again. During that time she was kept locked in her room, where she longed to be out in the warm spring sunshine that beckoned brightly from her narrow window.

To keep Anne entertained, Ian MacDonnell spent hours regaling her with tales of her mother's childhood. She hung on his words, listening with rapt attention while she learned more of her MacDonnell kin than her mother ever had told her.

In turn Anne spoke of her life in England, wisely dwelling on those happy times when her father was away. She could tell her words eased a heavy burden from MacDonnell's shoulders. "We were happy at Rosewood," she said softly, "though Mother was often homesick." She paused, remembering how as a child she had often awakened in the night to the sounds of her mother's crying. "Why didn't you come?" she asked abruptly. "There was never so much as a letter."

Ian's lips tightened and his lined face suddenly seemed far older than his years. "It wasn't my choice, lass," he said, returning her look. "Glenkennon forced Mary to break all contact with us after he took her off to England.

For a time I wrote. I even tried to see her once and almost lost my head for my troubles. The bastard threatened . . ."

He broke off, gazing at Anne strangely. "Ah, well, it's all over and done now, lass, and I doubt your mother'd be thankin' me for stirring up troublesome history." He studied his hands as if the past might be read there. "Believe me, Mary knew the silence was not of my choice."

Anne stared at him wordlessly, feeling a deep pity for the man and her mother and the many unhappy years behind them. Why had her mother married Robert Randall and abandoned her family? The marriage was no love match, of that Anne was certain. She longed to ask, but some nameless dread held her silent. Perhaps some things were best left unmentioned, as Ian had said.

When her uncle could not be with her, Donald or Kate kept Anne company, and from them she learned much about the current chief of Clan MacLean. Francis had inherited the title early in life when his father failed to return from a fierce clan skirmish. At the tender age of eighteen, he had been pitchforked into leadership of a powerful clan in one of the most turbulent times in Highland history. Now, some eight years later, he had successfully led his clan through political upheavals and border wars and was revered by many of the clans with a near worshipful awe.

He was known in nearby parts as a loyal and honest friend but a dangerous enemy for any man to have. A powerful and canny fighter, he was as sharp of wit as he was quick with his sword. No one who asked his aid met with disappointment—or so his loyal followers protested. The more Anne heard, the more confused her feelings became.

From her window, she had watched him come and go with his men a handful of times since the morning of her arrival. She had also heard his firm tread in the hallway and did not know whether to be relieved or sorry when it always passed her door without stopping.

Finally, just when she thought she would go daft from her forced inactivity, the footsteps halted outside and an impatient knock sounded. At her word, MacLean strode in, his restless personality filling the large room, which seemed far too small to hold him.

"Well, Mistress Randall, if you've recovered from your ill temper, I've come to take you riding," he announced, tapping his whip impatiently against his boot.

Damn the man for being so provoking just when she was most disposed to think well of him. "I've ridden with you once, sir, and I've no mind to endure the ordeal again," she said coolly.

He smiled so engagingly the room seemed to brighten. "Come, lass. A short ride about the moor will do you good. 'Tis a lovely day, and I took pity on you, locked away indoors. You need a bit of sunshine and wind to blow away your ill humor." He paused. "Of course, if you're afraid to go, we can forget the whole idea."

It was a lovely day, and Anne could not stand the thought of another minute spent indoors. Besides, she'd not have him thinking she was a coward. "Of course I'm not afraid. If you'll take yourself off, I'll be ready in fifteen minutes," she stated, dismissing him by walking to the press for her habit.

Ten minutes later, MacLean was hurrying her down the steps and out into the courtyard while she struggled to finish buttoning her sleeve. The horses were saddled and waiting; he had been sure of her all along.

She was glad to see he had chosen the same bonny mare she had ridden into Camereigh. He must at least have trusted her horsemanship if she was to ride Cassie again.

Stroking the mare's glistening neck, Anne watched in fascination while MacLean's nervous black stallion quieted quickly beneath his hands. A horsewoman herself since she had been old enough to toddle about and demand a pony, Anne spoke in unthinking admiration, forgetting she was still angry with the man. "Donald isn't the only one who works magic here. You've a way with horses, sir."

"Oh, Leven's not a mean sort," Francis said, running his hand appreciatively along the stallion's muscular shoulder. "He just needs a firm hand on the reins now and again."

He assisted Anne in mounting, then swung onto the stallion's back, nudging the impatient animal through the gate and down the road leading from Camereigh. Avoiding the trail they had taken on the day of Anne's arrival, they swung instead along a narrow track leading down toward the sea.

Anne rode silently beside MacLean, content, for the moment, to soak up the rich beauty of the day. Gone were all feelings of anger and fear. The cool wind blew against her face and whipped her cloak from her shoulders like a proud, dark banner. The sun shone with a clear, golden light, shimmering over the greening forest, gilding everything it touched with a special brilliance. Even the air smelled sweet and cool. She breathed in great lungfuls, conscious of a reasonless happiness spreading within her chest.

The lazy murmur of the sea beyond them grew nearer with each step the horses took. Rounding a bend in the trail, they passed through a stand of scrubby ash to find the brilliant blue sea stretching endlessly before them.

MacLean reined in, gazing calmly out at the glittering panorama. The white-crested waves rolled gently up the rocky beach, dropping tiny shells and pebbles as they retreated along the shore. Urging Cassie past him, Anne rode to the sea's edge, mesmerized by the rhythmic rise and fall of the breakers and the graceful dance of the gulls, swooping and climbing in the eternal pattern of their lives.

"It makes you realize how small and unimportant you really are, doesn't it?" Francis asked softly, still gazing at the shimmering face of the ocean. "I come here sometimes . . . it helps me to sort things out."

Anne nodded, longing to freeze this moment in time

like a jewel she could hold in her hand and enjoy forever. She closed her eyes, feeling the warm sun on her face, hearing the murmur of the sea, smelling the sweet tang of the air. She committed each sensation to memory, knowing instinctively that she might have need of this peace in the days to come.

Opening her eyes, she found MacLean watching her lazily, his own eyes as blue and calm as the sky above them. "I knew you'd like it," he said smiling. "I've another place to show you. Come."

They rode slowly along the coarse sand, the tracks of the horses quickly disappearing as the surging waters erased all signs of their passage. Following a narrow, rocky trail, they wound precariously up a steep hillside. To the right a solid granite cliff crowded over the path while to the left, the trail fell away—a sheer drop of several hundred feet led to churning waters beneath. Great slabs of gray stone lay piled and broken at the foot of the cliff, dislodged by some turbulent occurrence in the earth's history thousands of years before. The green waters tumbled about the rocks in a white froth while the ocean lifted and fell in lazy billows.

Reaching the crest at last, MacLean dismounted. He led the horses over the rocks, pushing aside the scrubby bushes clinging tenaciously to the clefts in the buffeting wind. Pausing in the shelter of a large jumble of boulders, he tied the horses to a stubby tree.

MacLean helped Anne from her mount, then took her hand in a natural gesture, leading her up the rocky face of a sloping cliff to the very summit of the headlands. At the top, Anne caught her breath. The rugged coastline stretched away as far as the eye could see in either direction.

"Gull Point," MacLean murmured. "Where sea and sky and land all meet, and wars and politics have no place in time."

She nodded wordlessly, watching the snowy gulls hang

motionless in the surging updrafts sweeping about the headland. Leaning against the hard stone, she was grateful for its protection from the fierce wind.

She gazed thoughtfully at MacLean's strong profile. He was not the man to enjoy the political intrigues her father seemed to thrive on. Ian had assured her that only his concern for his family had made him stoop to her kidnapping. "I'm sorry about the Camerons," she said softly. There, it was out. She had wanted to tell him ever since she had learned the truth.

"Who told you, lass?" he asked, never taking his eyes from the sweeping scene.

"It doesn't matter."

"I'll wager it was Donald," he said with a half smile. "The man's always too busy about my interests."

Anne studied him silently, an answering smile curling her own lips. "He couldn't bear I should think so poorly of his Laird."

MacLean's smile broadened, and he shook his head. "My people attach more honor to my motives than I can justly claim."

"Your people trust you. 'Tis no small thing when the welfare of so many depend on you. The responsibility must be irksome at times."

"Aye, but I'd no' have it any other way." He gazed out over the broad expanse of rugged shoreline. "Do you realize there've been MacLeans standing on this spot for over three hundred years? This was my father's land, and his father's before him and so on back through untold numbers until the fourteenth century. That's a heritage to protect, lass."

Anne studied his proud, dark head and the arrogant set of his wide shoulders, thinking the future of his clan was in very good hands. She leaned back comfortably against the rocks, thankful he had brought her to this secret place at the top of the world. If only she might have stayed there, away from the loneliness and confusion below. Unwillingly, her thoughts turned to her father and his treacherous dealings. "Why does my father hate you so?"

MacLean scowled and the peaceful magic of the day shattered abruptly. "The man wants the whole of Scotland beneath his heel. He tolerates those who cower and submit meekly to his orders. But if a man stand up and dare to act a man, he's like to find himself branded traitor or have his family dragged off to prison on any trumped up charge."

Gazing at MacLean, Anne couldn't imagine him cowering before anyone. The thought of him in her father's power was like the sudden, sharp throb from a painful wound. "Donald says my father plans to hang you," she ventured. "Won't your raid give him added reason?"

"Glenkennon needs no excuses for what he does. God's blood, if he gets his hands on an enemy, he simply invents a crime they're guilty of! Convenient, is it not?" he questioned with a harsh laugh.

"Will he be coming for me soon?" Anne gazed across the rugged headlands, finding the thought far more unwelcome than it had been just three days earlier.

"He doesn't know where you are yet, lass," MacLean said low, the mocking smile returning to his face. "I decided we'd let him fret a while before sending him news you're happily visiting relations here in the North."

"And if he harms your family meanwhile?"

MacLean gave her a flinty smile. "He won't dare." Standing abruptly, he drew her to her feet, steadying her with a hand against her shoulder. His penetrating eyes scanned her face, an unreadable expression burning in their depths. "You'd best be prepared to stay with us several weeks, Anne Randall. Do you think you can stomach me?"

"If you'll remember your manners, sir," she quipped, stepping back.

He threw back his head with a hearty laugh. "I'll do my poor best, mistress, but I make no rash promises." He took her arm as though to lead her back to the horses, but for several seconds neither one moved.

Anne met his eyes uneasily. As she explored their blue depths, the world around her seemed to fade so that even the eternal sound of the wind ceased to be.

The easy laughter disappeared slowly from MacLean's dark face. He leaned toward her, his strong fingers tightening around her arm, drawing her closer. His eyes half closed, their intensity shadowed by a sweep of heavy lashes no man had the right to have.

For a moment Anne was capable of no rational thought. Leaning forward instinctively, she was aware only of the pounding of her heart and of a sudden lack of air to her lungs. Then the feel of his hands on her arms reminded her of another afternoon—another day on a windswept moor when she had skirted the edge of disaster by a narrow margin.

At the memory, a wave of suspicion swept her. MacLean was her enemy, sworn to revenge against her father. And she was a fool for riding out with him alone. Stumbling back, she jerked against his hold.

MacLean released her abruptly. She backed away a few paces, gazing up at him with wide, distrustful eyes.

"Forgive me, lass, I'd no desire to frighten you," he said softly.

Seconds passed. The silence stretched uncomfortably between them. He turned toward the horses, casually holding out an arm. "Come lass, take my hand," he said, matter-of-factly. "Your boots weren't meant for climbing, and we'd best be getting back."

Returning to Camereigh by another path, they traced their way through rich, pine-scented woodlands. Golden sunlight filtered through the canopy of interlaced branches, dappling the tongue-tied riders with scattered patches of light and shadow.

Francis contemplated Anne's stiff profile as they came out onto the open moor south of the castle. He'd not meant that scene up at Gull Point—but the girl's loveliness made it hard to remember she was naught but a temporary guest.

Temporary, he reminded himself. She would be gone once her purpose was served. Still, he did not relish the knowledge that she was afraid of him. He had enjoyed those peaceful moments with her far more than he cared to admit. Drawing rein, he cast about for something to say or do that would wipe the dread from her face. "What say you to a race, mistress? I'll give you a headstart to the bottom of this hill and still beat you to the gates."

Anne glanced up. "Done, sir." She sent him a quick smile, glad to feel the strange tension melting away.

At MacLean's nod, Anne put her heels to Cassie's sides. Despite the speed of the mare and a generous headstart, the stallion caught her easily long before the castle came into sight. They raced along side by side, checking slightly only when they entered the narrow gates.

At the stables, Francis swung down from the dancing stallion, laughter making his face come alive. Anne could not halt the swift surge of her own blood or the laughter that tumbled from her lips when he caught her from the saddle and swung her down beside him.

"I'd have caught you long before that damned ravine had I been on this black devil the other day," he said with a laugh.

She grinned up at him impudently. "But then you'd have missed the pleasure of being so angry."

He laughed easily, pleased to see the sick fear gone from her face. Tossing their reins to a waiting stable boy, MacLean took Anne's arm, and they walked together through the narrow door into the hallway. Pausing in the entrance to the great hall, he rubbed his chin. "I'm in a muddle as to what to do with you, lass," he said with a slight frown. "I'd give you the run of the castle if I could be sure you'd not attempt to leave us again."

His right hand still rested on her arm. It was warm and

possessive, and she felt its power through the cloth of her habit. That warmth seemed to spread from his hand to her blood, making it course through her body with a vigor that dared her to step beyond her fear.

Thinking quickly, Anne looked across the room. Once given, her word would bind her to whatever choice she made. "I give you my word...," she began softly. She glanced up, meeting his eyes. "I give you my word I'll not try to escape—so long as you deal honestly with me."

MacLean smiled. "Done, lass. We've a bargain."

In that moment, Anne was aware of being unpardonably foolish, but she found, to her amazement, that she didn't really care.

The following morning brought a return of the dreary weather known as spring to the inhabitants of the western Scottish coast. A dense fog rolled in from the sea and the low-lying clouds trailed heavily across the sky, mingling with the fog to shroud the upland peaks in silent mystery. A damp chill crept into Anne's bedchamber, causing her to snuggle more closely beneath the covers on her bed.

A sense of excitement filled her, and she felt fully alive for the very first time. She thought with surprise of the remarkable change her life, aye, even her personality, had undergone in less than one short week. From the sheltered, uneventful existence of Lincolnshire, she had been thrust into this unbelievable escapade—and was actually enjoying herself!

She laughed aloud at the thought of what the very proper Philippa would have said about the idea of Anne's sleeping on the moor with two men. Her girlhood had been so confined. Few young men visited them in Lincolnshire, and she had scarcely been allowed to speak to the ones who did without a chaperone in attendance. But she had been aware, even then, of the interested looks, of the eager glances cast her way by the young men who visited Lord Randall at Rosewood.

Strangely enough, not all the speculative glances of her English admirers had shaken her as much as one boldly appraising glance from the MacLean chief. She shivered at the thought of what might lie behind that look, wondering with the perversity of her sex if she dared provoke it again.

She swung her legs out from under the covers and danced over to the fireplace. Quickly adding peat to the smoldering coals, she soon had a merry fire crackling behind the grate. Would she ride with MacLean today? she wondered. Did she dare—or ought she make up some excuse?

Huddled in front of the fire in the sable-lined robe Kate had found for her, Anne idly chewed a nail, trying to decide what intrigued her about MacLean. He frightened her, she admitted. There was a feeling of inexhaustible energy about him, of carefully leashed power held in check by a thin rein. She longed to catch just a glimpse of the world she sensed he could show her—yet she was more than a little afraid he might take her further than she wished to go.

Hearing the muffled stirrings of her charge, Kate knocked softly, entering with a brief curtsy. "Good day t'ye lass—though it be such a drear, cold marnin' I'd hurry you back ta bed if you dinna look wide awake as the cat in the kennel."

Kate walked to the press, eyeing Anne's meager array of clothing distastefully. "I suppose it'll be the green wool again today, though you've worn it already this week like the others. Mayhap the girls will have finished the new gowns by tomorrow. We'll have the fittings this afternoon, most like."

Anne's head jerked up. "What new gowns?"

"Why you dinna think we expected you ta wear these four makeshift garments forever did you?"

"But I'll not be here long enough to warrant having new dresses made," Anne said. "Tell the seamstress to stop. Sir Francis may be angry."

"While we've got ye here, you must be dressed," Kate said inarguably, "and dressed as befits your station. Sir Francis himself ordered it," she added as a clincher. She looked at Anne measuringly. "Aye, the gold silk will be perfect. I'll be sure the girls have it ready for the festivities tomorrow night."

Anne glanced up. "What do you mean?"

"Sir Francis invited the families within a day's ride of Camereigh here tomorrow. They'll be feasting and drinking, aye, and there'll be music and dancing too. You'll turn heads, lass, that's for certain," Kate prophesied with a sly look. "I'll wager you'll not find yourself sittin' out many of the tunes."

Anne's mind whirled. A party was going to take place there—the following night. "But my father may well be on the way with an army. How can Sir Francis dare?"

Kate chuckled and shook her head. "Those that live under Sir Francis MacLean stopped questioning his crazy starts long ago. The lad'd thumb his nose at the devil then outwit 'im behind his back. There's none of us as spend a sleepless night with so canny a chief to lead us." She kept her eyes carefully on the green dress she was shaking out. "He's even managed to avoid the matchmaking skills of all the fond mamas—a feat that's no' so easy. Aye, they'll be asimperin' and flirtin' in all their finery tomorrow atryin' to catch his eye."

With a gasp, Anne flew to Kate's side. "But I've nothing to wear," she groaned, vowing silently to remain in her room rather than wear any of the madeover garments before a host of arrogant Scotsmen.

"Dinna fash yourself, child. I've found just the thing. 'Tis a lovely gold silk cut to a pattern for Lady Janet—her that's Sir Francis's sister. It was never finished though. The lass found the color or some such dinna become her and 'twas put away to be forgot till this week when I was searching for dresses for yourself. With a little touch here and there, it'll be perfect."

The two continued their discussion of the coming evening while Anne consumed a hearty breakfast of warm milk and fresh oat cakes brought in by a maid. After dressing in the green wool, she set out down the stairs in search of her uncle or Donald. Perhaps they could tell her more of Sir Francis's plans. MacLean had said nothing to her—perhaps she was not to be included.

She did not find them among the dozen clansmen idly dicing beside the fire in the great hall. Moving down the corridor to the smaller private hall of the chief, she paused anxiously outside the door. What if MacLean were alone in the room? In spite of her earlier brave thoughts, she found herself loath to entertain him alone. She eased the door open a crack, relieved to find Donald and Ian arguing good-naturedly over a game of chess. "Am I interrupting anything?"

"You're as welcome an interruption as a ray of sunshine on a drear wintry day, lass. Do come in," Ian invited.

She flashed him a grateful smile and crossed the room to perch on the arm of his chair. Studying the chessboard critically, she looked at Ian in pity. "You're about to be had, Uncle."

He raised a finger in admonition. "Watch and learn, my girl, watch and learn." With those words, he moved unexpectedly, seizing a strategic player in MacLean colors.

Donald waved a hand unconcernedly. "A temporary setback only, lass. Nothing to worry about."

The friendly rivalry went on, with Anne pulling for first one man and then the other as the fortunes of the game fluctuated. "How could you turn against blood kin in support of this scoundrel?" Ian asked accusingly when she cheered as Donald took a man.

"I owe Donald a debt of gratitude," Anne said, laughing. "He saved me from Sir Francis's wrath on that ride through the mountains."

"Only because you wrapped him around your pretty finger."

Anne glanced up in surprise. MacLean lounged in the open doorway, thumbs hooked in his belt, amusement dancing in his eyes.

"Ah, Ian . . . 'tis a sad sight to see an old soldier brought low beneath the foot of a conniving wench," he added, advancing into the room.

Anne frowned, wondering how long he had been there and trying to remember exactly what she had said. "Those who eavesdrop seldom hear good of themselves," she remarked. "You should announce yourself instead of creeping up on people."

"I don't *creep* in my own house, mistress," he said, throwing himself lazily into a chair beside Ian. "And hearing people speak unguardedly is a good way to learn their true feelings. It's an excellent method of determining which are friend and which are foe, wouldn't you agree?"

She stared at him silently, wondering if any special meaning lay behind his words.

"Speaking of true feelings, what think you of Camereigh now you've been freed from the dungeon?"

"I've seen very little of it yet, though what I've seen has been impressive," she answered cautiously. "I was going to ask Donald to show me about when I came upon this game."

"So you wish to be shown about." MacLean raised an eyebrow. "Do you seek to spy out our weaknesses for Glenkennon?" His indolent smile mocked her, and she was suddenly unsure of her position. His words and the searching look that accompanied them made her uncomfortable. They were enemies, after all.

"Why, of course, my lord. For what other reason?" she said haughtily. "Will it be back to my room now you've discovered my plot?"

MacLean laughed at her obvious ire. "I doubt your tale is true, lass. You'd not know a weakness in this castle's construction if you saw it—and besides, Camereigh has none. Poke about in every corner that you will. I'm only sorry I haven't time to show it off myself. Donald must do the honors."

Rising to leave, he smiled down at her. "Enjoy yourself this morning, and ask Donald for anything you wish. Think of my house as your own."

The chess game was put aside as Donald began to tell Anne the history of the house and of the MacLeans who had built it. The original fortified tower house had burned long before but there were sections of the stone walls and foundation that had stood against the ire of man and nature for nearly three hundred years.

The oldest part of the castle was the three-storied north tower, its walls ten feet thick with corners carefully rounded to prevent damage from the dreaded battering rams of attackers. That structure was joined to the more modern south tower by a wing of barracks and servants' quarters, while the stables, bakehouse, and brewhouse made up a fourth side of the quadrangle. The jumble of buildings had been added to and remodeled numerous times over the years, but the current living quarters of Sir Francis and his household staff were well kept and furnished with all the modern conveniences from England and France.

Anne walked through the castle with Donald, poking about in the original structure, much of which was closed now in preference to use of the more modern wings. They avoided the unused dungeon in the stone vault of the north tower, moving on to view the immense, well-stocked storerooms before returning to the main keep two hours later.

MacLean, Ian, and a half-dozen clansmen were drinking and swapping tales about the fire in the great hall when Anne and Donald returned. As Anne joined the group, MacLean poured a glass of wine and held it out to her. "To my favorite spy," he whispered, lifting his flagon in salute. "May a man's enemies always be so bonny." His eyes rested steadily on her face, but she could see a teasing light in them.

She nodded in acknowledgement, a half smile tugging at her lips. "I've taken careful note of every door and window, but I shall take pains to dissuade Glenkennon from laying siege. From the look of the storerooms, you could hold out a twelvemonth or more."

"Oh, at least," Francis agreed amicably, leading her to a seat beside his own.

A cold rain fell outside and a ghostly shroud of white still clung to the trees, but indoors the warm fire crackled and laughter rang from the rafters as the men vied for the attention of the lovely, golden-haired lass in their midst.

CHAPTER SIX

*D*inner that night was a boisterous affair with cups lifted and jests tossed about. The golden light of the flickering torches cast a warm glow over the hall, and the fire in the cavernous hearth snapped and popped cozily. Anne sat quietly between her uncle and Donald, enjoying a curious sense of belonging as she watched the servants come and go and listened to the laughter of the men.

Hearing a burst of familiar laughter ring out above the din, she glanced down the table in search of MacLean. He was seated informally with his men, his dark head tilted in close concentration on a tale one fellow was spinning.

Would he ever listen to her with that rapt look, a small, betraying voice questioned. Of course not; nor did she wish it. It would be dangerous to take his fancy.

She firmly banished the memory of the exciting afternoon she had spent with the man. It was only natural that she should find pleasure with these lighthearted people after the dismal months just past, she told herself. There was nothing dangerous in enjoying the company of the engaging MacLean chief—as long as she kept him at arm's length.

"Are you looking forward to your first Scottish revel, Anne?" Ian MacDonnell's words broke abruptly into her thoughts. She turned reluctantly from her study of Mac-Lean.

"There's no doubt you'll enjoy yourself," Ian continued. "Camereigh's always been famous for its hospitality. And Francis makes it a point of honor to keep up the tradition."

"But I don't know I'm invited," she said bluntly. "Sir Francis hasn't spoken of it yet. You forget . . . I'm no ordinary guest."

At MacDonnell's exclamation of protest, Anne's eyes flew to his. "In truth, perhaps it's best I not join the company. It can't be wise for so many to know of my presence here. There might be some loose tongues. The report could get back to my father."

"Nonsense!" Ian cried. "You'll be openly introduced as my niece. It's been put about you're visiting me with Glenkennon's blessings. The man dare not refute the story lest he risk your reputation—something he can't do if he wishes to get you a rich husband. Glenkennon can ill afford scandal now," he added with a grin.

On Anne's left, Donald rose and moved away down the room. After a glance in his direction, she turned her attention to her plate, thinking of the planned celebration with a longing that surprised her. There had been few chances to enjoy friends at Rosewood, and she and her mother had always dreaded the state affairs when Glenkennon forced them to entertain some pompous company.

The wooden bench shifted suddenly beneath Anne as someone took the empty place at her side. Glancing up, she found MacLean beside her.

"I hear you question your welcome tomorrow night, lass," he said, settling himself backwards on the bench and propping his elbows on the table. "God's foot, you'd think after the trouble I took to get you here, I'd need say little else to assure you you're wanted."

She shrugged and managed a light tone. "I did think a prisoner might not be welcomed among your friends."

"But you're the guest of honor, lass," MacLean said solemnly. "Of course you must come."

She stared suspiciously into the deep blue of his heavily lashed eyes, noting the mischievous twinkle in them. Was he serious or making a jest? "I suppose I'll come for a time, then," she said carefully. "My uncle tells me his son Eric will be here. I'd like to meet my cousin . . . and the rest of your friends, of course."

"Then I'd best ask you now before Ian's lad steals a march on me. Will you honor me with the first dance, lass? We'll show 'em all how it's done."

A smile of quick pleasure lit Anne's face before she could control it. "I'd be pleased."

MacLean found his own lips curving upward in response to the girl's winsome smile. Lord, but she was a lovely thing! He fought the urge to brush a silky tendril of hair from her face, studying instead the soft curve of her cheek and the way her long, sooty lashes curled upward toward her brow. Her full lips parted invitingly as she spoke over her shoulder to Ian. He noted the creamy perfection of her throat, his warm gaze following that line until it disappeared beneath the rounded neckline of her gown. He studied the ample swell of her breasts beneath the cloth, remembering all too well the feel of her pressed against him on the moor.

Drawing his eyes reluctantly from their pleasurable study, he took a draught of ale. The girl was Glenkennon's prize. A lovely lass, yes, but not for him. He would enjoy her company—as he always did that of beautiful women—but he'd venture no further. Besides, Anne was the kinswoman of one of his closest friends. He'd not insult Ian by trifling with the girl.

The meal was almost over when an unexpected commotion sounded in the courtyard. An outer door banged shut, and the door of the hall swung wide, sweeping a breath of wet night into the room.

"Janet!"

MacLean sprang to his feet and hurried forward to meet a tall, dark-cloaked woman before she had taken a half-dozen steps into the hall.

As they stood together in the flickering torchlight, the resemblance between the two figures was striking. Anne needed no introduction to recognize MacLean's sister, wife to his ally Jamie Cameron.

The woman threw off her cloak and walked to the table beside her brother. Even from that distance, Anne could see that her lovely face was worn with worry and travel, and her eyes were swollen, as if from the ravages of recent tears. The woman took a fortifying drink from the silver flagon MacLean held for her and closed her eyes.

"You must do something, Francis!" Janet said finally, anger and despair giving her voice a thrilling urgency in the hushed room. "Glenkennon had them publicly beaten at the Mercat Cross three days ago!"

At her words, an angry growl from the men rumbled around the tables. MacLean held up a commanding hand. "All?" he questioned with deceptive softness. "Even the boys?"

"Not Evan," she whispered, her voice breaking from worry and strain, "but Will was considered a man."

MacLean took her hand and pushed her down onto a bench. His face was cold and hard, his voice harsh with fury. "Glenkennon will pay for this!"

Anne felt a shiver of dread go through her. Her stomach twisted at the thought of her father beating a helpless child. Surely there was some mistake!

MacLean raised his head, his voice rising so all in the room might hear. "Glenkennon will pay. I swear it this night before you all!"

Turning to Janet, he placed a comforting hand on her shoulder. "Randall's but venting his spleen," he explained with forced calmness. "At present, we have him neatly trapped. He dare not proceed further. We'll have Jamie and the boys back to you soon now, Janet."

He called for food and wine, placing it before his sister while they talked quietly together. Gradually, the buzz of angry voices rose again in the hall. Anne shrank toward her uncle, longing to flee the hostile room. At MacLean's command she'd been treated with kindness there. But what now? What if he withdrew his protection?

Suddenly Janet's voice rose as if in argument with her brother. She leaped to her feet, glaring furiously up the table toward Anne. "How dare you seat her at your table and treat the creature with such courtesy!" she spat. "Do you think my husband dines so well on Glenkennon's hospitality?"

Anne glanced quickly from Janet's hostile face to MacLean's. He looked grim, his dark brows drawn down warningly until they almost met above the bridge of his nose.

"Sit down, Janet. Mistress Randall cannot help who she is anymore than you or I," he said sternly. "At the moment she's a guest in this house and will be treated accordingly."

"I'll not sit at table with that bastard's spawn! Get her out of my sight."

Francis shot a glance at Anne's pale face. He rose to his feet, his eyes blazing dangerously. "I give the orders in this house, woman, not you!"

He leaned across the table. "I've said the girl is a guest, and that's enough. You'd best remember that if you plan to remain." He straightened and took a deep breath, continuing more gently, "I know you're upset, Janet, but I'll not have a kinswoman of Ian MacDonnell abused in this house."

Anne pushed back from the table and rose to her feet. "It's of no matter, m'lord. I understand Lady Cameron's feelings. I'm sure my own would be the same were our situations reversed." She glanced at Janet. "I can't make excuses for my father. There can be none for his actions . . ." She hesitated, then raised her head proudly. "Yet he is my father, and I've no wish to hear him abused. If you'll excuse me now, I'll go upstairs."

MacLean's troubled eyes searched her face. "You needn't go, lass."

"I'd rather, m'lord."

He nodded in understanding.

Anne dropped a curtsy in Janet's direction. "Lady Cameron." Turning without a backward glance, she made the long walk across the hall under the curious stares of all in the room.

Francis turned to his friend. "My apologies, Ian. I'd not have had that happen."

"I think the lass said it all," Ian said quietly. "We can easily understand Janet's wrath. Now if you'll excuse me, I'll go to Anne."

"Forgive me, Ian," Janet said, wearily holding out a hand to her friend. "I was thinking of Glenkennon only . . . not of you."

He took her hand and squeezed it in his own. "I know Janet, but 'tis a damnable situation we're caught in."

While Janet finished her meal in stony silence, MacLean frowned thoughtfully at his slowly warming ale. Anne was probably frightened half out of her wits. He took a deep draught of ale, hating the idea of her weeping alone in her room. Ian would comfort her, he told himself firmly; after all, it was a kinsman's place.

When Janet was done with her meal, MacLean led her to his private hall. Entering the room, he moved slowly across the floor, bending in silent concentration to stir up the dying fire.

Janet threw herself into a chair to one side of the fire, holding out her feet toward its radiating warmth. "Oh, all right, Francis," she said, breaking the tension between them. "I know I made a scene. Don't treat me to any more of your silence. I'd sooner have your temper than those cold looks. I'm sorry if I offended Ian, truly I am. But you should have warned me before I had to come face to face with the girl. I spoke without thinking."

MacLean straightened slowly. "I'd have you apologize to Mistress Randall. She didn't deserve that tongue-lashing."

Janet stared at him incredulously. "What! Apologize to Randall's daughter? You must be mad! Oh, I know none of this is her fault," she put in quickly, "but at the moment, I'm enjoying hating everyone who bears his name."

Francis leaned his broad shoulders against the massive oak mantel, the taut muscles in his face unyielding. "That girl is more innocent in this than all of us, including your lads, Janet. She's been raised in England knowing naught of this feud till I dragged her across half of Scotland under the worst circumstances you can imagine." He turned and shifted a log in the fireplace with his booted toe. "She's had a hard time of it since arriving . . . and will have worse once we return her to Glenkennon. She'll have that apology," he finished firmly.

Anne sat before the mirror, combing her hair abstractedly as she thought over her plight. What if her father did harm his prisoners? Her blood ran cold at thought of what anger could goad him to do. The youth and innocence of the boys would be no protection.

And what of her own innocence? Would the angry men downstairs take it into consideration? Thank God for her uncle! He had promised that MacLean meant her no harm . . . and Sir Francis had been quick to defend her, despite his obvious fury with her father. Surely he'd not use her to take revenge upon Glenkennon.

A light tap of unfamiliar footsteps caught her ear. A moment later, a soft rap sounded against the door panel. "Who is it?" she called.

"'Tis Janet Cameron. May I come in?"

Anne admitted Lady Cameron into the room warily, bidding the woman be seated in the chair she drew up before the fire. The two looked each other over. "I've come to beg your pardon," Janet said coldly. "My brother insisted."

Anne gazed into the hostile blue eyes, so like MacLean's in their shape and color. Sir Francis's sister was a lovely woman, but the weeks of fear were taking their toll. Tiny lines formed themselves about her wide mouth, and she had a haunted look that spoke of many anxious, sleepless nights. Anne knew the helpless fear of losing a loved one, and her heart went out to the woman in spite of the unpleasant scene earlier.

"Your brother is kind," she said softly, "but a forced apology means nothing. However, before you go, there's something I'd like you to know."

She turned to the fire, absently poking at a block of peat, searching for words of explanation. Strangely enough, she wanted Janet Cameron to understand; she didn't want this woman thinking she was like her father.

"You probably know Glenkennon as well as or better than I," she began. "He visited us so seldom I scarcely knew him as my father until I was six or seven years of age. And he was so cold even then. I remember as a child how badly I wanted to please him, yet the harder I tried, the more distant he became."

She paused, watching the shifting flames engulf the block of peat. "Things were . . . uncomfortable whenever he was at Rosewood. My mother and I were always relieved when he'd finish his business and go away again. He and Mother were not . . . were not close," she said, faltering. "She was afraid of him—and so were my brother and I."

She glanced down at Janet. "I've heard from him only a half-dozen times in the last three years. He didn't even come when my mother lay dying. I believe he cares little for me, despite the fact that his blood is my own." She smiled bitterly and gazed into the fire. "I've been here less than a fortnight, yet I've felt more warmth from my uncle than my father will ever show."

She stared at her clenched hands, suddenly feeling foolish baring her soul to a woman she had just met. Lady

Cameron would never understand. She had a husband, sons, and a brother who loved her. How could she understand how terrifying it was to be so alone? She swallowed the lump slowly forming in her throat. "I'm sorry for you and your family, but I doubt you've anything to fear. Your brother will get them back; I'm sure Sir Francis can do anything he sets his mind to." She glanced up with a twisted smile. "And then I shall return to Ranleigh."

The hostility drained slowly from Janet's face. Why, the girl was naught but a child—a lonely, frightened child. Taking Anne's clenched hand she squeezed it comfortingly. "Forgive me, mistress," she said softly. "I'd no right to speak as I did. My fear has made me act the fool."

MacLean's guests began arriving well before noon the following day. From the vantage point of her window, Anne watched the ladies and gentlemen dismounting amid the general confusion of arrival. With nothing to do, she paced restlessly about her room—from the chair to the fireplace, then back again to the window.

She was bored with the needlework Kate had found, but she did not feel like reading either. She hated shutting herself away, yet dreaded the possibility of another hostile confrontation such as the one the night before.

A vague depression settled over her. The unpleasant scene had burst the happy bubble she had been living in those last few days. It reminded her of the reason for her sojourn at Camereigh. She was there as a hostage—and only temporarily. She would soon be returning to her father.

From the window, she stared at the sky, drumming her fingers restlessly on the stone casement. Longing for a companionable talk with her uncle or Donald—even more for a fast gallop over the moor with Sir Francis Mac-Lean—she watched the gray clouds scudding rapidly before the wind. Somehow her worries fell away when she was with MacLean. He had a way of obtaining the best from each moment, of distilling the very essence of life so that he lived it to the fullest in a way Anne greatly envied.

Turning from the window, she sighed aloud. Perhaps a visit to the stable and a chat with Cassie would restore her spirits. Anything was better than remaining in her chamber. She slipped out the door and down the hall to the servants' stair. Making her way carefully down its narrow spiral, she came out in an open area where a maze of corridors intersected in front of the kitchen. She was surprised by the frantic bustle of activity taking place. Harried servants dashed this way and that, making rooms ready for arriving guests and preparing the feast for the evening.

Above the babble of noise, Anne heard her own name sounded. Turning, she caught sight of Janet Cameron carefully dodging servants who carried baggage and great silver trays of wine and ale.

"Anne, praise God I've found you!" Janet said, making her way determinedly through the press. "Francis has dropped this whole affair in my lap and is down at the stable now getting up a hunt. A hunt! With a dinner and guests to see to. I could strangle the man!"

Anne choked down the laugh that bubbled up in her throat. How like Francis MacLean to stir up this tempest and saunter off about his own business. She stared at Janet uncertainly. "Is there anything I can do to help?" she asked, fulling expecting the woman to repulse her offer.

"Do you know enough to organize the kitchen? Francis failed to mention his plans to Cook until yesterday. I fear the staff may wash their hands of the affair any minute." At Anne's nod, she smiled. "Good! I'll get the rest of the guests to the rooms we've prepared. I'll send Kate to you if I can free her from upstairs."

In less than a half hour, Anne had the frantic activity in the kitchen organized and running smoothly. She reminded the rattled servants that they had only to prepare one meal at a time and set them to their tasks accordingly. One group prepared refreshments for the arriving guests while the remainder concentrated on preparations for the evening meal. By the time Kate finally arrived, it looked as if a dinner might yet be served.

With the kitchen in Kate's capable hands, Anne slipped out into the courtyard, grateful to escape the stifling heat of the numerous fires. She leaned against the wall, the cool wind whipping her skirts as she watched the final preparations for the hunt. Some twenty horses stood stamping in impatience, their riders giving final checks to saddle girths and weapons. The panting hounds strained at their leashes, adding to the din by barking excitedly and attempting to wrap themselves around one another and their keepers.

How she longed to ride out with the men! To feel the wind in her face and a good horse beneath her stretching his muscles in a reckless race over the moors. She searched the crowd, finally sighting MacLean, his head thrown back in ready laughter as he made the rounds among his guests.

Their eyes met across the crowded space. MacLean nudged Leven over beside her. "How go the preparations indoors?"

Anne shook her head, repressing a strong urge to laugh. "'Twas a wicked thing you did in there, Francis MacLean."

"Janet needed something to keep her mind occupied. Do you think she's busy enough?"

"Quite," she responded, a tiny gurgle of laughter slipping out. "She's so busy planning to strangle you, she's forgotten about wanting to do away with me."

Francis smiled but said seriously, "Janet's hot-tempered at times, but she has a good heart. She didn't mean what she said last night."

Anne nodded. "We've made our peace and are now united in thinking men the most thoughtless creatures imaginable."

"A worthy sentiment, but one I'll make you retract

when we bring back enough venison to feed this army for the next few days."

"I wish I could go," she said wistfully, gazing across the courtyard of tangled men and animals.

"This will be a rough hunt, else I'd take you with me, lass."

"I know . . . women aren't supposed to do such things!" she exclaimed, a hint of bitterness sharpening her voice. "We're only here to see to the household tasks. Believe me, I've been well versed in all a woman's duties, and I wish I were a man!"

At his surprised exclamation, she glanced up in embarrassment, silently cursing her impulsive tongue. "I . . . I didn't mean it," she floundered. "Forgive me, m'lord. I'm just . . . restless today."

MacLean's warm gaze slid over her slowly, finally coming to rest on her painfully flushed face. "There are womanly duties that aren't considered boring, lass . . . or so I've been told. But I doubt you're as well versed in them all as you believe."

His knowing smile caused her flush to deepen.

"I, for one, am glad the situation stands as it is," he added. "'Twould have been a terrible waste the other way."

Leaning over, he flicked her cheek with one finger. "Be patient, lass. If you'll behave yourself tonight, I promise to take you tomorrow for a ride wild enough to satisfy even your restless spirits. As I remember, you've a marked liking for reckless rides in unthinkable territory."

They gazed at each other, eyes locked, each unable—or unwilling—to look away. As on that day at Gull Point, the clamor of noise and movement about them faded, and Anne was aware only of the lingering resonance of MacLean's deep voice and the warmth of her cheek where his finger had touched her skin.

Impatient at the delay, the stallion reared, shaking his head in mock anger. MacLean brought him down easily and wheeled him around. "Remember, Anne Randall," he said, still smiling. "You've promised the first dance tonight to me."

Anne nodded mutely, her eyes held prisoner by the excitement burning in his. Francis raised his hand, giving the order to sound the hunting horn. At its deep wail, the pack of hounds broke into frenzied barking, and men and animals streamed through the gate, leaving a confused and very unhappy young woman staring disconsolately after them.

CHAPTER SEVEN

With the fall of evening, a light mist moved in from the sea, shrouding the dark stone of Camereigh with a clinging veil of mystery. In startling contrast to the shadowy world outside, the interior of the castle blazed with light, from the windows of the highest turret chamber to the farthermost corner of the kitchen, and the sound of happy laughter echoed in every corridor.

Anne tried to sit quietly while Kate added the finishing touches to her hair, but the combination of excitement and fear knotting her stomach made her shift uncomfortably. She had looked forward to this evening with anticipation, yet once the time was upon her, she wished she did not have to go downstairs. She knew none of those happy, laughing people and was acutely aware that her name would make her less than popular among MacLean's guests.

"There," Kate said, stepping back in satisfaction. "We'll slip you into the gown, and it's an angel people will be takin' you for, I'm thinkin'."

Anne rose from her stool and moved woodenly toward the bed where the garment lay like a shimmer of liquid gold reaching to the floor. She'd not tried on the dress since its completion. In the hectic bustle that afternoon

Kate had forgotten to bring it to her. Perhaps it would not fit. That would give her an excuse to remain in her room.

Kate held the exquisite gown, easing it carefully over Anne's head, her nimble fingers deftly fastening the back. She tugged at the skirt with a sigh of satisfaction. "'Tis a perfect fit, and I had no doubt. 'Twas me what had the finishin' of it this afternoon."

"Oh, Kate . . . but I can't wear this!" Anne gasped, staring down at the ample amount of bosom showing to advantage above the plunging neckline.

"Nonsense," Kate admonished. "You're a woman now, not a child, and high time it is you dressed as one. 'Tis not near so bold as some you'll be seein' tonight . . . and on women who've no business wearin' such! At least we'll no' be havin' to pad the top as some will have to do," she added dryly, a twinkle in the eyes she raised to Anne.

Anne moved to the mirror, staring at the stranger she saw reflected there. The woman looked back, confident, sophisticated, worldly. There was no hint of the lonely child outcast from her father's love these eighteen years.

A slow smile spread over Anne's face as she studied her reflection. Perhaps the gown was not too daring after all —and it was so lovely. With one finger, she traced the fluid line of the cloth where it draped from the creamy ivory of her bare shoulder to plunge to the becomingly low neckline. Her hands slid slowly over the pearl-studded bodice, noting how snugly it fit her tiny waist. Whirling before the mirror, she watched in satisfaction while yards of iridescent gold cloth rippled from her hips in shimmering waves. An unexpected thrill raced through her veins. What would MacLean think of the gown?

"Is it really me?" she whispered, touching the loose curls that fell against her neck from the elegant twist at the crown of her head.

"Aye, and it's fine you look, sweet. Though no finer than I knew you'd be," Kate added in satisfaction. "Your dear mother'd be proud if she could see you tonight. I used to dress her hair in just that way; I knew it'd become you."

Anne's startled eyes met Kate's in the mirror. "You used to wait on my mother?" she asked in surprise. "Here?"

"Aye, and a sweet lass she was, too," Kate said, remembering. "She and Sir Francis's mother were the best of friends, you ken. Laughing, silly girls, both of them..."

Kate broke off as Janet poked her head around the door. "May I come in?"

"Please," Anne invited. "See what Kate's done to me."

Janet looked at her and gave a low whistle. "Kate, you've outdone yourself tonight. I've never felt so old and ugly in all my life! Thank goodness I'm dark and you're fair, Anne. At least I won't show to such poor advantage."

Anne stared at Janet in surprise. The woman was gowned in a becoming sapphire-blue velvet with a neckline every bit as daring as her own. Her glossy black locks were swept upward about the crown of her head, making her striking blue eyes appear even larger in the perfect oval of her face. "But you look lovely," Anne protested, thinking the dark beauty of the older woman far handsomer than her own.

Janet paid her no attention. Frowning, she rummaged through the jewel chest she carried. "There it is!" She lifted out an exquisite necklace of rubies set in a heavy rope of twisted gold studded with pearls. "There should be a pair of earrings here too. Ah... here they are! This should be perfect with that gold."

Anne was surprised—and touched. "But I can't wear your jewels," she said with a rueful smile. "I've already stolen your dress."

Janet waved the comment aside with a laugh and clasped the necklace about Anne's throat, ignoring her protest. "You must wear them," she said in a tone that brooked no argument. "This gown demands jewels. And don't worry about the dress. It was horrid on me! The color made me look pasty as dough!"

Janet held the earrings out on her palm. "I'd really like you to wear them," she said softly. "You were a help this afternoon . . . and after last night . . ." Her words trailed off, but her questioning eyes held Anne's own.

The crimson stones seemed to glow with an inner fire as Anne reached for the earrings. Her answering smile satisfied Janet's wordless inquiry. "I enjoyed working. It helped to pass the time."

Kate fussed over Anne another minute. Then, with a last anxious pat to their hair and gowns, the ladies rustled out the door and down the back stair to a small parlor where the family was to gather.

Four men were standing around a side-table, making good use of a decanter and glasses when the ladies swept in. Donald halted in the act of pouring out wine, his eyes widening at sight of the two women.

The experienced Janet paused just inside the room for effect, her mature beauty making the perfect foil for the golden girl at her side. Anne hesitated nervously on the threshold, unaware of the picture she made as the candlelight gleamed on her gown and the shining gold of her hair. She glanced at the men, quickly distinguishing MacLean's tall frame before her courage deserted her and she looked away.

"Oddsblood, Janet!" Ian MacDonnell exclaimed. "I thought no lass could rival you for beauty, but I fear my niece may give you a race."

Janet took his hand with a laugh. "You're kind Ian, but that's a race I'd no' be such a fool to enter. I've a son no' so many years younger than your Anne."

Ian turned, sweeping Anne with an appraising look. "You're as lovely as your mother, lass, and proud I am to claim you." Taking her hand, he turned toward a straight young stranger standing quietly by the table. "And I've someone here wanting to meet you. Anne, this is my eldest son, Eric. Eric, lad, come and meet your cousin, Anne Randall."

Anne studied the young man. He was a thinner, younger version of her uncle and appeared near her own age. Pleasant blue eyes appraised her with a look of such open admiration that her spirits soared with the first stirrings of self-confidence she'd had all evening. "I'm pleased to make your acquaintance," she said, dropping into a low curtsy.

"The pleasure's mine," his deep voice intoned. Extending a hand, he clasped hers firmly and lifted her to her feet. He smiled easily, and she found it no trouble at all to return the lonk.

For his part, MacLean scarcely noticed the introductions taking place. He drew a deep, unsteady breath, his eyes traveling slowly over Anne's face, noting the excited look in her wide-set eyes, the delicate blush of pleasure along her high cheekbones. Her wide, generous mouth was slightly parted, her full lips provocative, tempting . . .

His gaze dipped lower, lingering along the full, womanly curve of her breasts. He imagined the feel of her in his arms, her mouth crushed beneath his. Without warning, the blood surged hotly in his veins, and he knew a familiar tightening in his loins. Damn, but she was more beautiful than he could have imagined! His hands literally ached to touch her.

Becoming aware of his steady regard, Anne glanced across the room. MacLean looked devastatingly handsome that evening in a doublet of crimson velvet, its sleeves slashed to reveal undersleeves of shimmering silver. Her look collided abruptly with his. His eyes were intense, unreadable—dark as the murky pools in the peat bogs on the moor. He started toward her, and she glanced away, her stomach twisting nervously.

"You're a fair sight for a man . . . lass," he said, stopping before her, his husky voice making the words a caress. He took her cold hand and lifted it to his lips, kissing her fingers lightly with a practiced grace. "A lovely lass with hands as cold as ice. You need something to warm you, but I'm afraid a bit of wine is all I can offer at the moment."

Her heart stopped... then began to beat again wildly, and her surging pulses pounded loudly in her ears. A warm, tingling sensation spread slowly up her arm from the point where his lips had burned against her skin, making it difficult to think clearly. She attempted to pull away, but MacLean only grinned and tightened his grip, tucking her hand possessively within the curve of his arm.

She gazed at him uncertainly, feeling her heart bolt like a frightened filly at his intimate smile. She was being ridiculous. MacLean would tease her unmercifully if he knew how easily a few compliments had shaken her. "I'd like some wine," she managed in a steady enough voice.

MacLean tore his eyes from her and shot a look at Eric. "What do you say we break out another bottle and drink a toast to the two most beautiful women in all the Isles... my sister and your cousin."

"You'll get no argument from me, Francis," Eric replied with an admiring glance at Anne.

Eric poured the wine while Ian cleared his throat loudly. "To the two loveliest lassies in all the Isles... and the four men who can't be with us tonight. May they soon return for a celebration we'll remember for years to come."

There was a serious moment as everyone raised a glass in silent salute. "We'd best drink to five men," Francis said, amending the toast. "Conall's in Edinburgh watching Glenkennon's every move. The lad'd not take kindly to being left out of our plans."

Ian grinned. "If I know Conall, he's got his own revel going in some snug little inn."

"Not this time," MacLean said seriously. "Conall's got his work cut out for him."

Janet's smile trembled, but she raised her glass high. "Aye to Conall. May God give him aid."

MacLean gazed at his sister affectionately, then returned to his pleasurable perusal of Anne. He took a slow sip of

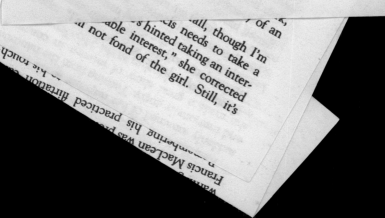

wine. "Do I recognize Mother's necklace?" he asked, abruptly changing the subject.

"Of course," Janet said lightly, making an obvious attempt to put her worries away. "It seems you forgot Anne's jewel box . . . along with the trifling matter of her clothing. I've made her a loan for the evening."

MacLean moved closer to Anne, as if to study the jewels, his eyes dropping to the rounded fullness of her breasts. "That was always my favorite necklace." He raised his hand, catching the flashing stones.

The warm brush of his fingers against the naked skin of her throat sent a strange feeling skittering along the edges of Anne's nerves. Her knees felt suddenly shaky and her heart missed several beats. It did not matter that he touched her, she assured herself. It was only an accident; he had meant nothing by it.

MacLean saw the pulse leap in her throat and longed to press his lips against the spot. He studied the necklace silently, then lifted laughing eyes to hers. "I don't remember the thing ever looking so fetching on Mother."

Anne felt a blush steal over her cheeks. She was unsure what to say to MacLean in his present flirtatious mood. He seemed different tonight, and besides . . . his proximity was having a strange effect on her heart. She longed to move away, but his fingers clasped the chain and kept her effectively beneath his hand.

"Francis, mind your manners!" Janet reproved embarrassing the girl." She shook her head nore him, Anne. I promise the other gentlemen, even if their host is

MacLean ended his inspe vious reluctance, allow Anne's throat. Sh knowing ins adept at tie

or why she was there. Determinedly banishing the thought of Elizabeth and MacLean, she began to enjoy herself.

The first strains of music were beginning when MacLean pushed his way through the crowd to claim her hand. "I believe I'd the promise of the first dance," he reminded her with a smile.

"Don't regard it," she said, forcing herself to speak pleasantly. She cast a significant glance toward Elizabeth. "I'll not hold you to your promise."

MacLean noticed the look but chose to ignore it. "You'll not get out of it so easily, lass." He took her arm, leaning toward her so closely she felt the warmth of his breath against her ear. "I've looked forward to this all night. You're caught, lass. You might as well come peacefully."

Throughout the dance, Anne refused to meet MacLean's eyes, replying to his polite attempts at conversation with brief answers. She had been foolish to dance with him. He was much too close, and the warm feel of his fingers clasping her own sent her emotions whirling. She was hot and cold at the same time—and aware of her feelings as she hadn't been before.

"Given the chance to guard your bath again, there might be a different tale to tell," MacLean murmured after a long silence. "I've been wishing this night that I'd not been such a gentleman."

Anne's eyes flew to his, then away to a couple on her right. "Lower your voice," she whispered. "I've no wish that the entire company hear that tale. Besides—" She sent him an arch smile. "I doubt you'd know the difference between a gentleman and a knave."

He caught her hands and turned her deftly about in front of him, pulling her closer than the movement of the dance required. "I'll be happy to show you the difference, lass," he threatened softly in her ear.

Anne forced herself to smile and curtsy as the dance ended. Francis MacLean was an accomplished flirt; she had seen evidence aplenty of that tonight. Why, he must have had half the women in the room languishing and sighing, certain he was in love with them.

And he planned to wed Elizabeth Macintyre, Anne reminded herself. He was only amusing himself with her and countless other fools. She turned quickly, before she could betray her feelings, leaving him in the middle of the floor without a backward glance.

For the rest of the evening, she stayed as far away from MacLean as possible without causing comment. She danced every dance, letting the lively music and the laughter and compliments of her partners ease the ridiculous ache beneath her heart. She kept her eyes resolutely away from her host—especially when he danced with Elizabeth and leaned his dark head down toward hers.

She was dancing a spirited reel with Eric when Francis maneuvered into position beside her. Forced to encounter him in the movement of the dance, she smiled and spoke in passing. At the end of the dance, he caught her before she moved away. "I'll see to Mistress Randall," he said with a curt nod of dismissal toward Eric.

Taking her arm, he edged through the crowd toward a line of benches along the wall. "You've been avoiding me all night. Shall I beg pardon on bended knee? I only spoke my thoughts honestly."

Anne wished for something polished and worldly to say, but could think of nothing. "Oh, did you?" she asked lightly. "I doubt you do anything honestly, Francis MacLean."

He halted abruptly, a look of incredulous surprise sweeping all signs of amusement from his face. "What, lass?"

Anne glanced away, knowing she needed to escape before she said something she would regret. "Excuse me, m'lord, but I've promised a dance to—"

"Not now," MacLean interrupted. "We must talk." Unmindful of her protest, he dragged her along in his wake. Waylaying a passing servant, he thrust a glass of wine into her hand and seized one for himself. Still holding her elbow, he steered her down the uncrowded corridor to a curtained alcove which serviced the hall.

The cool emptiness of the room was a welcome relief after the heated press of the hall. Anne picked her way between two narrow tables covered with unused trays and scattered tankards, holding her skirts carefully away from contact with three dusty barrels of ale waiting to be broached. Turning, she faced MacLean warily across the short space.

"I'd like to know your meaning just now," he said, his eyes following her every move.

She took a slow sip of wine before placing the glass carefully on the table, buying time while she searched for words that would not sound foolish. It was none of her business whom he fancied—and for all she knew, it was the practice for gentlemen to flirt outrageously with every woman who crossed their path. She had never been so miserably aware of her own inexperience.

"Don't regard it," she said, leaning back against the cool stone and closing her eyes. "I didn't mean it the way it sounded . . . and it doesn't matter anyway."

"But it matters a great deal to me," MacLean replied. He leaned forward, catching her bare shoulders and sliding his hands caressingly down her arms until his thumbs gently stroked the sensitive skin at the base of her wrists.

At his touch, Anne felt a pleasurable stir begin inside her, but the image of Elizabeth Macintyre materialized to spoil the feeling. She jerked away. How dare he try to make love to her now. She was no such fool! "How can you touch me like this when everyone knows you're to wed Elizabeth Macintyre?" she blurted out.

"Sweet Jesu, Anne, where'd you hear that tale?"

"From your sister. And half the other women in the room. It's common enough gossip."

"Women must always be gossiping, I suppose," he said calmly, "but there's no truth to the tale. I've no plans to wed Elizabeth, nor have I ever indicated any such intention. Her father is one of my oldest friends. I suppose her frequent presence here has given rise to the talk."

Anne felt a ridiculous happiness sweep over her, which must have shown immediately in her face. MacLean smiled. "And as for touching you like this," he continued, leaning closer and sliding both hands slowly along her arms, "why, I'll be damned if I can do otherwise."

He was so close that she could see her own image reflected in the dark pupils of his eyes. Her gaze dropped to his mouth . . . to the hollow of his suntanned throat where the rapid beat of his pulse was plainly visible . . .

His grip tightened on her arms, drawing her closer. This time she would not pull away. Closing her eyes, she surrendered to the powerful surge of excitement washing over her. He was going to kiss her . . .

"So, here you two are!"

Anne's eyes flew open in dismay. Elizabeth Macintyre stood in the doorway, Eric fidgeting uncomfortably at her side. The woman's cold, hazel eyes glittered dangerously, but she forced her tone to one of teasing playfulness. "Janet is looking for you, Mistress Randall. She sent Eric and me to see you weren't getting into mischief." She flashed a sidelong glance at Francis. "Someone should have warned you about the dangers of these hidden spots after a few glasses of wine. Francis, shame on you for disappearing without a word—and with such an innocent!"

"We were just cooling off after the heat of the dance," MacLean replied. "By the way, I don't think you two have met."

He performed the introductions with an unruffled composure Anne greatly envied but could not emulate. She was intensely uncomfortable under Elizabeth's assessing stare. Her hand trembled as she reached for her glass. How could she have been caught in this compromising position?

Elizabeth laughed brittlely and placed an elegant, jeweled hand possessively on MacLean's arm. "Father has been asking for you, but I told him you were occupied. I promised him I'd tear you away if I could . . ." She glanced at Anne and let her words trail off suggestively.

Anne could bear it no longer. With a mumbled excuse, she turned and fled. Eric hurried along beside her, finally catching her arm and pulling her to a halt just inside the hall. "Don't mind Elizabeth," he said, with far more understanding in his voice than she wished to hear. "She's had a yen for Francis these two years I'm aware of. She's unbearable whenever he's flirting with a new beauty."

Anne glanced up into his serious face. "And does that happen often?"

His eyes dropped from hers and he shifted uncomfortably. "About as often as a new beauty comes along."

The words were nothing more than she had expected, but they held a strange power to wound her. "I see," she replied, carefully composing herself. "How sad for Elizabeth."

The party broke up soon after, with the guests congratulating MacLean and Janet on the success of the evening. Anne should have been with them, but she had slipped away up the back stair to her room.

She undressed hurriedly, putting the gold dress carefully away. If only she could put her thoughts away so easily. Why had she allowed MacLean to drag her away like that? She knew better! She stared at her reflection in the polished glass. Elizabeth Macintyre obviously thought she was no danger. Humph! It would do the woman good to have some competition—not her of course, but someone more experienced, someone able to deal with MacLean's lovely lies.

She jerked the pins from her hair and brushed it viciously. It didn't matter to her whom Francis MacLean wed! He was an accomplished flirt. Even her cousin had seen fit to warn her of that. She resolved to think no more of the matter as she blew out her candle and settled into bed.

In the darkness, the curtains rustled softly against the

wall like whispering children. A soft night breeze wafted the heady fragrance of spring through the open window. The sighing winds must have blown away the mist, for the moonlight spilled into the inky blackness of her room like a pool of molten silver. Anne tossed about uncomfortably, but sleep was far from her. Finally, she got out of bed.

Leaning her forehead against the cool stone of the window facing, she was aware of a painful emptiness in her chest and a strange longing she couldn't identify, much less understand. Something was missing; some important part of life was passing her by. She was consumed by an urgency to fill the void in her life with the feeling of belonging she'd had at Camereigh. Soon she would be back under the dominion of her father and there would be little enough of laughter or love. These short days might be all she would have to guard against the loneliness of a lifetime.

She closed her eyes, remembering that strange moment with Francis when he had almost kissed her. She had made no effort to stop him; she'd even believed his honeyed words. Lord, but the man could be convincing!

Still—how would it have been to feel his lips on hers, his strong arms around her? Her heartbeat quickened at the thought, and the strange longing within her twisted more sharply. Now she would never know. . .

Unable to face the thought of trying to sleep, Anne lit a single candle, dressing hurriedly in the first garment that came to her hand. She dared not walk outside the castle at this hour, but perhaps a turn about the battlements would calm her restless spirits.

Leaving her hair flowing loosely about her shoulders, she caught up her cloak and moved toward the door. Turning the latch quietly, she slipped down the murky hall, thankful that torches still flickered in the wall embrasures in honor of the numerous guests.

Since her room was on an outer wing, she had little difficulty reaching the heavy door to the stairs leading to the battlements. It was unbolted and slightly ajar. Some careless guest must have taken an evening stroll and forgotten to secure it. Careless or drunk, she mused, climbing the steps in the moonlight. The wine had certainly flowed freely. She had even imbibed more than was wise herself. Perhaps that was the reason she had responded as she did to MacLean's touch.

Reaching the top of the stairs, she caught her breath at the beauty of the scene. The meadow stretched out in the moonlight like a placid, silver sea, the dark shadows thrown out by the castle walls looming in stark contrast.

Trailing her hand against the rough wall, Anne moved along the battlements, contemplating abstractedly why she felt such discontent. She leaned against the parapet, feeling the cool fingers of the night wind ruffle her hair.

She thought again of Elizabeth Macintyre, wondering unhappily if MacLean would wed the girl despite his protest. The Scotswoman was a beauty; there was no doubt the two made a striking couple. She stared into the darkness, disliking Elizabeth intensely at that moment. MacLean had kissed her—Anne knew it. She hated the thought of the dark-haired beauty in his arms.

"And of what does Mistress Randall think in the quiet after a ball?"

With a cry of alarm, Anne whirled toward the sound, instantly recognizing the tall outline of Francis MacLean when he stepped from the shadows. "You startled me," she uttered breathlessly. "I never dreamed anyone else would be here at this hour."

"I couldn't sleep, either," MacLean said, crossing the narrow space to the wall. He leaned against the parapet, so close his forearm brushed against hers. She could smell the clean, woodsy fragrance that clung about him. It brought back memories of the night of her capture, when she had slept in his arms as they traveled through the night.

"I meant what I said earlier tonight, Anne," MacLean said abruptly, breaking the short silence between them.

"Oh? And what was that?"

"You know what I mean. I'll play no games with you, lass."

She stared resolutely across the meadow. "Mistress Macintyre obviously thinks you belong to her," she stated bravely, wishing that she could calm the frantic pounding of her heart. "You must have given her some reason for that belief. No woman goes after a man who's given her no encouragement."

"I'm afraid you know little of your own sex, sweetheart," MacLean said, with what she knew must be a smile. "Elizabeth and I have known each other since childhood, and she's quite capable of going after anything she wants. She's been after me this last year. Not for any very flattering reasons, mind you, but because she sees me as an unending source of gold to ease her wants.

"And I won't say I've not considered making her my wife," he admitted after a short pause. "I want a family, Anne. I need sons to carry on my name. I thought she'd fill the need as well as any other."

"'Tis a common enough reason for marriage," Anne said carefully, "but I'd not have thought it of a man like you."

"I'm near twenty-seven years of age, Anne, and I've had more women than I can remember," MacLean said with a bluntness that made her face burn in the darkness. "I'd determined I wasn't the kind to have more than a passing interest in any woman . . . but now I'm not so sure."

Anne stared determinedly across the meadow, gripping the stone wall until its cold roughness cut painfully into the flesh of her fingers. She didn't dare consider the implication of his words. After all, Eric had said . . .

The thought died beneath the gentleness of Francis's touch. Catching a stray curl, he pushed it behind her ear, his strong hand sliding beneath her chin and lifting it toward him in the moonlight. He pushed the hair back tenderly from her brow, his touch so amazingly gentle she felt her fear and distrust slipping away. He stroked her hair, moving his hand down her shoulder until it rested lightly upon her waist. Drawing her into his arms, he held her against the hard length of his body while he gazed intently into her upturned face.

Anne closed her eyes instinctively. The cool brush of the night wind caressed her face as his lips, soft and tentative as the touch of a butterfly, met hers.

All her childish imaginings had not prepared her for this moment. His lips covered hers, softly persuading, his moist tongue slipping expertly along the barrier of her closed mouth. All distrust and resentment were forgotten as her lips parted beneath the growing pressure of his. He probed deeper, tasting the sweetness of her mouth, moving with a rhythm that evoked a surprisingly pleasant sensation in her. His hands moved down her back, pulling her closer, while her arms slid up to cling about his neck.

The pleasurable kiss ended long before Anne was ready. Burying her face against the rough linen of his shirt, she drew a deep breath to quiet the erratic pounding of her heart. His arms held her close. She was warmed by the heat of his body and the spreading warmth in her own blood. In that moment she knew a contentment no traitorous thought could mar.

"I've wanted to do that for a damnably long time now," Francis said unsteadily. "I'd not have held off had you not looked at me as if I were a villain each time I glanced your way. What frightened you so, lass?"

She shook her head, unable to speak or meet his eyes. How could she tell him that she had admired him from that first night—that his dangerous intensity had been like a beckoning flame to a foolish moth? She couldn't admit that the fear he had seen in her eyes those last days had been a fear of her own weakness: a woman didn't say that to a man.

At her silence, Francis slid his hands inside her cloak, putting his arms around her more intimately and bending down to catch her lips once more with his own. His mouth was more demanding this time. She felt an increasing excitement flowing through her as she responded instinctively to the feel of his body against hers, his hungry mouth upon her own.

His warm lips caressed her eyelids and her brow, and he whispered soft words she didn't understand against her hair. Her senses reeled and an irrational happiness swept through her, shutting out all thought of the world beyond his arms. So this was what it meant to be loved by a man like Francis MacLean, she thought exultantly.

After a long moment, Francis lifted his head. "I've longed to see you like this again, with your hair down as it was that morning on the trail." He buried his face in the fragrant mass. "Had Donald not been along, I can't say what might have happened."

"Why were you so angry that morning?"

His knowing fingers moved gently through the silken curtain of her hair, pausing to massage the sensitive skin at the nape of her neck. Anne closed her eyes with something akin to a contented purr.

"I was doing my best to remind myself you were an enemy . . . and you were making it damned hard to keep that thought uppermost in mind," he answered with a chuckle.

She smiled, lifting her hand to run a timid finger inquisitively along his smooth chin and up across the hard line of his jaw, satisfying a sudden need to touch him. Her exploring fingers discovered a tiny scar above his ear. She traced it into his hairline, running her hands through his thickly curling hair before returning to linger along the line of the scar.

"A souvenir from a battle I almost lost as a boy," he responded in answer to her unasked question.

"Was it bad?" She shivered slightly as he caught her open palm and pressed a kiss against it.

"Not so bad as it could have been. They were trying to

cut my throat, but I was too quick." She could hear the smile in his voice at the memory.

"What happened?"

"I got away and learned to be a bit quicker in my sword play. Practice keeps a man's head on his shoulders in these parts—unless, of course, he loses it to a pretty lass. Something I've not done above once before in my life."

An unexpected stab of jealousy pierced her. She tried to push him away, but his strong arms captured her waist, holding her tightly against him. "She was a chamber maid of amazing talents," he whispered laughingly, "and I believe I was all of fifteen at the time. My heart was near broken when I realized there was more than one man in her life . . . but I recovered!" Her laughter blended with his until he lowered his mouth to hers, abruptly ending their amusement.

The intimate claim of his mouth upon hers silenced any protest she might have made as his hands boldly caressed the curves of her body. Anne closed her eyes tightly, giving herself up to the intense pleasure of his kiss, her own hands tentatively exploring the muscular expanse of his broad back. His lips left hers, tracing downward to press hotly against her throat, flooding her nerves with a warm pleasure unlike any she'd ever known.

His experienced hands moved slowly, sensually, igniting a flame that flickered up from somewhere deep inside her and began to burn with a sweet intensity. She had tried to imagine his touch earlier, but her fantasies had fallen far short of this! She was aware of nothing save the hungry weight of his body against hers, and of his heart thudding heavily through the thin cloth between them.

Without warning, Francis released her and drew back against the wall. "I think I'd best get you back inside, lass," he said, drawing an unsteady breath.

Anne struggled to regain control of her own cartwheeling senses. His abrupt withdrawal surprised her. She swallowed hard, suddenly aware of the danger with which she had so recklessly flirted.

Leaving the moonlit battlements, the pair descended the darkened stairs, pausing only long enough to secure the outer door. Neither spoke as they moved along the hallway, but Francis's possessive touch was reminder enough of what had passed between them.

When they reached her chamber, Francis opened the door and followed her inside. Lifting a hand to her cheek, he traced the angle of her jaw with one gentle finger. "No more fears?" he said lightly.

Anne stared at him, amazed at the joyous rush of feeling inside her. She boldly threaded her fingers through the cool silk of his hair, drawing his dark head down to hers and meeting his lips with her own. "None," she whispered when he released her.

Francis leaned back against the door, tiny flames flickering to life in the depths of his eyes. His lips curled into a bewitching smile. "I think I'd best leave you now, lass, else you might get more than you've bargained for this night."

With that he was gone. Moments later, she heard his door close softly down the hall. Hugging herself in jubilation, Anne whirled madly about the room, finally falling into bed with a smothered giggle, the feel of his lips still warm upon her own.

CHAPTER EIGHT

$\mathcal{T}$he morning was well advanced when Anne awoke. A brilliant ray of sunlight streaming unchecked through her window reminded her instantly of the evening just past. She had forgotten to draw the curtain, she realized with a sleepy smile—but curtains had been the last thing on her mind that night!

Closing her eyes, she gave one languorous stretch and then lay still. An overwhelming happiness welled inside her, submerging every other thought beneath the incredible memory of that hour alone with Francis. She could still feel the heat of his mouth upon hers, the wild throb in her veins that began the moment he stepped from the shadows. She wondered at the strange power he held over her, that even now the memory of his touch set her body atremble.

She laughed aloud, filled with a confidence in the future she had never before possessed. No longer was she friendless and alone; with Francis beside her, the dread thought of her father might even cease to haunt her.

With a gasp she sat bolt upright, dismay flooding over her like an icy bath. Glenkennon would never countenance a match between his daughter and the rebel chief of the MacLean clan. How could she have forgotten?

Francis's words came back to her with a haunting clarity:

". . . your value to him in cold, hard gold." Her father needed her for the gold and for the alliance she could bring through marriage. Such arrangements were to be expected for women of her station.

Suddenly her dreams seemed naught but the foolish fancies of a love-struck maiden in the throes of her first affair. Her father would take delight in thwarting Francis and would care little if he broke her heart in the process. Glenkennon could be ruthless in achieving his ends. She had learned that lesson early and well.

She tried to think calmly, but her earlier confidence was shaken. Nagging doubts slipped into her consciousness like creeping trails of mist settling over the moor. Francis was a canny Scotsman, by all accounts. He'd not underestimate Glenkennon's determination to use her to his advantage. And if she realized the futile chance of a match between them, certainly Francis had foreseen its impossibility.

But the man never mentioned marriage, a small voice whispered to her. Slowly the warmth drained from her heart to be replaced by a cold, empty ache. Perhaps Francis planned to enjoy her company only until such time as she left for Ranleigh. Had he not warned her himself that he was seldom interested in a woman for long?

Her cheeks burned at the memory of the way she had responded to his touch. He would consider her an easy conquest—an "innocent," as Elizabeth had called her. And what better way to be revenged upon Glenkennon, the nagging voice whispered. He could easily ruin her and spoil her chances for an advantageous marriage.

Closing her eyes tightly, she took a deep, calming breath. She'd not believe it. Perhaps Francis had forgotten what having the full enmity of the king's representative would mean. Perhaps he had been caught up in the magic of the moonlight, as she had. It was easy enough to see only what one wished on such a night!

But now it was morning, and the seductive glimmer of moonlight no longer hindered her thinking. Francis had to see to the best interests of his clan, and she must return to her father and the marriage he would plan for her. She had to be practical. Regardless of the feelings on either side, this affair ought go no further; it could only end with hurt on both sides. Anne would not have Francis endangered because of her, nor did she wish to become more deeply involved with a man she could never marry—if marriage had, indeed, been his intention.

She rose and dressed slowly, the cold weight of despair hanging heavy on her rebellious heart. She would avoid Francis for the day, she determined. It ought not be difficult in the press of his many guests. Elizabeth Macintyre could occupy his time easily enough if given half a chance.

A brief knock interrupted her ruminations, and Kate entered, carrying breakfast.

Anne forced herself to smile. "It's kind of you to bring up my breakfast, Kate. I know you've more important duties with the house so full of guests." She took the tray with a show of interest. "I should have been made to wait till noon since I've slept away half the morning."

"'Twas the chief's orders," Kate returned. "You wasn't to be 'wakened due to the long night you had, and I was to bring your breakfast once I heard you astirrin'." She looked at Anne speculatively. "The laird seems to be in marvelous good spirits this morning for a man who danced the night away and was up again at the crack o' dawn."

So Francis was in a good mood that morning. Anne imagined how he would look at her with that hint of a smile dancing in his eyes. Pain stabbed her heart. Ignoring him was going to be more difficult than she had imagined. "Thank you, Kate," she said quietly. "And where is Sir Francis now?"

"The last I saw, he was in the hall with MacDonnell and MacInnes. They were refightin' the battle of Byrely Moor, though God knows it couldna' ha' been planned better than the way the chief ordered it near five years ago." Kate chuckled and left the room, shaking her head.

To Anne's surprise, the remainder of the morning passed easily enough. Discovering that Francis had ridden out with several of the men, she went to work helping Janet entertain those ladies of the party who were not yet preparing to depart. It was not until midday that she caught sight of Francis's broad-shouldered frame. He stood laughing with her uncle halfway across the room. She had only a moment to prepare herself before he turned, his face lighting at the sight of her. A small, private smile, little more than a change in the expression of his eyes, altered his face subtly and found its way into her heart. It almost drew an answering smile from her.

Francis shouldered his way through the press of friends, moving quickly to her side. "You missed a glorious morning, sleepyhead," he teased softly. "I was hard pressed not to wake you when I passed your door at dawn."

She ignored the unmistakable intimacy of his whisper and the heart-shaking smile he seemed to wear just for her. He's a master at this kind of thing, she reminded herself, summoning up all her pride to give him only a slight smile. "Kate was foolish enough to let me sleep half the day, leaving poor Janet to attend all your guests. As a matter of fact, I'm on an errand now for Lady MacInnes. Pardon me, but I've tarried overlong as it is." Sidestepping him, she moved quickly away, but not before she noticed the look of hurt surprise that registered fleetingly in his eyes.

By practicing the utmost caution, she managed to keep from running into Francis for most of that long, wretched afternoon. There were several close calls, but she kept herself occupied in remote parts of the castle whenever he was indoors. Even Kate, sent by her chief to discover Anne's whereabouts, was sent away with the lame excuse that she was "busy."

By late afternoon Anne was thoroughly sick of feigning a gaiety that she did not feel among a host of people with whom she was scarcely acquainted. Her head ached and she longed to be alone. Slipping out the postern door, she moved disconsolately across the courtyard toward the stables. She had not seen Cassie in two days; the mare would forget her if she was not careful.

She passed out of the harsh daylight into the musty dimness of the stable. The place was devoid of humans this afternoon, its only inhabitants contentedly munching the fragrant, dried meadow grass or stamping sleepily in their stalls. The warm, familiar smell of horses and manure engulfed her and, for a moment, she was transported to a simpler life when she had played in the stables and counted her father's knowledgeable stable hands the only men worth knowing.

She walked slowly along the aisle until she reached Cassie's stall. The mare nuzzled her hand, pressing a warm, inquisitive nose against Anne's pocket, her velvety muzzle sniffing out the dried fruit Anne had taken from the kitchen larder.

She stroked the mare's satiny neck, combing the tangles from the heavy black mane with her fingers. "You're a beauty, sweetheart, and I'll hate to leave you when I go. Will you miss me?" she questioned, looking steadily into the great, liquid, brown eyes that stared at her soulfully. She smiled as the mare nuzzled her arm, looking for more treats. "Well, you'll miss the things I bring, anyway. You'll just have to make up to someone else when I'm gone."

"And do you think you're going somewhere, mistress?" Francis's voice cut in coldly.

Anne turned in surprise. Francis was leaning against the stable wall, his dark garments blending perfectly with the shadows. It was no wonder she'd not seen him when she left the blinding sunshine of the courtyard.

She studied him wordlessly. His face was hard, the corners of his fascinating mouth set and unsmiling. She felt a quick pang at the possibility she might cause him hurt. "I suppose I'll be going sooner or later," she said, turning back to the mare before she could betray herself.

"You'll go when and if I choose and not before," he said

softly, moving away from the wall to within a few threatening inches. "I've been trying to see you all day, mistress. You can't have been unaware of the fact."

His voice was carefully controlled, yet she read the anger beneath its surface calm. "I've been busy helping Janet," she said, feeling the pace of her own heart quicken. "There are tasks to see to. She shouldn't have to handle them all herself . . ."

"I'm aware of that," he broke in curtly, "but I doubt they'd have kept you from a moment with me had you been so inclined. What is it, lass?" he questioned, sudden tenderness blunting the edge in his hard voice.

Anne's gaze shifted nervously from his, dropping to focus blindly on the rough wood of the stall. "Nothing," she replied, shrugging her shoulders with feigned indifference.

"Be bloody damned, woman! What kind of game are you playing?" Francis exploded. "Did I dream last night or do you just enjoy making a fool of a man?"

Underlying the obvious anger in his voice, there was something else. Was it pain, she wondered. Perhaps Francis hadn't been deluding her for the sake of revenge on her father. Perhaps her doubts were unfounded.

But if that were the case, it was all the more imperative to break off this misbegotten relationship. She could bring the MacLeans nothing but trouble.

"Last night was the result of too much wine and moonlight," she said with a shaky laugh. "This morning I found I'd changed my mind. I'm sure you understand. It . . . it just happened." She turned to move away from him, catching her breath at the look of cold fury on his face. "If you'll excuse me," she said nervously, "I think we've said all that needs saying about the matter."

A hard muscular arm shot out, blocking her way. "But I've not yet had my say," Francis whispered silkily, his dark face close to hers. "Is this the way you tease a man, lass? Christ, I'm sorry I left you last night!" Without warning, he jerked her against him, one arm clamped tightly around her slender waist, the other behind her head, fingers digging painfully into the tender flesh of her neck. His mouth descended angrily upon hers, bruising, hurting, demanding.

For a moment Anne struggled futilely against his rough embrace, so different from the tenderness of the night before. Then, abruptly, the struggle ended. The feeling of his muscular body pressed against her, his hard, unyielding mouth claiming hers, assaulted every sense with an urgency for which she had not been prepared. Her lips opened beneath his of their own accord, her tongue moving experimentally against the ravages of his. Her fingers crept slowly up the hard expanse of chest she was crushed against, one hand moving to stroke the corded muscles at the back of his neck then lose itself in the thick mass of his softly curling hair.

A wild thrill surged through her as his arms held her close, his mouth and hands touching a primitive chord she had not known existed in her until that moment. All resistance forgotten, her lips clung to his. She leaned instinctively into his body in passionate disavowal of the words she had uttered just moments before.

His crushing grip slowly eased. His angry, hurting mouth ceased its assault on hers, and his kiss became slower and more tender. His hands slid along her sides, brushing lightly against her breast before gently cupping each side of her face. He pulled his lips reluctantly from hers, studying her in perplexity. "Do you just enjoy living dangerously, lass, or are you playing some deep game with me?"

She felt strangely bereft once his lips no longer moved on hers. Nothing had changed, yet she was more certain than ever that she belonged in his arms. The harsh reality of the situation swept over her, and she closed her eyes against a sense of overwhelming hopelessness.

"What is it, Anne?" Francis asked gently, a note of concern sharpening the husky timbre of his voice. His thumb caressed the delicate line of her jaw, and he continued to hold her upturned face close to his.

She took a deep breath, struggling to speak around the constriction in her throat. "My . . . my father will never countenance anything between the two of us, and you know as well as I my time here is growing short. It's best we end this thing before it's begun."

"Do you wish to leave?"

Her eyes flew open, and she stared at him in amazement. "You must know I don't," she choked out.

A satisfied smile spread over his face. He leaned down, kissing her with a thoroughness that took her breath away. "You've nothing to worry about, lass," he said, raising his head after a long, pleasurable moment. "Let me take care of Glenkennon; I'm already working on a plan."

"But I'd not have you in further trouble on my account."

"I've been in trouble since the day I was born," he returned lightly. "If you don't believe me, ask Janet. Father used to beat me at least once a week."

She opened her mouth to protest, but Francis placed a silencing finger over her lips. "I told you once I wasn't afraid of your father. It's only a matter of outfoxing the fox, and I've had years of practice at the game." He smiled at her in a way that melted her heart too easily. "Trust me," he said softly, drawing her into his arms so that she forgot everything but the reality of his touch and the demand of his mouth upon hers.

The sound of someone noisily clearing his throat filtered vaguely through the haze of passion that rapidly engulfed Anne. The sound came again, followed by Donald's amused voice. "Pardon, sir, but the Lady Janet and Ian MacDonnell are looking for the both of ye. I told them I'd seen ye heading for the stables."

Anne froze in embarrassment, burying her flaming face against Francis's chest. He lifted his head, keeping his arms casually looped around her. "Thank you, Donald. I suppose we'll have visitors here in a few moments then."

"Aye, that's what I was thinkin'."

Francis's firm hand on Anne's elbow turned her around so that she faced the grinning Donald. She raised stricken eyes to his amused ones, feeling another hot blush sweep over her.

Francis slid his arm down to encircle her waist familiarly. "Don't mind Donald, lass," he said comfortingly. "He knows all my secrets and is as good a confidant as man or woman could wish. He's saved us a far more embarrassing confrontation with my sister and your uncle. He might have even saved me a deadly encounter with Ian. I can see him playing the irate kinsman if he thought I was trifling with you."

Anne smiled as he had meant her to, and the three were innocently discussing the merits of Highland-bred horses over those imported from England and France when they were joined by Janet, Ian and Eric.

The little group walked slowly through the stables, inspecting Camereigh's fine stock of mares and spring foals. They emerged from the cool dimness just in time to see a heavily lathered horse being led toward them by a clansman. Francis stopped short, eyes narrowed as he took in the significance of the worn animal. None of his men abused their animals in such a way unless—

He was away across the courtyard at a fast sprint.

Anne reached out a hand to the suddenly pale Janet, the same cold fear in both their hearts. Something must have happened to the Camerons! With a silent prayer, the women gathered up their skirts and followed Francis and the MacDonnells across the courtyard at an unladylike run.

Francis reached the steps just as the worn, muddied messenger burst through the door in search of him. He had time for one quick question, then the rest of the group converged upon the stairs.

"Is it Jamie?" Janet asked breathlessly, her eyes wide with fear.

"No. There's no word on your husband."

Janet gave a ragged sigh and closed her eyes, relief making her lean weakly against Anne for support. "Thank God," she murmured as Anne slipped a comforting arm around her.

"Well, what is it, man?" Francis asked gruffly. "What brings you to my door in such haste?"

"It's Charles Randall," the man replied in a voice hoarse with exhaustion. "He's close on my heels and not sparing his mount."

Anne's eyes widened in surprise. "Charles?" she whispered. "Coming here?"

"How many men-at-arms?" Francis's voice cracked like a whiplash into the stunned silence.

"Less than a score, sir, but heavily armed, all of them."

Francis's eyes half closed while his nimble mind leaped ahead to the possibilities. "He doesn't come here for a fight. He's far too few men with him. Not even that hotheaded young fool would attack Camereigh with a force of that size." He rubbed his chin thoughtfully "Of course, it could be a trick." His eyes snapped open and he studied the messenger. "Why do I receive word so late?"

"Glenkennon and his advisors are away at Edinburgh," the man replied. "Young Charles arrived unexpectedly from the Borders. I suppose 'twas then he learned of his sister's disappearance, for he tarried only long enough to eat and change horses and was away again with his guard. We discovered his intentions by the merest chance, sir. I'm ahead of him only by dint of a fast horse and no rest."

At that moment, Donald appeared with a tankard of ale which the man accepted gratefully. With a nod Francis gave him leave to drink. "You've done well, lad," he said shortly. "So the young pup acts on his own initiative and Glenkennon knows nothing of it. Excellent! We may win a point this game."

He turned toward Anne. A cold smile twisted his lips

but didn't reach his eyes. "Will you be pleased to see your brother, mistress?"

Anne felt a flicker of animosity at his tone and was reminded again of the gulf that yawned between them. Could this hard, dangerous man have kissed her so tenderly only a short while before? She raised her head a notch to cover her confusion. "Why, yes, I think I shall," she said, matching his own cold tone.

He turned to Donald. "Get a full score of men up here. Let them be armed, but not overly so. I want them in the hall at their ease playing dice and such, but they're to be on the ready. There's to be no fighting unless it's begun by Randall. Let them understand I'll break the first man that picks a quarrel."

"Janet." He turned to his sister. "Get the women out of the hall and upstairs. Tell them we're having unexpected company, but don't alarm them unduly. If the men stay, be sure they're armed. We'll not invite trouble, but by God, we'll be ready if it comes!"

They moved forward into the hall, and Anne watched in growing dismay while Francis ordered them all about. Men scrambled to obey his terse commands. Even her uncle seemed loath to question his friend in this ruthless mood. She thought of her younger brother, hurrying headlong into a trap. "And what orders do you have for me, my lord?" she asked tensely. "Surely you've some part planned for me in this game, as you call it."

"You'll be upstairs with Donald, Ian, and me," he said without glancing in her direction. "I want you beside me."

Turning away from her, Francis slipped his sword from its sheath, testing the weight of the steel before slipping it back into place. Anne licked her lips nervously. Surely he didn't mean to kill Charles!

"What do you plan to do with my brother once you have him trapped?" she asked. "He's hopelessly outnumbered; you said so yourself." She stared as though mesmerized by his sword. "It would be cold-blooded murder, and you know it, Francis MacLean!"

The angry accusation in her voice caught Francis's attention. He frowned, eyebrows lowering in displeasure. "I don't plan to do anything to the lad save offer him a drink and some hospitality. But a man doesn't ride through the countryside armed to the teeth without something important on his mind." His cold stare held hers unwaveringly. "Life in the Highlands teaches a man to be suspicious, sweet. I've learned to take care of my own."

With a chill dread in her heart, Anne followed Francis up the stairs to the laird's room. A fire blazed warmly in the great fireplace, but she didn't dare try to reach it with her knees trembling so. Sinking gratefully into a velvet-cushioned chair, she tried to convince herself Francis meant Charles no harm.

A few moments later the clatter of the arriving band sounded. A quick look passed between Donald and Francis, and the older man slipped out to see to the preparations below. Ian stood beside the window gazing down at the activity in the courtyard, but Francis leaned casually against the wall beside the fireplace . . . waiting.

An uncontrollable shiver ran down Anne's back, and her hands felt so damp she dried them on her skirt. Wringing the rich cloth between nervous fingers, she glanced toward Francis. He was watching her impassively. Immediately she released her skirt and sat up straighter.

The hard lines of his face softened. "I've no desire to harm the lad, Anne . . ."

The tramp of boots upon stone wrenched her gaze from his. She stared anxiously at the door. The clatter of spurs rang just outside.

The door flew open abruptly. Charles strode angrily into the room, Donald hard on his heels. The boy was a handsome young giant, tall and straight, looking far older than his seventeen years. At the sight, Anne's heart swelled with pride. Charles had grown up in the years since she had seen him. There was now little trace of the boy she remembered save the dark auburn hair and shrewd gray eyes of their father.

"Charles," she whispered, scarcely believing her eyes.

He turned, crossing the room to her in a few long-legged strides. Catching her hand, he drew her into his arms for a quick embrace. "So you *are* here!" he said, his voice harsh with relief. "I scarcely credited the rumor." His eyes searched her face anxiously. "Are you well? Have you been harmed?"

"No, Charles. I'm well, truly I am," she said quickly. "It's good to see you, though."

His fingers tightened convulsively on hers, and he turned toward the two men across the room. "What infamy is this, MacLean? Do you stoop to kidnapping innocent women for sport now in the North? I've heard many disreputable tales of you, but to now I'd not believed them."

Francis leaned his broad shoulders against the lintel, calmly surveying the seething young man. "I'd be careful how I spoke of infamy were my name Randall," he drawled softly. "The imprisonment and beating of two innocent men and a couple of lads would go well under that name."

"They attacked and murdered a half-dozen men," Charles returned, still angry but obviously less sure of his ground.

Francis snorted derisively. "Not even you can believe that tale, my lad. Those were trumped-up charges, as well you know."

Anne saw her brother's hand slide toward his sword. She caught his arm in both hands. "Please Charles, there's no need for trouble. I swear I've not been harmed, but have been treated with the greatest courtesy here. We've even two of our kinsmen here to see to my honor."

"Well, I'm here now to take you home," he declared. He glared at Francis, daring the man to contradict him.

"I don't think the lass has finished her visit," Francis

stated softly. "We're enjoying her company, so we'll not suffer her to leave us just yet."

"Meaning you'll try to stop me from taking my sister out of here."

"I won't try," Francis promised with a dark smile.

Ian MacDonnell stepped out from the wall. "Come nephew, sit down and have an ale. Let's discuss this situation like civilized men. The lass has not been harmed, so you've no cause to go fondling your sword hilt as if you'd enjoy nothing better than to run us through."

Charles turned toward Ian, his gray eyes cold with disdain. "I'm disappointed you should countenance this, Uncle—disappointed, but not surprised. When I see you traffic with this unprincipled blackguard, I hate to admit our kinship."

MacDonnell's eyes glinted steely blue and the muscles of his jaw tightened visibly. "Aye, lad, but blood's blood, whether you will or no, and there's no changing the fact no matter how ashamed a man may be of his kin."

The tension in the room tightened like a vice. Anne had to get her brother out before violence erupted. "Charles, listen to me," she said, forcing herself to speak calmly. "I swear I've not been treated with any discourtesy. I've my freedom about Camereigh—I don't mind staying longer."

She turned toward Francis, casting him a look of entreaty. "Sir Francis, let me speak with my brother alone. I'm sure once he understands, you can discuss this more calmly."

"No."

She stared at him in surprise. "Francis, please, I—"

"I said no!" he interrupted in a harsher voice than he had ever before used with her.

His rough tone acted like a lash to goad further Charles's anger. "So you plan to continue holding her prisoner here?" he questioned. "What do you think to accomplish by it?"

Francis moved deliberately across the carpeted floor. Catching Anne's chin between his long, tapering fingers, he twisted her head away as if to study her profile. "Your sister's a very lovely woman, boy," he said consideringly. He dropped his hand before Anne could turn away. "I'm sure I can think of some use for her," he added, a sardonic eyebrow raised in Charles's direction.

Anne stared at Francis in amazement, unable to believe his deliberate baiting of her brother.

"Come, lad," MacDonnell put in hurriedly, "your men and horses are spent, and you need a good meal under your belt. Rest here tonight, and perhaps we can come to some agreement on the morrow."

Charles glared from one man to the other, his blazing eyes speaking his fury. "You may have little concern for your honor, Uncle, but I'll not spend an unnecessary hour with this whoreson of a Scotsman."

Francis's hand flew to his sword, and Anne caught her breath as the gleaming blade slid a few inches from its sheath. Charles rested his hand on the basket hilt of his own muddy blade. The room was so quiet, Anne could hear the ticking of the ornate French clock across the room. The sound hammered against her ears while the two men glared furiously at each other across the narrow space.

Finally, Francis shoved his weapon back into its scabbard with a decisive click. "I'll not stand accused of murdering foolish children," he said, controlling his temper with obvious difficulty. "But take care you don't try my patience further. I'm like to turn you over my knee and give your backside quite a thrashing."

Charles moved forward until he stood directly before Francis. "I'm not afraid of you, MacLean," he said so softly Anne had to strain to hear. "You may laugh at me for a youth, but if you hurt one hair of my sister's head, I'll come after you . . . and you'll pay."

An unexpected smile spread slowly over Francis's face, relaxing the taut muscles along his jaw. "You're game, lad,

I've no doubt of that. I think you've more MacDonnell blood than you care to claim just now. Don't let that rash tongue get you killed before you learn a bit of wisdom, though; Scotland has need of lads like yourself." He stepped back and his hand swung away from his sword. "Now be gone before I forget my quarrel's not with you."

Charles gazed at Francis in stunned surprise, obviously uncertain what to do. He glanced at Anne, then back to Francis.

"Go on lad," Ian said softly. "Anne'll come to no harm."

Charles turned and strode to the door. "We'll have you out of here before long, Anne," he said, pausing in the doorway. "I promise."

Anne heard his tramp on the stairs, then the sound of his voice in the courtyard calling clipped orders to his men. Weak with relief, she flew to the window, scarcely able to believe he was riding out of Camereigh unharmed. Turning, she glared at Francis. She could not reconcile the laughing, tender man of last night with the cold-blooded devil who had used her just then to move her brother to justifiable anger. Any contest between the two would have ended little short of murder.

With a sick feeling in her stomach, Anne turned away from Francis and walked blindly out the door. She pushed past the anxious Janet, ignoring her questions and slamming the door to her chamber.

Alone in her room, she paced the floor, desperately trying to resolve the conflicting desires within her. In the last twenty-four hours she had run the gamut of emotions from despair to joy and back again, and she felt exhausted by the tumult of feelings in her breast.

Just what did Francis want from her—and what were his motives? Had he only been acting for her brother's benefit, or had his real performance been the past night, when Anne had been so easily convinced of his sincerity by a kiss? Poisonous arrows of doubt darted through her. Francis was using her. Thank God her eyes had been opened so soon!

The afternoon waned, and Kate came to call her to supper. Pleading a headache, Anne remained in her room, thankful to the ever-dependable Kate for a tray of soup and bread. She tried to eat, but each bite choked her, and she finally shoved the tray away in disgust.

Wearily, she dressed for bed, knowing sleep would be long in coming. She gathered up her embroidery, but it lay untouched in her lap. Why had Francis acted as he had? And what part did he mean her to play? What schemes really lay behind his tender words? There was no trusting the man, she told herself. He was as changeable as the Scottish weather.

A loud knock at her chamber door broke the silence. Startled, she dropped the needle she had taken up. "Who is it?" she called.

"Francis."

She swallowed hard. Francis was the last person she wanted to see at that moment. "I've retired. It must wait till morning."

The door swung open. Francis strode into the room without hesitation. "I think not. We'll talk tonight."

"Well, do come in," Anne snapped, jerking her robe more closely about herself. She rose to her feet. "After all, I'm your prisoner; I can't lock you out. You might even think of some use for me if you put your mind to it!"

Francis folded his arms across his chest, gazing at her impassively. "I think you've sulked long enough; it's time we got things straight between us."

"I have the headache," she informed him.

He lifted an eyebrow. "So we were told." He crossed the floor until he stood before her. "The truth is, you're angry with me and have kept to your room in a temper."

"Angry . . . yes, I'm angry!" she threw back furiously. "You used me deliberately to anger Charles when we could have easily explained everything. And what's more, you enjoyed it! You enjoyed manipulating us both!"

His narrowed eyes held her own, their cold expression unchanging. "It's time you faced the truth, Anne. You and I belong on opposite sides; strictly speaking, we're enemies. My first loyalty must be to my family and my clan. The lives of too many people depend on me for personal considerations to matter. I'll do anything I must to win the freedom of the Camerons. Do you understand that?" he asked, dropping his voice. "Anything!

"I couldn't let you talk to Charles alone for fear you'd give away too much. We don't want Glenkennon to think you're safe and comfortable here. I wanted to shake them up, make them worry about your well-being. I must keep them anxious enough to release their prisoners in exchange. After Jamie and the boys are back, we'll have time to work out whatever's between the two of us."

"But I'll be back at Ranleigh then," she protested.

"Not necessarily." The trace of a smile warmed the wintry blue of his eyes. "I plan to hold onto you for a while."

She moved toward the fire, wishing she could steady the erratic beating of her heart. Coldness filled her. "Even if I wish to go?" she whispered.

"I'm afraid so. I'm an unprincipled blackguard, you know."

At his words, her anger flared again. "Do you think if you keep me here I'll just fall into your arms at the snap of your fingers? God, I know I was easy last night. Do you really think after today it'll be that easy again?"

He took in her angrily flushed face and flashing blue eyes, the golden mass of hair hanging in a luxurious curtain about her quivering shoulders. His heart ached at the mistrust in her voice and the hurt mirrored in her eyes.

"No, I don't think it will be easy . . . for either of us," he said softly. "But there's something between us we can't deny. I can no more stay away from you than you can from me. God knows, you're the last woman in the world I need to be involved with . . ." He paused, staring at her intently. "But I can't stop myself, and I've given up trying."

He closed the distance between them with one long stride. Placing a gentle hand on her shoulder, he turned her around. "Do you understand, Anne? This is the way it has to be for now." He tilted her face up, his eyes searching hers for any hint of understanding. "I can't promise I'll never hurt you. I may have to, as I did today. But I give you my word I'll do what I can to limit the harm to you and your brother. And when this mess is over, we'll have time to pursue our own future."

It was happening again. She was falling back under his magical spell. It mattered not that he had used her, that he had just told her he might have to again. He pulled her close against his chest, his strong arms holding her comfortingly as he gently stroked her hair. He did not kiss her or even speak a word—just held her tightly in the haven of his arms. Anne closed her eyes, knowing it was enough —that he would always have the power to bring her back into his arms.

CHAPTER NINE

$\mathcal{B}$y noon the next day, the guests had departed, leaving the echoing halls of Camereigh empty save for the boisterous MacLeans. Standing in the open gateway between Francis and Janet, Anne strained for one last glimpse of Ian's vivid plaid as the MacDonnells disappeared among the far trees. The sun shone hotly against her face, and the breeze across the meadow smelled of spring flowers and greening forests, but inside she felt a spreading, wintry hollowness.

It seemed Anne was always saying good-bye to the people she loved. First Charles, then her mother and Philippa —now the MacDonnells. Would she ever see them again? Ian had been terse making his last good-byes. Did that question haunt him also?

As if in answer to Anne's bleak thoughts, Francis placed a comforting hand upon her arm, drawing her closer. She turned toward him. His eyes were steady on hers, his touch reassuring. "You'll see them before long, lass. Scotland's no' so broad a land a determined man can't cross it." He drew her beside him toward the stable. "Come, let's have a smile. 'Tis too bonny a day for that dark frown."

Anne's spirits lifted at the promise in his eyes. He was right—it was too lovely a day for brooding. Ian would soon return as he had promised. Besides, how could she be unhappy with Francis beside her?

Janet caught the look that passed between Francis and Anne, and her eyes narrowed in sudden concern. She had seen that look on her brother's face before and knew where it led. She watched the two move together across the courtyard, shoulders touching, heads bent close in conversation. Had she been blind to what was happening beneath her very nose?

Francis had a way with women, she'd not deny, but she did not like to think of Anne falling victim to his easy charm. It would be dangerous for the MacLeans, and besides, she'd not like to see the girl hurt. She bit her lip thoughtfully. It might not be her place to interfere, but she would have a word with Francis before riding for home in the morning.

Janet got her chance to speak with her brother after the evening meal. Sitting comfortably in his private hall, she considered him silently, uncertain how to bring up the touchy subject.

Francis grinned down at her from his place beside the fire. "What's to do, sister? You seemed so anxious to talk with me at dinner, yet now you sit as though you've nothing to say. Come, it can't be so bad as that."

Taking a deep breath, Janet plunged in determinedly. "What is Anne to you, Francis?" she asked bluntly.

Francis frowned in surprise, then raised an imperious eyebrow. "And what business is that of yours?" he countered.

"I like the girl in spite of who she is. I'd not see her hurt . . . even by my own brother."

He scowled at her wordlessly, then turned, drumming his fingers irritably against the mantel.

"It'd be easy for her to fall in love with you," Janet continued, picking her words carefully. "In fact, I'd wager it's happened already. You can't make her your mistress,

Francis. She's not the type. Anne doesn't even know the rules to these games you play." She paused, then finished softly. "I'd not like to see you ruin her... or be ruined by her father."

"Oddsblood, Janet!" Francis snapped, giving her a hard look. "You paint a pretty picture of me. I don't believe I've ever been known as a seducer of innocent virgins."

"I mean no slander," she replied, returning his angry stare evenly, "but I've seen the way you look at each other. I'm not such a fool that I don't know what it means. Anne's a beautiful woman, but there are others just as bonny who could easily fill your needs."

"Spare me your sermons," Francis returned, flinging himself into a chair across from hers. He crossed his long, muscular legs and scowled intently at one boot. "I've no intention of harming the girl. The last thing I want is for Anne to be hurt." A wrinkle of concern creased his brow. "Honestly, I'd tell you if I knew, Janet, but I'm not certain of anything yet. I can promise you this, though... I'll not make her my mistress though the temptation's enough to break a stone. The cost to her might be too dear."

Janet stared at him in amazement. Could he possibly desire something more than a quick tumble with the girl? "Francis," she whispered, "you can't be falling in love with her—not Glenkennon's daughter!"

He grinned sheepishly before turning back to the well-studied boot. "I'd not say that yet, but I'd no' be ruling it out either. Anne's different from the other women I've known. I enjoy her company in a way I never thought to do... a way I can't even explain."

"You'll not jeopardize Jamie and the boys?" She stared at him, her large, expressive eyes dark with fear.

Francis's heavy brows lowered. "Jamie and the boys come first, Janet. You should know better than to ask that! I'll get them back no matter the cost." Taking her hand, he gripped her fingers painfully. "But is it wrong to hope for some happiness for myself—to gamble everything if I deem it worth the price?"

"Glenkennon will destroy you, Francis. You'll be giving him just the excuse he needs!" she began desperately. "Then the MacDonnells, the Camerons, and a host of others will rally to you. Would you start another war with England and bring about the ruin of us all?"

Francis leaned back wearily in his chair, allowing Janet's hand to slide from his grasp. "I hope it doesn't come to that. I'm not afraid of Glenkennon and his mercenaries, but I'd not like to drag the clans to war." A vicious, well-placed kick sent the three-legged stool beside him careening across the floor. "Damn it, Janet . . . you know as well as I, if not Anne it'll be some other matter that causes this pot to boil! Glenkennon will force a fight before long."

Janet bit her lip, studying her brother's troubled face. There was nothing she could say; she knew his words were true.

She recalled her own stormy courtship near fifteen years earlier and her love for a man who was not her father's choice. Francis had helped her persuade their father to the match. Rising from her chair, she moved to his side, placing a comforting hand on his shoulder. "You know Jamie and I will be behind you no matter what. And I'll warrant every other clan in these hills will side with you should the earl force you to war."

He caught her hand, pressing it tightly against his shoulder. "Thanks, sister dear, I do hope you're right." Smiling, he unfolded his length from the chair, the roguish gleam back in his eyes. "Don't fret, Janet. We've no way of knowing if the lass will even have me. Donald says I've too dark a face and rough a manner to interest any decent wench."

"I don't doubt she'll have you. If Glenkennon doesn't have your head first."

"The man will pay dearly if he tries," Francis said with a

confident laugh. "But no more of this dark talk. This is your last night at Camereigh. Let's join the others."

Anne was to look back on those carefree days as the happiest in her life. She abandoned all worry and care into Francis's capable hands, trusting him to solve the confusing riddle of her future. She had no idea how he would bring about the miracle that would free her from her father, but she gave the matter no further thought. Francis would see to it.

The days swept by in an idyllic blur of companionable rides, romantic picnics, and long walks beside the sea. Even the weather conspired to make the days seem magical, for there was an unheard of stretch of golden days beneath a dazzling, cloudless canopy of blue over Camereigh.

The nights were even more unforgettable. The two ate together and played chess beside the crackling fire; sometimes they talked for hours, ignoring the silent servants and the knowing winks of Francis's clansmen. Lost in their own enchantment, they even managed to overlook Donald's disapproving frown and the worried looks he and Kate exchanged while they went about their duties.

Mindful of his promise to Janet, Francis clapped a resolve of iron over his body, restraining the powerful urge to take Anne's innocence and teach her the ways of love. He spent many a sleepless night as a result, tossing and turning in his lonely bed in a room so close to hers, cursing himself for creating his own torture.

He awoke early one morning after a restless night, his mind still fired with images from the stirring dreams he had enjoyed. The thought of Anne lying asleep down the hall was enough to drive the last vestige of sleep from his brain. He tossed back the covers and got up, crossing the floor on well-muscled legs to stand naked before the window in the predawn chill.

Just what did he feel for the girl besides the desire to

take her to bed? She would come to him willingly. He sensed a slumbering passion in her that fanned the flames of his own desire each time he took her in his arms. But there was more than that, he mused, else he would have had her long before. She trusted him, and he felt bound by some feeling that would not let him cause her harm. He wanted . . .

He drew a deep breath. What did he want? Struggling, he put his formless feelings into thought. He wanted to love her—to keep her safe beside him . . . always.

An inexplicable joy welled up inside him at the thought. He gazed out the window at the shadowy countryside. The sunrise would be a glorious one, and he wanted to share it with her.

In the dim light, he fumbled into his clothing and hurried down the inky corridor. Pausing outside Anne's door he listened, then slipped inside.

He stood for a moment watching her sleep, a curious tenderness stealing over him at the sight. Sitting gingerly on one side of the bed, he leaned down to press a kiss against her lips.

Her heavy lashes fluttered against the creamy alabaster of her cheek. Slowly her eyes opened. She smiled at him sleepily in recognition, then sat up with a start as she came fully awake. "What's amiss?" she asked sharply, blue eyes wide with alarm.

"Nothing." He placed a silencing finger over her lips. "Hush, love, or you'll wake Kate, and that harridan will run me out on a broom."

"But what are you doing here?" she asked, still befuddled by sleep.

"Why, I came to see you," he teased. "Do I need another reason?"

Unmindful of her scantily clad body, Anne slipped her arms around his neck and leaned against him with a sigh, closing her eyes in contentment while he crushed her against his chest. "It sounds like a perfectly good reason to me," she said sleepily, wondering if it had only been wishful thinking on her part, or if he had really used the word "love" a moment before.

Francis felt the soft swell of her breasts against him through the thin cloth of her shift. Her arms clung trustingly about him and the intoxicating smell of her rose up to fill his senses. He pressed his lips against the tempting hollow of her throat, trailing moist kisses along her shoulder until he felt her quiver in his arms. He eased her yielding body down onto the soft pillows, forgetting the reason he had come.

In the courtyard below, the clatter of a pail dropped by a sleepy servant brought him back to his senses. The servants would soon be about the halls, and he had best not be caught in Anne's room. Lifting his head with a sigh, he pushed a silken strand of hair back from her flushed face. Capturing a willful curl, he lifted it to his nostrils to inhale its heady fragrance.

Anne belatedly drew the covers across her chest, amazed that she should feel so comfortable with Francis beside her like this. "I fear your notions of propriety seem strange to a poor English lass, m'lord. Back home I wasn't allowed to speak to a man alone—much less entertain one in my bedchamber." Her eyes twinkled. "I may like this Scotland of yours after all."

He tweaked the curl, then gave her a wicked grin. "I'll have you know I've behaved with every consideration of propriety. Janet threatened me with direst consequences if I stepped beyond the line!"

"And is this within the line?" she asked, indicating his reclining position beside her on the bed.

"I only came to invite you for a ride," he said, slipping to his feet. "How was I to know you'd still be asleep on such a fine morning?" He glanced toward the window where the glow of dawn lightened the sky. "If you can be dressed and downstairs in the time it takes to saddle two horses, we might still make Gull Point. Daybreak's an unbelievable sight up there."

She was up and fumbling for her habit before his steps died away in the hall.

That was but one perfect day among a dozen that swept by on swift, silent wings. Anne lived for each moment, foolishly refusing to think about the future while she basked in the warmth of her first love.

But the spell could not last. Her serenity ended abruptly one afternoon as she sat in a small glen studying the intricate design of a tiny, star-shaped wildflower she had picked. Francis lay on his back beside her, one arm thrown lazily over his eyes to shield them from the brilliance of the sun.

"Glenkennon's coming tomorrow," he said, breaking the peaceful stillness of the day as a stone tossed into a pool shatters the calm surface and ripples to the shore. It took a moment for his words to sink in. Anne stared at him in surprise, dismay written on her face.

"Don't look so stricken," he said gently. "I've no intention of letting him take you."

Still she did not speak. She had ignored the thought of her father so long that this abrupt reminder literally took her breath. Glenkennon coming—it couldn't be!

Francis rolled onto his stomach, catching her hand in his. "Don't worry." He grinned. "I'll not let him eat you."

"But I didn't know you'd heard from him," she protested, finding her voice at last.

"Oh, I've had several messages, each more arrogant and impatient than the last. We've arranged a prisoner exchange to our mutual satisfaction." He smiled shrewdly. "What he doesn't know is that we plan to free his prisoners tonight while they lie at Ginahea Castle. Come the morrow, the man will have nothing to trade."

Anne shredded the flower in wordless abstraction. Rising nervously, she moved away across the clearing. She leaned her arms against the gnarled branch of a spreading oak, staring into the greening forest. The shady depths of the woodland seemed suddenly menacing.

"Why didn't you tell me you'd heard from him? I . . . I'd almost forgotten."

"I knew you'd have asked if you wanted to know, lass," Francis answered softly. "You seemed to be enjoying yourself best not thinking about the man."

She nodded, acknowledging the truthfulness of his words. She had deliberately refused to think about the future, hiding her head from every unpleasant thought. Now it had come upon her with a vengeance. "Must you ride to Ginahea tonight?" she asked, a new fear chilling her blood.

"No. Donald made me think better of that plan. Unfortunately, my face is well known in those parts, and my wretched size makes it difficult to avoid attention. One glimpse of me and the whole place would be up in arms." He smiled at the sigh of relief that escaped her.

Rising quickly, he crossed the ground to her side. Catching her by the shoulders, he shook her gently. "You must learn, lass, that raiding and stealing are a part of life here. A man's not even considered a man until he's raided his first horses. God grant you see me ride out on many a raid . . ." He lifted her chin with a gentle hand and brushed a kiss across her lips. ". . . and return to find you waiting here at Camereigh."

She searched his face anxiously. "Are you sure the plan for tonight will succeed?"

He shrugged his shoulders, taking her hand and drawing her toward the horses. "Of what can a man ever be sure save that he's born to die? We've laid our plans well and have brave lads to carry them through. With a bit of luck you'll be meeting my impish nephews on the morrow."

The household dined that night to an unusual absence of laughter and merriment. Men spoke to their neighbors in hushed whispers or brooded in anxious silence over their slowly warming ale. Torches flickered uncertainly, throwing dancing shadows across long, unsmiling faces in the dim light. At the chief's table, Donald and Anne spoke little, and even Francis seemed distracted and untalkative. One thought troubled the minds of all: somewhere in Ginahea Castle a brave MacLean masqueraded as an English guard, and the lives of four innocent men rested in his hands.

Following that cheerless meal, Anne trudged slowly up the stairs to her bedchamber. She could not shake the sense of gathering danger that had troubled her since hearing of Glenkennon's coming. She longed for reassurance, for the feel of Francis's arms around her and the sound of his easy laughter to drive away her fears. He had seemed so preoccupied. She wondered a little at his brusqueness in sending her away to bed. Was he already regretting his dangerous entanglement?

It was late when she heard his familiar step in the hallway. Her candle had burned low, but she'd not dressed for bed, knowing the evening wasn't done. The brisk steps halted and his knock sounded softly against the panel.

She swung open the door, her heart beating unsteadily as it always did upon coming face to face with Francis after even so short an absence. Leaning against the door frame, he regarded her somberly, no hint of a smile lurking anywhere in his dark countenance.

"There's a full moon tonight, lass, and I feel a need to walk beside the sea. Will you come?" He seemed curiously vulnerable, standing there in the shadows, that strange, shuttered look masking his expression.

She nodded wordlessly and turned aside for her cloak. The breeze would be cold along the cliffs.

They slipped through the sleeping castle, Francis propelling Anne silently with a hand at her back. He unbarred the great door, and they stepped into the cool spring night, then walked across the shadowed courtyard to the gate.

After a low word from Francis to the guards, the gates swung open, and the pair walked out onto the damp grass of the meadow. Anne wondered what the men made of her midnight stroll with Francis. No doubt they thought it a lovers' tryst and herself the mistress of their chief. She smiled, realizing she did not really care. It was enough that Francis wanted her with him, that they walked together in the moonlight with the damp night smell of the moors rising about them and the soft murmur of the sea vaguely discernible in the midnight quiet.

Francis took her hand when they entered the shadows at the edge of the woodland. He drew her along beside him, leading the way with sure steps. They walked along a rocky path before descending carefully along the cliffs to the sandy crescent of beach below.

The moon rode high over the sea, larger and brighter than Anne had ever before seen it. The water shimmered beneath, reflecting the silvery light from its calm, glassy surface. Small swells crested and rolled lazily up the beach in a shower of dancing silver sparks as each drop of salt spray captured the moonlight, reflecting it back from the water's multifaceted surface. Anne felt an ache in her chest at the beauty of the scene—and at the fear that she might be taken away from it all. As though he sensed her feeling, Francis moved closer, wordlessly putting his arms about her shoulders and pulling her against his chest.

Anne leaned her head against his shoulder, gazing up into the black velvet of the sky where stars twinkled like a million tiny diamonds flung across the heavens by a generous hand. Her eyes closed in contentment as his lips traced the curve of her cheek to the sensitive space behind her ear. He kissed the nape of her neck, then traced a line back to her ear with his tongue. Anne shivered uncontrollably.

"Cold?" he whispered softly against her ear.

She shook her head so vehemently that he chuckled.

He drew her comfortably into the curve of his shoulder, and they walked the water's edge. After a few paces, one wave edged farther than its companions, wetting her feet. She hastened to higher ground, pausing to inspect her damp slippers. There was no sense ruining her shoes, she thought, removing them with her stockings. The sand was still warm from the heat of the sun and felt wonderful beneath her feet. She wriggled her toes delightedly in its grainy warmth.

"What are you doing, lass?" Francis inquired.

Her only reply was a lighthearted giggle. She stepped into the edge of the advancing waves, splashing playfully in the shallow water. "It's wonderful, Francis," she gasped. "Take off your boots and come out here . . . if you dare." Raising her skirts about her knees, she laughed aloud as the cold waters rushed and swirled about her naked calves.

Francis watched in amusement while Anne played, finally removing his own boots to join her in the dancing shallows. They wandered the beach arm in arm, finally reaching the looming darkness of the granite cliffs which marked an end to the narrow stretch of rocky beach.

He purposefully led her out of the bright moonlight into the deep shadows cast by the towering rocks, his eyes burning with a warmth even the night could not hide. Taking her cloak, he spread it beneath them on the sand, wordlessly drawing her down into his waiting arms.

For a moment, they lay together in contentment, side by side, watching the great, billowing ocean rise and fall in easy, rhythmic swells. Then his hands began to caress her sides. He bent his head, nuzzling the hollow of her throat, his warm lips sending a multitude of pleasurable sensations radiating along her nerves.

"Umm . . . you taste good, lass."

Gently loosening the gold clasp restraining her hair, Francis fumbled for the pins that held it in place. It tumbled down her shoulders in fragrant golden waves. Unable to stop himself now, he tangled his fingers in the luxuriant mass, holding her head still while his mouth buried itself in hers with a message old as time.

Anne leaned against him eagerly, trembling at the unexpected excitement of lying against his muscular length. Her tongue touched his tentatively, playing about his lips until he drew it into his mouth, caressing it with his own.

With a groan he shifted slightly, drawing her beneath him, pressing her down on the warm sand. His tongue probed deeper, as if he would taste all of her, know all of her, through the passion of their kiss.

She met his desire with a growing hunger of her own, her blood surging with a cadence more powerful than that of the rolling breakers. Clutching his broad shoulders, she drew him closer, moving her body instinctively to fit the curve of his.

His hands moved with tantalizing slowness in ever narrowing circles about her breasts, his thumbs gently stroking her suddenly sensitive nipples. She did not understand the wild excitement pulsing through her veins or the wealth of sensations shooting through her body. She only knew that carrying his unfamiliar weight felt right—that the pleasing touch of his hands could not be wrong.

Beneath his knowing fingers, the crest of each aching breast grew taut. His tongue teased her lips, then explored more deeply the welcoming recesses of her mouth. In and out, in and out, with a rhythm that did strange things to her heart—and to a deep, secret part in the very center of her being.

Drugged with passion, Anne made no protest when Francis lifted her against him to unfasten her gown. She dimly noticed the cool caress of the night wind against her skin. His trembling fingers slipped the dress from her shoulders, then tugged the straps of her shift down her arms, dropping it to join her gown in a crumpled heap at her waist.

He gazed at her silently, lifting a shaky hand to caress

her cheek, her throat, the velvety softness of her breast. The creamy perfection of her naked shoulders gleamed against the dark backdrop of shadowy rock. With a groan he lowered his mouth to hers in an all-consuming kiss, his hands gently cupping the ripe fullness of each breast.

She shivered with delight at the warm touch of his fingers against her skin. Then all rational thought ended as his lips left hers to follow the wanderings of his hands.

An explosion of feelings swept her as his searing mouth spread an arching flame throughout her body, igniting the slumbering passion that had never before been touched. His lips toyed expertly with the taut crest of first one breast and then the other, sending a flood of sensations through her that left her breathless and eager for more. The flame within burned higher and hotter with each exquisite movement of his mouth, leaving her with a desire she could not long deny. A low moan escaped her, and she half rose against him in ecstasy.

Francis tried to go slowly, but his own loins ached with the throbbing pressure of desire. He felt drunk with passion for the woman in his arms. For a month now he had watched her close about and had denied himself release. The past fortnight had been a real struggle for self-control as Anne had teased him with her innocent kisses, and her beauty had haunted him night and day.

Now he held her yielding body so closely that he could trace every curve, and he felt her quiver in excitement with each touch of his hands. His heart slammed crazily against his ribs and his breathing grew ragged and uncontrollable at the thought of slaking his desire with her. His hungry lips slanted across hers; his starving senses drank their fill of her eager response. Sliding one knee between her parted thighs, he pulled her into a more intimate position against him, already imagining the thrill of their lovemaking.

Anne felt the swell of his manhood against her, but she had no thought of stopping him. She longed to know every inch of him—to love every inch of him. Slipping an eager hand beneath the cloth of his shirt, she stroked the rippling muscles of his back. His skin was warm and smooth, inviting the play of her fingers. Her hands slid lower, caressing the flesh along his ribs, stroking down along his taut belly...

With a sharp intake of breath, Francis flinched from her touch. Sitting up, he fumbled with the lacings of his shirt, then flung it away onto the sand beside them. Never before had he been so aroused. Even in her innocence, Anne could excite him more than the experienced hands of any of his previous mistresses. The blood pounded in his head and surged hotly through his body. Throwing himself back down beside her, he drew her against him with an urgency heightened by the teasing touch of her breasts against his naked chest.

"God, Anne," he mumbled hoarsely. "God, I want you!"

His mouth moved over hers again, leaving her weak and helpless with desire. She arched her body against his with no thought save an incredible yearning to be even closer to him. His hand crept down over her hips, pushing aside her skirt to stroke boldly along the inside of her thigh.

An unfamiliar tension was building within the lower reaches of her body. She twisted beneath him, restless and uncomfortable in his arms, longing for something she hardly understood. Nothing seemed important but the one primitive urging that bid her seek release from the exquisite torture of his hands.

"Anne, I need you," Francis whispered against her throat. "I need you, and before God, I can wait no longer."

She stared into his eyes, black now in the shadows. He waited for her answer; he'd not take her against her will despite his desire. Her heart swelled with love, and she ached to fill his need. "Francis, I love you more than life itself," she breathed. "Make me yours now. I want to belong to you. I'd give anything to make you happy and would count the cost as nothing."

At her words, Francis's eyes snapped shut, and he winced as if she had struck him. Glenkennon would kill Anne if he discovered that Francis had lain with her. Releasing her abruptly, he sat up with a groan, head and arms propped against his knees. He sucked in rapid breaths of the cold night air, clasping his knees tightly, fighting hard to regain control.

Anne clutched her dress about her shoulders and sat up beside him in alarm. "What is it, Francis?"

There was no answer save the sound of his labored breathing in the strained quiet.

"Did . . . did I do something wrong?" she asked humbly, quick tears of humiliation starting to her eyes. Dear God, in her innocence she had done something to disgust him!

"No lass, no," he whispered, quickly reassuring her. He ran a finger along her cheek. "You please me greatly, love. So much, in fact, I near broke my word."

At her puzzled look, he smiled grimly and shook his head. "There's too much unresolved between us. To take advantage of your willingness now would be the act of a scoundrel." He took a deep, shuddering breath. "But damn it, woman, you're enough to make a monk forget his vows!" Pressing a quick kiss against her forehead, he rose to his feet. "Wait here," he commanded.

Bewildered and strangely disappointed by his abrupt ending of their play, Anne watched as Francis walked to the water's edge and began stripping off his breeches. Blushing at her own unmaidenly curiosity, she studied the picture he made, muscles rippling along his hard body, poised against the backdrop of sand and sea. The vision of his naked maleness branded itself across her memory. He was beautiful—like some exquisite god about to command the sea to give up its treasures. She blinked and he was gone, diving into the crest of a wave while she watched anxiously for the reappearance of his dark head.

The cold surge of water took his breath away, but it succeeded in cooling the hot throbbing of Francis's blood. He swam hard against the current, working his tense muscles, finally finding some relief from the tension within him in hard physical exercise.

He swam twenty minutes before leaving the icy water. The sea had refreshed him, and he was once more in command of himself. Shaking the shining droplets from his streaming body, he stepped back into his clothing and rejoined Anne beside the shadowy jumble of rock.

"Ah . . . that was good, lass," he said, a shake of his head making the water fly in all directions. He dropped to his knees, pulling her roughly against him and kissing her warm lips.

"Francis, you taste of sea water!"

"And so would you had you just been for a swim," he returned. "Wouldn't you care for a dip? I promise it's most refreshing." Placing one arm under her knees and the other behind her back, he swung her up into his arms and made as if to carry her to the water.

"No, Francis. No!" she protested laughingly. Placing a hand upon his chest, she pushed against him. "I find your method of swimming too bold for me. Put me down."

He dropped the arm from about her knees, letting her body slide against the damp length of his. His mouth caught hers in a smoldering kiss, reminding her how quickly he could rouse that trembling excitement in her blood. Lifting his head, he gazed down with a rakish grin. "Did I shock you, lass?"

The vision of his nakedness bloomed in her mind, but there was nothing shameful in it. "No," she whispered, made suddenly bold by the laughter in his voice and the night shadows that hid her face from his. She grinned and ran a teasing finger through the intriguing mat of hair on his chest. "To be honest, I was admiring your figure."

He raised an eyebrow at her answer, then smiled with a

look that quickened her pulses. "As I'd like to admire yours, lass, but I suppose it'll have to wait."

With a sigh, Francis picked up his shirt, slipping it over his head and lacing it tightly as they walked the beach in search of their shoes. Fully clothed at last, they left the beach reluctantly and climbed the path back to Camereigh.

CHAPTER TEN

$\mathscr{O}$nce indoors again, Anne felt the cold slap of sanity with the closing of the door. Head lowered in embarrassment, she hurried along the hallway ahead of Francis, aghast at what had occurred upon the beach.

She had offered herself to him—God forbid, she had even begged him to take her! She had spoken her feelings aloud, yet no word of love or commitment had passed his lips. She writhed inwardly. What must he think of her now!

Reaching her chamber, Francis opened the door and ushered her inside. Unable to face him in the light, Anne made a great task of removing her cloak and placing it in the press. Seconds ticked by while she fiddled with her wrap. She felt his eyes upon her, warm and curious. His hand caught her elbow. He turned her about, a look of tender amusement warming his face. At his knowing expression, she turned miserably away, a hot blush staining her cheeks.

"'Twas a most interesting walk, lass. Mayhap we'll go for another soon," he teased.

Keeping her eyes downcast, she attempted to shift out of his grasp.

"Come, Anne, don't get missish on me," he continued with a grin. "There's naught to be ashamed of when a man and woman want each other. 'Tis the most natural thing in the world."

"But it's wrong, Francis," she murmured, still unable to meet his gaze. "I don't know what madness overcame me that I didn't... didn't even stop to think... about anything." She could not add that three simple words from him would have made all right in her eyes.

"It's a madness that happens to men and women sometimes if they're lucky," he said with a chuckle. He placed a finger under her chin, forcing her head up to study better her unhappy look. At her shamed expression the laughter drained from his face and his voice sharpened. "You've not yet experienced the full extent of that madness, sweet, but I tell you this: I'll not always be bound by my word. I'm no gawking lad to be led about by a smile and the promise of a kiss. I've more on my mind than that, and I'll make no pretense to the contrary."

His harsh tone reminded her of the ruthlessness she had glimpsed the day of Charles's visit. Would he be that relentless in taking her? He wanted her, but he had never said he loved her. Could she trust a man who changed so radically in the blink of an eye? She pulled away from him, vowing silently that she'd not blunder again so foolishly.

"Do you think this feeling between us is wrong?" Francis questioned, visibly angered by her withdrawal. "Is it because no words have been spoken over us? No vows exchanged before the Kirk?" He snorted derisively. "Such things are worthless in my eyes. If a man and woman care for each other, the vows between them are the only ones that matter. Not a hundred churchmen can bless the union of two who've not pledged themselves from their own hearts."

He caught her arm, drawing her roughly against him. "You belong to me, Anne Randall, and you have from the first. You feel that now, though you'll not yet admit it for the truth."

Her lips opened in angry protest, but his mouth swooped

down, silencing her with a kiss that burned away all reasonable thought. Despite her resolve to remain cool to his touch, her arms slipped around his neck, drawing him closer, while her body molded itself willingly to his. A million pleasurable sensations shot through her at the taste and smell and feel of the man. She could no more deny him than she could her need for breath.

Releasing her reluctantly, Francis smiled. He traced her full lips with a gentle finger, his face softening with a tender, unguarded look she had seldom seen. "I'm the luckiest fool in all Scotland," he said huskily. "Some men search a lifetime and never find the right woman—and I wasn't even looking when you happened along."

She pressed her cheek against his shirt. The faint odor of sea and sand clung to it, reminding her of the pleasurable hour they had spent. Francis loved her; she was sure of it. A contented sigh escaped her and she snuggled closer in his arms. There was no shame in loving him. She was only sorry their time together had been so short.

"I think you have your answer, sweetheart," Francis said softly. "Here, give me one last kiss and send me on my way, else neither of us will be fit to match wits with Glenkennon on the morrow."

He pressed a quick kiss upon her brow before striding purposefully toward the hall. Turning in the doorway, he gave her a reassuring smile. "Don't fret, Anne. I promise you'll have no cause to regret what's happened."

Francis closed the door and hurried along the hallway, feeling as if his feet scarcely touched the cold stones. He wanted to whistle and sing and shout out his happiness to the world. Anne was his, and nothing would change it!

A golden shaft of light spilling beneath his door brought him back to earth abruptly. He had left no candle burning that evening. Pulling the familiar dirk a few inches from its sheath, he placed his hand on the door, thrusting it open. Three men sat at a table on the far side of the room.

They looked up in surprise as he paused, braced for action, on the threshold.

"It's about time you brought yerself home, lad," one of the men said gruffly. "We've searched the castle high and low fer ye, and now you saunter in as if you'd just been ta take tea with Jamie Stuart hisself."

Francis smiled at the impatience in the voice of Colen MacKenzie, an old ally and close friend from the wilder reaches of land farther north. It was this uncouth laird of Clan MacKenzie he had fostered with several years as a boy in the exchange so common among the clans. With the MacKenzies he had learned the all-important skills of raiding and fighting necessary to survival in the Highlands.

He slipped his blade back into its sheath, surveying his rough visitor with a grin. "I've been for a swim along the beach, man. 'Twas too pleasant an evening to remain indoors." Francis held out his hand to Colen, then nodded toward James MacKenzie beside him.

"'Tis bad news we bear, Francis lad, and sorry it is I be the one ta tell it," Colen stated bluntly.

Francis caught a chair and flipped it backward to straddle before the table. "Well, out with it, man. I've been concerned since that cursed moon rose, giving enough light to pick a man from a horse at a hundred paces."

"Glenkennon outfoxed us, MacLean," James stated simply. "He never went near Ginahea Castle. He swung northwest instead and is resting the night on Dunolly Moor. He has enough men-at-arms about to garrison a large stronghold. 'Tis impossible to get in to James Cameron, much less get out again."

"Are Conall and the others safe at Ginahea?" Francis asked sharply.

"As far as we know."

"It seems you must abide by Glenkennon's terms after all," Colen put in, "though it's loath I am to see you give up that ring in his nose you hold in keeping the girl."

"I don't plan to give her up."

James MacKenzie leaned across the table. "MacLean, there's no way we could wrest the Camerons from Glenkennon by force. He'd kill them in a minute if he sensed a trick. You'll have to trade the girl if you want them back safely."

Francis lifted his dirk, toying with it absently while his quick mind raced ahead, formulating a new plan. "I don't mean we won't trade," he said with a grim smile, "we'll just snatch her back later along the trail."

Colen and Donald exchanged glances. "I've not told you the worst of the news, laddie," Colen said wearily. He put a large paw on Francis's shoulder in rough sympathy. "Glenkennon has petitioned the king for a writ of treason against you using a tangle of lies and half-truths. And God knows Jamie sees a traitor under every bed and basket since this cursed union took place." He scowled darkly. "Chances are good that unnatural son will have you put to the horn. It won't help yer cause if the earl can complain of another raid, and he'd scream to high heaven if his daughter was involved again."

Stunned by the unexpected news, Francis made no answer. He had been a fool not to foresee Glenkennon's action. Still, the writ was seldom granted except against the most dangerous of traitors. If passed, it would brand him a hopeless outlaw, giving any man the right to kill him with impunity. His lands would be forfeit to the king and put under the administration of the king's representative in Scotland—Glenkennon himself in this instance. Camereigh would be put to the torch, and no man would utter Francis's name on pain of death.

He shook his head stubbornly. "Jamie Stuart won't do it. But if he does . . . Randall can try and take me. I'll not give her up!"

"Christ's blood, man, are ye daft?" Colen exploded. "I dinna believe Donald when he warned us you were caught in the girl's net. 'Not Francis MacLean, of all men,' I said.

I've seen good men ruined by the lure of a pretty face, but never did I think ta find you caught in that trap! Ach, man, there be plenty of other winsome faces and willing bodies to warm yer bed at night. Forget her! You'll find another soon enough."

In a flash the gleaming blade that had lain so innocently between Francis's fingers quivered upright, buried an inch deep in the center of the oak table. He turned toward Colen, his eyes narrowed and cold. "I'll not allow such talk from any man, Colen MacKenzie...not even yourself." He pushed his chair back from the table and surveyed the surprised man coldly. "I plan to make the girl my wife."

Colen's eyes opened wide in obvious dismay. His mouth snapped shut, and the muscles of his throat tightened visibly as he swallowed his surprise. "Now, Francis, lad, you know I mean no harm," he said hurriedly. "I dinna know that was the way of it. I apologize for my witless outburst, but by God, man, think on what you're about! I look upon you as one of my own, lad. I'd never forgive myself an I made no move to prevent yer seeking out disaster!"

Francis took a deep breath and forced himself to relax. "Ah, Colen, forgive me...I know you're concerned." He grinned. "I am, too, but I must do as I think best."

James MacKenzie leaned forward. "Francis, listen to me. You may not care for your safety or even the danger to your clan, but have you thought of the effect this may have on the girl? If you marry her in Glenkennon's teeth, do you really think he'll ever let you be? He'll hound you to all the corners of hell until he brings you to ground and has your blood. Is that the kind of life you want for her and for your sons? You'll have to drag them with you as you run, or else leave them to fall back to Glenkennon...and then, what in God's name did you accomplish in the first place? Think on it, man!"

Francis stared into the anxious faces around him, seeing Anne's image receding further and further from the realm of possibility. He turned to Donald, eyes silently pleading for some argument in his favor.

"Would ye see history repeat itself, lad?" Donald asked softly.

A long look passed between them. With a deep sigh, Francis rose and walked stiffly to the window. An unspeakable weariness weighed down his limbs, paralyzing his very thoughts.

"You're right, of course...all of you," he said finally. "I'll send her on her way on the morrow. I've been unpardonably foolish, but no real harm's been done." He stared out into the night. "Donald, see these gentlemen to bed and attend their needs."

The noise of chairs scraping across stone filled the room. Heavy footsteps moved across the floor to halt uncertainly behind him, and a powerful hand, clumsy with sympathy, descended on his arm.

Francis gripped Colen's arm, feeling the wordless understanding that passed between them. In a few moments he heard the door close softly, and he was alone with the specter of a fair maid with laughing lips and sparkling eyes that gazed trustingly up at him.

Dawn broke that morning cloaked in a pallid gray that did little to raise Anne's spirits. At the thought of disobeying her father, a sick feeling of dismay churned in her stomach. Francis would laugh at her fears and rally her on her timid disposition, she thought with a smile. But then, he'd not been raised to fear the earl's slightest displeasure.

Her thoughts flew back to their words the night before. Though Francis had spoken no word of it, she was certain he loved her. His look, his touch, the very tenderness in his voice told her all she needed to know. And if the words of a minister were unnecessary to him...well, so be it! She was his, even as he had said the night before.

With a mind calmed by those reflections, she descended the stairs, turning into the hall in search of Francis. She hesitated at sight of two strangers seated at table with Donald. Francis was nowhere in sight.

The conversation of the men stopped abruptly. Rising to their feet, the two strangers regarded her with undue interest while Donald hastened to make the necessary introductions. "Mistress Randall, may I make these gentlemen known to you? Colen MacKenzie, chief of Clan MacKenzie, and James MacKenzie. Gentlemen, Mistress Randall."

Anne gave the men a brilliant smile. She had heard Francis speak of his adventures with these two, and she felt an instant liking for the great ox of a man who stood before her, bare knees peeking from beneath the bright tartan of his kilt. "I'm pleased to make your acquaintance," she said, addressing her remark to the still tongue-tied Colen. "Sir Francis has spoken of you often."

Colen squirmed uncomfortably beneath her friendly look, and the men exchanged sheepish glances. "Will'y breakfast with us, lass?" he asked, still staring admiringly.

At her nod, James drew out the bench and called for more food and ale. As the servants moved hastily about with steaming platters, Anne turned to Donald. "When will Francis be joining us?"

He stared at her nonplussed for a moment, then shifted his gaze unsteadily. "Have ye not seen him then this morning, lass?" he countered, carefully evading her question.

"No, not since last night. We went for a walk on the beach."

"Uh . . . I believe he went out earlier. He should be back soon," Donald mumbled around a piece of bread hastily shoved into his mouth.

"Well, I hope so," she replied. "I don't relish the idea of meeting my father alone—especially when he learns I'll not be leaving with him."

Donald choked on his food, and the MacKenzies were still pounding him on the back when racing footsteps sounded in the corridor. Moments later Francis threw open the door.

"The English have come," he informed them. "They'll be before the gates in another ten minutes. You men come with me. Anne..." He threw her a brief glance. "Get upstairs and stay there till you're called."

She leaped to her feet, quick to obey that tone in his voice without question. She hurried up the stairs, worrying as she went. The plans to spirit the Camerons away from Ginahea must have gone awry.

The men took the stairs two at a time on their way to the castle battlements. All about the walls, the heavily armed MacLean clansmen leaned over the parapets, eager to go at the men below. Francis scanned the soldiers drawing up on the meadow; there were now near four score men covering the grassy plain. He could make out the Camerons easily, but his searching eyes found no sign of Glenkennon. "The bastard didn't come," he said bitterly. "I can see Charles and that fool Kincaid, but the devil himself is not in sight."

"Perhaps the jackal's afraid ta show his face," Colen suggested. "He might be dragged into a fight and soil the lace on his sleeve."

Francis continued his scrutiny of the group below. "Don't be fooled, Colen. Robert Randall's no coward, and he can account himself far too well to fear setting foot on my land. No, the devil has some obscure purpose for not showing himself—you can depend on it."

One well-dressed rider emerged from the group and advanced purposefully toward the gates. Francis jerked his head toward Donald. "See to that messenger and have him brought to me in the laird's room." He glanced back at the MacKenzies. "I'd be obliged if you two would keep an eye on things from up here. There's no telling what tricks the bastards may be up to. Bring me word at once if you see anything suspicious."

To the anxious Anne pacing restlessly in her room, each minute seemed an eternity while she waited for news. Her

straining ears finally caught the sound of scurrying footsteps outside her door, and she flung it open in the face of
a startled servant. He nodded. The men were ready.

She followed the hurrying servant down the hall, trying
unsuccessfully to still the trembling that began deep inside
her. Pausing before the door, she took a deep breath. If
only she could have had a few minutes with Francis before
having to face Glenkennon. She was afraid of him; she
always had been. She was not ready to withstand his fury.
Wiping her sweating palms on her skirt, she reached for
the door, cautiously pushing it open.

The sight was not what she had expected. Only three
men stood within the room. One, obviously an English
courtier by his rich dress, conferred quietly with Donald,
while Francis stood behind the desk, his dark face impene-
trable as he studied a series of papers the Englishman had
brought.

A wave of relief surged through her. She'd not have to
confront her father after all.

The tall Englishman turned at the sound of her entry,
his brown eyes widening with pleasure in his squared,
tanned face. "Mistress Randall?"

She nodded. He bowed his dark head with practiced
grace. "Nigel Douglas at your service, m'lady. I'm come
from your father to escort you from this place. He's most
anxious for your return."

She acknowledged his speech with a polite smile, waiting expectantly for some word from Francis. The silence
stretched interminably in the room. She glanced toward
Francis. He seemed completely absorbed in the study of his
pen, his expression aloof and unapproachable as she had
seen it only twice before during his coldest moods.

She turned to Donald. His grizzled face was impassive,
but the pitying look in his eyes made her heart miss a beat.
Her eyes widened in a look of desperate inquiry. He gave a
slight shake of his head.

"Well," Douglas said, breaking the awkward silence, "I

suppose there's nothing more to be said. I'll give the word for the Camerons to be brought to the gates, and the lady and I will be on our way." He looked warningly at Francis. "MacLean, I need not remind you any tricks will be dealt with most harshly."

"I've given my word, Douglas. You'll find that's a binding agreement in the Highlands, though it may not be where you come from."

The Englishman swallowed the insult with good grace and turned to Anne. "I'll be waiting for you below, m'lady," he said kindly, "unless you wish me to remain with you now." His dark eyes flickered questioningly toward Francis.

"That won't be necessary," Anne murmured. "I . . . I'll be along."

"Very well, then. I'll expect you to join me in the court-yard." Douglas made a half bow in MacLean's direction and turned toward the door.

"Donald, see Kate has Anne's things packed . . . then get to the stables and bring around her horse."

"Aye, Francis." With a quick glance at Anne, Donald, too, was gone.

In the hollow silence after the slamming of the door, the two stared warily at each other. Francis would have an explanation, Anne told herself desperately. This was all part of a trick for the Englishman's benefit. In a moment he would explain, and they would laugh together over how easily Douglas had been taken in.

"Well," Francis began after a moment, "so ends a pleasant month. Between the two of us we've managed to beguile the days." His eyes lowered to the pen in his hand. "I trust you've not spent your time altogether unpleasantly."

Anne stared at him incredulously, unable to make sense of his words. "I'm afraid I don't understand, Francis," she whispered. "What do you mean?"

He laughed harshly then, his words deliberately cruel. "Come, Anne, don't be such an innocent. We've had an agreeable time of it together, you and I, but it's time you returned to your world and I to mine. We're enemies, you know. I've reminded you of that once already, as I recall. Surely you've not forgotten."

"But . . . I don't understand," she repeated. "Last night you said . . ." Her words trailed off beneath the cold contempt of his gaze. It chilled her heart, slowly freezing the blood in her veins, paralyzing not only her limbs but her tongue as well. She could think of nothing to say to this tall, cold stranger who looked so like her Francis.

"A man says many things when he walks in the moonlight with a willing lass," Francis said indifferently. "We've had an agreeable flirtation, but now it's at an end. You were sweet, lass, sweeter than most. But I've time for nothing more."

Her heart pounded so loudly in her ears she could scarcely think. "Was that all it was to you? A flirtation?" she whispered dazedly. She swallowed around the lump in her throat, clasping her hands tightly together to keep from flinging herself into his arms. Her throat ached violently with the strain of swallowing back tears. She dared say nothing more.

Francis stared down into the pale face before him, the stricken eyes she raised to his, bright with unshed tears. Involuntarily his hand went out to touch her, but he jerked it back with a silent curse. "Yes, that's all it was," he said harshly, "and when you've seen more of the world, you'll understand the games men and women play."

His eyes shifted from hers to focus unseeingly on the square of blue outside the window. "In a few months you'll have half the men in Scotland dancing to any tune you name. You'll be glad I sent you on your way," he added, unable to suppress the bitterness that crept into his voice.

She shook her head wordlessly, fighting the threatening tears and the pain in her throat that kept her dumb.

A mocking smile suffused his face. "I've had a bit more

experience than you, sweet. I know the truth of what I say."

"For God's sake, Francis, tell me what's happened! Why are you doing this?"

He turned from her impatiently and flung open the door. Damn it, another minute of this and he would break. He could not stand the anguish in her voice or the look of hurt disbelief on her face—yet he could not tell her the truth! He could not send her back to Glenkennon nursing any partiality for him. The earl would not hesitate to abuse her to get to his enemy—and Francis was one who knew to what lengths Glenkennon might go.

Leaning against the door facing, he looked determinedly down the hall, refusing to look at her again. "Kate should have your things packed," he said stiffly, ignoring the anguished cry that still quivered in the air between them. "Have a pleasant journey. Perhaps we'll meet again."

Anne studied him wordlessly. She wanted to say so many things, but there was no softening anywhere in his hard face to encourage her to linger. She gazed across the floor to the waiting hallway, knowing she must walk through that doorway alone, fearing her legs would not carry her there. So this was how it ended.

Nothing was left her now save a shred of pride. Raising her head, she pulled herself together and stumbled through the door. One step and then another. Don't look back. One step and then another . . . *Dear God* . . .

Somehow she made it through the door and up the stairs. She turned blindly into her chamber, slamming the door behind her and leaning back against it, trembling hands held tightly to her mouth as if she might hold in the long scream that was building inside her.

The sound of the door halted Kate's frantic packing. The woman rose to her feet, a frown of concern on her wrinkled face.

"No," Anne said distinctly, stopping Kate with one outstretched hand. She regained a measure of control. "Cease your packing. I'll take nothing from here save what I wore when I came."

Holding herself tightly in an unthinking void, Anne left the rose-colored room. If she didn't think, she might just make it . . .

Descending the central stair, she found Donald awaiting her. He stepped forward and touched her shoulder, his gray eyes warm with sympathy. "Life's no' so easy a thing at times, lass," he said softly. "I doubt you'll understand now, but this be for the best."

She jerked away from him. Donald must have known Francis was lying all along. It must have been a good joke. How they must have laughed at her ignorance!

At thought of his betrayal, black fury surged up inside her and she drew back her hand to strike him. He faced her unflinchingly, returning her glare with compassion. The tight knot of anger in her chest slowly dissolved, leaving only pain and bewilderment in its wake. Not Donald. She would believe it of them all—but not Donald.

Her fist dropped to her side and she ventured a slight smile that went painfully awry. "I . . . I think you'd best get me to horse, Donald, else I might embarrass us both."

He nodded in understanding. Flinging open the door, he followed her out to the waiting horses.

In the courtyard several waiting clansmen milled about, one holding Cassie's reins and those of a dark, liver chestnut she did not recognize. Nigel Douglas helped her into the saddle, then mounted the chestnut beside her.

She gathered up her reins mechanically. He was not going to come. The thought was an icy needle of cold despair threading her heart. The wild hope that Francis would prevent her departure at the last moment—that this was all a trick to best her father—shriveled and died a painful death in her breast.

The castle walls teemed with armed MacLeans—nearly three score pairs of eyes gleamed down at her curiously.

The thought stiffened her backbone. She squared her shoulders and lifted her head.

"Give my love to my uncle," she said, leaning toward Donald, "and thank Janet and the others for all their kindnesses." She wrinkled her brow in concentration, struggling to resist the urge to gaze once more at the window fronting the laird's room. "I can't remember taking leave of Kate. Thank her again . . ."

"Aye, lass, I'll give everyone your regards," Donald said, one hand on her stirrup as if loath to let her go. "Don't be frettin' yerself now . . . and take care."

She nodded, swallowing hard. Turning Cassie's head toward the gate, she put her heels to the mare's sides.

"God go with you, lass," Donald muttered under his breath as Douglas swung out after the girl.

Anne paid no heed to the scores of burly soldiers they rode through, nor did she notice the four horsemen who galloped past her into the gates of Camereigh amid the cheers of the exultant MacLeans. Charles spurred to her side, and she found herself making mechanical answers to his anxious inquiries, thankful his questions were mercifully few due to the need to get the army around them on the move. Ignoring the host of curious stares, she concentrated on keeping herself in the saddle and holding back the tears that threatened her feigned calm.

She was leaving—actually riding away from Camereigh. She'd not be seeing Francis again. She'd never again see the quick laughter that gleamed in his eyes long before it reached his lips or ride beside him across a windswept moor. She was leaving. The words spun around and around in her mind as if by repetition they might become believable.

Francis had used her, her mind cried accusingly. He had been lying to her all the time. She closed her eyes tightly against the pain, trying hard to understand. How could she have been such a fool; how could she have been so terribly wrong?

She longed to be alone, to give up the battle for self-control that cost so dearly. Her stomach churned, and she wondered vaguely if she were going to be ill.

Content to let Cassie pick her way, she rode blindly along the trail after her father's men. As the miles slipped by, she began to achieve some order to her spinning thoughts. Francis had tired of her quickly enough—perhaps he had already found another woman to share his days. He had stopped short of taking her virginity—perhaps he feared the consequences had he sent her back to Glenkennon carrying a bastard of his making. Her face burned—or perhaps she had been so easy the night before that he had lost even the slightest interest in her.

The misery swept over her in waves, but she steeled herself against each new surge, determined to show a mask of cool composure to the curious men who rode all around her. She would be able later to think about it rationally, she reasoned. She would be able to understand it all—later. Somehow she would survive this blow, as she had survived the other blows life had dealt her, and she would work to see Sir Francis MacLean hurt as he had hurt her. Somehow, she would see him brought low.

Beneath Anne's anguish, the first stirrings of hatred began. Hate was as strong an emotion as love, she reasoned. Perhaps even stronger. For the moment her mind still reeled in confusion and disbelief, but tomorrow, she told herself, tomorrow she would begin to lay her plans.

CHAPTER ELEVEN

A brisk wind drove the scattered clouds across the sky, whipping Francis's hair into his eyes as he strained for one final glimpse of Anne's blue habit among the trees. Leaning against the stone parapet, he watched the last of the English soldiers disappear into the forest. An overwhelming feeling of loss swept through him, submerging for a moment even the deep hatred he felt for Glenkennon.

The colorful banners atop the wall fluttered in the sea breeze, snapping loudly through the quiet. The men about him exchanged glances and shifted uneasily. He turned away from the empty meadow, his bleak face a study in rigidity. "Dugall, bring in your men and choose a score to man the walls. The rest may take their ease, but keep them ready. I want three score up here tonight."

"D'ye expect a trick then, sir?" Dugall asked, brown eyes narrowing beneath heavy, graying brows.

Francis shrugged. "I expect anything from Randall."

Turning, he made for the stairs, scarcely hearing the victorious shouts of his men welcoming the Camerons and Sir Allan MacGregor in the courtyard. He would go below soon, Francis told himself, but for the time being he needed a moment alone.

Reaching the seclusion of the empty laird's room, he poured himself a stiff draught of whiskey, tossing it off in a gulp that burned its way to the pit of his stomach. It steadied him, easing the constricting band across his chest. God, but that scene with Anne had been hell! He rubbed his eyes tiredly, wishing he could erase the image of her white face and tear-filled eyes. He had done his job well —she would hate him now for sure. With a heavy sigh, he turned toward the door.

Upon reaching the hall, Francis was met by an exuberant shriek from a small whirlwind that launched itself across the floor and into his arms. "Uncle Francis, I knew you'd save us—I knew it! I told them so all along," young Evan shouted triumphantly.

Francis gazed down into a pair of worshipful blue eyes and tried not to remember another pair that had stared up at him so trustingly. "Of course, lad." He smiled fondly at the grimy face of the boy. "You didn't think we'd leave you there to become good Englishmen, did you?"

"Evan would have it you'd tear down our cell stone by stone," William Cameron stated with an affectionate grin at his younger brother.

Francis tousled Evan's dark hair. "That would have made a magnificent rescue, boy, but only think how fatiguing. This way I didn't stir from my door. I let Glenkennon deliver you straight to my gates."

Francis held out a hand to Will, carefully searching his nephew's tired face. The boy looked different in a way that had nothing to do with the dirt matting his raven-black hair or the dark circles ringing his vivid blue eyes. The fourteen-year-old Will had lost the last vestiges of childhood in the festering dungeons of the Tolbooth. "And how does it feel to be a man, lad?" Francis asked softly.

"To tell the truth sir, 'tis a bit painful."

Francis's grip tightened on the boy's hand and the smile left his face. "Glenkennon will answer for every stripe he laid on your back, son. That I promise."

James Cameron stepped forward and caught his brother-in-law's arm. "Don't leave me out of your plans, Francis.

I've a few scores to settle with Glenkennon and will take ill if you keep the fun for yourself."

"Count me in," MacGregor threw in from his chair beside the fire. His over-wide girth had narrowed considerably since Francis had last seen him, and his usual plump, good-humored face was stiff and hard. "The MacGregors will be happy to extend some hospitality to the earl and his cutthroats. Just give the word, MacLean."

"Aye, I'd a hunch you'd both be eager," Francis said, "but we must pick our time carefully lest we find ourselves fighting a royal army instead of Glenkennon's rabble. I've no wish to be hanged for treason for defending my land."

James Cameron nodded in agreement, then glanced around questioningly. "Where's Janet?"

"I sent a messenger to her with orders not to set out till morning. I didn't want her here if things turned ugly today." A slight smile lightened Francis's harsh expression. "If I know my sister, she'll start out tonight, calling it morning, and be here by early afternoon tomorrow."

"It'll be good to see her," Cameron said simply.

The afternoon passed quietly as the newly released prisoners accustomed themselves to freedom. They bathed, ate, slept, and rose to eat again with many a humorous comment regarding the not-so-humorous conditions of the prison they had just left.

Because Francis half expected a raid, supper was a quiet celebration. The men consumed their ale temperately, then retired to rest or take their turn upon the walls. Francis and his guests withdrew to the laird's room to talk privately of Glenkennon's treachery and the king's indifference. The boys listened avidly to the talk until shortly before midnight, when young Evan's heavy lids and drooping chin betrayed him.

"Off to bed with you, lad. You're three parts asleep already," Francis said with a smile, leaning over to give the boy a shake.

Evan sat up with a jerk. "I wasn't asleep," he denied hotly. "I was just . . . leaning my head on my arm to rest."

Jamie Cameron gazed at his youngest son fondly, trying hard to suppress a smile. "It's long past time you were abed, boy. That's the third time I've seen you nod off."

"But Will doesn't have to go yet. Please, sir, can't I stay up until he has to go—he's not so much older than me."

"We'll all be turning in soon," Francis assured him. "I, for one, will be seeking my bed in no short order. Besides, I don't relish listening to your mother if she sees those circles under your eyes." He stood up. "Come along, and I'll see you upstairs."

The fresh linen sheets on the bed were turned back invitingly when Francis and Evan entered the boy's chamber. A small nightshirt of approximately the right size lay across the pillow. Silently blessing the efficiency of his resourceful staff, Francis helped the boy out of his clothing and into the great bed.

Extinguishing the candles, he hesitated beside the bed while his eyes became accustomed to the faint light spilling into the window. In another hour it would be shining directly in the boy's eyes. He reached up to draw the curtain.

"Please, sir . . . don't . . . don't close it."

"The light will be in your eyes in another hour, son," Francis said softly. "'Tis like to keep you awake."

"No, it won't. I'll turn on my side, like this," Evan said, demonstrating. "I . . . I like the light."

Francis nodded and started toward the door.

"Sir . . ." The voice was even smaller now, and a sob trembled behind that short syllable. "How does a man learn . . ." he sniffed, "t . . . to be a man?"

Francis stopped short, the question and the sob catching him completely by surprise. "Well, 'tis a thing that comes upon a man so gradual like, it's hard to say how it happens." He moved to the edge of the bed, seating himself beside the small, huddled figure. "A man's shaped by what he sees, what he's taught, and the experiences life brings him. It's not something that's done in a day."

"But I'm not brave enough," Evan confessed miserably. There was a long pause. "I was scared, Francis. I was scared the whole time. Father and Sir Allan weren't. And Will wasn't scared... leastways not till the soldiers dragged them out." He sniffed. "We thought they'd be h... hanged. Even then Will didn't say a word."

Evan sat up in bed, clasping Francis's arm urgently. "I don't want to be a coward, sir. There's nothing worse! Tell me how I can learn not to be afraid. And, please, sir... please don't tell my father!"

Francis put a comforting arm about the boy's shoulder, drawing him into the shelter of his arms. "Being a man doesn't mean you're never afraid, Evan," he said quietly. "Only a fool is never afraid—and fools don't live long. Fear can be good if it makes a man canny."

"But you're not afraid of anything."

Francis smiled into the darkness, carefully weighing his words. "At risk of disillusioning you lad, I'll tell you I'm oft afraid."

"I don't believe you," Evan said suspiciously. "You're just saying that. You never act scared!"

"Ah, but how a man acts is a whole different subject now, lad. What a man feels and how he acts are often separate matters. A man may oft be afraid, but he bears himself proudly and doesn't let his enemies know. You're not a coward, lad—not by a long shot," Francis said bracingly. "You felt nothing your father and MacGregor didn't feel. They've just had more practice at covering up the signs of fear."

"You really think my father was afraid?"

"I'm sure he was—a little. I'd have been, in his shoes. You men were in a damned tight spot!"

"But how can I learn not to act afraid," Evan persisted. "I'd like to be like Father next time... or even Will."

"Please God, there won't be a next time. At least not

like that!" Francis said with a laugh. "Evan, you've a lot of promise, but you can't expect to have the control of a man full grown by age ten. As the years go by, you'll handle what life brings you, and one day you'll wake up and find yourself a man without ever knowing how it came about. Remember, fear can be good if it makes a man shrewd. The danger comes if he allows it to grow and take control."

Evan sat quietly digesting the information. "Well, I think I acted brave enough when the English were about," he said finally. "Deep down I knew you'd get us out." His small arms went around Francis's neck and he leaned his head trustingly against Francis's chest with a sigh. "I knew you wouldn't let Glenkennon win. I told myself that over and over again in the dark when everyone else was asleep."

Francis pressed his face against the boy's hair, holding him tightly while he struggled with a surge of guilt. How could he have found pleasure in Anne Randall's arms these last weeks while this small lad waited so trustingly in the hell of that notorious prison? How could he have forgotten his kinsmen, even for a moment, while he schemed to keep Anne from returning to Glenkennon?

With a final hug, he pushed the boy down onto his pillow and tucked the covers around his shoulders. "Go to sleep now, lad," he said, rising from the bed.

"Oh, sir, you can close the curtain now," Evan said sleepily. "I think you were right about the light."

"Aye, lad."

Once outside the door, Francis paused, reflecting on the wisdom it must take to be a father. He remembered his own father well and marveled at the man's patience and his understanding of the knotty problems facing a boy forced into manhood early by the violence of his day. Suddenly, he felt a longing for his sire's rich wisdom in a way he had not in years. What decision would Colin MacLean have made in his position?

Francis had done what he had to do in bartering Anne

for the freedom of his kinsmen. His people were his first consideration; there had been no other choice. Yet there was no relief in that decision, no lightening of the ache in his chest. He sighed heavily, wanting his father's counsel or, even more, the gentle understanding of his mother.

As a boy, he had carried his hurts to her, and she had patched them up using her healing arts not only on the cuts and scrapes inevitable to an enterprising lad but on his wounded pride and faltering ego as well. She had been his trusted confidante, an infallible being who always knew what to do.

Katherine MacPhearson MacLean had loved her husband and family with all her heart, and she had borne the tragedies life dealt her with a quiet dignity and an unshakable faith in the Almighty. She had seen the death of three of her offspring, two at birth and another in his first year of life. She had borne even the death of her husband in a manner that put Francis's own actions to shame. It was Lady MacLean who had ordered the defenses of Camereigh and repulsed the Campbell attack while the eighteen-year-old Francis stood in shock beside the mangled corpse of his father. She had comforted him, he remembered, instead of requiring the comfort and support of her devastated son.

He shook his head silently at the memory. Yes, she would have understood what he was feeling and would have had a word of comfort. But he was a man now, and his family and clan depended on him for wisdom. He prayed to God that he would have enough of it.

The gentlemen were still sitting in conversation when he opened the door. "Has that pesky boy of mine been plaguing the life out of you, Francis? I was on the verge of sending Will to rescue you from his infernal questions," James Cameron said with a smile.

"Not at all. Evan's a fine lad 'Tis pure pleasure for me to have him about." Francis glanced toward Will. "You've two find lads. They're a credit to your house."

Will flushed bright red at such unexpected praise from his idol, but Jamie only smiled and laid a hand on his son's arm. "Aye, Francis, 'tis proud I am of all my children, including the girls back home." He raised an eyebrow. "But I'd say 'tis time and past you were setting up your own nursery and praising sons of your own."

"But we'll have to find him a wife first," Will teased.

Colen MacKenzie choked on his ale, but Francis only smiled at the boy. "That's not always the case, lad. Has your father not talked with you man to man?"

Will acknowledged the hit with a rueful grin, then pursed his lips into a prudish line. "Of course I'd know nothing of such things, but Mother's suggested that's desirable."

Cameron turned from his son with an indulgent grin. "Speaking of wenches, Francis—tell us, what thought you of Glenkennon's girl? The talk in Edinburgh is that she's wondrous fair. I'm sure the gentle Robert was in a quake knowing, as he must, your penchant for the lassies."

There was an almost imperceptible stiffening along Francis's spine. He turned, pouring himself a draught of whiskey from the flask on the table. In the sudden quiet, Donald cast a frown at Cameron, then quickly dropped his eyes.

Francis studied the amber liquid sparkling in his glass. "She's wondrous fair, easily the fairest woman of my acquaintance," he said smoothly. "And no faint-hearted English lass either. She does her MacDonnell blood credit . . . though little good it'll do her in Glenkennon's house." He tossed off half the drink, then moved to the window, staring out into the night. Donald deliberately began another subject, and the conversation floated easily around the men once more.

After a few moments, Colen MacKenzie heaved himself out of his comfortable chair, smothering a ponderous yawn. "Well, lads, James and me must be up betimes if we're to reach Shieldaig by tomorrow next. We bid you good rest now and sweeter dreams than you've had in many a night."

Francis rose with the MacKenzies. "I'll say good night, too, and see to my men. We may have word from our patrols. If you've need of anything, Donald will see to it. Sleep well."

Francis escaped the confines of the room gladly, breathing in the sweet night air while he made his way across the battlements. The wretched moon was pouring out its silvery radiance in a repeat performance of the previous evening. He had no doubt that should he walk the beach, the dancing waves would again curl refreshingly about his feet and the stars above would twinkle just as brightly as they had the night before. Only one thing would be different— Anne would not be beside him.

He swore softly into the darkness, clenching his fists atop the wall in an effort to get hold of himself. He was acting like a besotted schoolboy, he told himself disgustedly. He must keep his mind on other matters.

"Did'y call, sir?" a familiar voice questioned.

"No," Francis snapped. "That is . . . Dugall. I was looking for you. How goes the night?"

"All's quiet. Nothing's stirred save a few deer that ventured into the meadow."

The two men stood quietly, peering out into the moonlight. "He'll not come tonight," Francis said softly. "Glenkennon's too canny. He knows I'd be ready for him now."

"There be no tellin' what that devil'll do," Dugall replied sourly. "Why for all we know he could as easily be snug between the covers at Ranleigh as out there in the dark."

Francis stared into the shadows of the nearby wood as if his eyes could truly pierce the darkness. "He's out there all right; I can feel it," he said with an eerie assurance. "He wants me badly, but he'll take no risk till he's sure he can't lose."

The old soldier felt the hairs prickle along the back of

his neck. There was some what said young MacLean had the Sight, others that he dealt in witchcraft, so canny was he in anticipating the moves of his enemies. He squinted back into the night, wondering what the laird really did see.

With a few hastily issued orders, Francis retired to his chamber. The room had never seemed so uninviting as it appeared now in the flickering light of a single candle. Shrugging out of his clothes, he threw himself wearily onto the great, curtained bed. He had spent a day exhausting to body and mind and had not had a wink of sleep the night before.

Staring up into the darkness of the velvet canopy, he wondered where Anne was camped for the night. Was she wide awake and thinking of him—or had she already dismissed him from her mind? Her thoughts of him would not be kind. He had hurt her deliberately, thinking she would get over him more quickly. There would be nothing she might romanticize and regret. Anger would soon take away the sting of her loss—but what would help him?

He thought again of the words of James MacKenzie. He'd had no other choice. The life of an outlaw was not for a woman. God's blood, it was scarcely one for a man! But was the life Glenkennon planned for her so much better?

He ground his teeth in frustration at thought of Anne married to a man such as Percy Campbell or the sniveling Howard laird. Well, if the worst came, and she were endangered, he could always snatch her back. His sources kept him well informed of the happenings at Ranleigh.

But did he have the right to endanger the well-being of the entire MacLean clan? His thoughts swam hazily and his head ached with a vengeance. There seemed to be no satisfactory answers to the questions crowding his mind. He closed his eyes against the pounding in his head, and sleep mercifully overcame him.

* * *

True to her brother's prophecy, Janet arrived at Camereigh just after noon the next day. Her party was sighted by the watchful patrols, so that the Camerons were lined up in the courtyard when she entered its narrow gate.

Never had she seen a more beautiful sight! Her eyes flickered over her tall sons anxiously, then came to rest on the gaunt, pale face of her husband. His brown hair was long and in woeful need of a trimming, but the piercing gray eyes beneath his shaggy mop were the same as she had loved these fifteen years.

She slowed her mount, and Jamie stepped forward, his powerful arms sweeping her from the saddle before the animal came to a halt. All the anguish and uncertainty of the past month faded as she lost herself in his arms.

Releasing Janet reluctantly from his crushing embrace, Jamie smiled at her. "Come love, you musn't weep over us." He brushed a tear from her cheek. "I'm afraid the boys won't like it above half."

"Oh . . ." she gasped. "I . . . I didn't mean to cry."

He gave her shoulder an understanding squeeze, turning her to greet their sons. Evan flung himself into her arms, but stopped short of letting her make a fuss over him in the presence of the men of Camereigh.

Will hung back shyly. "Hello, Mother," he said, but his heart was in his eyes. "It's good to see you."

She stood on tiptoe to kiss his cheek, gazing at him through tear-drenched eyes. "It's good to see you again, too—all of you."

Turning to her brother, she searched for words. "How can I ever thank you, Francis?" she asked unsteadily.

"By keeping this bunch of reivers out of mischief."

"But . . ."

He cut short her thanks by putting an arm around her and sweeping her up the stairs in advance of her family, calling for refreshments as they turned into the hall.

For more than an hour the group ate and talked, the story of their adventures shaded for the ears of their wife and mother. Janet listened intently, reading much between the lines but never letting on by even the flicker of an eyelash that she knew there was more to these stories than was being so gaily recounted. She caught Jamie's hand beneath the table, a silent communion flowing between them while they laughed together at the antics of their lively sons.

The looks that passed between them were not lost on Francis, nor was the passion inherent in that first kiss of reunion. He stretched his long legs beneath the table, then pushed back and stood up. "Well, lads, I'm for a bit of exercise after sitting about all day. What say you to a ride and a bit of sword practice?"

Evan's blue eyes opened wide with delight. To get a lesson in swordsmanship from such a master as his uncle was a high treat indeed. Glancing back at his mother, he frowned abruptly. "But we shouldn't leave Mother so soon."

"Your mother's weary after her long ride. She needs to rest and freshen up. And I'm sure your father would enjoy some quiet conversation with her—just to get reacquainted, you know," Francis added. He flashed a conspiratorial glance at his brother-in-law.

Will caught the look. Grinning, he added his mite to the conversation. "Well, brat, you can sit here cooling your heels if you like, but I'll not miss a chance to go a round with Francis."

That was enough for Evan. His scruples overcome, he bounced down to the stables to order the horses. Will kissed his mother before leaving, a twinkle in his eye as he wickedly admonished her to rest.

Janet flushed scarlet. "Francis, you're a wretch," she hissed at his unrepentant back. As his laughter died away down the corridor, she turned shyly to her husband.

James Cameron gazed in amusement at his blushing wife. "A person'd think you were a newly wedded bride instead of a woman well married these fifteen years," he said softly. "Have you forgotten so much in only one month, lass?"

"Of course not," she said, tossing her head back in the saucy way he loved. "Only we shouldn't be carrying on in front of the boys."

"No," he agreed, "which is why your brother has taken them off our hands." He inclined his head toward the stairs. "Madam, shall we go upstairs and, ah . . . rest?"

Taking Janet's hand under his arm, he propelled her up the stairs and into his bedchamber. Closing the door behind them, he turned to her with a look in his gray eyes that made her heart race.

"I really should freshen up—" she began.

His hungry gaze slid over her. "Later," he said tersely, catching her shoulders and pulling her against him.

His mouth moved over hers, tender, compelling, speaking of emotions he could never say aloud. His warm lips slid down her throat and across her shoulder. Janet leaned against him, trembling in her eagerness, her body reawakening to the magic born between them. Shivering with suppressed excitement, she guided his impatient fingers as they tugged at the fastenings of her habit.

"I can't count the times I've thought of you in my arms like this," he murmured hoarsely. "That vision's all that kept me sane. Whenever the hatred and fear began to eat at me, I'd imagine making love to you." He laughed softly. "Sweet Jesus, I'm sure the guards thought me mad, sitting in that hellhole with a smile of pure contentment on my face."

His fingers tightened convulsively on her arms, and the garment slipped from her shoulders, falling to the floor in a crumpled heap where it lay crushed and forgotten for one suspended hour as a man and woman renewed the rapture of their love.

CHAPTER TWELVE

Anne huddled disconsolately before the fire, a borrowed cloak clutched tightly about her drooping shoulders. She gazed vacantly into the crackling flames, a strange numbness creeping over her, blunting the pain of betrayal and humiliation that had knifed through her all day. As if some instinct for self-preservation now deadened her senses, she felt nothing save an overwhelming weariness pervading body and mind. Strangely enough, she no longer even felt the urge for tears.

The sound of her name spoken in a pleasantly deep, male voice roused her. Lifting her head wearily, she blinked at Nigel Douglas in surprise. "I'm sorry, sir; I didn't hear you. Forgive me — my thoughts were elsewhere."

"Is there aught I can do to make you more comfortable, m'lady?" Douglas questioned. His dark eyes scanned her face. "Are you certain you're well?"

At his look of concern, Anne forced a wan smile. "Your interest is kind, sir, but I'm not ill, only tired. These last few days have been a strain . . ."

Douglas nodded in agreement. Squatting on his heels before the fire, he shifted the burning wood carefully. The flames licked greedily at the logs, sending out a wall of heat that Anne's chilled body welcomed eagerly. Finally satisfied with the fire, he shifted his attention to her.

"Are you certain you weren't mistreated?" he asked with another penetrating look. "You've but to say the word and I'll personally see the MacLeans are punished to the man." He paused, carefully measuring her reaction. "Sir Francis MacLean has a dangerous reputation, but he'll soon learn such behavior is no longer countenanced. James Stuart is tired of these petty chiefs and their petty rebellions. He has two bickering kingdoms to unite, and he intends to see peace established in the Highlands... at the cost of the blood of a few rebels, if necessary."

Anne stared into the fire, remembering the cruel words that had shattered her world just a few hours earlier. Francis MacLean had discarded her like a plaything he had wearied of, and the thought of revenge was sweet. She would give anything to see him brought to his knees.

Then other faces intruded. Janet, Donald, Kate, and the host of others who had been kind to her. She could not serve them such a trick because Francis had betrayed her.

"There's no need for that," she heard herself saying. "I took no hurt at the hands of the MacLeans. I was treated with kindness by the household, more like an honored guest than a prisoner. My uncle is a friend of the clan, and he and the Lady Janet Cameron saw to my safety."

"James Cameron's lady?" Douglas asked in surprise. "She was at Camereigh?"

"Surely you knew Janet and... and Sir Francis are brother and sister," Anne said, stumbling slightly over the name.

"I've only just come from England, m'lady, so I can't say that I did." His eyes narrowed in speculation. "So the Camerons are MacLean's kinsmen..."

He rose to his feet abruptly. "If you've no wish to press a complaint then, I'll stop intruding and take myself off. Perhaps your brother may be of more comfort than myself." Bowing slightly, he turned and disappeared into the night.

A great yellow moon was rising over the land, its golden light throwing soldiers into stark relief as they spread their bedding upon the moor. Gazing miserably over the scene, Anne compared this evening with the last night, the inevitable rush of memories reawakening a throbbing pain.

Was Francis walking the beach in the moonlight with another woman? She closed her eyes, trying to shut out the memory of those moments in his arms. Did he lie with another tonight—and were they laughing together over her foolishness? Why, she choked, dear God why had he done this?

Opening her eyes, she saw Charles moving toward her across the damp grass, two platters of food balanced neatly in his hands. He dropped to his knees beside her. "Anne, you're not coming down with the fever, are you? Nigel thought you looked unwell."

"I'm fine, Charles," she said, forcing a smile. "All I need is a meal and a good night's sleep and I'll be good as new." Taking the food, she forced herself to eat with the appearance of relish.

Charles watched in silence, then cleared his throat uncomfortably. "I'm sure you're wondering why Father hasn't come."

She stared at him in surprise. In truth, she had been so sunk in misery, she'd not thought of Glenkennon all day. After the events of the last twelve hours, her father had power to cause her neither dread nor joy. "I'd really not considered it, Charles," she said lamely. "I suppose he's too busy to attend to me as usual."

"He was supposed to be here by now," Charles continued in a puzzled voice. "He planned to leave his men and camp with us tonight."

"His men?"

"Father was certain MacLean planned treachery," Charles explained. "We divided our forces. I led the smaller group—only about three score—while he brought up a force double that. They stayed hidden a mile or so from Camereigh while we marched into the open. If MacLean tried anything, I was to retreat, leading him away from the castle while Father's men circled around to trap them outside the gates. We would have had them easily enough."

She stared at him in disbelief. "You planned to lure the MacLeans out so Father could ambush an outnumbered force?" The food shifted uneasily in her stomach, and she put her plate down in disgust.

"Only if they tried some trick. Christ's blood, Anne, you'd think you were on their side! You've acted damned strange about this whole affair."

She uncurled her clenched fists and took a deep breath. "Of course, I'm not on their side. I've just no wish for bloodshed."

"I guess a woman can't be expected to understand strategy." A boyish smile suddenly erased the lines of fatigue about his mouth. "I remember you always were too tender-hearted. You couldn't even bear to have the foxes killed that raided our poultry houses at Rosewood. Well, things are different here, Anne, and you'd best get used to it. There's little law and order in the Highlands, and force is often necessary. Especially with rebels like MacLean."

At her nod, Charles turned his attention to his meal with a gusto she envied. Sopping up the last of his food with a crust of bread, he put down his plate. "It's not that Father doesn't want to see you," he said, returning to their original topic of conversation. "But he's always busy. He holds the authority of the king here, and rebels like MacLean and Cameron make it difficult to carry out his duties. Father's a very important man," he added proudly.

Anne smiled at her brother's enthusiasm. "You needn't make apologies for him to spare my feelings, Charles. Father's never cared much for me—I was reconciled to that fact years ago."

"It's not that . . . Father often has no time for me either. I'm afraid I'm a bit of a disappointment to him," he admitted with a heavy sigh. "That's why every command he gives me is important. I have to show him I'm fit to lead men. If MacLean attacks us tonight, I swear I'll kill him with my bare hands if I have to!"

Anne glanced at her brother's eager face, at the length of his lean body sprawled on the ground beside her. Francis would make short work of him, she thought darkly. He would give no quarter—to any of them. She had certainly learned that to her sorrow. "I'm sure you can take care of us," she said soothingly, "and Father realizes that, too, else he'd not have trusted you with the task. I know he's proud of you."

"He's proud of the way I handle a sword," Charles said with a ready grin. "Even Father says I'm 'damnably good.' He taught me himself, and there's no better swordsman in all the Isles. You should see him, Anne," he added, his voice quickening in excitement. "His blade's pure poetry..."

He broke off, leaning back with a sigh. "Those are my happiest memories—working with him, learning from him. It's the only time I ever pleased him."

"I'm sure he just doesn't always tell you when he's pleased, Charles."

"Perhaps," he murmured, staring into the fire. Raising his head, he gave her a shy smile. "I'm glad you're here, Anne. I've missed you—you and Mother." He drew a deep breath. "I can't believe that she's gone—that I'll never see her again." He grasped his knees tightly, speaking with an obvious effort. "I wanted to come when she was taken ill, Anne, truly I did! Father and I had quite a row. He said we'd go later—when she was better. Sweet Jesus, I'll never forgive myself..."

Anne caught his hand, feeling the clutch of his fingers about her own. For a moment, he was still a small boy looking to her for comfort. "It's all right, Charles. Mother understood," she said softly. "She knew Father far better than either of us. She wanted to see you, but I know she understood."

"Was she in any pain?"

She shook her head. "She just went to sleep. She spoke of us and of her brother Ian. And at the very end she murmured a man's name . . . one I didn't recognize. Then she was gone."

Charles nodded his bowed head. "Good." He drew a long breath, then gazed around the moonlit campsite. "I must see to my men now, Anne. See if you can't get some sleep—we'll be riding again at dawn." Rising to his feet, he strode away, as though embarrassed by the emotions that had almost overwhelmed him.

Anne wrapped herself closely in the too-large cloak, curling up into a tired ball beside the dying fire. In spite of all her resolution, her thoughts flew back to her brother's words. Perhaps Francis had known of that second force waiting to destroy him. Perhaps he had learned of her father's treachery and for that reason had sent her away. He could be waiting out there in the shadows, even now planning his next move in this game of human chess he played with Glenkennon.

She tried ruthlessly to crush the hope that surged to life in her breast, telling herself firmly that it would only lead to further disappointment. Yet the thought would not die.

She closed her eyes wearily. Things would be better in the morning.

The journey to Ranleigh lasted four days, time Anne spent well in getting reacquainted with Charles. During all that time Anne did not see her father. The earl had sent word that he was riding for home and would meet them there. The tedious pace of an army on the move was not to his liking.

Anne, too, chafed at their slow movement, yet at her first sight of Ranleigh, she foolishly wished herself back on the trail. Reining in sharply, she gazed down on the pale stone of the harled walls and the slender arching towers of the twin keeps.

"'Tis a lovely sight, Ranleigh. I'm sure you're glad to be home."

She turned. Nigel Douglas had drawn rein beside her, his warm brown eyes regarding her curiously. Anne forced herself to smile. "I'm so weary of this saddle any rude hut would be heaven."

She stared down at the glistening blue waters of a small loch curving around two sides of the castle, remembering another expanse of sparkling water she had so recently enjoyed. But that had been another day, another lifetime—and that happiness had existed only in her own foolish head.

She must have sighed aloud, for Douglas leaned toward her with an encouraging smile. "Don't despair. You're home now, my lady."

Home—he had used the word again, yet there was no such place for her, she thought bitterly. She put her heels to Cassie's sides, following Douglas down the hill and over the wooden bridge after the soldiers.

The hooves of her mount sounded hollowly on the planks in echo of the hollow pounding of her heart. In the next few minutes, she would meet her father—and he would be furious with her for causing the loss of his hostages. In spite of the warmth of the midday sun, a numbing cold crept over her.

Dismounting in the courtyard, Anne followed Charles into the imposing double-doored entrance to Ranleigh. Servants swarmed forward to meet them, taking cloaks and gloves and offering silver tankards of ale and wine. She took wine gratefully, steadied by its sharp bite.

Moving into the hall with her brother, she gazed about in awe. The oak-paneled room easily could have held two hundred men. Its floor was not of stone but of a highly polished wood, which reflected the shine of silver from numerous sconces set into the walls. Cavernous fireplaces

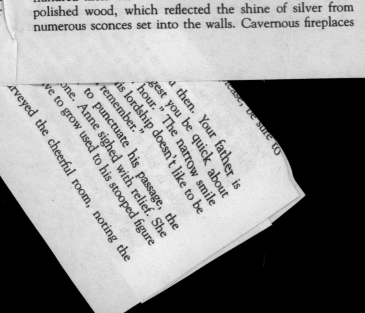

at either end of the room could have taken small trees in their gaping mouths, but no cheery fire burned to chase the chill from the room. Trestle tables stood along the walls, separated some distance from the raised marble dais and imposing table of the earl. And behind the earl's chair, the likeness of James Stuart, king of England and Scotland, gazed down in royal boredom from the wall.

Preoccupied by the study of her magnificent surroundings, Anne failed to notice the sudden hush as servants sprang to attention and the buzz of a dozen excited voices quieted. Charles glanced over his shoulder and stiffened. "It's Blake," he hissed into her ear.

Anne turned, following Charles's hostile stare. A thin, slightly stooped man with lifeless, straw-colored hair was making his way toward them. Dressed in a suit of somber brown cloth, he wore no hint of lace or jewels to relieve the monotony of his attire.

Blake halted before Anne, his transparent gray eyes looking out shrewdly from a pale, bloodless face. "I see you've brought her home at last, Charles." His voice was soft and caressing as a woman's.

Charles nodded stiffly. "Anne, this is Edmund Blake, Father's steward."

Anne forced herself to smile and murmur an acknowledgment, though she did not extend her hand. Some how she did not like the thought of this man touching h w

Blake studied her as if reading her mind. Hi mouth curled upward at one corner into a crook less smile. "You must be tired, mistress," he sa you'll follow me, I'll see you to the room we'

"Where's Father?" Charles asked. "I'd we've arrived."

"Your father is fully aware of your office at the moment, but he's aske He'll see you presently, I'm sure."

Turning in abrupt dismissal, door without a backward glan

opened the door of the massive
hung there as though they belonged.
Sinking down into a stiff-backed chair, she considered her
strange welcome to Ranleigh. Blake had assured her
comfort, yet the man made her uneasy. His perverse, col
orless appearance reminded her of nothing so much
blade of grass that had lain too long beneath a ston
Anne's dark musing was interrupted by a li
the door. At her word, a slight girl of al

* * *

In less time than she had imagined possible, Anne was standing outside the door to her father's office, watching Bess disappear down the corridor. This was the moment she had dreaded so long. Unbidden, the wish for Francis's steadying presence swept over her, but she thrust the thought angrily aside. She would never wish for him again —nor for anyone else, she vowed. With that rallying thought, she thrust open the door and swept into the room.

Robert Randall, fifth earl of Glenkennon, sat quietly behind his desk, busily writing among the stacks of paper scattered about. He did not look up as she stepped inside. Perhaps, Anne thought, he hadn't heard the door.

"Please come in, my dear; I'll be with you in a moment," he said, abruptly ending her cowardly thoughts of slipping unnoticed back outside. He continued to scratch busily, finally sanding and sealing his missive before raising penetrating eyes to hers.

He hasn't aged a day in the last three years, Anne thought, studying him dispassionately. He was just as she remembered. The thick hair was still a dark auburn; no hint of gray marred its smooth waves. The face was still as cold and impassive, the eyes as hard and flinty. They flickered over her now, measuring the changes of her face and figure over the last three years.

He must have been pleased by what he saw, for his lips turned up in the ghost of a smile, though the calculating expression in his wintry gray eyes did not change. "So we meet again at last," he said softly. "I was beginning to despair of ever welcoming you to Ranleigh."

He stood up abruptly, taller than her by a full head. "You've changed since I last saw you, Anne, but I must say it becomes you. Three years ago you were but a promising bud; now I behold the flower you've become." He scrutinized her carefully from head to toe. "I didn't think it possible, but you're even lovelier than your mother was at your age."

"I'm glad you're pleased with me, sir," she said stiffly. "The years have been kind to you also."

"Why, thank you, Anne." He moved across the floor with the peculiar, lithe grace she remembered so well. Pouring them both a glass of wine from the crystal decanter on the side table, he turned back to her. "Pray be seated, my dear. You don't look comfortable standing there in the middle of the floor."

Anne glanced about the room, finally selecting a high-backed wooden chair with carved, curving arms. She sank down obediently, though she could not relax against the chair's cushioned back.

Glenkennon crossed the room, pausing to hold out the glass of wine. Nervously, she noticed that the deep red of the wine matched the crimson velvet of his doublet. The color reminded her of blood, and she thought fleetingly of his plan to massacre the MacLeans.

"I'm relieved to get you safely here at last," he said smoothly. "I sorely regret the experiences you've had. That my own daughter cannot travel in safety. . ." He broke off as if it were an affront he couldn't bear to contemplate.

"I took no hurt sir, though I'm sorry I spoiled your plans," Anne said bluntly. "I'm sure you were wishing me back in England when you heard the news."

He looked at her keenly, as if wondering how much she knew. "It's no matter." He dismissed her statement with a graceful wave of his jeweled hand. "I shall have those rebels sooner or later—and I can afford to wait."

He returned to the chair behind his desk, gazing across its wide length at her. "You were at Camereigh quite some time, Anne. Charles states you told him you were well treated—that the MacLeans even gave you your freedom about the place. Is this true?" The expression in his eyes was unreadable, but some slight inflection in his soft voice kept Anne on guard.

"It's true," she said slowly, remembering those long rides with Francis, seeing his smiling face again in her mind's eye. She had never until then known such freedom—and doubtless never would again.

"I should like to question you in detail concerning things you might have seen—things you might have heard," Glenkennon continued. "You may think you noticed nothing of importance, but there are details you may have picked up. Details that could be of great interest to me."

Anne dropped her eyes, veiling her thoughts from his prying gaze with the sudden sweep of heavy lashes. There was a tiny pause. "I'll be happy to tell you everything I can remember, Father, though I doubt there's much to interest you. If it doesn't displease you, however, I'd postpone our talk until tomorrow. I've been in the saddle four days now and am so weary even my thoughts are confused."

Glenkennon was silent. Her heart fluttered wildly against her ribs, and a tell-tale dampness began spreading between her clasped hands. How dared she put him off? Should she not have blurted out all she knew about Camereigh and the MacLeans? She owed Francis nothing. Nothing!

"Of course, my dear," Glenkennon finally said with just the right tone of concern. "We shall speak of this later, after you've rested." He toyed absently with his glass, inspecting the carefully manicured fingers clasping its crystal stem.

An uncomfortable silence stretched between them so long that Anne jumped when he spoke again. "You know, women are adaptable creatures," he mused aloud. "Given time, they're capable of adjusting to any set of circumstances. 'Tis a most wonderful characteristic of your sex, my dear."

Anne swallowed to ease the growing dryness in her throat. She had no idea what he was getting at, but she did not trust his faintly purring voice or the calculating way he continued to regard her.

"You seem strangely loath to speak of your experiences, Anne. One would think you'd be ranting about your ill treatment at the hands of those outlaws or else prostrate with exhaustion and embarrassment. Since you're neither, I must wonder at your amazing fortitude." He raised a questioning eyebrow at her. "Forgive my foolishness, Anne, but could you possibly be seeking to protect those rebels?"

She forced herself to meet his gaze. "I fail to see how fainting at this point would improve matters, and as for ranting about my ill treatment, I've already told Charles I was treated with every consideration. I seek neither to protect nor harm the MacLeans."

"And were you treated with consideration by Sir Francis MacLean?" Glenkennon asked, immediately taking up her words. "'Tis rumored he's most considerate of the fairer sex—even his enemies. Many have been said to have, ah . . . shall we say, enjoyed that consideration."

The words cut painfully into Anne's heart, reminding her that she had been only one of many for Francis. She drew a deep breath, returning her father's stare unwaveringly. "I'm not certain what you're suggesting. What answer do you wish me to give?"

Glenkennon sipped his wine meditatively, his eyes downcast, veiled by hooded lids. "Let's not mince words, Anne." He placed his glass on the desk with deliberation. "Your stay at Camereigh has thrown doubt upon your reputation. I must know if you are still a virgin if I'm to successfully negotiate a marriage for you."

Anne stared at him, an angry flush mounting her cheeks. Francis had been right; her father did plan to sell her in marriage to the highest bidder. "And would it spoil your plans if I weren't, Father?" she snapped, anger making her foolishly bold. "Tell me, how much would my value decrease? How much gold would you lose if I were in slightly used condition?"

Glenkennon's eyes narrowed with displeasure. He leaned across the desk toward her. "You're being impertinent, Anne," he said smoothly. "I must assume you're so overcome with exhaustion you don't know what you're saying. I don't remember your being such a foolish girl."

The silken voice awoke a prickle of fear. She would be foolish indeed to defy him. He would only enjoy crushing whatever resistance she could muster. She clasped her hands tightly in her lap to still their trembling, hating herself for her helplessness—for giving in to him so easily. "You're right, Father, I'm so weary I can scarcely think," she said, her voice carefully expressionless. "You've naught to be concerned about. I'm still as God made me and have known the touch of no man—most certainly not that of Sir Francis MacLean."

Glenkennon leaned back in his chair, a faint smile playing about his thin lips. "It is well. I knew you'd not disappoint me, Anne. You may go now," he said, dismissing her abruptly.

She rose and moved hurriedly across the floor.

"Oh, and Anne . . ."

She turned back, one hand clutching the door knob.

"Be sure to get plenty of rest. I'd not see you again when your thinking is so disorderly. Impertinence in a woman is a trait I will not abide. I suggest you remember that."

She stood motionless, caught in his unblinking stare while the unspoken threat hung menacingly between them. Finally breaking free of his penetrating gaze, she gave a quick nod and slipped out the door. Pulling it shut behind her, she fled down the echoing hall as though pursued by all the demons of hell.

CHAPTER THIRTEEN

*F*rancis shoved a damp lock of hair back from his forehead. It had been a long, wearying morning of training. He glanced at his men, who sprawled tiredly in the shade at the edge of the meadow, many naked above the waist as they rested. Unfastening his leather jack, Francis drew his shirt over his head. The cool breeze at once began drying the sweat from his glistening body.

William Cameron lay beside him, eyes closed in exhaustion. Francis smiled at the boy. He had worked Will relentlessly that morning, but he had been pleased by what he had seen. The boy was tough. Will had not given up, even when his arm trembled so he could scarcely raise his sword.

Francis gave the boy a shake. "Come lad, don't tell me you're spent. We've only begun."

Will opened one baleful eye, then closed it again in relief at the teasing expression on his uncle's face. "I'm past spent, sir. I think I'm dead and gone to heaven this ground feels so good. If Glenkennon himself were upon us, I doubt I could pick up that sword."

"You did well, lad. Far better than I expected after a month's inactivity. It'll take time to regain your strength," Francis said encouragingly. "I don't like the way your mount shys from the ring of steel, though. If Jamie will allow it, I'll see to the mounting of you. It's often the mount that makes the difference in a fight."

"I'd like that," Will murmured, a smile curving his lips. "Find me something like that black brute you ride . . . then teach me to stay in the saddle."

Francis grinned at the compliment. "I'm afraid Leven has no equal, lad, but I'll see what I can do."

"Horsemen approaching!"

The shout rang out down the line, abruptly silencing the desultory laughter as every hand groped instinctively for a weapon.

After a moment Francis relaxed against the oak behind him. His keen eyes had caught the colorful flash of a lady's habit. Smiling cynically, he lounged at his ease though many of his men now stood to attention to meet the approaching riders.

Elizabeth Macintyre looked her beautiful best as she drew her spirited chestnut to a halt. Her emerald-green habit was cut simply enough, but fitted in a manner that drew a man's eyes to her attributes. Her luxuriant black tresses coiled demurely over one shoulder in a heavy twist that shone in the morning sunlight. The color of her cheeks was heightened by the day's exercise, and her brilliant hazel eyes sparkled with flecks of green fire. Seated expertly on her prancing mare, she was a picture to gladden the heart of any man.

Francis swung lazily to his feet, hatless and shirtless before her in the warm spring sun. "Good morrow to you, Mistress Macintyre. What fortunate wind brings you to us this morning?"

She flashed him a blinding smile. "I was on my way to visit a kinswoman and heard the good tidings of the Camerons. I hoped to enjoy a comfortable visit with Janet and rest the night before continuing my journey—if I might beg a place at your board . . ."

Francis swept a graceful bow which, oddly enough, wasn't incongruous with his state of undress. "We're honored, mistress," he drawled, blue eyes glinting up at her in amusement. "You're welcome, as always."

He lifted an arm encompassing his men. "Pardon our present state, but you find us resting after a morning of exercise. We aren't fit for a lady's eyes, I'm afraid."

Her eyes swept appreciatively over his finely muscled torso, noting the way the thick black hair curled on his broad chest and tapered to a fine ebony line against the dark bronze of his flat belly. "Oh, I don't mind," she said with a provocative glance.

Francis turned to Will, lips twitching at the spellbound look on the boy's face. "Elizabeth, you'll remember William Cameron here, Jamie's eldest boy."

Elizabeth leaned down, smiling at the boy in an intimate manner. "Of course, I remember you, Will, but I'd no idea you'd grown into such a fine figure of a man. 'Tis pleased I am to see you back safe and sound."

"My thanks, mistress," Will managed to get out.

Elizabeth turned her attention back to Francis, and the two exchanged a few more polite comments. Finally, with a nod at Will and another brilliant smile, she rode off in the direction of Camereigh.

"Sweet Jesus!" Will breathed, shaking his head after the retreating figure. "I can't understand why you remain unwed, Francis, with a carrot like that dangling before your nose." He shot a sly grin at his uncle. "And I'll warrant she's yours for the asking from the look of things."

"Ah, lad, you've not yet learned there's more to a woman than meets the eye. The wrapping's nice, but 'tis the substance beneath that must be worth the price of the package."

"I'd like a look beneath that wrapping," Will remarked, gazing hungrily after the disappearing riders.

Francis laid a hand on his shoulder. "You'd best leave that wrapping to more experienced hands," he whispered with a grin. "She'd eat you alive and be looking round for more."

"Is that so?" Will demanded indignantly. He punched Francis playfully and soon the two wrestled in the grass with the MacLean clansmen crowding around shouting their encouragement.

Elizabeth rode slowly toward Camereigh, smiling in satisfaction. So the rumors she had heard were true. The Camerons were free, and Glenkennon's daughter was gone. There would be nothing to keep Francis's attention from her any longer.

Her eyes narrowed thoughtfully. Marriage to Francis MacLean had been her goal for as long as she could remember. She must have been only nine or ten when she first had seen the magnificence of Camereigh, first had heard her mother whisper what a match she might make. As she had grown to womanhood, his name had been the one on every woman's lips, and he continued to be the prize every marriageable girl longed to snare. Even her father had encouraged her pretensions, proudly reminding her she was the most beautiful lass in all Scotland and frequently wishing aloud for an alliance with the powerful MacLeans.

But Francis had never shown her any peculiar mark of regard until the year past, when her family was visiting Camereigh. On that night they had walked in the garden, and Elizabeth had allowed Francis to kiss her in a way that left no doubt where his thoughts lay. She had teased him to the limit of his endurance before calling an abrupt halt to his passionate caresses. She had been certain he would soon ask for her hand, but strangely enough, no word had come. After that night, Francis had been a charming companion whenever they met, but she had failed to be with him alone long enough to provoke the response she desired.

She had come to the Camereigh revel a month earlier, determined to win a declaration from him. But that night his eyes had followed the Randall chit with more interest than Elizabeth cared to recall. Her fingers tightened on the reins and a fever of jealousy rose in her heart.

She wanted him. Since that night in the garden she had thought of little else. Other men had kissed her since then, but it was Francis she dreamed about, Francis she could not forget. And besides—he had all that lovely gold.

She smiled to herself. This time there would be nothing to stand in her way. She would spend a tiresome visit with her aunt until she heard the Camerons were gone. Then she would return, once again stopping to rest the night at Camereigh. Only this time, she would get Francis into bed with her. After he had bedded her once, or maybe twice if she could manage it, she would leave, returning later to claim she carried his child.

Francis wanted children, hadn't her father told her that often enough? A strange excitement tingled inside her. Perhaps she truly would be carrying his child by then, but if not, she could always stage a fall after the wedding and lose the fictitious child. She would be Lady MacLean of Camereigh then and rich beyond her wildest dreams.

Only one thought marred the beauty of the plan. Francis would be furious if he ever learned what Elizabeth had done. She gnawed the finger of one gloved hand thoughtfully, uncomfortable at the thought of his wrath. She must take care that he never suspected.

Francis did not return to Camereigh that morning. Seeking any alternative to an afternoon spent in polite verbal fencing with Elizabeth, he set out to find Donald. His clansman was establishing a warning system for his crofters to be ready should Glenkennon march on them again.

Francis had learned of the earl's frustrated plan to ambush him, and could only thank God he had not been mad enough to challenge Charles Randall's small force that day. Glenkennon was ruthless; he would stop at nothing to destroy the MacLeans. Yet he would do nothing rashly. When Glenkennon struck it would be with animal cunning, and Francis had to move carefully if he were to survive.

He caught up with Donald shortly after midday, just as his friend was sitting down to a meal of cold mutton pie and coarse oat bread. Never at a loss, Donald took one look at his chief and silently opened his pack to remove a whole meat pasty and a slab of hard cheese.

Francis tethered Leven in the sparse grass beside Donald's rangy gray, returning to sit cross legged beside his clansman. Donald passed him a hunk of bread with the pasty resting upon it and raised one bushy eyebrow. "Did you think I couldna do the job without help?"

Francis stuffed the food hungrily into his mouth. "No," he mumbled, licking his dripping fingers. "We've company at Camereigh."

"Well, now that explains it. Have you changed the rules of hospitality that the laird must leave when he's guests in his gates?"

Francis ignored Donald's wit. "It's Elizabeth Macintyre come to have a 'comfortable' visit with Janet."

Donald gave a rude crack of laughter. "Janet should love that—the two of them bein' bosom friends and all."

Francis's eyes twinkled at his friend over half of the pasty. "I judged it time to retreat."

"Oh, now...a pair o' bright eyes might be just the thing for you lad," Donald dared, gazing innocently across the hillside.

Francis propped his arm against his knee and leaned against the stone at his back. "The mood I've been in of late, I'm no fit company for anyone save an uncouth scrub of a Scotsman like yourself."

"'Twas a lass that put you into that mood. Mayhap a lass can pull you out again," Donald replied.

Breaking off a lacy frond of fern, Francis shredded it abstractedly. "So you and Colen are agreed I can find forgetfulness with—how did he put it? Another winsome face and willing body."

"I didn't say that. But for a time, you must just fill the days."

"But the days are empty, Donald," Francis answered softly, allowing the fern to slip from his fingers.

"Well, the days will go by, empty or no, and time will bring ease, if not forgetfulness. 'Tis an impossible situation, lad, as well you know. It'll do no good to dwell on it."

"But is it impossible, Donald? Couldn't there be some answer I've not thought of?" Francis asked, still gazing down at the fern.

"There's naught to be done, lad," Donald repeated slowly. "Much as I like the girl, she'd be the ruin of ye. We can't have ye outlawed now. Glenkennon's spoiling for a fight, and you're the best one ta lead the clans."

"God's blood, Donald! Why me?" Francis picked up the mutilated fern and began tearing at it again. "Maybe I'm not cut out to be the laird," he added harshly.

"But you are the laird, man, and 'tis a responsibility you wear well, though I know 'tis a heavy load at times," Donald said. "You may not believe it, but I heard the old laird voice that same doubt on occasion."

Francis's eyes flew to Donald in amazement. "Father?" He stared at his friend, unable to imagine Colin MacLean feeling unequal to any task.

"Aye, lad, your father was a man like any other. At times he felt weary and confused like you must now. I'm sure he'd tell ye to be gettin' on with yer life though, not pinin' over what canna be had."

Francis chewed the remainder of his lunch in thoughtful silence, giving a harsh laugh when the last crumbs were gone. "Wouldn't Elizabeth be disappointed if she achieved her goal only to find herself tied to a penniless outlaw a short time later? God, what a good jest," he snorted cynically.

"Mayhap you wrong the girl," Donald put in. "There may be more she wants than your gold. You've an ugly face and the manners of a knave, but for some reason you warm the lassies' hearts."

"If Elizabeth has a heart, it's beyond my ability to warm. But perhaps that's for the best. She'll not be plaguing me for something I can't give." He shrugged his shoulders. "If she bears me sons, she can take my gold and go her way, and I'll not interfere. You're right—I do need to get on with my life. Perhaps that's the answer for both of us."

"Don't do anything foolish yet awhile, lad," Donald cautioned. "Give yourself time. There's no hurry."

Francis's dark mood continued during dinner that night, and nothing pleased him save the hearty red wine. It went down easily; enough of it and he might forget the empty ache inside.

He refilled his glass often, finally catching Janet's worried glance. No doubt she guessed the cause of his temper. She had raised the subject of Anne only once during the last two weeks, and he had quietly explained the end of that affair. He had changed the subject abruptly then, his black look discouraging her from raising the topic again.

"Francis, would you pour me more wine?"

He turned his attention to the woman beside him. "Certainly . . . my pleasure, Elizabeth."

He took her glass, feeling the casual brush of her fingers against his, smelling the faint perfume of roses she always wore. He wordlessly poured wine from the crystal decanter at his elbow, recalling his earlier conversation with Donald. Perhaps a woman was the remedy he needed.

Returning her glass, he studied the delectable contrast of her flawless ivory skin and black hair. His gaze slid lower, to the ripe swell of her breasts above the moddishly low-cut yellow brocade she wore.

How could he look at such a woman and feel nothing but a slight stir of appreciation? The sight of her had used to send his heart racing, yet now he found himself comparing her unfavorably with a golden-haired wench who crept into his memory no matter how he tried to cast her out.

Damn Anne! She had made him into nothing more than a gelding! Tossing down the remainder of his wine, he placed his glass on the table. "It's a lovely evening, lass," he said abruptly. "I'm sure a walk in the garden would do us both good."

Elizabeth sent him a languid smile. "That sounds delightful, Francis."

Ignoring Janet's frown, Francis linked Elizabeth's arm through his and led her from the hall. Walking beside her in the warm darkness outdoors, he was haunted by memories of other nights and another woman who had walked these paths at his side. Lightheaded from the quantity of wine he had consumed, he felt an unreasonable anger with himself, but most of all with Anne.

He had lived the life of a priest too long. He had trembled and sighed and held himself in like a schoolboy unsure what to do with his first woman. Had he taken Anne as he had ached to do, perhaps he'd not have been so besotted with her when she was gone. After all, was one woman not exactly like the next?

Elizabeth stumbled against Francis in the darkness. Catching her instinctively, he drew her into his arms. He covered her mouth with his, kissing her brutally, as if he might punish Anne thereby.

Elizabeth was warm and willing and made no move to push away. Leaning her body into his, she followed the movement of his mouth with her own, her parted lips inviting the intimate ravages of his tongue.

Francis slid his hands from her shoulders, down her back—then lower, over the curve of her hips to mold her body against his loins. He felt nothing, damn it! Nothing but an overwhelming frustration and a rapidly building anger against himself and Anne.

Anne . . . Anne . . . she was beyond his reach forever! But Elizabeth was there beside him. He drew her out of the path into a shadowy corner of the garden. He kissed her again, slowly this time, his hands stroking her back deliberately, then moving boldly up to caress her firm breasts.

The low-cut gown scarcely impeded his exploration. He edged it off her shoulders, his roaming fingers discovering her nipples already hardened with excitement. She made no effort to stop him as his lips slid from her mouth to the hollow of her throat and lower. Instead, her hands moved teasingly along his ribs and down against his belly, urging him on.

His heartbeat quickened, and his blood began to surge at last. In his mind's eye he saw her spread naked across his bed upstairs. He would take her and be done with this celibate life. Perhaps his restless anger would ease with the physical release to be found in her willing body. After all, he needed a wife and sons to give purpose to his days.

Suddenly the image of blue eyes and honey-colored hair swam before him. Anne . . . Anne of the sweet smile and innocent kisses. Anne lying half naked beneath him, tangled in the silk of her own hair that last night on the beach. The thought drew a low groan from deep in his throat, and he lifted his head in indecision.

As though sensing his hesitation, Elizabeth slid her arms around his neck, drawing his head down against her naked breast. Overcome by her heady scent, Francis closed his eyes to the warning sounding faintly in the recesses of his brain. Her mouth sought his eagerly, and he gave in to his growing desire.

From somewhere in the darkness a small voice called his name. "Francis, Uncle Francis. Are you out here?"

Elizabeth froze in his arms. "God's body, I'll strangle the boy," Francis growled as she jerked away. She tugged the dress over her shoulders and began straightening her mussed hair.

"Over here, Evan," he called after a moment.

By the time the boy reached them, Francis was outwardly composed at least. "What is it?" he snapped.

Evan glanced from one dark shape to the other, as though wondering why they stood in the darkest part of the garden. "Well," he began hesitantly, "Mother's talking of leaving in a day or two, and you still haven't taken me fishing as you promised. I'm sorry to bother you out here, but . . . but Mother's sent me to bed now, you see. I wanted to ask you if we couldn't please go tomorrow morning?"

"A promise is a promise lad, so I guess that means we'll go," Francis replied shortly. "Now get yourself off to bed before you're caught out here instead of upstairs."

The boy gave a delighted yelp and danced off into the night, leaving Francis and Elizabeth standing together in uncomfortable silence.

"Janet should do something about those boys," Elizabeth said sharply. "They're spoiled beyond measure."

"I find them remarkably well behaved," Francis contradicted, eyeing Elizabeth's dark shape with sudden distaste. He shifted impatiently in the darkness, beginning to be thankful for the interruption.

"Perhaps you're right. I haven't been around children much," she returned, quickly realizing her mistake. She took a step toward Francis, leaning against him enticingly. "I just didn't expect anyone to follow us."

Francis stepped away. "Perhaps it's best someone did. I'm afraid I must beg your pardon, Elizabeth; I'd no right to treat you so. I've no defense save that of a man overcome by a woman's beauty." He glanced toward the castle door. "I'd best take you inside now before someone else comes to find us."

He parted from Elizabeth at the stairs, taking the hand she held out and holding it briefly. She smiled at him with a look that would have melted any other man, but he had seen her give that look to whichever of her court happened to be in favor. He watched her graceful ascension of the stairs, feeling vaguely unclean when he recalled the passionate scene in the dark garden outside.

Elizabeth could bring him only the most fleeting of pleasures. She was not the woman for him. Thank God for whatever providence had sent Evan to find him.

He wandered down the corridor toward the kitchen buildings. He had eaten little at dinner; perhaps that was why the wine had gone so quickly to his head. He would have a bite to eat, then find the Camerons. He was disgusted with his own company that night.

He rummaged through the kitchen, finally discovering a loaf of leftover bread. Tearing off a hunk, he washed it down with a draught of sweet spring water from the crock.

As he ate, a daring plan began taking shape in his head. Sweet Jesu, why hadn't he thought of it before? Quitting the room in haste, he sprinted up the stairs to the summer parlor where the family was wont to gather after dinner. He shoved open the door. Jamie and Will were playing chess at a small table, while Janet sorted threads for her embroidery.

Their conversation ended abruptly as Francis entered the room. "Where's Elizabeth?" Janet asked.

Francis sat down on the settle back, absently toying with the lace at his sleeve. "She's gone to her room," he said innocently. "By the way, Evan and I have hatched a plan to go fishing in the morning."

"And when did he plague you for that scheme?"

"Just now in the garden. Did you send the boy after me, Janet?"

"No, Francis, on my honor I did not!"

He smiled ruefully. "Well, don't scold him, lass. I think he may have done me a good turn the measure of which I may never fully appreciate."

Jamie gave a crack of laughter, his eyes twinkling in unholy amusement. "Francis, lad, that woman means business. You'd best stay out of her way unless you're ready to give up your freedom."

"I've no time for women now," Francis said brusquely. "I'm taking the fight to Glenkennon, Jamie. I'm going to meet him on my own terms."

"Francis, no!" Janet exclaimed. "Don't be a fool."

"I'll not sit waiting for Glenkennon to make his move. Why, I could wait in readiness all year only to get a knife in my back in some shadowy street in Edinburgh or Dundee," Francis said disgustedly. "No, thanks. I'll turn the tables on him, and let him wonder where and when the next strike will come."

"Is that wise at this time?" Jamie asked, his emphasis on the last two words reminding Francis of the charge he might be facing.

He shrugged his shoulders. "A small group of hand-picked men wearing no identifying markings, trained to strike silently in the darkness and disappear without a trace . . . we could inflict a great deal of damage on our wily friend. At the very least we'll make him angrier than a wingless bee when he finds he can lay no name to the raiders."

"Even a wingless bee can sting," Jamie said dryly, "and it's the odd raid that goes off without a hitch."

"Would you wait mewed up on your lands if the man meant to have you?" Francis asked, gazing steadily into his friend's worried face. After a moment of silence Francis smiled. "I thought not."

"May I ride with you, sir?" Will asked, moving eagerly to stand before Francis.

"No, lad, not this time."

"Is it because you think I'm too young, or am I just not good enough?" Will asked bitterly.

"You're old enough to be going on raids lad, and your skill is superior to most your age. I'll take you raiding with me this fall if your father permits, but these raids will be different from a friendly skirmish among the clans. There'll be no rules of barter and ransom should a man fall during a foray. If anything goes wrong, we'll be killed to the man and no questions asked."

Francis put his hand on Will's shoulder, remembering when he had stood on the brink of manhood, begging his father to take him along on a dangerous raid. "I've no sons, lad, no heir save you. If I don't return, the responsibility for my clan will rest on your shoulders." His grip tightened. "Do you understand now? I dare not take you with me."

Will stared up at him, eyes wide with disbelief. "But nothing will happen to you," he said in a tight voice. "It couldn't."

"Oh, but it could lad, and I'll not leave Camereigh without a man of MacLean blood to carry on."

Will swallowed against the sudden tightness in his throat, disconcerted by the thought of a world in which no Francis MacLean lived and laughed and ruled supreme at Camereigh.

CHAPTER FOURTEEN

The morning's driving rain had slowed to a steady drizzle that glanced off the outbuildings below Anne's window and collected in dingy puddles in the courtyard. Anne threw open the window, gratefully taking in a breath of the cool, damp air that rushed into the room.

The weather had turned inclement shortly after her father's departure for Dundee, making the castle dark and stale with the smell of a place too long closed against sunshine and wind. For days, Anne had thought of little but the urge to be quit of the place, to breathe fresh air and walk beside the loch without dozens of pairs of eyes watching her every move. If only her father had not forbidden her to go outside Ranleigh while he was away.

Her face flushed with embarrassment as she remembered the humiliating scene before Nigel Douglas and Captain Kincaid. "You're not to go outside the gates for any reason," her father had said coldly. "Not even if Charles returns from the south and offers to escort you. We'll most likely be entertaining guests on my return, and I can't afford to have you disappear again."

His eyes wandered over her dispassionately. "I'd see you in some new gowns, too. Something a bit more, ah... womanly." He raised an eyebrow. "No gray or black, mind you, and none of these high, starched ruffs you seem to have such a passion for. There's not a man alive who likes the things."

He smiled thinly, as if enjoying her discomfiture. "I've given the seamstress an idea of what I want, and there are trunks of material and trim upstairs. I'll expect to see you suitably dressed on my return."

Anne bit her lip painfully, recalling the cold way he had left her. And worst of all, he had set Edmund Blake to spy on her in his absence.

The thought of Blake sent a shudder of revulsion along her backbone. The man was everywhere about Ranleigh —most often when he was least expected. His disturbing gray eyes peered into every corner of the castle and into the lives of all its inhabitants. Of late she had felt she could not move without coming under his cold stare. But Blake had said he would be busy that afternoon updating the estate ledgers...

She sucked in her breath as a daring thought reared its head. If Blake were busy, no one would notice if she slipped out for an hour or so. After all, what harm could it do? Despite an uneasy qualm, she turned from the window, already planning her escape.

A short time later, Anne fled the cheerless confines of Ranleigh garbed in the rough cloak and brogues of a serving woman. Approaching the outer gate, she drew the frayed hood over her face, as if seeking protection from the inclement weather. The uninterested guards glanced her way briefly but did not comment as she passed.

It was a dismal day to be abroad, but she relished the scent of rain-washed countryside after nearly two weeks of being pent up inside. Head high, she followed a rocky track leading from the road down to the loch. The damp stones were slippery and forced her to step carefully along the water's edge as she made her way toward a large jumble of boulders at one end of the loch. The dark pile of granite was cold and uninviting, but she welcomed its protection from prying eyes.

She half walked, half slid down the rocky incline to the shore. Passing between two great boulders, she clambered atop a large, flat stone, polished to smoothness by the rains of a thousand years. Free—she was free at last, if only for an hour or so.

A cold breath of wind stirred a damp tendril of her hair and sighed brokenly across the loch, while from closer at hand the desolate wail of a curlew sounded from out of the mist. Her feeling of lonely isolation slowly grew, sending her thoughts slipping back to Camereigh.

What was happening there on that cool, damp afternoon? Were the inhabitants gathered snugly about a cheerful fire, laughing and telling tales? A sudden longing to be a part of it washed over her, and she pictured Francis as he had looked on such occasions, laughing down at her with blue eyes twinkling or those same eyes gone dark and tender with . . . with what?

"I don't believe it. I don't believe he didn't care," she whispered aloud. Unbidden, thoughts of the many tender moments between them came back to plague her. Why would he have lied to her, used her, pretending emotions he had never felt? Was it only to beguile the boredom of a few spring days?

She had been over it again and again, only to end with the same unanswered questions. Perhaps Francis had cared for her, but the feeling had been short-lived. Or perhaps he had cared but had determined the consequences of angering her powerful father more than he wished to bring upon his clan. He might well have sent her away for such a reason. Or perhaps—perhaps it had been just as he had said that last unforgettable morning.

She stared down at the muddy-brown water lapping at the rocks beneath her feet. Whatever Francis's motives, the results were the same. That happy time was over. Any day now her father would be returning, and a round of entertaining would begin that would soon see her wed to some wealthy lord of his choosing. She must put away the memories of a moonlit beach and the way it felt to lie in a man's arms and count the world well lost. She must try to meet halfway the man her father would choose, and perhaps in time the images would fade.

She closed her eyes tightly, swallowing back the bitterness of shattered hopes and betrayal. Why had she been granted that one glimpse of freedom, that one taste of life as it was meant to be lived? It was as if a bird, raised in captivity from birth, had been allowed to soar across the heavens, to marvel at the sensation of flight and freedom for a few days, only to be brought down once again, have its wings clipped, and be put back into its cage. Anne's taste of the sweetness of life had been so short. Empty days stretched endlessly ahead of her, and she marveled that life could go on when all that made it worth living had ended.

The wind picked up, groaning restlessly around the great stone slabs lying stark and upended against the lonely water's edge. She clutched her cloak tightly about her as the fine mist changed again to a mizzling rain. It was time to be getting back.

Moving quickly up the path, she slipped into the postern door without incident, creeping stealthily down the dim corridor toward the western stair. She had almost reached her destination when a cold voice sounded from the gloom above the stairway. "Well, mistress, I trust you enjoyed your walk. I should hardly think the weather auspicious for such activity . . . but then, I'm certain you had your reasons."

Anne stood rooted to the spot, one foot upon the stairs as Edmund Blake's pale face materialized above her. He had watched her—he had been spying on her all the time!

She drew herself up as proudly as she could in light of her clumsy shoes and tattered cloak. "Yes, thank you. I enjoyed my walk well enough. There's something invigorating about the wind and mist, don't you agree?"

Blake blocked her path at the top of the stairs. "Do you really think it wise to invite your father's displeasure, mistress?" he asked softly. "There are many who could have seen you out this afternoon."

She halted one step below him. Their heads were almost on a level, his unusual gray eyes riveting hers. "But no one did, save you," she returned, "though I'm sure you'll enjoy recounting the tale to my father at the first opportunity."

"Perhaps . . . and then again, perhaps not," he replied smoothly. His pale, lashless eyes flickered with an emotion she could not read. "I might just manage to . . . forget your activities this afternoon."

His words and the twisted smile that went with them made her go cold with dread. Holding her breath, she pushed past him without reply. Blake would expect something in return for his silence, and she'd no wish to bargain with a man of his ilk. Better her father's displeasure, terrifying as that was. Forcing herself to walk calmly down the hall, she ignored the cold weight of Blake's gaze upon her back.

The earl of Glenkennon arrived with his men on the following afternoon. From the gateway, Anne peered down the road, shading her eyes from the slanting rays of the afternoon sun as she tried to make out the identity of the approaching riders. A dark, bearded man rode beside her father. Even from this distance she could tell he was a gentleman of importance by the luxury of his dress and the blooded bay he rode.

All was confusion as the riders entered the courtyard teeming with servants, children, and barking dogs. Anne hung back until the worst of the chaos subsided, then stepped forward dutifully to greet her father and the stranger at his side.

"Anne, my dear, you can see I've brought guests," Glenkennon said, turning his attention upon her. "Sir Percy Campbell and his men will be staying with us several days. Campbell, I'd like you to meet my daughter Anne."

She cast a quick look at the man before dropping into a

curtsy. She had a fleeting impression of dark hair and eyes, and a well-trimmed beard with a moustache curling above thin lips. He had been handsome once, she thought, though lines of dissipation were already beginning to ravage his narrow, pointed face.

"I'm pleased to meet you, mistress," Campbell said smoothly. "I've been looking forward to a visit to Ranleigh, but now I'm doubly glad I've come." He took her hand and lifted it to his lips before training his dark gaze upon her again. "Your father may have great difficulty driving me away . . . now."

The brush of his beard against her skin was unpleasant, and Anne barely restrained the impulse to jerk her fingers from his grasp. She did not like the flare of interest in his eyes or the way his bold gaze lingered along the curves of her body.

"We shall be pleased to have you as long as you wish to stay, my lord," she replied. "The honor will be ours."

Drawing her hand firmly from his, she turned to her father with a forced smile. "You must be hot and thirsty after your ride, Father. I've refreshments waiting in the hall. You may rest there while I see rooms are made ready for our guests."

She led the men into the hall, then slipped away to her room to change for dinner. Sir Percy Campbell—she recalled the name. Glenkennon desired closer ties with the powerful Campbell clan.

Her father needed her for a marriage alliance and gold —cold, hard gold, Francis had said. The memory of his words sent a shudder down her spine. She would be sold to the man now drinking below if he thought her desirable enough to meet her father's price. Such transactions occurred every day. Marriages were made for wealth and power—and nothing more.

"Bess," she said suddenly, turning toward the girl, "what can you tell me of Sir Percy Campbell?"

"Campbell? He's well known in these parts," Bess remarked. "He's master of several large estates, though his principal residence is Dunbarton, northwest of here."

Seeing the girl intended to say nothing further, Anne prompted her. "But how is it he has no wife? He's well past thirty if I'm any judge."

"His wife's dead—from an accident near a year ago," Bess said slowly. For a moment, she recalled the tales that had circulated about Campbell then quickly dismissed them from her mind. Servants' gossip, she told herself, and not the kind of talk her dear, sad mistress needed to be hearing.

"She was a wealthy Campbell heiress, but a frail lass who bore him but one sickly daughter. The bairn lived scarcely a sixmonth." Bess lifted speculative green eyes to Anne's. "'Tis said he's looking about now for a young wife to bear him sons. He's a wealthy lord and not at all ill-favored," she added helpfully.

"Yes, he's well to look at I suppose," Anne remarked, "and not as old as I feared." She rose abruptly and crossed to the window, leaning her elbows on the polished stone. "And there's always the chance he won't like me," she whispered, trying desperately to banish the image of a man whose eyes twinkled bluer than any summer sky and whose smile made the sun seem cold in comparison.

"And what would you be wearin' tonight?" Bess questioned briskly, seeking to divert her mistress from an unhappy train of thought. Carefully removing several new gowns from the clothespress, she held them up for Anne's inspection.

"I don't suppose it matters, Bess. You choose."

Bess quickly selected a gown of rich crimson silk with long, fitted sleeves and a panel of Flemish lace sewn about the deeply scooped neck. The lass needed the deep shade to bring out the color in her pale cheeks, Bess decided.

She laid the lovely garment across the bed, then turned to dress Anne's hair. Braiding the long strands expertly, she wove slender ribbons of deepest wine through the braids, then twisted the thick mass about the crown of Anne's head and caught it with a pearl-studded clasp.

"'Tis lovely you look, mistress," she said, stepping back with a proud smile. "The gentlemen will lose their hearts tonight and no mistake."

The words were a good omen, it seemed, for when Anne entered the parlor a short while later, Glenkennon looked up and smiled at her in approval. "Good evening, my dear. You're looking most fetching tonight." His glance shifted from her to Edmund Blake. "Blake here has been telling me all ran smoothly while I was away."

Anne forced herself to smile and murmur an assent. She didn't dare glance at Blake; he would probably consider her indebted to him now in some strange way.

Glenkennon winked at his friend Campbell. The man had risen at Anne's entrance and was studying her with open admiration. "I can't tell you, Percy, what a comfort it is to have a daughter see to my household. Anne keeps things running smoothly."

"There's little to see to here," she said, gratefully accepting a glass of wine from Nigel Douglas. "The servants know their tasks and Ranleigh runs itself, even in Father's absence."

"A woman who's as modest as she is lovely," Campbell said archly, stepping forward to take her hand and draw her toward a seat beside his own.

Anne sent a longing glance at Nigel, wishing she might sit beside him and discuss news from Dundee. While the men were away, she had missed his easy wit and the amusing tales he recounted of his recent service in Jamie Stuart's court. She couldn't recall laughing even once since he had been gone.

But Campbell was waiting. Turning obediently, she followed Sir Percy to the settle. "Tell me, my lord," she said, seating herself with a rustle of silk skirts, "were you in

Dundee on business, or was it chance that brought you together with my father?"

"The former, I fear. We've had raiders plaguing us of late," Campbell replied. "We've lost mainly horses and sheep at this point, but the outlaws are getting more daring all the time. Sir Alexander Dorsett lost a quantity of silver en route to your father not a fortnight ago. And just a week earlier, a large quantity of powder was destroyed at an English outpost. Those of us who've suffered met in Dundee to discuss what might be done."

"Does no one know their identity?" she asked.

"Not yet. They strike in the dead of night and leave no sign capable of being followed over a few miles." Campbell smiled at her arrogantly. "But we'll catch them soon enough. Even crafty men make mistakes and these will hang by a piece of good rope soon enough, I'll swear."

"It's MacLean, I've no doubt," Glenkennon said calmly. "He's behind these raids; there's none other among those uncivilized northern fools who could have planned the attacks."

Anne's heart lurched painfully, then began to beat so wildly she could feel it pounding in her ears. She studied her clasped hands carefully, not daring to look up.

"They're far too widespread to be the work of any one man," Nigel Douglas put in, pouring himself more wine. "It's more likely the work of several rebels seeking to profit at the expense of England and those loyal to the king."

"It can't be MacLean, much as I'd like to see him swing," Campbell agreed. "Are you forgetting I saw the man myself? He was roistering about town with a wench on each arm the very night of that raid on Mayburn."

Campbell chuckled. "MacLean may deal in witchcraft as they say, but even he can't be in two such distant places in the same evening. Besides, the landlord himself told me MacLean had been drinking, wenching and spending his blunt freely in his house the past week. That was just the time the outpost was struck. No, it can't be MacLean," he repeated, "though if you'd like to hang him for the fun of it, I for one wouldn't object."

A wench on each arm . . .

Anne continued staring carefully at her hands, concentrating on keeping that blank, interested smile that seemed to please her father. So Francis had been wenching and carousing about town, she repeated to herself dazedly, considering her very different activities of the past few weeks. Had she really believed he might yet care—that he might still come for her?

She had been a fool—a complete fool! Francis had not cared for her in the least, and it was senseless to delude herself with any hope to the contrary. She could not blame him for her disillusionment this time. He had spoken the truth to her on that last morning, and it was she who had believed against all proof that there was more behind his words—that his actions might yet be some trick to best her father.

Somehow she survived the endless evening, retiring immediately after supper with the complaint of a headache. Once in bed, she leaned against the pillows dry-eyed, watching a friendly moonbeam creep slowly across her chamber floor.

Hope was over now—entirely so, and she couldn't even wish for any spark to keep it alive. While she had lain shedding hot tears in her bed, Francis had been out drinking and spending his time with cheap women. She clenched her fists in an agony of jealousy and ire until the nails of her fingers cut painfully into her palms.

She bitterly reviewed every hurtful word he had uttered to her. Ironically enough, they gave her the inspiration for her plan. He had always seemed well informed of the happenings at Ranleigh. Well, let him hear of the advent of Anne Randall upon the midlands. Let him hear that the beautiful daughter of Robert Randall had all of Scotland at her feet.

In the morning she would set out to charm Sir Percy.

Other guests were arriving the next week, and she had no doubt that she could win them, too. She did not care that she would be playing into her father's schemes, she only knew that she wanted Francis to hear of her success.

Lying back upon her pillow, she stared grimly into the night, hoping Francis MacLean would have abundant time to regret what he had lost before her father put a rope about his neck.

CHAPTER FIFTEEN

Francis was once more in residence at Camereigh. Alone in the laird's room, he leaned an elbow lazily amid the clutter of ledgers on his desk, abstractedly studying the glass of wine in his hand. It had been a most successful six weeks—five highly profitable raids against the English without the loss of a man.

With a satisfied smile, he raised the glass in a silent toast to his men's success. Yes, it had been a profitable six weeks—Glenkennon must have been in a continual rage those days.

Lowering the empty glass, Francis thought fondly of the rough, hard-bitten clansmen who had ridden with him. They had obeyed his orders unquestioningly, even when Conall had taken command on those occasions when Francis had made a point to be seen in Dundee.

He and Conall had hatched the plot between them after learning that Glenkennon and his loyal lords would be meeting in that coastal town. Francis had assured himself a place in the memory of several local innkeepers by dropping his coins freely and buying numerous rounds for his "friends."

He closed his eyes contentedly. Now that the immediate danger was over, he could allow himself to think on other matters. At once, memories of Anne came stealing back to haunt him as they had so often during the past weeks. He had attempted at first to fight the visions that plagued him as he lay sleepless on the hard ground or sat his mount amid the whirling mists. But little by little, he had come to welcome her presence in his thoughts and to while away many dull hours in contemplation of her comely face and laughing voice.

He had yet no conscious plan for taking her against all odds and reason, for he knew it was impossible. But when he thought of his future, it was with her at his side, and that vision brought peace to his previously troubled mind.

"Am I interrupting anything?"

Francis jerked upright, his hand groping instinctively for the dirk at his belt. "Conall, for the love of God! You'd best learn not to startle a man so, else you'll grow no older!"

Francis relaxed against the chair back, gazing into his friend's clear gray eyes, which gleamed now in fun beneath his crop of dark, unruly red hair. "I'd ask you to come in," he added dryly, "but since you've already done so, make yourself useful by bringing that decanter along."

"By the look of bliss on your face, I must have caught you contemplating the good Robert's downfall," Conall ventured. He advanced across the room with a slight detour to pick up the wine and an extra glass.

Francis chuckled and shook his head. "Far from it, lad. I'm contemplating a much sweeter face than that of Glenkennon."

"Ah, a lass then, is it? 'Tis the only thing sweeter than the confounding of a man's enemies." Conall made an exaggerated pretense of looking about the room. "Where have you got her hid? I've a great need to see a softer form and sweeter face than those I've ridden with these last weeks."

"Do you think I'd be fool enough to have her here at Camereigh with an unprincipled rogue like yourself about?" Francis shoved his glass across the table for Conall to fill. "The sweetest face we've had about the place in weeks is Donald's, now he's finally shaved his beard. Nay, lad, I keep this lass only in my mind."

"Humph," Conall snorted, "an image can do a man little good. Come, let's get to Dundee or even Edinburgh, if you'd rather, and find a flesh-and-blood woman to help us while away a pleasant evening or two."

"I've already been to Dundee and found nothing to my liking. Go if you like, but take my men in case you need rescue from a jealous husband."

"You found nothing to your liking!" Conall repeated in astonishment, nobly ignoring the latter half of Francis's statement. "You weren't used to be so hard to please, Francis. Come, this must be serious. Tell me about it—or wait—let me guess! Have you finally offered for Elizabeth Macintyre as all the gossips have been claiming this last year?"

"No, and you'd best not be spreading that tale," Francis said with a quick scowl. "Comparing Liz to my lass is like comparing a candle to the sun."

The teasing grin on Conall's face disappeared. "May I ask the lady's name?"

"Aye Conall, you've a right to know. The lass's name is Anne Randall."

Conall's eyes widened in disbelief. "Are you ale-bitten, man?" he gasped. "At this time of the day?" At Francis's continued silence, Conall gave a low whistle and dropped abruptly onto a stool beside his friend. "Well, I'll say this, you don't take the easy road."

He took a long swallow of wine, eyeing Francis gravely. "You know there's nothing I'd rather see happen, if we could pull it off . . ." His words ended abruptly and his narrowed gaze shifted from Francis to the floor. Suddenly, he threw back his head with a rude crack of laughter, slapping his muscular thigh in merriment. "Christ's bones, it'll infuriate Randall . . . and damned if I won't help you to it."

"Hold on, Conall. I'll do nothing outrageous yet. I've no wish to get a price on my head if I can help it."

Conall sobered immediately. "I'd forgotten that little matter of Glenkennon's petition to the king."

"Your concern for your laird is touching," Francis said dryly. "Were it you about to face your future hanged, then drawn and quartered as a traitor, I'm sure you'd not be so quick to forget."

"Ah, lad, the time's not so long past when I faced the same. They have to catch you first," he added, his ready grin reappearing, "and I've no doubt we could outfox simple Englishmen. Come now, let's drink a toast to Mistress Randall. I've developed an overwhelming curiosity to see my fair kinswoman."

The next two weeks passed pleasantly enough, with Francis and his men resting and relaxing before beginning to lay plans for a series of autumn raids. The golden July days slid by like warm honey, and since nothing was heard from Glenkennon, the thought of danger from that quarter slipped to the back of men's minds. But on a beautiful summer's afternoon, Francis was reminded all too well that Glenkennon had not forgotten the MacLeans.

Returning from a morning's hunt, Francis and ten of his men ambled slowly along a sun-dappled trail, arguing good-naturedly over an unfinished game of chess. Above the laughter, a high-pitched shout rang out ahead. "A'Maclean . . ."

The laughter ended abruptly as all ears strained the silence. Another shout, the unmistakable noise of clashing steel—sounds of battle—carried faintly on the summer wind. Francis instinctively slid his sword from its sheath and spurred Leven ahead through the trees.

Galloping over a rise, he drew rein abruptly at sight of the desperate scene in the glen below. Three of his clansmen were backed against a steep hillside, fighting for their lives with a half-dozen heavily armed horsemen. Even as

Francis watched, one of his men went down, and another wavered unsteadily in the saddle.

Francis let loose a bloodcurdling clan roar, raising his sword on high as he and his men surged down the hill. The attacking horsemen turned to flee but weren't quick enough to reach the dubious protection of a heavy stand of birch at the edge of the glen.

Hurling himself into the fray, Francis cut and slashed his way through the thrashing melee, downing one man and carelessly trampling him beneath Leven's plunging hooves. The men were English he noted through the red haze of his fury—undoubtedly Glenkennon's men.

He ducked a length of gleaming steel meant to sever head from shoulders and swung Leven so that the stallion crashed into the oncoming Englishman's mount. The smaller animal scrambled for his footing. Francis made a quick thrust with his sword, disarming his enemy with a blow that cleaved the shoulder joint. The man's lips drew back in a grimace of agony while he frantically sought to control his plunging mount with his good arm.

Francis offered no quarter. Raising his arm to deliver the final blow, he was stopped by the sudden report of a pistol fired from close range. Flinging himself along Leven's neck, he swung about.

Instead of the English army he expected, the sight of one lone rider met his eyes. At the edge of the trees, Charles Randall sat his mount, a smoking pistol held aloft in one hand.

"What in the name of heaven goes on here, MacLean?"

"You tell me," Francis snarled. He wheeled Leven out of the press of men and animals, his sword dripping red with English blood. The white heat of anger surged through him, and he felt an incredible desire to destroy these men who profaned his very soil with their presence.

"Hold them, lads," he ordered his men tersely. "We'll deal with the cowards later."

"Two to one, MacLean. Are those the kind of odds you

favor?" Charles taunted. "These men didn't have a chance!"

"I've just come upon three of my men fighting for their lives with seven of your dogs at their throats, Randall," Francis bit out. "And you're right . . . they'd have had little chance if we'd not happened along."

He gazed at the English soldiers, their badges and colors conspicuously absent. "It looks as though my men had the misfortune to stumble upon your little spying expedition." His narrowed gaze shifted back to Randall, and he jerked his head in the direction of his fallen clansman. "If my man lies dead, I'll see every last man of you cut to pieces for it, so help me God!"

"My men wouldn't attack without reason, MacLean. They'd orders to start no trouble," Charles snapped, his own fury matching MacLean's black rage. "I've no idea what started this, but you'll cut no one to pieces if I can help it. You may have the advantage of us in number, but if you've no wish to be called a coward to your face, you'll meet me now."

"Done," Francis growled, sliding from his mount and tossing the reins to one of his somberly smiling men. He wiped the blood from his blade and handed his dirk to another of his men. He felt no compunction at the thought of killing this man. Charles Randall had led men to spy on Camereigh, and his men had ambushed and attempted to slay three clansmen who had stumbled innocently on their activities. For a moment all his hatred of Glenkennon centered on the man before him, and he felt an overwhelming eagerness to slip his blade into the lad's black heart.

Charles faced Francis warily. He had challenged MacLean on impulse, but now he felt an eagerness to match his sword with that of the man who was fast becoming a legend throughout the Highlands. His own anger rode him hard, but he controlled it, knowing he must keep his head if he were to have any hope of surviving this encounter.

MacLean moved to the center of the clearing, sword pointing carelessly downward to the dirt. Charles shifted into position facing him, searching for any hint of weakness.

MacLean's hard face gave him little satisfaction. The man was completely in command of himself now, his dark face betraying nothing of the violent rage that had gripped him moments before. MacLean would give no quarter— nor would he, Charles thought grimly, lunging forward in an attempt to catch the Highlander off guard.

Francis parried the lunge neatly, following with a quick feint to the right that brought him close against Charles's blade. Steel grated harshly against steel as the boy recovered quickly and the fight was on in earnest. The pair circled each other warily, engaging in several quick exchanges as each attempted to measure the abilities of the other. The ring of steel echoed hollowly in the hush, the men moving tirelessly for many long moments on end.

The sun beat down, flashing blindingly along the gleaming length of blades as the combatants continued to engage and thrust and test. Sweat beaded Charles's brow and began to trickle down his forehead into his eyes. His lungs burned with the effort of taking slow, controlled breaths, and his arm began to tire, the great sword growing heavier though he lifted it doggedly to parry MacLean's blows.

He faced the Highlander defiantly, but a tiny fear began forming in the pit of his stomach. MacLean still matched his blade with an unhurried and negligent skill, his breathing strong and even. He was not even winded, Charles realized desperately.

Suddenly MacLean altered the pace. His dancing blade was everywhere at once, and Charles found it increasingly difficult to defend himself. He felt the sharp bite of steel once, then again and again as Francis toyed with him. The hilt of his sword soon grew slippery with his own blood, and his legs responded sluggishly to the commands of his brain.

Francis abruptly ended the game. Lunging forward, he tripped Charles and threw him to the ground in a maneuver learned from Colen MacKenzie and his wild clansmen in the North. He held his bloodied sword to Charles's heaving chest, pressing down until a bright red stain began spreading in widening circles about the point.

The boy winced as cold steel slid through the cloth of his shirt into living flesh. His eyes, large as saucers now, lifted from a surprised contemplation of the great sword to Francis's face. He drew a deep, ragged breath, managing one last defiant look at his executioner.

Francis suddenly eased the pressure on his sword. Something in that boyish gaze stayed his hand. Blue eyes locked with gray while Francis searched for the trick of expression that had suddenly reminded him of Anne. Sweet Jesus, he couldn't kill Anne's brother! No matter the provocation, she would never forgive him that!

The sound of galloping hooves echoed in the strained silence. Francis glanced from Charles to the approaching horseman. "How do they fare? Have we dead men to avenge?"

"They live, though Naill be cut up badly," the clansman reported. "I've a mind the wound's too high to cause lasting harm, though it'll trouble him sore for weeks to come."

With an expert flick of the wrist, Francis sent his blade skittering down the boy's midline, opening Charles's shirt to the waist and leaving behind an angry red line. That done, he held the blade point down in the dust and leaned upon the hilt.

"Get up," he ordered coldly. "Bind up your wounds and be thankful the fool who struck my man had no aim. Had he a better arm, you'd be leaving here slung across your saddles."

Charles sat up warily, pulling together what was left of

his bloody shirt while he struggled to control his uneven breathing.

Sraightening, Francis gestured with his sword toward the waiting men. "If I catch any such parties on my land again, I'll accord them the same welcome they gave my clansmen. I give you warning though, we've much better arms. Not one will we leave to tell the tale."

"I'm responsible for these men, and we hold no commission to murder," Charles said evenly. He stood up, trying to achieve what dignity he could while his furiously pounding heart began to slow to a more normal pace. "If I find they deliberately set upon your men unprovoked, I'll punish the guilty."

"Aye, but do you have anything to say in the matter, lad?" Francis asked shrewdly, raising one sardonic eyebrow.

A slow flush crept over Charles's face, and he clenched his fists against his side in helpless rage. "You've shown you've nothing to fear from my sword, so you may insult me now as you please, MacLean. I don't give a damn what you think, but I'll see to this matter and take what measures I see fit."

Francis silently studied the boy so long that Charles shifted uncomfortably beneath his stare. "Aye, I believe you will," Francis said. "When will you leave that scheming crowd you run with, lad? Your father doesn't deserve your allegiance."

"Your opinion is of no interest to me," Charles snapped with an assumption of haughty dignity that brought the ghost of a smile to Francis's face. "If you've done with your insults now, we'll be on our way."

"Not so fast." Francis turned to a clansman. "Bruce, collect the weapons save that of young Randall here. Take a half-dozen men and personally escort these..." he paused meaningfully, "...gentlemen from our land."

"Aye sir," the man responded with a delighted grin.

As the weapons were collected, Charles saw to the binding of his men's injuries. Several of them were serious

wounds though only one man looked as though his hours
might be numbered. The men mounted up as best they
could and rode out under the gleeful MacLean escort.

Charles's thoughts were bitter as he rode at the head of
his battered patrol. His arm throbbed painfully from one
deep slash, but he scarcely noticed that physical ache
while he writhed from the humiliation he had just suffered
in front of his men. What his father would say when he
heard the tale he hated even to imagine. He had failed
again.

Still and all, he and his men had gotten off better than
he had expected. According to the Highlanders' savage
code they should by rights have been dead—and he had
come perilously close.

Reliving that moment beneath MacLean's sword, a fresh
sweat broke out on his brow. The man had planned to kill
him. What chance thought had meant the difference between life and death?

He recalled every agonizing detail of that humiliating
scene. It would take months, perhaps even years, to live it
down. Suddenly he wondered if he hated MacLean the
more for leaving him alive after all.

Francis and his men limped slowly into Camereigh carrying their wounded. Faces were grim as the story raced
through the castle, then spread quickly through the cot-
tages of neighboring crofters.

Donald began at once to treat the more seriously
wounded, but Conall pulled Francis aside and whispered
"Your man from Ranleigh's arrived. He's big with news,
but the fool will tell me nothing! He just grins and says,
'It's Sir Francis himself I'm wantin' and I'll speak to none
other,'" Conall mimicked.

Francis glanced at his men. Donald was ordering the
cleansing and binding of their wounds; they were in good
hands. He followed Conall out the door, heading down
the corridor to take the turret stairs two at a time. It had

been almost a month since he'd had news from Ranleigh. He had become so eager for word, he had been half inclined to ride there himself.

"What news, man?" Francis asked, breaking in abruptly upon the startled messenger. "I've been waiting for you a damnably long time."

The man's grizzled face split into a wide grin at sight of his chief. "We was in daily expectation of news from England, sir. I was bid to wait."

Francis felt his stomach lurch sickeningly. His heart pounded rapidly, sending the blood surging in his head. News from England could mean only one thing—Glenkennon had heard from the king. "Well?" he asked, his world hanging in the balance.

"Randall got his news from King Jamie on the last ship what came into Leith." The man raised his eyes to Francis, his face wreathed in a smile. "You've not been put to the horn this time, sir. Jamie Stuart denied the bastard's petition, so all his cursed scheming went fer naught!"

Francis closed his eyes, releasing his long-held breath in one quick sigh. He felt Conall's hand, warm and sympathetic, on his shoulder. Of all men, Conall best knew what he was feeling now.

"Let's sit down," Francis said quietly. "Conall, pour us an ale from that pitcher yonder. It's good to feel a free man again."

Francis and Conall listened quietly while the courier recounted the remainder of his news. They laughed delightedly at Glenkennon's frustration over having no identity to lay to the raiders terrorizing his supporters' estates. But Francis's amusement faded when he heard of Percy Campbell's frequent visits.

"The earl's entertaining now," the man continued. "'Tis rumored he hopes to snag a rich husband for his girl. As a matter of fact, there's a week-long round of entertainment planned for all his fancy lords and ladies in honor of her nineteenth birthday."

Francis frowned darkly. "That whoreson would sell her to the devil if he thought he could wrangle an additional piece of gold." He rose and paced the floor. "I've heard Glenkennon's not paid his troops in months, and they're growing more discontented by the day."

"Aye, the king's sent no payment since the first of the year. 'Tis said he's angered his English nobles using the treasury to redecorate the clutch-fisted Elizabeth's state apartments." The man snickered. "The earl will have to marry the girl in haste . . . and to someone who can afford to pay through the nose."

"When's this celebration to take place?" Conall asked thoughtfully.

"In another week," the man replied.

Francis took another hasty turn about the floor. "I've a sudden urge to attend a party," he mused. "What think you, Conall? Could you behave yourself in polite company if we paid a visit to Glenkennon?"

"I'd not miss it for the world," Conall replied.

CHAPTER SIXTEEN

⁓

$\mathcal{D}$inner was long over and the dancing far advanced when Francis and Conall bluffed their way through Ranleigh's gates and strode confidently up the stone stairs into the castle. Well-trained servants sprang forward at their approach, taking their cloaks and leading them down the oak-paneled corridor toward the great hall.

Following the lackeys, Francis took careful note of the number of branching hallways and the dearth of windows. It would be difficult to escape should the earl choose to take them. If he had miscalculated Glenkennon's reaction, he and Conall would soon be cooling their heels in the dungeon below.

The sounds of music and laughter eddied through the open doorway ahead. Francis pushed past the liveried servant, his gaze sweeping the crowded room for any sign of Anne. A sea of dancers swept by in a kaleidoscope of shifting colors: ladies in shimmering silks and satins, men in rich velvet and the snowiest of linen, all bedecked in jewels of every description, which winked in the light of a hundred candles set in sconces of polished silver. Anne was somewhere amid this glittering throng, and he'd find her—if he lived the night.

His searching eyes came to rest on a tall, well-proportioned figure attired in a doublet of black velvet and fashionably padded velvet breeches. Even from the back, Francis recognized that arrogant stance. His heart quickened its pace and a thrill raced along his sword arm. Robert Randall—he'd know the devil anywhere.

As though drawn by the intensity of Francis's gaze, Glenkennon stiffened and swung toward the door. Gray eyes dueled with blue across the space, and a look of black hatred registered fleetingly on the earl's face. Quickly schooling his features into a politely smiling mask, he moved forward to meet his unexpected guests.

"Sir Francis MacLean. What a pleasure! It's been far too long since we've seen you," Glenkennon said smoothly. He raised an arched brow. "Of course we do hear of you occasionally in the North."

Francis swept an elegant bow. "I agree, my Lord Glenkennon. It's been too long since we've met." A polite smile curved his lips but his frozen gaze didn't thaw. "I've been pleased to entertain several of your family, of course. By the way, how is your son?"

"Ah, Charles... I'm afraid the lad's a disappointment to me. But then, I've learned a valuable lesson—a boy shouldn't be sent to do a man's job."

"I'd say it would depend rather on the boy... and the job," Francis responded curtly. He nodded toward Conall. "Allow me to introduce my kinsman, Conall MacLean, to your notice."

Conall sketched a half bow. "Your servant, m'lord."

Glenkennon scarcely acknowledged Conall's salutation. His shrewd gray eyes remained fixed on MacLean.

Francis glanced pointedly at the guests thronging the large room. "I can see we've come at an inopportune time, my lord. We'd hoped to discuss a bit of business, but we've no wish to trouble you now. Perhaps you could suggest a date we might return."

Glenkennon feigned surprise. "Come, come my friends, I'll not hear of your leaving! You must remain... as my honored guests of course. We're celebrating a great occasion—my daughter Anne's nineteenth birthday." He smiled thinly. "You'll remember Anne, I'm sure."

"No man could forget such a charming young lady. I wish her joy of the day."

"My thanks." A slow smile curled Glenkennon's hard mouth, and a flicker of anticipation glittered in his eyes. "I really can't allow you to leave, MacLean—not until we've enjoyed a pleasant week together." His voice dropped. "I'm certain we can find entertainment of an appropriate sort—even for such enterprising gentlemen as yourselves. We can discuss your business at a later date, if you're still inclined."

"Your kindness is gratifying, but you needn't trouble yourself to contrive amusements for us," Francis replied politely. "Conall and I can entertain ourselves easily enough."

"Oh, but it's my pleasure," Glenkennon protested. "My daughter and I shall spare no pains to make your stay at Ranleigh one you'll remember . . . for as long as you live."

Francis ignored the double-edged words. "We'll take advantage of your hospitality then, but pray excuse me now." He grinned and lifted one dark brow mockingly. "I've just caught sight of your daughter, m'lord. I'd best pay my respects, or the lass will think I've forgotten her. You know how women are."

Without bothering to observe the earl's reaction, Francis pushed past him into the crowd, sending a ripple of excitement spreading across the room as his tall, powerful figure was recognized.

He strode purposefully across the floor. Anne was standing with her back to the doorway and probably had not even seen him come in. He paused just behind her, his heartbeat quickening at the thought of seeing her again—of ending this misunderstanding between them. "I hope this day is, indeed, a happy occasion for you, Mistress Randall," he murmured.

Anne froze. In the sudden stillness following his words,

it seemed even her heart had ceased to beat. She recognized Francis's low, husky voice with its lilting Highland burr: she would have known it though she had not heard it for a score of years or more. As if in a dream she turned to see his hard, handsome face, the tiny flames leaping to life in the depths of his blue eyes.

Unable to find her voice, she stared at him foolishly, drinking in the sight she had longed to see for so many weeks: the thick, black hair above his strong forehead, the eyes so intensely blue against the deep tan of his face, the sensual lips smiling now in that tender way she had used to think meant so much.

The room began to whirl sickeningly and Anne's heart, which she was sure had stopped a moment earlier, leaped and pounded frantically in her throat. The blood drained from her face, and even her knees felt like jelly.

"Don't faint, lass," Francis said low.

His fingers closed around her wrist, warm and strong, and the tilting, lurching room steadied beneath her feet. She blinked and his hard, dark face came into clear focus.

The sudden memory of their last, painful meeting swam before her. "Take your hand off me," she gasped, jerking her arm from his with a force which surprised her. Her hatred surged like an engulfing flame, and her cheeks burned with an angry heat. "How dare you... how *dare* you come here!" she bit out.

"Why, I've come to bring you best wishes," he said softly. "Did you think I'd forget?"

Only Francis MacLean could have stood within the stronghold of his bitterest enemy and asked such a question. "You're not wanted here. Go away!" Anne demanded, her voice perilously unsteady.

"Ah, but you're wrong there, lass. Your father has kindly invited me to stay the week."

Her eyes widened in astonishment. "My father knows you're here?"

A mocking grin suffused his face. "Surely you'd not have

me backward in any attentions to the earl? Conall and I paid our respects as soon as we arrived."

"Is this man annoying you, Mistress Randall?"

The tense words shattered the spell which held her. Anne turned to Nigel Douglas, struggling for composure. "No . . . no, Nigel. I'm just surprised he has the audacity to come here."

Nigel's eyes slid suspiciously from Anne's flushed face to MacLean's impassive countenance. One hand hovering near the polished dirk at his belt, he appraised the Highlander.

Francis gave him a contemptuous smile. "I'm merely giving the lass my best wishes, Douglas. I've no intention of staging a kidnapping from this gathering. That might be a bit difficult even for me."

He turned to Anne. "By your leave, mistress." With an elegant bow, he strode away, leaving Nigel feeling vaguely foolish and Anne shaken and angry.

The evening was ruined for her, and all her pleasure in the dancing was gone. She could scarcely keep her attention on the movements of the dance or follow the conversation of her partners. She was left instead with a sick urge to seek Francis out whenever he left her sight and an even more painful ache as she reviewed every humiliating detail of her shameful conduct at Camereigh the past spring.

Over the shoulder of her partner, she watched Francis making his way among the guests—her guests—renewing old acquaintances and flirting shamelessly with all the loveliest ladies as if he hadn't a care in the world.

He looked incredibly handsome that night, she admitted grimly. The rich, crimson velvet of his doublet fit becomingly across his broad shoulders, and a riotous cascade of Belgian lace fell away down the front of his shirt contrasting markedly with the dark bronze of his throat. A richly jeweled dirk flashed at his hip, but it could not match the sparkle of his smile.

A false smile, Anne reminded herself quickly, as false as

the sweet lies that tripped so easily from his tongue. Damn him, damn him, damn him, she raged. Why had he come? He had some dark purpose, of that she was certain.

Smiling and nodding, she forced her attention back to her partner, though she had no inkling what the man had said. She would ignore Francis MacLean, she vowed. She'd not voice even the slightest curiosity as to why he was there. That would be the best way to counter his arrogance. She would show him that he was nothing to her—that she had recovered from his betrayal quickly enough.

For his part, Francis was pleased with the assembled company. There were plenty of Glenkennon's henchmen to be sure, but there were enough good men to raise an outcry should the earl proceed against him without cause. It was just as he had anticipated. Glenkennon could do nothing at present, at least not openly.

"Sir Francis, my boy! What in God's good name are you doing here?" a deep voice boomed.

"I could ask the same of you, MacCue," Francis replied, smiling at the short, rotund figure of a man who had been a long-time friend of Francis's father.

"God's body, I'd no choice in the matter," MacCue grumbled. "Every lord south of Stirling was commanded to attend. Things have come to a pretty pass indeed, when a man fears to be branded a traitor unless he obeys the commands of a thief!"

"Not so loud, MacCue," Francis whispered. "At least not while you're with me—guilt by association, you know."

Sir Evan MacCue smiled briefly, but his dark eyes were troubled. "Why did you come, lad? I could scarce believe my eyes when I saw you standing there grinning like the devil hisself. Don't you ken Randall would like nothing better than to see you dead—and that in as miserable a way as possible?"

"Aye, but I've no plans to oblige him," Francis said dryly. "With men like you and Stewart and Galbraith about, the earl won't move unlawfully. And I've a few tricks of my own should the occasion warrant."

Another guest wandered up to speak to Sir Evan, and Francis moved away toward a corner table set with pitchers of ale and trays of empty tankards. Conall joined him, and the two drank deeply of the bitter brew.

"Well," Conall said, wiping the foam from his lips with the back of his hand, "we've made it in alive, and so far things have gone as you planned. But I can't help wondering what our next move should be." He grinned at Francis over his mug. "I was watching Mistress Randall when she saw you. To my mind, the lass didn't look overjoyed."

Francis laughed. "She's laboring under a slight misapprehension concerning my character. I've but to convince her I'm no' so bad as she believes."

"Faith, it should be an interesting week then," Conall said in amused exasperation. "We've but to make the lass agreeable, avoid any number of men who'll be trying to slit our gullets, and escape from a well-guarded stronghold. 'Tis easy enough when all's said and done."

"Leave any time you like, Conall."

Conall shook his head. "Nay, lad. I've waited too long for the chance to bring Randall low, and I'd not miss any opportunity to annoy the bastard. And besides," he added with an impudent smile, "now I've seen the lass, I'm not above trying to cut you out."

"You concentrate on keeping the knives from our backs and how we're to walk through these walls at the end of the week. I'll see what I can do to make the lass change her mind," Francis said, lifting his tankard to drain the last of the ale.

"You'd best get in line, then." Conall jerked his head toward the cluster of gentlemen around Anne. "It may take her the better part of the week to get round to your suit."

"We'll see," Francis rejoined softly. Placing his empty mug on the table, he headed toward the group. The music was beginning again, and a dance with Anne might be the best chance he would have for private conversation. He pushed through the half-dozen men making up her court. "Your pardon, gentlemen, but I've a promise of the lady's hand."

Anne smiled sweetly, but the look she sent Francis spoke of a very different emotion. "I'm sorry, sir, but my hand is promised to Walter Murray for this dance."

"Aye, MacLean. You'll have to wait your turn like the rest of us," a male voice piped up.

"I'm afraid it's you, Murray, who'll be waitin' your turn. I've the promise of the lady's hand from her father. I'm sure none of you will be wanting to annoy the earl in his own household. I know I'd never dream of it."

"I fear you're mistaken, m'lord," Anne repeated firmly. "My hand is already promised for the rest of the evening." She raised one delicately arched brow and met his gaze coolly. "But let me introduce you to any fair lady of your choice. I'd be delighted to find you a partner."

Francis's eyes gleamed in amusement. "I'll take advantage of your offer later, but Glenkennon promised you to me this dance." He held out his hand. "Come, lass. We'll be late joining the set."

Anne stared at his strong, brown hand, remembering the shameful pleasure he had brought her that last evening on the beach. Her face burned at the memory. "I don't believe you spoke to my father at all," she breathed, her eyes glittering dangerously. "I doubt he even knows you're here!"

"Shall we ask Glenkennon then, lass?"

"You wouldn't dare."

Francis did not hesitate. Swinging about, he raised his voice above the din in the room. "My lord Glenkennon, we've need of you here!"

The laughing voices about them suddenly hushed. The earl glanced up in surprise, his eyes shifting from the stormy face of his daughter to that of the grinning Mac-

Lean Chief. He moved deliberately across the floor toward them. "What seems to be the trouble?"

"My lord Glenkennon, I hesitate to trouble you, but we've a slight misunderstanding here," Francis said gravely. "Mistress Randall is under the impression you take no pleasure in my company. Being such a dutiful lass, she refuses to dance with any man of whom her father disapproves." He sent Glenkennon a challenging look. "But perhaps I was mistaken in your own warm welcome. Conall and I can be on our way on the moment—we've no wish to remain where we're not wanted."

Glenkennon studied MacLean thoughtfully. The man was taking a perverse pleasure in forcing the issue, yet it would be best to keep him happy for now. If the Highlander tried to leave, he would be forced to seize him, and he did not want to show his hand just yet—not until he could talk to Blake and determine how best to use this to their advantage.

"My dear Anne," he said softly, "I fear you're being rude to one of our guests—and after I expressly promised him all the entertainments Ranleigh had to offer. Please make him welcome at once. I'm sure these gentlemen will understand if you dance with him now."

Anne swallowed hard, choking down the hot words of refusal that sprang to her tongue. Lowering her eyes, she dropped into a respectful curtsy. "Of course, Father. I meant no offense to your guest." She turned to young Murray. "Pray hold me excused, sir. I shall hope to dance with you later."

Francis extended his left arm graciously. "If you'll allow me, mistress."

Inwardly seething, Anne placed the tips of her fingers on his muscular arm, allowing him to lead her onto the floor.

"What a dutiful daughter. Do you always obey your father so readily?" Francis inquired, covering her cold fingers with his own.

"Do you think I've any other choice?"

His clasp on her hand tightened and a look of quick sympathy crossed his face. "Has it been hard for you, lass?"

She ignored the caressing note in his voice and stared at a point beyond his shoulder. Her father might have forced her to dance with Francis, but by God she'd not be used again! She was done being a pawn in this twisted game between them. "That's none of your concern," she said coldly.

The movement of the dance separated them, and Francis silently cursed this ill-conceived attempt at private conversation in a room filled with upward of two score dancers. He needed to see Anne alone if he was to successfully explain his actions in the spring.

"Janet sends her best wishes," he tried again as they once more moved together. "And Donald and Kate bade me give you their regards."

She nodded. "I've missed them. They were so kind last spring, I . . ." Flushing again, she broke off, cursing herself for bringing up that painful time.

If Francis noticed her confusion, he ignored it. "You're seldom seen outside the gates, lass. I hope you've not been ill."

She dared a slanted glance upward. He was gazing at her with such tender concern her heart missed several beats. "I've been well," she said shortly. Damn the man! Damn him for his black heart and the charm he used so ruthlessly.

But how did he know she had been shut up inside Ranleigh? He must have spies in their very household! The thought reminded her of his encounter with Charles, the memory successfully destroying any last possibility of a truce between them.

For as long as she lived, she would not forget that terrible scene when Charles and his band of bloody, exhausted men had slunk through the gates of Ranleigh. Charles had stood quietly, blanching before Glenkennon's rage as he recounted his tale, trembling with fatigue and loss of blood, yet stubborn in his assertion that his men had been wrong. Glenkennon had stormed out in disgust, leaving Charles to stumble up the stairs with his sister's support. Raging aloud against Francis while she worked, until Charles tiredly commanded her silence, she had tended the ugly wounds, finding none so bad as they had looked beneath the mixture of blood and dirt.

"I'm afraid my brother hasn't been so fortunate though," she said, throwing back her head to meet his gaze accusingly. "His health has caused me grave concern."

"Your brother is lucky to be alive."

"So you don't deny you attempted to murder him."

"I made no attempt to kill the lad—else he'd be dead," Francis replied bluntly.

"Sir Francis, the merciful..." She laughed bitterly. "Come my lord, I'm no longer so naive. If you let him go, I'm certain it was for your own benefit. You're bold enough in taking advantage of women and helpless boys..." She smiled mockingly. "Could it be you're afraid of my father, despite all your brave claims?"

"We can both attest to the fact I don't take advantage of women, be they ever so willing," Francis said, stung by her words, "and anyone less like a helpless boy I've yet to see. Charles has the best arm I've come up with against in a twelvemonth."

His harsh expression softened and his voice lowered caressingly. "I may have hurt Charles's pride, but I didn't harm the lad unduly. I made you a promise I'd minimize any hurt to you and your brother, lass, and I've kept my word. The fact that Charles is alive after ambushing my men should tell you something, if you would care to look beyond your own wounded pride."

Her face flamed, but Anne ignored his painful probing at the root of their argument. "Charles wasn't involved in that ambush and you know it!"

"Any leader is responsible for the actions of his men,

even if he isn't personally involved," Francis explained patiently. "Charles understands that, though you aren't reasonable enough to do so. One of my men almost lost his life, Anne. As it is he'll be long recovering. You might remember the lad," he added. "'Twas Naill MacLean your brother's men nearly murdered."

Anne bit her lip and looked away. She remembered Naill well. The laughing young clansman had strummed the lute and sung for her on several rainy afternoons at Camereigh.

"I'll not stand by and see my people murdered, even for you," Francis said softly, "but I didn't let Charles go because I've any fear of Glenkennon..."

"Then you're a fool," she interrupted. "Father thinks you're behind those raids. If he has his way, you'll not leave here alive!"

"And would you be so indifferent to that as you pretend, lass?" Francis asked unwisely.

Anne sucked in her breath. The man's arrogance was unbounded—he obviously thought he still had her under his spell. "Indifferent?" she repeated. "Why, no, m'lord. I'd consider the day's work well done to rid the world of a lying rogue like you!"

The music had stopped, but neither Francis nor Anne was aware that they had stopped dancing long before its end. For a moment, they glared at each other, then Francis turned on his heel and stalked away.

Edmund Blake stepped from the shadows along the wall, his eyes following MacLean as the Highlander strode angrily across the room. His sinister smile flashed once as he moved to join Glenkennon. "A most interesting development, my lord," he said softly. He took a glass of wine from a passing servant, then waited until the man moved away. "What think you of our uninvited guests?"

Glenkennon laughed aloud. "Here I've been wondering how to get into MacLean's impregnable fortress, and what happens but he shows up in my own. God's blood, but the luck is with us tonight!" he exclaimed gleefully. "Christ! Has the lamb ever come more willingly to the slaughter?"

"I've already ordered the guard doubled and have chosen a room where our two young friends may stay."

"Yes, that's good. We must keep them happy until we can come up with something that isn't too obvious."

"Perhaps you'd best speak to your daughter then, my lord," Blake remarked, glancing back at Anne. "From the look of things just now, she's in no mood to humor the man."

"Anne will humor any man I tell her to, no matter her mood," Glenkennon responded carelessly. "The girl's even more manageable than her mother was."

"Do you wish me to continue to watch her then, my lord?"

"Yes . . . and be sure to let me know if she's discourteous to our friend." Glenkennon smiled darkly. "Perhaps my lovely daughter can make the condemned man's last week a trifle more pleasant."

Francis's anger scarcely lasted as long as it took him to cross the room. After all, what had he expected from Anne? The girl had every right to hate him after his words at Camereigh. He wished now more than ever that he could have explained, but the truth would have served no purpose at that moment and might have been dangerous for Anne. As it was, their best protection from Glenkennon lay in her apparent dislike of him.

Since Anne was in no mood to listen to his explanations, Francis left the hall, wandering down the corridor to the rooms set up for dicing and cards. He strolled among the tables, speaking to acquaintances and watching the luck of the dice.

"Well, Sir Francis MacLean. By all that's holy, I didn't expect to see you here!"

Francis stiffened, immediately recognizing the insolent voice. Turning slowly, he swept the seated man with a contemptuous glance. Percy Campbell sprawled back in his chair, his long, pointed face flushed with the effects of too much wine. "Ah, Sir Percy, my good friend. I should have known I'd find you at cards. I hear it's all the excitement you can stand these days."

Campbell kicked an empty chair back from the table. "Do sit down, MacLean. Take a hand and tell us what you're doing here. It's rare, isn't it, for you Highlanders to venture out of your fortresses save to rob and steal?"

He paused, studying his cards before glancing up. "But you do get to town occasionally, don't you, to drink and brawl in the streets." His narrow mouth turned in a condescending smile. "I hope you're not planning to embarrass yourself with such barbaric behavior here."

The man standing nearest the table melted away, while those seated held their breaths and did not move. Francis considered the pleasure he would take in sending Campbell headfirst over the table but decided against it. A brawl would accomplish nothing and might give Glenkennon an excuse to clap him in irons. The cowardly Campbell laird wasn't worth it. Besides, he could pain the man more by pricking his overblown conceit.

"Why, Sir Percy, I'd not think to sit down to cards and take more of your gold." Leaning across the man, he thumped the small stack of coins at Campbell's place, tumbling them across the table. "I can see your luck is on the ebb."

Resting his palm on the table beside Campbell, he shifted so that their eyes were on a level. "And as to why I'm here—why, I've come in search of you, man," he said in a voice so low none but Campbell might hear. "You boasted aplenty of your desire to cross swords with me, and your words have reached my ears. Well, I'm at your disposal, Campbell . . . and I'm no' so helpless as some you've abused!"

Campbell's face reddened, his dark eyes staring out at Francis with hatred and fear. Pushing backward, he overturned his chair in his haste to draw his jeweled dagger. The earl...f...fetch the earl," he stammered, glancing desperately at the men around him. His eye fell on Charles Randall. "Fetch your father. Quick boy, before this brigand runs me through!"

Francis still leaned carelessly upon the table, making no move to reach for his dirk despite Campbell's action. "Calm yourself, Campbell. You're safe enough. I'd no' so abuse Glenkennon's hospitality as to draw steel in his house." He smiled thinly, his blue eyes blazing with contempt. "I'll be guilty of no so barbaric a behavior."

Straightening away from the table, he turned his back on Campbell's blade. Ignoring the curious stares, he sauntered toward a corner table where Sir Evan MacCue and Lord Galbraith were playing cards. Slowly the men in the room resumed their previous activities, leaving Percy Campbell standing alone, foolishly clutching his dagger in one hand.

From his place across the floor, Charles Randall watched MacLean's dark, aristocratic figure with reluctant admiration. He had encountered him once already that evening. Fully expecting to feel the bite of the Highlander's caustic wit, he had been surprised when the man had merely spoken politely and moved on past.

MacLean might be a rogue, he thought wryly, but the Highlander was a man! Better an enemy of his caliber any day than a brace of allies like the blustering Campbell. For a moment Charles wondered what it would be like to ride beside MacLean instead of against him, then quickly banished such a dangerous thought.

Hours later, the wasted hall was awash in a flickering dimness, the candles guttering and dying one by one. Tired servants trailed out, removing flagons of wine and empty glasses, rearranging the tables for the meals which would follow in a few short hours.

Anne gave the servants her last orders, then crossed the

empty floor toward the doorway where several women still clustered as if reluctant to retire. Why didn't they go on to bed, she wondered wearily. Her own head pounded and she was so exhausted she doubted she could climb the stairs.

As she reached the doorway, a familiar laugh rang out, and she realized at once why the women still hovered there. Francis and his handsome friend stood just outside, entertaining the fools with their glib nonsense. Her throat tightened suddenly, and tears of frustration and weariness stung her eyes. God, she couldn't bear another confrontation with Francis that night! She was not adept enough at this verbal fencing to hold her own with so skilled an opponent.

Pushing past the women, she attempted to slip through the doorway, but Francis stepped into her path. "Mistress Randall, my compliments on a wonderful evening's entertainment."

She drew a deep breath and looked up. His eyes were warm and steady on hers. In that moment she hated him —hated him for his insincerity, for all the looks, for all the smiles, for all the lies she had wanted so desperately to believe.

"Alas, the evening's done and we must seek our beds," he said softly, "but before you slip off, I've something for the occasion." Reaching into his doublet, he drew out a velvet bag, placing it in her hands before she could protest.

"I don't care for your gifts," she said churlishly, attempting to give it back.

He held up his hands. "It's not from me, lass, but from Janet. She'll be offended if you refuse. It's a little something she's been wanting you to have."

She nodded stiffly, turning the package over in her hands. "Very well. Give her my thanks."

Francis stepped back, allowing her to reach the stairs. "Pleasant dreams, mistress," he called after her.

In the privacy of her chamber, Anne sank wearily into a chair. For a moment she simply stared at the bag, feeling its warmth from where it had lain inside his doublet next to his heart. Loosening the strings, she turned it upside down.

A shimmering flash of blood red stones tumbled into her lap. She caught her breath in amazement. It was the necklace Janet had lent to her that long-ago night at Camereigh.

Tired as she was, it was dawn before Anne slept.

CHAPTER SEVENTEEN

 $\mathscr{A}$ nne awakened reluctantly to Bess's insistent hands shaking her from the depths of a deep sleep. Sitting up with a groan, she pushed the hair back from her eyes and attempted to listen to the words the girl repeated.

"Your father insists you come down now, mistress! The gentlemen are a'ready about the hall." Bess rolled her green eyes expressively. "My lord Percy Campbell is askin' for you, and—" Her gaze fell upon the heap of glittering jewels on the chair, and she broke off abruptly. "Oh, mistress," she breathed, lifting the sparkling chain to the light, "is this the earl's gift for your birthday?"

"No," Anne said crossly, the reminder of the necklace flooding her thoughts with all the misery of the evening before. "Sir Francis MacLean gave it to me—or rather, his sister did," she corrected herself. "It's too valuable a gift to accept, of course. I must give it back as soon as possible."

Bess peered at her strangely. "'Tis a shame to return so lovely a gift . . . but I'm sure you've the right of it. It'd cause trouble for sure, if your father got wind of it."

Anne leaned forward and took the necklace, staring as if bemused by the sparkling stones. Why had Francis given her such a valuable heirloom? Did he think to buy back her regard? Did it please him to think of wounding her yet again? Her eyes flashed at the thought, and she thrust the necklace into Bess's hands. "Here, take it! Get it out of my sight until I can return it to that arrogant man."

Bess blinked in surprise at the flash of bad temper from her mistress. She silently took the necklace, hiding it away among Anne's clothing.

Tossing back the covers, Anne stumbled to the wash basin and splashed her face with cold water, hoping to shake off the dread that weighed her down that morning. There was nothing wrong, she told herself firmly. If she felt miserable, it was justly due to the precious few hours of sleep she'd had.

Entering the hall a short time later, she was relieved to find several other women already present. Lady Dorsett, Lady Galbraith, and Lady Galbraith's two daughters were engaged at a table with several gentlemen. There was much laughter and good-natured bantering as Anne sat down.

Casually joining the conversation, she scanned the room for a tall, familiar figure. Her search was unsuccessful; neither Francis nor Conall was anywhere in sight. What if something had happened to them during the night? It was entirely possible, and though she told herself it would not matter to her one jot, the thought became a nagging fear that grew as the morning progressed.

By midday most of the guests were up and accounted for, but there was still no sign of the two MacLeans. Several gentlemen had gone hawking with her father, but she doubted Francis would have made one of that group.

A careful hostess, she moved about the hall, seeing to food, drink, and entertainment for Glenkennon's guests. She forced herself to chatter with the other women, yet her eyes lifted anxiously to the doorway at the sound of each new arrival.

It was afternoon before she heard the deep voice she had listened for all day. Unable to help herself, she turned to stare, a strange sensation surging through her at the sight of Francis very much alive and well and headed in her direction.

As he halted beside her, all her well-rehearsed phrases fled her mind. "I appreciate Janet's gift," she began stiffly, "but you know I can't accept it. You must take it back."

Francis grinned. "Nonsense lass, 'tis a gift, and I'll no' be takin' it back."

"But I can't accept it," she repeated stubbornly.

Under the guise of requesting food and drink, Francis took her arm and drew her away from the nearest table. "You accepted it last night, if memory serves me."

"But I didn't know what it was last night," she protested. When he did not reply, she added pettishly, "If you don't take it back, I'll sell it."

Francis shrugged his shoulders. "'Tis yours to do with as you will, though if it's money you're needin', lass, you've but to say the word and all I have is at your disposal."

She stared at him in surprise, shaken as much by the words as the look that went with them. "You're . . . you're impossible," she snapped, finding her voice at last. "You're a lying—"

"Hush, lass," Francis interrupted, his eyes dancing in amusement. "You can discuss my character later. For now, just listen—I've something of importance to tell you. Where can we meet this afternoon?"

He was close—so close she could see the tiny lines about the corners of his eyes, so close she could feel the warmth of his breath against her cheek as he bent toward her. The touch of his hand on her arm caused a familiar trembling to begin deep inside her, but the knowledge of her weakness only stiffened her resolve. "There'll be no meeting, Francis," she flung back, steeling herself against his charm. "You told me enough last spring."

The smile left his face. He angled his head back to better observe her. "You're wrong, Anne," he said softly. "I didn't tell you nearly enough that day. That's why Conall and I are here. Now where can we meet?"

Her defenses began to crumble before the intensity of his gaze. Blessed Lord, she actually *wanted* to believe him!

What was the magic of the spell he wove that she was ready to fling away her pride yet again?

The sudden recollection of what she had heard of his amorous adventures in Dundee saved her. "You must think me a fool to fall for the same trick twice," she hissed. "Save your sweet words for your other women. I'll have none of them! I'll not meet you today, nor any other day. Nor do I care why you're here. I wish you'd go away!"

"You're a stubborn lass," he said shortly, "and you think you've reason to hate me." His eyes narrowed darkly. "I don't remember ever giving you cause to fear being alone with me though. Ten minutes is all I ask."

"I'm not afraid . . ." she began, only to end her speech abruptly as Percy Campbell approached.

"Why, Anne," Campbell said, "how lovely you look today. None would believe you danced away the entire evening."

"Thank you, m'lord," she replied, turning away from Francis in relief. She was surprised at Campbell's free use of her name, but she had seen a quickly concealed flare of anger in Francis's eyes at the sound of it and knew he disliked it far more than she. It gave her a strange pleasure to provoke him. She smiled brilliantly at Sir Percy. "Where have you been all morning, sir? I feared you might have left without bidding me good-bye."

Campbell shot Francis a triumphant look. "I've no intention of leaving yet, and I'd certainly not depart without seeing you, my dear. No, I've been with your father."

His eyes traveled slowly from the wide skirts of her peach, silk gown to rest admiringly on the swell of her breasts above the gown's fashionably squared neckline. "Glenkennon described the beauty of his rose gardens and recommended I see them under your guidance."

He took her hand and lifted it to his lips. "Would you care to show me about, Anne? I don't believe I've ever seen the gardens in their glory."

Anne turned her back pointedly on Francis and gave Sir Percy an adoring look. "I should enjoy that, my lord."

Campbell placed her hand in the crook of his arm. "I'm sure you'll excuse us, MacLean," he said brusquely.

Francis made a half bow. "Of course, m'lord. The roses are indeed lovely today. Just take care you don't end in a thorn bush."

Anne breathed a sigh of relief as Campbell led her outside the hall into the warm sunlight. Francis had put her into such confusion she scarcely knew what she felt anymore. The sight of him, the familiar feel of his hand upon hers reawakened memories of both pleasure and pain that made it difficult to think clearly.

She despised him; she was sure she did. When she recalled that final interview at Camereigh, she felt the hate rising inside her with a physical ache. Yet there were so many other times, so many other memories associated with the man. What if he were telling the truth? What if there had been more behind his words that last morning?

"Why so thoughtful, Anne? It's a lovely day and you should be wearing a smile instead of that frown," Campbell said, squeezing her arm.

She threw him a guilty look, searching her mind for an excuse for her pensive mood. "I beg pardon, m'lord. I fear I'm poor company this afternoon, but I'm trying to remember if I've seen to everything." She smiled and shook her head. "It's difficult running a household so full of Father's guests. I'm constantly afraid of giving offense. I should never forgive myself if I embarrassed Father."

Campbell smiled and drew her closer. "You've little to fear, Anne. Nothing you do could offend any of us here. You've everyone at Ranleigh in the palm of your hand— including myself."

Anne shifted away nervously at his intimate words and the sudden pressure of his hand on hers. Remembering the reason for their walk, she halted abruptly and began pointing out the beauty of the summer flowers, now in full bloom along the carefully manicured paths.

Taking his cue from her, Campbell spoke in a lighter vein, describing her guests in such a droll manner Anne began to enjoy herself in spite of her preoccupation with Francis. Sir Percy was an amusing companion when he chose to please, she thought, smiling at his comments. During his frequent visits, she had lost her fear of him, scarcely remembering she'd not liked him at the outset.

They strolled along between high yew hedges, finally reaching the end of the pleasant walk. The small area was carefully contrived to provide a narrow corner for privacy. They paused beside a stone bench, but instead of turning to retrace their steps, Percy moved closer, his hand slipping about her waist, deftly turning her into his arms. Before she could protest, his mouth lowered to hers, his tongue slipping easily between her numb lips. He greedily explored the moist cavern of her mouth, one hand moving down her back to press her stiff body against the eager heat of his.

For a moment, shock held Anne motionless. Campbell wouldn't treat her like this—he was her father's friend! She pushed wildly against his chest, attempting to twist away from his unwelcome kiss, but her struggle seemed to inflame him the more. His mouth slanted across hers, smothering her frightened protest.

After what seemed like forever, he lifted his head and she was free to breathe. He stared down at her, his dark eyes moving hungrily over her face, dropping to the white expanse of her throat and heaving breasts.

"My lord, please!" she gasped, thoroughly frightened by the look on his face as he continued to hold her crushed against him. "Let me go . . . let me go or I'll scream," she threatened breathlessly. "I swear it!"

She pushed against his chest with all her strength, and he released her so suddenly she stumbled, almost losing her balance. Instinctively she backed away, poised like a wild animal ready to flee if he made the slightest move in her direction.

"Anne, is it possible your father hasn't spoken to you?" Campbell asked, his eyes narrowing in anger at her obvious aversion. "You were so eager to walk out with me. I thought surely he'd—"

He broke off, and drew a deep breath, his sharp features smoothing back into a deliberate smile. "I'm terribly sorry, my dear; I didn't mean to frighten you. But you're so lovely, you steal a man's reason." He held out his hand with another smile. "Believe me, Anne. I've no intention of harming you—far otherwise, if the truth be known."

Her breathing began to slow. "You surprised me," she said softly. "I didn't expect . . . I mean you shouldn't—"

"I've frightened you half to death when I'd no intention of doing so," Percy put in smoothly. "I beg your pardon again. I've never blundered so foolishly." He smiled ingratiatingly. "I hope I've not ruined our friendship."

"No . . . no of course not," she said, glancing longingly up the path toward Ranleigh. She wanted to be away from this hidden place and the smiling, bearded man who blocked her way.

His gaze followed hers. "Come, my dear. I'll take you inside and fetch you a glass of wine, and we'll not speak of this again." He reached for her arm, but she moved away, unwilling to have him touch her again. His lips tightened angrily, but he bowed with a flourish. "After you, then," he said pleasantly.

She set out up the stone walk, holding herself to a lady-like pace though she longed to gather up her skirts and flee. Campbell moved beside her, repeating snatches of court gossip for her amusement as if nothing out of the ordinary had happened. When he finally left her in the hall, she could almost believe she had imagined the whole unpleasant scene.

She was now more confused than ever. Campbell had hinted at marriage, had practically told her Glenkennon knew of his suit. All this she had expected, but the thought of becoming Campbell's wife was suddenly so repugnant she almost burst into tears.

What was wrong with her? Campbell was not unattractive, he was rich, and he'd always been courteous until this instance. And what had happened in the garden was most likely her own fault. She had flirted with him openly in front of Francis, so he had naturally thought her willing.

She closed her eyes against the sting of hysterical tears. She was only distraught from the pressure of entertaining and from lack of sleep. She would be fine if she could only get away for a few minutes of quiet.

But there was little hope of any privacy then. Composing herself with difficulty, she spotted Lady Galbraith and sat down beside her to watch the antics of a troop of jugglers. At least she'd not be forced to make polite conversation for a while.

The afternoon sped by, and as the sun slipped toward the western horizon the urge to get away from the constant company became more pressing. She needed to be alone —to sort through the confusing web of emotion and doubt that entangled her more firmly with each passing hour. Her father and a party of men were out riding, and she'd not seen Blake all afternoon. It would be the perfect time to slip away. After all, she had done it before.

She hurried to her room and pulled out the ragged cloak she had hidden in the bottom of a chest. Taking the servants' stair down to the postern gate, she was soon slipping down the trail to the rocky shore.

The loch lay still in the hush of evening, the blue of its waters deepening to a smoky slate as the shadow of the castle fell full across its face. She half slid down the steep trail to her favorite perch. Ducking between the large boulders, she breathed deeply of the damp evening air, willing her mind to absorb the tranquillity of the scene.

Her whirling thoughts gradually quieted as she watched the terns fishing in the still waters and heard the tiny wavelets lap against the shore. Francis's arrival had set her on edge, she admitted. His presence was a continual reminder of the foolish way she had behaved in the spring. It was especially humiliating since he obviously believed she would succumb again as easily to his charm. That was it . . . it was only her pride that rankled. She did not care a rap for Francis MacLean!

But what about Sir Percy Campbell? She shuddered in revulsion at the recollected feel of his hands and mouth upon her. She could scarcely believe his actions; he had always been so charming, so carefully correct in his treatment of her. His behavior this afternoon had frightened her—yet surely he meant her no harm.

With a deep sigh, she pulled her knees up against her chest and clasped her arms about them. Across the loch, the golden sunlight of late afternoon still shone on the far meadow, but the stillness of evening lay upon her there in the shadows. She closed her eyes tightly, listening to the sounds of twilight.

A loose pebble tumbled along the trail, and she sat up in alarm. The soft crunch of boots upon rock followed. The next moment, Francis stepped around the huge boulder screening the path.

For a moment the two simply stared at each other, each held motionless by the surprise of this unlooked-for meeting. Then in a scramble of petticoats Anne was up from her undignified position to face Francis haughtily.

"Well, by all that's holy! What a piece of good fortune," Francis remarked, propping his foot on a stone and crossing his arms upon his knee.

Anne forced herself to remain calm; it was the only way to handle Francis. "I was just on my way back. I won't spoil your solitary ramble," she said coolly.

His hand shot out, closing upon her wrist like a vice. "Not until I've had a word with you, lass. As I told you this morning, I've something most pressing to say."

"And I told you this morning I'd no wish to hear it," she snapped, attempting to twist out of his grasp.

"For Christ's sake, Anne! Conall and I have risked our lives to come here to talk to you. You can spare me a moment. You've certainly plenty of time to spend with Campbell!"

"I'll spend time with anyone I please, but it'll not be you! And I don't care a rush that you're risking your life. I didn't ask you to come here, did I?"

"Spend your time any way you want, but don't think to spite me by encouraging Campbell to dangle after you," Francis retorted. "You're playing with a kind of fire you don't know how to handle, lass."

"Oh!" she gasped, furious he had put his finger on her very ploy. "You're the most conceited, most arrogant..." Powerless to twist from his grip, she struck his hand with all her might, wincing as the pain radiated up her arm into her shoulder.

Francis seized her flailing limbs and dragged her into his arms, his long submerged passions flaming to life at the feel of her against him. He crushed her struggling body to his, his mouth moving boldly over hers, sure of his welcome. The wild, sweet taste of her sent a rush of sensation pouring through every inch of him, making him forget the need for explanations.

Anne's lips opened instinctively beneath the onslaught of his, her mind tumbling in confusion as she struggled not only against his strength, but against the deep aching need within her. Every nerve, every instinct urged her to yield all pride and resistance. It was as if she came to life in his arms and had no feeling apart from his touch.

Slowly her struggle ended, but a disturbing image took shape in her mind. She could see the dark-haired Macintyre beauty lying passionately in Francis's arms. There had been many women for Francis MacLean, Anne reminded herself—and damn him, she'd not be another! The thought effectively cooled the fire in her blood, and she stood completely unresponsive in his arms.

When Francis finally released her, she pulled away, forcing her face to a mask of frozen indifference so he would not guess how deeply he had shaken her. Drawing back her hand, she dealt him a ringing slap across the face, not realizing the extent of her folly till seconds later.

His cheek reddened slowly from the blow. His eyes glittered like shards of splintered ice, though he stood painfully still, the muscles of his jaw tightening visibly with his effort at self-control. "I'll allow you that, Anne. I know you think I deserve it." He drew a deep breath. "But I'd not advise you to try it again."

Trembling with anger, Anne longed for a pistol, a sword, any weapon with which to fight him. Restraining the impulse to fly out at him with her fists, she battled him in the only way she knew. "If you're quite through making a fool of yourself then, m'lord, I'll be on my way," she said, forcing all the contempt and loathing she could muster into her voice.

Francis bowed to the impossibility of talking reasonably with her then. "Very well. Despise me if you will, Anne, but step carefully where Percy Campbell's concerned. He's no' so patient as I, lass, and I'd not see you hurt."

Anne hesitated. She'd not forgotten the look on Percy's face that afternoon.

"And what have we here?" a soft voice called from the rocks above. "Is this a private conversation, or may anyone join?"

Anne stifled a groan. Was there anything else that could go wrong that wretched day? How long had Edmund Blake been standing there, and how much had he seen? Surely not even Blake would have stood by and watched her struggling in Francis's arms—but then, he was such a strange little man.

The stones rattled beneath Blake's feet as he made his way down to the two standing guiltily below. "I suggest you get back inside as fast as possible, mistress," he said coldly. "Your father has arrived and will soon be calling for you. And as for you, sir," he swung toward Francis, "I shall be pleased to accompany you back to Ranleigh—now, if you don't mind."

Francis put on a brave show of innocence. "I was but taking a walk when I came upon this lady unattended," he began. "I was attempting to persuade her to accompany me back when you arrived. Allow me to suggest you provide her escort. Then I'll continue my walk in peace."

Blake smiled thinly. "I'd not dream of leaving so important a guest unattended. We'll not have you thinking our hospitality so lacking, m'lord. And as it will do the lady no good to be seen in your company, I suggest we abide by my suggestion." He turned toward Anne. "Be gone now, mistress," he said impatiently.

She threw one last look over her shoulder at the two standing stubbornly face to face in the twilight, then fled up the path, leaving Francis to handle his predicament as best he might. Had he deliberately set out to make as much trouble as possible for her, he could not have succeeded any better, she thought bitterly. What her father would do when he heard she had slipped away with Francis MacLean, she shuddered even to think.

Francis threw himself into a sturdy chair in the sparsely furnished room he and Conall shared, cursing himself aloud for the opportunity he had bungled that evening. If he had spent his time explaining things to Anne instead of trying to kiss her, she might even then have been in his arms.

It had been a close-run thing, he mused as he tugged off his heavy boots. A few minutes one way or the other and he would have been found out. Several lives might hinge on his actions—not the least of which were his own and Conall's and possibly even Anne's if he didn't succeed in convincing her that Campbell was not what he showed himself to her.

He frowned darkly, recalling the ugly rumors surrounding the death of Campbell's first wife. It was said he had murdered her in a fit of rage and then contrived to make the death appear an accident. Francis did not doubt it—it was in keeping with Percy Campbell's personality. His lips drew back into a soundless snarl—he'd kill the bastard before he would let him get his filthy hands on Anne!

Francis flexed the muscles of his shoulders and sighed wearily. It was not going to be as easy as he had anticipated. Time was passing swiftly, and he had not yet told Anne why he had sent her away. And he had ruined his best chance so far to speak to her alone.

The sound of light footsteps outside heralded someone's approach. He swung expectantly toward the door, dirk in hand. Relaxing at the sound of Conall's special knock, he crossed the floor to admit his friend.

"I've everything arranged for our escape," Conall said, moving into the circle of candlelight. "But we have to act within the next evening or two, else the guard will be changed."

"Aye," Francis acknowledged. "I'd not give a ha'penny for our chances should we be inside these walls at the end of the week. Don't concern yourself lad—we'll be gone."

Conall left, and Francis wearily finished preparing for bed. Snuffing the candle, he stared grimly into the darkness. He had to find another way to talk to Anne alone. Though her cold response that morning had surprised him, he refused to believe she was as indifferent as she claimed.

CHAPTER EIGHTEEN

An uneasy wind keened about the walls of Ranleigh that night, like so many homeless spirits loosed upon the moor. Exhausted as she was, Anne tossed and turned uncomfortably, listening to the eerie wail of the wind in the turrets until sleep finally claimed her.

Even in sleep, troubled thoughts pursued one another across her consciousness, and she dreamed she stood beside her father in a circle of stern-faced soldiers in the courtyard. Everything about her was dark and drear: a gray mist fell from the gray sky, sifting down to wet the slippery cobbles beneath her feet and the somber cloak she had pulled about her as protection from the damp.

The heavy, scarred door of the guardhouse swung open and a dark figure swathed in a hooded cloak stumbled out. She knew it was the figure of a man, though she could tell little more. The wretch's hands were bound, and he walked with the stooped, halting gait of one too long without hope. She held her breath as he shuffled along before his guards—something about the figure was hauntingly familiar.

A bitter wind knifed through her, flinging damp tendrils of hair across her mouth and tugging the man's hood back from his face. Though the features were pale and altered by exhaustion, she recognized Francis MacLean.

Numb with disbelief, she watched him stagger past, his attention riveted upon something behind her. Slowly she turned, following the line of his gaze. A gibbet reared its gaunt head high above them, its hangman's noose swinging menacingly in the wind. Her father began to laugh roughly beside her, and the words of Sir Percy Campbell echoed through her mind. *"If you want to hang him for the fun of it . . . for the fun of it . . . for the fun of it . . ."*

She struggled to go to Francis, to call his name, but she could not move or make a sound. She watched helplessly while the rope was placed about his neck. Glenkennon lifted his hand in signal to the guards, and a door dropped beneath Francis's feet, his weight jerking the rope taut with a sickening thud.

Anne opened her mouth to scream, but no sound came forth. She was fighting to go to him, fighting to breathe. Sitting up with a gasp, she peered frantically about but found nothing save darkness and the empty lament of the wind outside her window.

Her breathing gradually steadied as she realized the images had been naught but a dreadful nightmare. She could still feel the smothered scream choking in her throat, still see Francis's lifeless form dangling limply from the gibbet as her father stood laughing beside her. Tears slipped unheeded down her cheeks, and she leaned weakly against the bedpost, whimpering like a frightened child for her mother.

Fingers trembling, she lit the candle beside her bed. Its wan, flickering light was as welcome as the golden sunlight of a summer's day. The shifting flame cast long, changing shadows about the room, and even her well-known possessions suddenly took on a sinister cast. Yes, it was a dream, but one that she knew might easily come true.

She struggled to shake off the feeling of horror and loss that still enveloped her. Francis might be in danger even then—but what did she care, anyway?

Her feigned indifference did not help. Pulling the blankets closely about her shoulders, she called to mind those times she had been frightened as a child. Then her mother would come to her, and together they would read aloud from a great, gilt-edged Bible. She remembered the comfort of her mother's soft voice and warm arms, a comfort she associated with the sound of the Biblical words long before she had been patiently taught their meaning.

An overwhelming urge to read those same soothing passages rose inside her. She could dimly recall seeing a dusty Bible and several prayer books upon an unused shelf in one corner of Glenkennon's large library. It was ridiculous to leave her warm bed to wander about the dark corridors in search of a Bible, yet even as she chided herself for her foolishness, she was donning robe and slippers, preparing to venture forth.

Candle in hand, she let herself out the door into the dark hallway. Shielding the dancing flame with one hand, she moved quietly along the passageway, negotiating the dozen stairs and making a sharp right turn into the hallway where her father's offices and library were housed. A cold draught of air slipped beneath her robe and she shivered, more certain than ever of the folly of her errand.

She squinted down the long passageway, attempting to pierce the darkness beyond the dim circle of light she moved within. A narrow ribbon of light spilled out along the doorway of Glenkennon's office.

Abruptly extinguishing her candle, she remained motionless in the heavy blackness that immediately enshrouded the hallway. If Blake had found the opportunity to describe her meeting with Francis, Glenkennon would be furious. She did not feel up to facing his wrath on the heels of that terrible nightmare.

As she turned to go, a faint murmur of voices rose from the room ahead. She cocked her head toward the sound. Who did her father find it expedient to meet in the dark stillness after midnight when all others had sought their beds?

Surprised at her own audacity, she crept forward until she was near enough to recognize the voices. It was Edmund Blake's soft tones she heard, though she could not make out his words. She edged closer shamelessly, resting her face against the smooth, oak panel of the door.

There was a long moment of silence, then her father's voice carried easily. "I want to take him alive, Blake. I've waited years to get my hands on the man and I'd like to savor the victory now." He laughed harshly. "It'd be such a pleasure to force a confession of treason from MacLean before I hang him!"

Anne closed her eyes, holding her breath against the sudden wave of nausea that assailed her. Blake was speaking again, but though she strained her ears desperately, she could understand little of his reply.

"You've said all this before, Blake," Glenkennon interrupted. "I know James is growing tired of the unrest, and he's like to become suspicious of us before long." There was a short pause. "Oh, all right then," he said irritably. "I'll agree to the hunting accident, since we've not proof enough to take him with these witless fools about. This man of yours is good, I know, but he'd best keep his mouth shut. He's been well paid in the past. Just remind him what he's got in store if a word of this leaks out. And mind . . . not a penny till MacLean's cold in his grave."

Anne drew back from the doorway and leaned weakly against the wall. Her father was planning to have Francis murdered in cold blood! She drew a steadying breath, then edged carefully back down the corridor into the protection of another doorway. Seconds later, the earl's office door opened, spilling a shaft of light into the passage and illuminating the very spot where she had been.

For an instant, Blake stood outlined against the light. Then he closed the door, plunging the hall into a deep, oppressive blackness. Anne pressed herself into the doorway, holding her breath. She strained for any indication of movement, but all was silent.

Seconds ticked by like hours. Her straining ears caught the muffled tread of Blake's shoes when he passed, so close she felt the wind stirred by his passage. Slowly, she fought down her terror of the darkness, of Blake, and the sickening plot she had overheard. She forced herself to concentrate on one thought: she had to warn Francis.

Pushing away from the doorway, she gazed into the yawning darkness of the corridor. Glenkennon might leave his office at any moment, and she doubted that he would be so obliging as to travel without a light. If he caught her there, he might guess that she had overheard his plan.

Placing a hand against the cool roughness of the stone wall, she stepped forward bravely into the blackness. She forced herself to move quickly, desperately trying to ignore the thought of running into Blake in a dark passageway ahead.

The comforting solidity of the wall ended abruptly. Anne stopped, her fingers groping in midair. She had reached the open waiting area before the stairway, she told herself, edging forward blindly, hands outstretched. She did not remember its being so wide; it seemed forever before her searching fingers were rewarded by the smooth feel of the polished stair railing.

Edging her way carefully up the stairs, she hurried along the hall, her fingers raw and burning from their constant contact with rough stone. She counted the doorways from the stairs. Blessed Lord! Was hers the seventh or the eighth? She had never counted before.

Holding her breath, she lifted the latch and entered the eighth door. The faint starlight spilling into the room illuminated a familiar table and chair and a length of embroidery she had carelessly left out that afternoon. With shaking hands, she slid the lock in place.

For a moment she could not move. Then reaction set in and her knees trembled so that she did not dare try to reach a chair. Her father was an evil man—evil far beyond her worst imaginings—and Edmund Blake was in league with the devil himself!

She pushed away from the door and sank into a chair. There were several hunts planned for the week, including one in the morning. How could she warn Francis in time?

To go herself would be the surest way of attracting unwanted attention, but if she sent Bess with a note and it fell into the wrong hands, they would both pay dearly. She rose and took a turn about the room. She would not chance missing Francis that morning before the hunt. She would send the note; she would take any risk to keep him alive.

Hard on the heels of that discovery came the staggering realization that she was still very much in love with the man. There was no denying it when his life was at stake. That she could still care so much after his betrayal was incredible, but her heart did not respond to the cold demands of logic. She was a fool, she admitted it readily, but the thought mattered little weighed against his life.

Armed with a new determination, she picked up paper and pen and began to write. "Sir," she began. "You are in grave danger. There are those here who plan your death. You are to fall as if by accident this morning during the hunt. As you value your life, do not ride out this day." She signed it only: "A Friend."

Returning the pen to its place, she folded the note and placed it in her pocket. Pacing the perimeter of the room, she gazed at the dark courtyard below, wondering how long she must wait before Bess came to awaken her.

Francis awakened long before dawn, all his faculties immediately alert. He and Conall had talked long into the night laying their plans, and they quickly put them into action. While darkness still cloaked the hallways, Conall stuck a loaded pistol into his belt and a dirk in his boot. "I'll see to your horse," he said softly. "I seem to have more luck with my tasks than you, Francis, lad. Perhaps you should send me to woo the lass."

Francis grinned and shook his head. "I've gone about it all wrong, Conall, but I've still time. At least I will have if you're successful," he amended. He gave his friend a long look. "Take care, lad. Don't take any foolish chances."

With a jaunty wave of his hand, Conall slipped out the door, and Francis settled back onto his bed to wait.

He had no idea how long it had been when a knock sounded, so low he scarcely heard it. He swung to his feet, quietly reaching for his sword. Damnation! He should never have let Conall go out alone. "Who's there?" he called sharply.

"'Tis only the maid with some fresh towels, m'lord."

He flung open the door, fully expecting to see Glenkennon's men come to seize him. Surprisingly enough, there was only one very frightened young woman standing uncomfortably before him.

"Please m'lord. May I come in? I've a message for you," she said, casting a nervous glance down the empty hallway.

His eyes narrowed suspiciously, but he stepped aside, allowing her to pass into the room. Turning, he closed the door, leaning his shoulders against the door frame. He studied the girl in the light of the single candle. He had known eager wenches before, but this was—

Suddenly recognizing the girl, he leaned forward intently. The wench was Anne's maid—could the lass have changed her mind? Why else would this one be here with a message?

At his eager look, the lass took a step back and swallowed convulsively, her wide green eyes trailing from his tall boots to the broad expanse of his shoulders.

"I believe you spoke of a message . . ." he prompted.

"Oh." She fumbled for the note and held it out.

He took the paper, reading it over quickly, then studying it more closely. "Are you aware of the contents of this?" he asked sharply.

"No, m'lord. I do not read."

"How came you by this paper?"

"A gentleman gave it to me with a shilling and ordered me to deliver it this morning before the hunt."

"Describe this gentleman to me."

She hesitated, then caught herself smoothly. "He was short of stature, reaching scarcely to m'lord's shoulder. He wore his hair and beard close cropped and it was brown in color." She frowned as if struggling to recall the man. "That's all I remember, sir," she ended apologetically. "I've not seen him before, but I'd recognize the man again, I'll be bound."

Francis barely controlled his urge to laugh. He reached into a pouch beside the bed. "Here, lass, a little something for your trouble," he said soberly, holding out a silver coin. "If you should see this...ah...gentleman again, please be sure to give him my thanks. The information is extremely valuable."

She took the coin, staring first at it, then back at him. Her face split into an enchanting smile, and she dropped a quick curtsy. "Thank you, m'lord. I must go now."

He made her a short bow, gallantly holding the door while she slipped into the corridor. She gave him one last appraising glance, then hurried away down the hall.

Closing the door, Francis gave in to an overwhelming urge to laugh. "Oh, Anne, you ridiculous creature," he whispered. He lifted the paper to his lips, then ignited it in a candle flame burning nearby.

Anne paced the floor, anxiously waiting for her maid's return. It seemed like hours since the girl had gone, though she knew by the dawn light little time had actually passed. A soft tap sounded on the door. She flung it open, instantly relieved by the triumphant smile on Bess's face. "You found him?"

"He was still in his room, so there was no trouble in that," Bess replied, closing the door behind her. "I gave

him the paper. He read it and gave me this." She gazed
wonderingly at the coin, turning it over in her palm. "He's
a most generous lord, mistress."

"Yes, but what did he say?" Anne asked impatiently.

Bess glanced up. "He asked where I'd the note from, and
I answered as you'd told me. Then he asked me to describe
the man." She frowned. "I made up a description. It must
have satisfied him, for he asked no more questions."

She gazed at Anne consideringly. "He told me, if I saw
the gentleman again, I was to give him his thanks and say
the information was of great value."

Anne nodded, closing her eyes in relief. Francis had
been warned; it was up to him to get out of the tangle. He
must leave soon if he were to stay alive. But then she
would never see him again...

When Anne opened her eyes, Bess was regarding her
curiously. The girl must have been mad to know what was
afoot. "You've done me a great service, Bess," Anne said
softly, "but it would endanger us all if it came to be
known."

"It'll not be known through me, mistress. And I've no
doubt the man can keep a secret. He looks the type."

"Aye, he's the type," Anne echoed.

With Bess's help, she dressed hurriedly in a new fawn-
colored riding habit, then made a quick breakfast from a
tray the girl brought. Composing herself, she made her
way downstairs to the hall, where men and women were
already gathering for the hunt.

As she entered the room, she caught sight of her father
and Campbell standing off to themselves, speaking intently together. Was Campbell one with her father and
Blake in this plot against Francis? The thought sickened
her, and she hastened to move outside before either of the
men noticed she was there.

"I believe we'll have a fine day for the hunt, despite the
rain during the night."

Anne turned at the sound of Francis's voice, smiling in

spite of herself at sight of him squinting up at the sun as if he had nothing more important to think of than the weather. "Yes, it'll be a fine day," she replied, drinking in the details of everything about him for what might be the last time.

Francis shifted his gaze to hers, a slow smile warming his face and spreading to his eyes. Without another word, he took her arm, leading her to the edge of the crowd of milling horses and groomsmen. To her surprise, Conall leaned casually against the wall, the reins of Cassie and two other mounts held fast in one hand.

"I can see you've taken good care of my horse. Cassie looks rested and ready for a good run, though I can't say the same of you, lass." He raised his hand and touched her cheek with a gentle finger. "There's a look of strain about your eyes I don't remember seeing at Camereigh."

She jerked her head away, belatedly remembering she should still have been angry after their meeting the previous evening. "I've the headache," she snapped, pulling away from the treacherous warmth of his hands.

"Again? Is it a real one this time?"

She gave him a look of such withering contempt, Conall chuckled. Turning away, she began pulling on her gloves, searching the crowded courtyard for a glimpse of Nigel or Charles.

"A good gallop in the fresh air is all you need to chase away a headache," Francis offered blandly. "As a matter of fact, I'm counting on it to clear my own."

She turned to him in surprise, noting for the first time that both men were dressed for riding. "But you're not going," she protested.

"Why, I'd not miss it, lass," he said, catching her about the waist and lifting her easily onto Cassie's back.

Ignoring the intimacy of his hands, Anne gazed down into his smiling face. Could Bess have played her false and not taken the message—or did he simply refuse to believe the warning it had contained? "Well, you're not wanted, sir," she snapped, gathering up her reins to cover her confusion. How could she stop him, short of telling him the truth?

He leaned against the mare's shoulder, gazing up at her in tender amusement. "Ah, but you're wrong again, sweet Anne. Lord Robert has expressly invited me to make one of this party." He grinned knowingly. "You might even say this hunt is held in my honor."

She stared at him helplessly, realizing at once that Francis knew the danger. He knew and was deliberately courting disaster by making one of Glenkennon's party. "Francis, don't be a fool!" she whispered, the words wrenched from her unwillingly.

His eyes held hers. "Don't fret, lass. All will be well."

Over his shoulder, she saw Percy Campbell heading toward them, an angry frown creasing his brow. She glanced at Francis and then away. "Release my reins," she said loudly, "and if you must ride today, please refrain from bothering me again."

She swung Cassie toward the Campbell chief. "Oh m'lord, here you are," she said, forcing a smile to her face. "Would you be so good as to help me with the length of this stirrup? It doesn't feel right."

The hunt was away soon after that, the hounds loudly voicing their excitement, and the horses tossing their heads eagerly against the bits as they trotted slowly through a dense woodland on the way to an open field. The first good run of the day soon took place with the animals stretching their muscles across the open ground and rising easily to leap the low, stone walls separating a series of small crofts.

The riders paused at the last wall to breathe the horses as the hounds coursed for scent on the dewy grass. Anne moved close enough to keep Francis in sight. She had ridden with her heart in her throat, wondering where the attempt on his life would take place. Her eyes followed him in the crowd of men around her father as he swung down from his big chestnut.

He knelt in the grass, lifting the animal's left foreleg and inspecting it intently. Surely nothing had happened yet, Anne thought. Her father would not dare act in such a crowd.

Noticing the movements of his guests, Glenkennon moved toward MacLean. "Is there a problem with your animal, Sir Francis?" he inquired politely.

"I'm afraid so. The brute stumbled just as we took that wall, and now he's limping badly." He led the animal forward a few steps to demonstrate the painful hobble. "I fear my mount has strained a tendon, m'lord. The hunt's over for me."

"Nonsense," Glenkennon said briskly. "Douglas, exchange mounts with our guest." He smiled down at Francis. "My man can lead your horse back to the stable, and we can continue the hunt."

"I'm obliged," Francis remarked, "but I make it a point to care for my own animals. I'll take him back myself. I've no wish to interfere with the pleasure of the rest of your party."

By this time nearly a dozen gentlemen had gathered around and were loudly voicing their suggestions for treatment of a bad leg. "Come now, MacLean," Glenkennon said with a thin smile, "surely you're not suggesting my people can't take care of a simple strained tendon."

"No, m'lord, only that I prefer to see personally to my mounts."

"That's absurd. I'll not permit you to leave for this ridiculous whim," Glenkennon said, still struggling to remain pleasant. "I know you're an excellent sportsman, MacLean, and we've yet to hunt together."

"I'm grateful for this unusual interest, m'lord, but in spite of your insistence, I must hold by my original plan. I'll see to the leg myself." Francis lifted one dark brow challengingly. "I know you'll not wish to press me further."

Glenkennon's eyes narrowed, but he smiled his most gracious smile. "Very well, MacLean, if you feel so strongly about it, you must certainly see to your mount. I'm sure we'll hunt together again soon.

"Douglas," he snapped, turning to the waiting man. "Take two men and accompany our friend. See he receives whatever help is necessary." He nodded coldly toward Francis, then spurred his horse impatiently away toward the sound of the distant hounds.

Anne released her breath slowly. Francis could take care of himself, and Nigel would see that nothing happened in the short distance to Ranleigh. Perhaps Francis and Conall would make their escape then while most everyone was away with the hunt.

As the last of the riders disappeared over the rise, Francis set out, leading his hobbling animal. Conall rode ahead to ready the mud packs they would need, leaving Francis with Nigel Douglas and the two English soldiers.

Dismounting, Nigel waved Glenkennon's men on ahead. He walked beside Francis in silence the length of the first field. "You know your life's not worth a damn here, MacLean," he said at last. "You'd best be gone while you have the chance."

Francis shot him a penetrating look. "Are you attempting to frighten me, sir, or uncover my plans for your employer?"

"Neither. I just hate to see a good man killed for no reason. And to set the record straight, I'm Jamie Stuart's man," Nigel said bluntly. "I'd not work for the likes of Robert of Glenkennon!"

Francis laughed outright. "I take it Glenkennon doesn't suspect you of any willingness to aid the enemy or he'd have ordered a guard upon us both. As it happens, I'm fully aware of the danger, but I've not yet concluded my business here."

"I confess I haven't a clue as to your business, and neither does Glenkennon," Nigel said slowly. His shrewd brown eyes probed Francis's face. "I trust it's nothing to do with treason."

"Rest easy, man. Not even the most fanatical of Jamie's supporters could catch a whiff of treason in my current pursuit."

Frowning, Nigel considered Francis's words carefully. "I've spent a great deal of time since my arrival in Scotland attempting to discover where your loyalties lie, MacLean. I was much disposed to brand you traitor at the start. The tales we hear at court are most unfavorable."

"I'm flattered by your interest, Douglas. Need I hazard a guess as to who supplies Jamie and his counselors with those accounts?"

Nigel smiled grimly. "Aye, you've the right of it there. Glenkennon's complained long and loudly against all you Highlanders. In all fairness though, you must admit you're not a pillar of support for the Union of the Crowns."

Francis stopped abruptly and leaned down to inspect the chestnut's injured leg. Straightening, he turned to Nigel. "As a lad, I swore my loyalty to Jamie Stuart as king of Scotland, though I personally despised him as a coward and a dupe of the English. When the two kingdoms made this unholy alliance and he won an English throne, I repeated that vow." His level gaze held the Englishman. "I've told you once, Douglas—we Highlanders take our word seriously."

"'Tis a difficult line to walk between loyalty to the king and disobedience to his representatives," Nigel said slowly. "I'd not like to face you across that line, MacLean."

"I've no quarrel with the king or his policies," Francis put in, "and if he called on me tomorrow, I'd be there with my clan. But I'm a man, Douglas, and I'll not stand by and watch my family beaten and murdered and see my lands go to feed the greed of a bastard who claims to speak in the king's name. If that makes me guilty of treason in your eyes, then so be it!"

"I understand your sentiments. Damn it man, I even agree! But others may brand you traitor if you don't take care."

Francis pursed his lips thoughtfully. "I'll be careful, Douglas. I've even less desire now than most men to end up on a traitor's tree."

They continued in thoughtful silence until they reached the stable where Conall waited anxiously with a stable hand and a bucket of slimy mud. Francis handed the reins to his friend, then turned to Douglas. "I've no idea why you've come out on my side, Douglas, but I thank you for the warning. And I'd give you back your own advice," he said softly. "Be careful . . . I'm not a popular man to champion."

"You don't rate me of much account, do you, MacLean?" Nigel inquired. His dark eyes narrowed thoughtfully. "Should the time come, I think you'll find I'm a man who can take care of himself. And I choose my fights carefully . . . for an Englishman."

Francis grinned. "Let's just say you've yet to show your mettle, Douglas." He nodded and turned aside into the stable while Nigel moved away toward Ranleigh's entrance.

Neither man noticed the slight movement of a curtain at a window across the courtyard, where Edmund Blake had stood just moments before—watching them.

CHAPTER NINETEEN

$\mathscr{I}$t was the end of another incredibly long and agonizing day for Anne—a day in which the minutes of each hour multiplied a hundredfold and the hours were as long as days. It was a day in which her body and mind separated, the one smiling and talking with her guests while the other raced back through the woodlands with Francis, wondering frantically if he might not lie stretched out beside the trail, a victim of her father's uncanny ability to succeed despite her meddling.

The knowledge of her duplicity taxed her taut nerves to the breaking point, for she was certain Glenkennon's cold gaze fell upon her more often and more suspiciously than usual. He'd not yet spoken to her concerning her meeting with Francis, yet Blake must have told him of it. Would he link the meeting with his foiled plot to murder the Highlander? Perhaps Blake had even seen her in the darkness of the corridor.

She'd not been much relieved when the hunt returned and she saw Francis about the hall. Why hadn't he escaped while he had the chance? Did he intend to lurk about making her miserable forever? She almost wished her father had succeeded in his plans!

Supper and the brief spate of dancing that followed had held little pleasure. Throughout the evening she had found herself searching the crowded room for a glimpse of Francis's tall figure, so easily visible since he stood a head above the other gentlemen. Yet when he approached her, she had snapped at him so rudely that Lord and Lady Galbraith had gazed at her in surprise. He had not attempted to approach her again.

Now the evening was over, and she stood alone in her bedchamber. She struggled to unfasten the tiny jet buttons running down the back of her gown, pettishly wishing she had refused Bess's request to tend a sick cousin. The maid's soothing words and gentle touch would have been welcome.

But even in her absence, Bess made her comforting presence felt. She had left word with another servant to have water heated for her mistress's bath, and now the tub steamed in warm invitation behind the curtained alcove.

Finally succeeding in releasing the last button, Anne dropped the gown over her hips, dragging her heavy silk petticoats after it. The air in the room was chill, raising gooseflesh along her arms. She paused only long enough to hang the gown in the press instead of leaving it on the floor as she was half tempted to do. Shivering in her nakedness, she hurried around the corner into the steaming tub.

Anne eased herself into the warm, scented waters, leaning against the rim of the tub, eyes closed, seeking to still her tumultuous thoughts. But even in the privacy of her bath, Francis haunted her. Why couldn't he just leave her alone? He did not want her for himself, yet he could not be content unless he could whistle her back to heel. Perhaps his tremendous self-esteem demanded that he prove himself irresistible to her again.

Anne splashed the water angrily, remembering the confident way he had kissed her beside the loch. He obviously thought she would fall back into his arms anytime he was ready. Damnation! She had been forced to admit that she still loved him, but she would take care that he never knew. She'd not be made a fool of twice by the same man!

Despite Anne's brave thoughts, a bitter anguish welled inside her as she remembered her own response to Francis's most recent advances. Perhaps he had good reason to believe she would be an easy conquest.

She thought of his embrace, recalling the feel of his lips upon hers, his arms holding her fast against his heart. Even now her treacherous body betrayed her with a powerful yearning she could not suppress. She would just have to keep away from Francis until he left Ranleigh, she told herself firmly.

It was well past the time she should have been abed when she finally stepped from the tepid water. Reaching for the towel, she draped it around her shivering form, looking uncertainly about for her nightwear. She had not brought it with her; she must have left it on the bed in her hurry.

Rounding the curtains in search of her robe, she halted in surprise. Francis was lounging coolly at his ease on her large bed, looking as if his presence there were the most natural thing in the world. She stood frozen, unable to move or speak or even to think as she gazed at him in disbelief.

"Good evening, lass. I trust you enjoyed your bath. You certainly took the devil's own time about it," he remarked, smiling that lazy, calculating smile she remembered so well as his eyes traveled appraisingly over her scantily clad form. "Had you lingered longer, I'd have joined you."

"Francis . . . get out of here!" she hissed, finding her voice. She clutched the towel more tightly to her breasts. "If you're not out by the count of five, I'm going to start screaming and not stop till the guards drag you away. One . . . two—"

"Scream if you like," he interrupted calmly, "but I'm not leaving until I've said what I came to say."

She was tempted to shout for help. He did not believe she would do it . . .

He watched her wordlessly, still lounging against the pillows.

"Say your peace then and be gone," she snapped. "I'll not have any man dead because of me . . . not even you."

He caught up her robe and held it out. "Then oblige me by putting this on, lass. Clothed as you are, you make it damned difficult for a man to keep his wits."

She jerked it from his hands, then stood uncertainly, refusing to drop the towel to slide into her robe.

"Shall I turn my back as I did one cold morning not so long ago?" he suggested. His warm gaze traveled the length of her long legs, caressing the shapely contours revealed by the damp, clinging towel. His eyes lifted to hers and he grinned mischievously. "God's blood, had I known what a comely sight I was missing, I'd have peeked at least once!"

"Close your insolent mouth . . . and turn all the way around," she ordered, watching to see he did as she commanded. She dropped the towel, slipping quickly into the robe and wrapping it tightly around her. "I don't even want to know how you managed to get in here, but you're a fool, Francis MacLean! Someone could walk in at any moment and you'd be a dead man."

"Were you expecting a lover? He'll get a surprise . . . I locked the door."

"You said you had something important to discuss," she said pointedly. "Say it, and be gone. I'm tired of your prattle."

He turned around. "I'd not have chanced this had there been any other way, lass." He leaned forward, suddenly serious. "Glenkennon's watchdogs have made it nigh impossible to speak to you privately, but I had to see you again . . . to tell you what happened last spring."

His eyes were dark, compelling, binding her gaze to his. The old need to touch him rose up in her as a throbbing ache. She turned abruptly away. "I don't want to know. It's over and done with, Francis. Leave it be."

"Damn it, Anne! You'll hear me out if I have to tie you in that chair," he exploded, coming halfway off the bed. "Now sit down!"

For a moment their eyes clashed angrily. How dare he order her about like one of his clansmen!

Francis settled back onto the bed. His voice dropped. "Please, lass . . ."

Her fingers traced the carved oak of the chair back uncertainly. "Very well, then." She eased into the chair. "If you promise you'll leave Ranleigh afterward."

"About last spring," he began softly, "it wasn't as I said that day at all. Everything between us was real, lass, but the MacKenzies brought news that changed all my plans. Glenkennon had petitioned the king for a writ of treason against me, and there was a good chance I was to be put to the horn."

Anne's eyes flew to his in stunned disbelief. Camereigh —he would lose Camereigh. "Was it . . . granted?" she asked, holding her breath.

He shook his head. "Nay, lass, though at the time it seemed likely I'd soon be on my way to France."

She dropped her eyes, quietly releasing her pent-up breath.

"Colen was waiting for me with the news when we came in from the beach that night." He rose and paced the floor. "Maybe if there'd been more time I could have thought of something, lass. God knows I didn't want to hurt you, but I knew you couldn't stay at Camereigh." He halted before her chair. "Returning you to Glenkennon seemed better than dragging you into an outlaw's life. It wasn't what I wanted for you, Anne."

She kept her eyes focused firmly on her hands, trying hard to temper the wild exultation growing inside her. He hadn't wanted to send her away! Dear God, could it be possible that he loved her—had loved her all these miserable months?

Don't believe him, a warning voice whispered. He's too glib, too easy with words. He's fooling you again. Remember how he acted, what he said.

"Why didn't you tell me the truth then? Did you think me so stupid I'd not have understood . . . or did it just take you this long to come up with a good tale?"

"I said what I did because I thought it would be easier for you. I didn't want you hurt any more than necessary, and I thought it best to end the thing quick and sharp, so there'd be no lingering regrets on either side. And I was afraid for you, lass—afraid of what Glenkennon might do if he knew you cared for me." He gave her a rueful smile. "I thought your pride would get you over the affair quickly enough."

"And it did," she said, rising unsteadily and starting past him toward the window.

"But I overlooked one thing," Francis added, catching her wrist as she passed. He swung her into his arms. "I hadn't counted on not being able to get over it myself."

He gazed at her hungrily, his eyes holding hers in a gaze she could not break. "You've haunted me night and day—every moment since I sent you away. Every inch of Camereigh, every foot of that damned beach remind me of you! I can't escape you lass—you give me no peace." He drew her close, burying his face in her hair. "For Christ's sake, Anne, I love you," he breathed, "and in spite of Glenkennon and all the English in Scotland, I'll have you!"

His mouth sought hers with an eagerness that sent her heart pounding, making her forget all thought of resistance—all thought of sanity—as her lips opened beneath the pressure of his. The kiss was hard, brutal with a passion that seared her soul. The world whirled around her, then steadied, narrowing until his mouth, his hands were the only reality. There was no thought of pride or anger, no thought of prudence or fear as her body arched against his of its own accord and her arms slid up to draw him closer, touching him, holding him as her entire body came alive to his caress. He loved her, she exulted. He had never said the words before, not even that night on the beach.

She could feel the muscular hardness of his body straining against hers through the thin cloth of her robe. His powerful hands were strangely gentle as they slid along her waist then up to cup each breast, shifting the cool satin of the robe back and forth across each crest until she groaned deep in her throat and pressed against him eagerly. His questing hand found its way inside her robe, caressing the satin of her naked hip, pressing her hard against his rigid thighs.

His mouth left hers, trailing a line of warm, moist kisses against her throat and shoulder. "Anne, Anne...I've loved you so long, wanted you so long," he breathed. She felt a shudder race through his body, then he swept her up in his arms and carried her, unprotesting, to the bed.

Laying his burden down gently on the coverlet, he was beside her in an instant. He buried his lips in hers, kissing her until she was dazed with passion and longing. Her robe slid open obligingly beneath his roving hands, and she gasped with pleasure as his lips traced down the line of her throat to the soft fullness of her breast. Beneath his knowing hands, she responded as she had that long-past night on the beach, unconscious of any feeling save the racing blood in her veins and the flash of desire that spread like a flame throughout her body at his touch.

She moved beneath him, aching in a way she could not understand as his mouth took hers once more and his hands moved over the silken length of her body with an intimate knowledge of the pleasure a man can give a woman. It seemed as if she were drowning in his kiss. She cared for nothing save the ecstasy promised by his touch as the weight of his body pressed her down into the softness of the bed.

The tension was building between them to an unbearable degree. Francis paused, lifting his head to gaze unbelievingly at the beauty of Anne's naked body in the warm glow of the candles. His breath came raggedly, and he found himself shaking as he fought to control his own raging desire. She was warm and willing now in his arms, but he was determined to go slowly. He'd not hurt her for all the world.

He began unbuttoning his shirt in trembling haste, pausing in surprise as Anne reached up and deftly slipped the buttons loose. She looked wordlessly into his eyes, her hands slipping across his naked chest.

He groaned savagely, rapidly losing his battle with himself. His fingers caught in the wild profusion of her hair, which spread like a surging sea across the pillow. Jerking her head toward his, he crushed her lips beneath his own, sweeping her mouth with his tongue, unable to get enough of the sweet taste of her.

A sharp knock sounded on the door, abruptly rending the haze of passion engulfing the pair. Cursing softly and fluently, Francis was off the bed and onto his feet in an instant. Anne gasped and rolled to her feet, pulling her robe about her with trembling hands as Francis disappeared behind the curtains of the bathing alcove. She stumbled to the door, trying desperately to pull herself together and order her whirling thoughts.

What if it were her father, come with some late-night message as he had once before? Or worse yet, what if he knew Francis was there? Her heart thudded painfully against her ribs as she opened the door.

"Did I get you out of the bath, mistress?" Bess stood in the doorway, her questioning eyes searching Anne's flushed face. "I saw your candle was still lit, so I thought it best to let you know I'd returned. I knocked once before, but you didn't hear."

Anne sagged against the door in relief. "Ah . . . yes. I

was just getting dressed... for bed," she said, making no
move to step back from the door to allow the girl inside.

"The messenger was mistaken. My cousin wasn't sick at
all." Bess smiled and shook her head. "I can't imagine how
such a thing happened." She craned her neck, attempting
to peer around Anne. "I know it's late, but would you like
me to finish straightening the room and help you to bed?"

"No! That is... I'm sure you're tired after your trip to
the village," Anne said quickly. "I shan't need you tonight.
I'm ready to put out the candles now."

Bess stared at her strangely, then nodded and turned
away. Anne closed the door and leaned against it, her
trembling limbs ready to collapse now as the threat of the
moment passed.

Francis put his head around the curtain. "If you're going
to consort with Highlanders, you'd best learn to be more
glib with your lies, lass," he said with a grin. He moved
toward her across the floor, his eyes still warm with desire.
"Since it's my life resting in your hands, I suppose I must
teach you the way. Come here, and we'll begin our les-
sons."

He reached for her, but Anne drew back, shrinking
away from him against the wall. How many lies had he
told her? Was his declaration of love moments earlier just
another lie to get her into his bed? Hadn't she promised
herself she'd not be made a fool of again? Dear God! Why
hadn't she thought of that before her passionate response?

"What is it, lass?" Francis asked, halting as she cringed
away from him.

"You're so practiced at lying I can never tell whether to
believe you or not," she blurted, closing her eyes miserably
against the sight of him. "Get out! You should never have
come."

"When have I lied to you, Anne?"

"When have you what?" she gasped, opening her eyes in
astonishment. "How should I know? For all I know every
word you've ever said is false!"

He frowned. "As God is my witness, Anne, I've never lied to you save that day I sent you from Camereigh. Every word I've spoken here is the honest truth. This is no game we're playing—I'm in dead earnest. I love you, and I want you to be my wife despite Glenkennon and his plans." He paused, but she made no effort to speak.

"I'll not beg, lass," he said, drawing himself up proudly though the bleakness in his face betrayed his pain. "This is the last time I'll ask you, for Conall and I must soon be gone if we're to keep our heads upon our shoulders. I've no time to convince you. You must choose to trust me or no'."

Anne gazed at him as a drowning man stares at nearby land just beyond his reach. There were so many reasons it was impossible to love him. She bit her lip uncertainly. In a few minutes he would walk out of her life forever if she didn't stop him.

She suddenly knew there was only one answer she could give. It did not matter if he were lying or telling the truth. She no longer cared about her own injured pride or even the many reasons she had fashioned for avoiding him.

With a strangled cry she threw herself across the few feet separating them and into the haven of his waiting arms.

He held her tightly, raining gentle kisses upon her face and hair. "I'm still waiting for your answer, love."

"What answer?"

"I asked you to be my wife." He chuckled. "Did you forget a'ready?"

She closed her eyes, burying her head against his chest and breathing deeply in an attempt to steady her voice. "You must know my answer a'ready."

"But I'd like to hear it from you, lass."

She gazed up into his face, amazed by the tenderness she saw reflected there. "I love you, Francis MacLean," she whispered, "and I'll marry you despite all those who'd say us nay."

His hands contracted against her back in a brief, involuntary movement, and a flicker of some deep emotion sped across his face. Then his eyes went warm and bright with laughter, but he pursed his mouth into sober lines. "Then all that remains is to request your dear father's permission."

Though she knew he was teasing, she could not resist a startled gasp. "Francis, don't even joke about it!"

"Well, that's the way it's usually done," he protested innocently. "Can't you see me down on one knee before Lord Robert, imploring him to bestow your hand upon me?"

Anne choked at the vision his words invoked, and they laughed together as he further embellished the scene. Finally wiping the tears of laughter from her eyes, she sobered. "Really Francis, what are we going to do?"

"I'm going to take you away from here," he said simply, "though I need to know if you'd object to remaining another month. I've a few things to take care of before we return to Camereigh and commit ourselves to a siege." He searched her face. "Is it hard for you here, lass? Has Glenkennon threatened you in any way." His eyes narrowed in concentration. "It'd be difficult, but perhaps I could arrange to take you with me when Conall and I leave."

She resisted the temptation to beg him not to leave her. "Of course, I'm safe here. You're the only person at Ranleigh who's ever threatened me," she said with a smile.

He laughed and drew her close, dropping his head to kiss her again with a slow thoroughness that set her blood singing. Finally raising his head reluctantly, he released her and stepped back. "I must go now. I've been away far longer than I intended, and Conall will be imagining me with a dirk in my back."

Turning to leave, he cast an expressive look at the bed. "I've a strong desire to strangle your maid, lass. I thought she'd stay in the village."

He opened the door a slit and peeked into the blackness of the hall. "Remember, sweet," he whispered, turning back, "you must still act the shrew tomorrow."

She blew him an airy kiss. "I'll be as rude as ever!" Her smile faded. "Be careful, Francis."

He winked at her, then slipped through the door, and the empty room seemed barren and cold without the warmth of his presence. She leaned her head against the bedpost and smoothed the rumpled coverlet. "Oh, please be careful, my love," she whispered into the emptiness.

CHAPTER TWENTY

$\mathscr{G}$lenkennon paced the floor of his office, eyes narrowed in concentration. "I tell you Blake, he'd best not slip through my hands!" he growled, whirling to confront his steward. "I wonder if we shouldn't take him now, before he has a chance to play off his tricks."

Edmund Blake pressed his palms together and studied his thin fingers imperturbably. "Of course, you, my lord Glenkennon, know best, but I can't help wondering at the outcry if you were to throw MacLean into prison now—with no proof of any wrongdoing. The king would hear of it."

He glanced up. "Of course, we could dispose of him long before the case could be investigated, but his death might cause suspicion—suspicion we can ill afford."

The earl released a heavy sigh. "You're right, Blake. The most obvious solution is seldom best. But, damn, it puts me on edge to have him strolling about when I've no idea what he's up to!" He paused, staring blindly out the window, where the morning rain splashed grayly against the glass.

"You'll have him m'lord. But why this haste? It isn't like you."

"I've waited a long time to have Scotland secure," Glenkennon said softly. "Once we dispose of MacLean, we'll break the back of the opposition. Without him, those half-clothed savages in the North will fall in line."

"Yes, but no hint of blame must fall on you," Blake reminded him. "I can arrange for the accident we discussed." His mouth twisted slyly. "It can take place during the hawking party tomorrow as easily as a hunt."

"MacLean's a known enthusiast of the sport. Yes... it should work," Glenkennon mused. He whirled from the window. "That is, if his horse doesn't strain a tendon. Christ's blood! Was there ever such luck?"

Blake shrugged his narrow shoulders. "If this attempt fails, we can seize him on some pretext or other before he leaves. I can find witnesses to swear to anything if we've gold to loosen their tongues. While it's not the most politic plan, at least we can keep our hands on him."

Glenkennon poured himself wine from a crystal decanter on an ornate chest. "Do you have him well guarded?"

Blake nodded. "I'm keeping MacLean and his friend under constant watch."

"But are you certain the guards can be trusted? I warn you, there must be no mistake."

Blake scratched his chin meditatively. "I'm using Godfrey, Smith, and young Donaldson for the job. Their work's been dependable before."

Glenkennon nodded. "They've served me well on past occasions." He stared into his glass in perplexity. "I wish I knew what MacLean was up to. He didn't come to Ranleigh to enjoy my company, and I don't believe his tale of business."

Lifting his glass, he gazed coldly over its rim at his steward. "I'll not be made to look a fool by that arrogant barbarian, Blake."

"Of course not, m'lord," Blake said smoothly, "but we've another problem besides MacLean. I hate to mention it, but I've received another bill from the merchant Murray MacDuff—this time with a letter insisting we make payment on the debt owed him. His tone is ill considered; he actually hints he might refuse you credit."

"Does he now?" Glenkennon said, smiling darkly. "The man's even more a fool than I thought."

"Yes, m'lord, I'm afraid so. I've taken the liberty of composing a letter to him and several other creditors, promising payment by next month. I've suggested they reconsider any hasty words. It should suffice for a time."

"Yes, by then I'll have the money," Glenkennon agreed. "I'll disclose the new tax levy to my lords tomorrow night. We should have the first payment within the fortnight."

Blake raised his colorless brows. "And if the lairds refuse to pay?"

"The tax will support my army, held here to protect them. They should pay it gladly," Glenkennon snapped. "Every man present shall affix his name to a document pledging support, else he'll not leave Ranleigh." He smiled sourly. "Their wives and daughters are here, Blake . . . I anticipate little trouble."

He moved to his desk and sat down, leaning back in satisfaction. "Then there's the payment we'll receive when Anne's marriage is arranged."

Blake glanced toward him curiously. "Have you received an offer?"

"I've been deluged with them all week," Glenkennon responded with a wave of his hand, "but none of the scale I desire. Percy Campbell continues to play a waiting game." He laughed coldly. "Christ's bones, you can simply look at the man and tell he's hot to bed the girl. I'm certain he'll come up with an agreeable offer by the end of the week."

"You might consider waiting until Sir Charles Howard returns from Court," Blake interjected. "I've word he's expected any day, and 'tis known he's on the lookout for a young wife."

"Howard's rich enough, and at an age he might be more willing to part with his gold," Glenkennon mused. "Be

sure we have immediate word of his arrival. If nothing
else, the hint of a rival might prod Campbell."

Blake nodded and began gathering up the letters he had
brought for the earl's signature.

Glenkennon sipped his wine meditatively, watching the
colorless dab of a man whose mind was as sharply devious
as his own. "And what of you, Blake? I've noticed you
watching Anne a great deal. Do you want my daughter for
yourself?"

Blake continued organizing the correspondence on the
desk, his manner poised, his movements self-controlled. "I
watch your daughter because you bid me do so," he said
without looking up. "My duty in that respect is a pleasurable one—the girl's lovely. But I've no interest in such
things. My life is devoted to service to my house and
lord..." He glanced up. "I've no time for such foolishness."

For a moment hard gray eyes clashed with orbs equally
flinty, and neither man looked away. Then Glenkennon
threw back his head and laughed in genuine amusement.
"God's body, man, were you always so cold-blooded a creature?"

"Always, my lord," Blake said softly, his mouth lifting
into its crooked smile, "I've a much greater goal than the
pleasure of a moment."

That night, Anne sat quietly in her chamber...
waiting. She had quickly snuffed every candle save one
after Bess left, placing it carefully across the room so its
tell-tale light would not be visible beneath the door. She
told herself it might be hours before Francis could come as
he had whispered he would at dinner, yet she started at
every sound as the household settled down for the night.

The minutes stretched into an hour... then longer.
Heavy shadows swathed the doorway and every corner of
the room. Anne closed her eyes, which burned from the

constant strain of staring at the door. Perhaps he'd not be able to come after all.

A draft of cold air swept Anne's legs. Her eyes snapped open. Francis stood casually beside the door as if he belonged there. He slid the bolt home, then crossed the floor to her in three long strides.

Anne rose to her feet, lifting a hand to caress his dark face, needing that touch to believe he stood before her.

"You've been worrying again, lass, probably imagining me dead at every turn." His slow smile fired a happiness that burst inside her like a flame. "What must we do to break you of that habit?"

"Take me away from here," she whispered, "and I promise I'll not worry so."

His tender gaze shifted from her eyes to her mouth then back again. "So I shall." He cupped her chin with both hands, bending to kiss her with an unhurried thoroughness that sent her world whirling. His arms slid about her, crushing her close, while his lips gently brushed her hair.

Warm and secure within the circle of his arms, she closed her eyes. "You don't take my father seriously enough," she murmured. "He's determined to be rid of you permanently, Francis."

"On the contrary, love. I take Glenkennon seriously." He took a step toward the bed and sat down, drawing her onto his lap. "He's a dangerous man to balk. If I'd not had a healthy respect for him since my boyhood, I'd be dead now, most like. By the way, tell me how you stumbled across his plan to do away with me."

"How did you know it was me?"

"'Tis easy enough to discover the maid to the lady of the house," he replied, smiling. "I doubted I'd any other friends here who'd have risked sending me such a message. But tell me, how did you learn the plan?"

"I couldn't sleep that night, so I decided to fetch a prayerbook." She looked away, remembering the lingering horror of that nightmare. "When I reached Father's office, the door was ajar. I could hear Edmund Blake's voice, so I listened, thinking he'd be telling Father about our meeting at the loch." She clasped her hands together. "That's when I overheard Blake and...and Father," she stumbled, "planning your 'accident.'"

"Look at me, Anne," Francis said softly, lifting her chin toward him. "You must promise you'll not wander about Ranleigh at night—for any reason. You must stay inside this room with the door bolted after dark." His arms tightened around her. "And you're not to make a move even if you think I'm in danger. I've good men about who'll see to my safety."

She shook her head stubbornly, knowing she would move heaven and earth to help him if he ever had need of her.

He took her face between both hands, his voice lowering earnestly. "Right now Glenkennon holds the one weapon he could use to destroy me, Anne—and heaven help us both if he should discover it. He'd not hesitate to abuse you to get to me. Now do you understand?"

"But he's my father, Francis," she protested. "Surely he'd do nothing to cause me serious harm."

His voice grew harsh. "Believe me, Anne, I know the man. He'd let no ties of any kind stand in the way of tormenting me. I wish it weren't so, but he'd cheerfully consign you to the devil if it'd give him his way."

"But what if I'd not warned you? You might be dead now."

"I already knew of his plan, lass."

"You knew!" She struggled out of his arms and stood up. "But how could you know?"

"I can't answer that, lass. Just be thankful I've my ways."

She shook her head ruefully. "All that worry, the risk I had Bess take—for nothing."

He caught her hand and drew her back beside the bed, his lips trembling on the verge of a grin. "Not for nothing, love. That note gave me hope. I was about to have done and go home, believing you wanted no more to do with me."

"You . . . give up? I don't believe it," she said, smiling.

He rubbed his cheek gingerly. "As I recall, you'd let me know earlier exactly what you thought of me."

She laughed softly, gazing down into her open palm. "I hurt my hand more than your face."

His hands shot out and caught her about the waist, toppling her across him full length upon the bed. Rolling quickly, he penned her shoulders against the coverlet. "I've been plotting my revenge these two days," he said slowly, tiny flames leaping to life in the dark depths of his eyes. "I must teach you that the proper manner in which to respond to a gentleman's kiss is not with a sharp hand across his face."

His look set her heart racing. She caught her breath, unable to force her lungs to function properly as his hands dropped from her shoulders to her waist, gathering her close against him. His mouth lowered slowly to make its claim, his lips teasing, tasting, his tongue moving tantalizingly from the rim of her mouth to its deepest recesses and back, sending a shiver of warmth and desire radiating through her body.

His tormenting kisses roused her. She needed more. Burying her fingers in the cool silk of his hair, she held his head against hers until his mouth gave her the satisfaction she craved.

He raised his head at last, his eyes dark with passion. "That, lass, is a far more acceptable way to respond to a man's kiss."

He did not kiss her again, though she wished for it with all her heart. Instead, he lowered his head to her breast, resting his face beneath her chin. She felt his breath, warm and steady against her throat. His hands stroked slowly along her sides, memorizing her form, moving in a way that awakened the familiar ache she had come to expect from his touch.

She cradled his head in her arms. "Could you stay . . . for part of the night, I mean?"

"Nay lass," he breathed, "it would mean my life. Conall's covering my absence, and I promised I'd not be so long tonight."

She closed her eyes, holding him tightly against her breast, refusing to dwell on what could happen if he were discovered. "When must you leave Ranleigh?"

"Tonight, lass."

The words struck her like a blow. "Tonight," she echoed, sitting up in dismay.

"Aye. Our plans are made, and I've but come to say good-bye."

She pushed the hair back from her face and regarded him distractedly. Not yet, she couldn't stand the thought of him leaving yet.

His eyes were steady and reassuring on hers. "I'll be back before you know it, lass. I promise," he said, catching her wrist and pulling her down against his chest. He wrapped his arms tightly around her. "You'll see me before a month is out, I swear. In the meantime, you're to remember your own promises."

She nodded, feeling the powerful throb of his heart against her cheek. She swallowed heavily. He was so alive —pray God he stayed that way.

"Keep in mind I've friends about. Little happens at Ranleigh I won't know in a week or ten days at most."

"I'll just have to find something to do to pass the next few weeks," she said, struggling to keep her voice light.

"Try planning your wedding," he whispered. "It's like to take place sooner than you think!" He kissed her again, then stood up reluctantly. "I must go now, lass."

She searched for something to keep him another moment. Moving to the clothespress, she rummaged for the ruby necklace. "Here. You must take this back to Janet."

Taking the chain of glimmering stones, Francis held it to the light. "Do you have any valuables of your own? Any jewels Glenkennon allows you to keep?"

She shook her head.

"Keep it then. You'd not believe the way a few coins or a sparkling stone will open doors if you've ever a need to buy your way from a tight spot." He reached into his pocket. "And take these," he added, holding out three gold pieces. "Hide them away just in case. No lass should be without a few coins to jingle together."

He walked beside her to the door. "I'll be back for you, lass. Remember that," he said, his hands grasping her shoulders almost painfully.

She tried to smile, but the growing tightness in her throat warned her she was losing control. She could not cry—Francis would hate it. "Be gone," she whispered, reaching up to stroke his somber face. Her fingers traced his frowning mouth. "And may God go with you."

He kissed her again, a hard, angry kiss, and she managed one last smile. Then the door opened a slit in the shadows, and he was gone.

The smile on her face crumpled slowly. Covering her mouth with her hands, she leaned against the door, sobbing silently.

The long golden days of late summer blazed across the Scottish landscape, drying up the lowland bogs and turning the winding roadways into thin, shifting rivers of dust which hung in the air long after a traveler passed, stinging the eyes and making the mouth taste of chalk. The sun marched across the sky with a maddening slowness, refusing to hasten its journey no matter how often Anne checked the time each day.

At night she lay in her bed, gazing wide-eyed at the ceiling, remembering those brief, sweet hours when Francis had lain beside her. She smiled to herself, and her heart beat faster as she wondered what the night would hold when he'd no longer rise to leave her side.

That first day after his escape had been the hardest, when she had been forced to cover her aching loss beneath an unconcerned exterior. The entire household had been in an uproar that day, with worried men standing in anxious groups, and Glenkennon seething beneath his forced calm.

By the whispered comments and speculative glances she had observed, Anne gathered that at least half the assembled gentlemen believed her father had foully murdered the missing men. It seemed the height of irony that what the earl had schemed to do by stealth, so as not to arouse suspicion, he now stood accused of by the very escape of the men he had planned to murder. She smiled to herself, knowing Francis had probably planned it that way all along.

By the time Glenkennon convened his council, there were several gentlemen openly questioning MacLean's disappearance. A none-too-polite request by Sir Evan Mac-Cue that Glenkennon allow an inspection of his prison did little to soothe the earl's rapidly fraying temper.

It was to this unreceptive audience that Glenkennon coldly announced the levy, and the resulting uproar occasioned the calling of his guard. Order was quickly restored, but the presence of armed soldiers couldn't quell the sullen looks on the men's faces or the whispered protests that rippled across the floor.

Even those men Glenkennon had always relied on— men like Sir Alexander Dorsett and Sir William Johnson —looked askance at the new tax. And Glenkennon had neither the time nor the temper to soothe them with promises of future largess.

But in the end, it was as the earl had foreseen, with every man signing his name to the paper and promising a portion of his worth in gold and silver. No man cared to risk defiance with his family's safety in Glenkennon's hands.

But if time moved at a frustrating crawl for an impatient Anne, such was not the case at Camereigh. In its Highland fastness, the castle hummed night and day with a frenetic activity as every stone and inch of mortar was checked for soundness. Weapons and ammunition arrived daily to be stockpiled, and the great storehouses of the castle were filled to overflowing.

Messengers came and went, stumbling over one another in their haste to follow the orders of the chief, as MacLeans from all over the Highlands and even the Isle of Mull were summoned to the laird and alliances were struck with a host of other clans. Closing his eyes only a few hours each night, Francis was a figure of perpetual motion as he drilled his men, saw to the stockpiling of food and weapons, or rode out personally to discuss an alliance with some proud Highland chief.

But the frantic activity was worth it. Before a fortnight was out, Francis had achieved his goal.

"It's done now, Donald," he said wearily, shoving a well-handled paper across the desk toward his friend. He raked a grimy hand through his tousled hair. "I've the signature of near every laird within a three-day ride and a pledge of as many men as they can put weapons to."

Donald scanned the list, his dour expression unchanging. "You've enough men to put up a fight, lad. They'll do."

"Aye." Francis retrieved the list and locked it carefully away. He rested his head in his hands and closed his eyes, trying to block out the dark images that had haunted him all day. "There are enough names there for Glenkennon to keep his hangmen busy for a week," he said softly.

Dropping his hands, he met Donald's gaze angrily. "I don't mind risking my own neck, but I'll be damned if I like the idea of bringing down my friends!"

"You're tired, Francis," Donald said. "You'll feel the better for a decent night's sleep."

Francis pushed his chair back and rose to his feet. The air was too close. The walls pressed in unbearably. "I'm going for a walk," he said abruptly. "I'll be back before dark."

He moved rapidly down the corridor, nodding curtly to a clansman who dared speak to him in his dark mood. He had no direction in mind as he left Camereigh, but his feet turned of their own accord down the well-known paths behind the castle. Coming out on the cliffs guarding Camereigh's back, he inhaled the pungent freshness of the ocean, tasting the salt spray in the wind that blew in from the sea.

The sun had dipped low over the watery horizon, bringing an end to the stifling warmth of the day. Above him a pair of gray herons flew up the coast, heads stretched in a graceful arc, wings beating in perfect unison against the wide backdrop of burning sky.

He frowned at the tranquil scene, wondering what changes another month would bring to that peaceful coast. It was an awesome thing to stir a people to rebellion.

He closed his eyes wearily. He had used every persuasive art at his command to unite the clans against Glenkennon. Some had joined him willingly, eagerly even, their hatred of the earl stirring them to embrace the cause with relish. Others had been fearful and cautious, hating the words which smacked of treason, but agreeing with him in the end.

Francis wondered tiredly where it all would end. How many of the men he had convinced would be alive come winter?

"Don't turn that dark scowl upon your lass, else you'll frighten her to the other end of Scotland."

At the voice, Francis glanced up, surprised to see Conall perched precariously upon the jagged rocks behind him. Frowning, he turned back seaward. "I've a right to scowl, lad. I've just succeeded in talking my neighbors into treason, and I'm wondering how many will be alive to curse my name a few months hence."

"'Twould be a grim thought indeed, if it were true," Conall said quietly, "but we've no quarrel with the king, so the word treason need not apply. We've only banded together to protect ourselves from a scoundrel."

"I'm afraid Jamie Stuart may not see the thing our way," Francis interjected. "Those will be his troops, and they'll be carrying the royal lions when they march over those hills to fight."

"You didn't begin this thing, Francis," Conall said low. "It began long ago, when you and I were both lads. Many families hereabouts have suffered from Randall's greed. Have you forgotten my parents were murdered, my name and lands taken while I fled for my life? Have you forgotten Mary MacDonnell . . . and Anne?

"You and your clan are next on his list," he continued. "And after you will come Ian MacDonnell, Colen MacKenzie, Jamie Cameron, and so on, until all the men with any backbone will be gone. Christ, Francis, were it not you, it'd be some other of us fighting to organize the clans! The man must be stopped, but it'll take a united front, else he'll pick us off one by one.

"If treason's the word used, then so be it. But at least we stand together instead of waiting for a false arrest or a knife blade in the dark. That's the way Randall prefers to work."

Francis studied the darkening sea. "I know, Conall. We must make a stand against him. But merciful God! Why can't the man contract the fever or take a fatal fall from his horse? 'Twould make my life so much easier."

Conall chuckled. "The devil protects his own, so they say. But listen! I've news." He stood up, resting his hands on his hips. "What would you say to word of a large shipment of gold and silver on its way to Glenkennon?"

"The tax levy for the outfitting of his army?" Francis breathed.

"The same. 'Tis said to carry a heavy guard, but there's no army moving with it." He raised a finger to his lips and grinned. "Hush, lad. It's supposed to be a secret," he whispered. "It's leaving Duncraig on Tuesday for Ranleigh."

"That'll mean Glencarry Pass on Wednesday evening—and there'll be no moon this week."

Conall nodded. "Glenkennon's creditors are openly badgering him now. And his soldiers have received no wages in months."

Francis threw back his head and laughed, his mood of depression scattered to the winds. "Glenkennon's mercenaries are poor soldiers at best, but with pockets to let, they'll be more than hesitant to cross into the Highlands. The good Robert may be hard pressed to force them onto our lands, not to mention into our swords. God's blood, the man will tear out his hair in frustration!"

He scrambled numbly up the rocks to Conall's side. "Your news comes in good time, man. We must ride tomorrow if we're to reach Glencarry ahead of Glenkennon's gold. Hurry, Conall! I want my raiders gathered. We must lay our plans tonight."

CHAPTER TWENTY-ONE

*G*lenkennon took the theft of his gold hard. He sat perfectly still while Blake gave him the news, his thin lips a tight, angry slash across the sudden pallor of his face. "Bring Kincaid here. That fool will answer for the loss!"

"Kincaid's dead," Blake replied bluntly. "He and two others died in the ambush—a dozen more are wounded."

Glenkennon's face contorted in sudden fury, the powerful muscles of his arms cording with his effort at self-control. "This wouldn't have happened if we'd taken MacLean as I wished to do weeks ago," he said through grated teeth. "But, no . . . I listened to my fool of a steward instead. Damn you to hell, Blake!" he shouted, striking his fist upon the desk. "I'd have had the man a confessed traitor and cold in his grave by now if not for you."

Blake stared at him impassively. "Just so, my lord."

Glenkennon rose and paced the floor, his fingers clenching into tight fists in his rage. "Have you questioned the men?" he bit out. "By God, they'll wish they'd died with Kincaid by the time I get through with them!"

"They were set upon in the dark by an undetermined number of men wearing no identifying markings," Blake replied calmly. He shrugged his shoulders. "To hear them tell it, there were upward of a hundred men in that glen."

"MacLean!" Glenkennon snapped. "I need no description or count. But how did he know? Who knew the route that gold was to take?"

"Any number of people," Blake answered. "It's impossible to keep news of that nature quiet. Kincaid knew. Nigel Douglas, who organized the collection. Several individuals in the household of Sir William Johnson, since the money was collected there. Your son, Charles—"

"I want MacLean," Glenkennon interrupted. "I'd have killed him before to get him out of the way. But now..." He smiled grimly, his dark eyes glittering with narrow purpose. "His death won't come easy, Blake. Everyone must know the fate of a man who tries to make me look the fool. If I accomplish nothing else in Scotland, I'll destroy MacLean. I swear it," he added softly.

He swung from the window, in command of himself once more. "Gather all the plate in the household—gold and silver in any form. I want it sold for whatever it will bring." He moved lithely to his desk and sat down, toying with the great ruby on his hand. "Sell my eastern holdings if you must, but get me enough coin to pay the back wages of my men, else we'll never budge them for this campaign." He glanced up. "And send Nigel Douglas to me. I want him on his way to England with letters to James. I'll not wait until the autumn rains make the Highlands impassable."

"You might question Douglas before sending him," Blake said carefully. "I've observed him with MacLean on more than one occasion. The men were too friendly to my mind... and Douglas knew of the gold."

Glenkennon bit his lip, his eyes narrowing thoughtfully. "Douglas is intrigued by the man, but he's too stupidly loyal to the Stuarts to throw in his lot with a traitor like MacLean. I've no fear of his tongue—and James may listen to him."

Blake nodded. "If you say so, m'lord." He turned to go. "I'll have an inventory of the household gold, silver, jewels, and saleable lands by tomorrow evening."

"Wait!"

Blake turned back.

A smile of satisfaction played about Glenkennon's lips. He settled back in his chair. "Get a message to Percy Campbell, ordering him to wait on me at once. You know, I was almost forgetting our most valuable property at Ranleigh."

Anne did not remain in ignorance of the turn of events for long. Nigel Douglas told her of the stolen shipment of gold and of Glenkennon's plan to raise money for his army before leaving with dispatches for England. Like her father, she had no doubt as to the leader of the raiders. It was Francis—pray God he was still safe!

Alone in her room, she considered her foolishness. She had fallen in love with a man who did not know the meaning of the word fear—she who had always quailed at her father's slightest frown! Francis would never turn his back on a challenge, no matter how dangerous—not even for her. As his wife, she would spend many anxious hours waiting for him to return from whatever daring escapade he had joined. She must accustom herself to this cold fear coiling about her heart.

Francis would never change—but she would not have made him over, even if she could have. A reluctant smile touched her face. She might more easily catch the wind which blew so freely over the Highlands than change Francis's nature. He would not be the same man who had won her heart were he to become hesitant and careful— even as the wind would cease to be once it was trapped safely inside a box. Francis would live as freely as the gulls soaring above Camereigh, and she would be thankful for whatever time she would have at his side.

The sudden clatter of horses' hooves in the courtyard drew Anne to the window. Sir Percy Campbell was dismounting in all his dusty splendor. She stepped back with a frown. Her father would expect her to entertain Campbell, and in light of Glenkennon's recent temper she did not dare protest. Yet it was growing more difficult to tolerate Sir Percy's sly looks and lingering caresses with any degree of composure.

She fortified herself with the knowledge that she had only to play this game a few more days. Francis had promised to return for her within the month. And on that promise she knew she could depend. She counted the days on her fingers, an exercise she found herself performing numerous times each day. Only four days remained— Francis must have been on his way to Ranleigh even then.

Hurried footsteps sounded in the corridor, and Glenkennon flung open Anne's chamber door.

She studied him warily.

"Campbell's here and in no good temper by the look of him," he snapped. "I want him coaxed into good spirits." He stared at her pointedly. "You're to apply yourself to that end in whatever way possible, my dear. I want the man happy."

A sudden surge of unfamiliar rebellion rose up bitter as gall in her throat. She crumpled the yellow silk of her skirt between her fingers, willing herself to hold her tongue . . . only four more days. "I'll do all I can to entertain him, Father," she said with an obedience she was far from feeling.

He nodded curtly. "Dress yourself becomingly then, and see to your hair." He frowned at the demure knot she'd gathered at the nape of her neck. "I'll expect you at dinner in an hour."

Glenkennon took a long sip of the fiery amber liquid in his glass, watching Campbell closely. The evening had gone well despite its unpromising beginning. Campbell was furious over the recent levy, though God knew the man could well afford to pay. He had been angered still more by the curt message ordering him to Ranleigh so abruptly. The circumstances certainly weren't the most auspicious under which to arrange a marriage contract, but Glenkennon vowed he would have the matter settled before Campbell left. He needed the money too badly to await the man's pleasure any longer.

He forced a bland smile to his face. "Another drink, m'lord?"

Campbell glanced from his empty glass to the sidetable of fine wines and brandy. "Aye. Just a wee dram more." He shook his head. "That's the finest dinner I've had set before me in a fortnight, m'lord. My compliments to your cook."

Glenkennon rose, his smile more genuine this time. He took Campbell's glass and crossed the office floor, tilting a liberal draught of his finest imported brandy into the goblet's crystal globe. Campbell had been expanding all evening under the combined treatment of skillful flattery and strong spirits. And it had taken only a smile from Anne and a fine dinner to coax the man into good humor.

Glenkennon held the glass out to his guest. "Nothing but the best for you, my friend. Your advice has been invaluable. You understand these mad Highlanders better than any man I know. But I've something else on my mind, Percy, and I think I'd best give you a hint." He raised wide, guileless eyes to Campbell's face. "Sir Charles Howard has requested an interview with me concerning my daughter." He sipped his brandy thoughtfully. "You seem to cherish an interest in Anne, and I'd not promise her to another without determining your feelings first."

Leaning back in the velvet-cushioned chair, Campbell studied Glenkennon's carefully blank face with a satisfied smile. "I'm not so drunk as you believe, so let's have the truth of it now, m'lord. On the one hand, you're desperately in need of gold to finance this campaign against MacLean before winter, while I've gold and to spare in my coffers. I, on the other hand, want your daughter to wife, but feel you've placed an exorbitant price on the arrangement."

He paused, warming the brandy between his hands. "I might decide to meet your price, but only upon my terms." Scarcely controlling his eagerness, he raised his eyes to Glenkennon's waiting face. "May I suggest we get down to business?"

It was impossible to identify the varying shades of scarlet thread in the candlelight, even with a half-dozen candles lit. "Bess, I think we'd best wait till morning," Anne said, watching the girl squint intently over the tapestry frame.

She rose and moved to the window while Bess put the work away. She was restless and uncomfortable that night, uneasy at the way Glenkennon had watched her throughout supper. She'd not liked the continual smile he had worn or the calculating look in his cold gray eyes.

Gazing into the darkened courtyard, she wondered where Francis was at that moment. What if he had been injured during that raid...or even killed? It might be months before she heard if anything had happened!

She clasped her arms about herself and drew a deep breath. Nothing had happened, and she was being unaccountably foolish to give in to such thoughts. Francis would be with her soon. After all, there were only four more days...

A sharp knock sounded, startling her from her reverie. She glanced at Bess, and the girl rose to open the door.

Before Bess could reach it, the door swung inward. She took a hasty step back, dropping a low curtsy as Glenkennon strode through the entrance.

Anne noticed the look of triumph glittering in his dark eyes and was immediately on her guard. Not Francis... dear God, let it not be Francis!

"You may go, girl. Your mistress won't need you further tonight," Glenkennon said, jerking his head toward the door.

With a quick glance of apology toward Anne, Bess bowed herself out.

Anne faced him, her heart quickening its beat as she prepared herself for whatever news he bore.

"I'm delighted to inform you I've completed the arrangements for your marriage, my dear child," he said smoothly. "Our friend Sir Percy Campbell has requested your hand, and it's been my pleasure to accept on your behalf. I know you're as pleased with the news as I."

Anne swallowed heavily, holding her breath to steady herself at his words. It was no more than she had expected, yet the sudden announcement made her blood run cold.

Campbell moved into the doorway behind her father, lounging against the wall while his dark eyes slid over her possessively. She knew some word of acknowledgment was expected, but she couldn't force herself to speak of happiness now.

"You may congratulate yourself, my dear, on having won such an ardent bridegroom," Glenkennon continued. He exchanged a knowing look with Campbell. "Sir Percy insists upon an immediate marriage. I've assured him you've no foolish desire for a large wedding; therefore the ceremony will take place day after tomorrow."

Anne reached for the chair back for support, struggling to control her features. It was absolutely imperative that she stop them now. "Father . . . my Lord Percy, I'm conscious of the honor paid me, but I must beg the indulgence of a few days to prepare myself." She forced a smile. "Couldn't we wait a week? Even a few days and I can be ready."

"This week, next week, it makes no difference to me," Glenkennon said impatiently. "But Percy wishes the day after tomorrow to be his wedding day, and so it shall be." He looked at her strangely, a hint of amusement curling his mouth. "I suggest that after tonight you get yourself wed as quickly as possible, my dear."

Her chest ached with the effort of taking controlled breaths. She would be married to Percy before Francis could even be told. She wanted to scream her refusal, yet she knew she had no choice in the matter. Better to bide her time and make plans right away. And Francis might come—dear God, please let him come—tonight!

"The marriage contract has been drawn up and signed and all the arrangements have been agreed upon," Glenkennon continued. "You're Lady Campbell in all but name now, and that shall be taken care of in another day. I shall give you into Percy's keeping as of this hour. You're to consider yourself under his protection and make yourself obedient to his wishes from this time forth." He cast a sidelong glance at Campbell. "I'll leave the two of you now to make whatever arrangements you see fit. You'll not be disturbed further."

Anne stared at him in disbelief, cold fear chilling her heart. She could not mistake that smug leer on Campbell's face or the finality with which Glenkennon had uttered those last words. "Father, you can't mean..."

She broke off, flushing painfully. "I...I need time to accustom myself to the idea of...of marriage. I..."

He was shaking his head.

Her heart left its usual place in her chest and pounded heavily in her throat. Though the room was warm, icy needles of fear crept along her spine. "Please, Father, we must discuss this further!"

Glenkennon paused at the door, turning back upon her with indifference. "There's nothing to discuss. You'll comport yourself now in a manner befitting an obedient wife. And you may consider yourself lucky in my choice of a husband for you."

She searched his cold face desperately for any hint of affection. Did he really hate her so? "Can you really give me to this man so easily...without benefit of marriage?" she whispered.

"The space of a day or two will make little difference, and in the eyes of the world you'll be his wife, and nothing more will be known," he replied. "I've given my word to the bargain, and as such it shall stand. This isn't so unusual as you might believe, Anne," he added coldly. "As a matter of fact, I'm certain it's the way you were conceived."

His words cut through her like a hot blade, severing her breath. She no longer needed to question her mother's marriage to such a man. The door swung shut behind him with an awful finality, leaving her staring in dismay at the solid oaken panel.

"Come, Anne, 'tis not so bad as you'd have it," Campbell stated, advancing toward her across the floor. "I'm sure we shall deal together very well."

His words jerked her back to the situation at hand. She studied Campbell now with an attention he had never before inspired. He was a tall man, heavy chested with powerful arms. There was no hope of overpowering him. She must stay calm—use her head to delay him.

She licked her dry lips. She must divert him . . . if only for a few hours. "My lord, please," she entreated, lifting one hand. "You're a gentleman. I know you'll not press your suit in this manner. Allow me a few days to accustom myself to the idea of our marriage. I assure you I'll meet you as a dutiful wife in every way." She wanted to smile at him, yet her fear was so great she could only stare in wide-eyed alarm.

"Your modesty is becoming, Anne, but I've done with waiting," he said softly. His eyes slid over her eagerly. "I've your father's blessing, and he's the promise of my gold— and a goodly sum I paid for you, too. You've no need to fear I'll go back on my word. I'll take you to wife on tomorrow next." He reached for her, but she sidestepped him quickly, putting a table between them.

A flicker of annoyance crossed his face, cracking the thin veneer of polished politeness she had always seen. He raised his arms from his sides, palms up, in a gesture of submission. "You've no need to fear me, Anne," he said soothingly. "Come, sweetheart, you know me better than that." As he spoke, he moved slowly toward the table.

She glanced frantically about the room. There was nothing at hand to use as a weapon. Her eyes darted longingly toward the door. She could never reach it.

Campbell lunged forward suddenly, seizing her wrists and dragging her around the table into his embrace. He held her tightly, then lowered his head, forcing his wet, suffocating kiss against her mouth. She attempted to twist away, but his grip on her arms tightened until she cried out in pain.

As he fumbled to unfasten her gown, unreasoning panic seized her. She struggled wildly to free her hands, but there was no loosening his grip. His mouth closed over hers, insolent, punishing. Like a frightened animal, she fought him, finally biting down hard upon his lip.

Percy jerked back with an oath, one hand held to his lip where a tiny trickle of blood began forming. Before she could move, he struck her hard across the face, twisting her head around with a snap and flinging her several feet across the floor with the force of the blow. She came up short against the wall, stumbling to her knees on the hard floor.

Through the blinding clouds of pain in her head, she wondered dully if her jaw were broken. She leaned against the wall, staring at Campbell in revulsion.

There was no one to come to her aid even if she screamed for help. Nigel was on his way to England, and Charles was somewhere to the south on business for her father. Had it been planned that way all along? She wanted to cower upon the floor and weep, but the very knowledge of her helplessness gave her unexpected strength.

Campbell grinned at her, his chest heaving with the rise and fall of his uneven breathing. "I never thought you'd be such a vixen, sweetheart. You've always seemed such an obedient creature."

He moved to the door and slid the bolt into place, the noise grating loudly in the silence. Anne closed her eyes and swallowed heavily, knowing that the sound would haunt her for the rest of her life.

Drawing herself slowly to her feet, she faced Campbell with forced calm. "I would have you know," she said evenly, "that if you continue in this manner, you'll ruin for all time any hope of a cordial relationship between us. I shall never come to you willingly after this."

He laughed harshly, as if amused by her ignorance. "I don't believe you understand, Anne. Your willingness is a matter of complete indifference to me."

There was nothing else to say. She closed her eyes as he reached for her, his brutal grasp on her shoulder triggering a sharp pain that shot through her but scarcely pierced her numbed disbelief.

As he drew her against him, she thought fleetingly of Francis and of those golden moments between them that would never come again.

CHAPTER TWENTY-TWO

*A*nne stared dully at a golden ray of sunlight that crept across her window sill to brighten the shadowy room. She had lain awake all night watching the darkness fade to dawn and the dawn to morning light. She had swallowed a sea of bitter tears, wondering what trick of fate had brought her to this—the end of all her hopes, of everything.

She shifted her head against the pillow, and a throbbing pain shot through her jaw to her temple. Glancing at Campbell, she wished for the thousandth time that her hair were not caught beneath his shoulder. She had lain beside him all night, not daring to move for fear of waking him, trapped so closely she could smell his unwashed body. A wave of nausea swept her, and she drew a deep, shuddering breath.

Percy stirred beside her, and she closed her eyes, feigning sleep. She felt a slight tug at her hair as he moved. The bed creaked. He rose and crossed the room to the chamberpot. Hoping he would leave without disturbing her, she kept her eyes tightly closed, forcing herself to breathe slowly and evenly.

The rustle of clothing told her he was dressing. She willed herself to keep still, even when she heard the sound of his footsteps moving nearer. He eased himself onto the bed, his cool fingers brushing her face.

Her eyes flew open and she jerked away. God, not again —please, not again! She studied him fearfully, her gaze never leaving his face.

Percy smiled. His hand dropped from her chin to caress her naked shoulder bared above the covers. "Good morning, Anne. I trust you slept well."

She stared at him, refusing to answer.

"I'd no idea what a pleasurable evening I'd find with you, my dear." His hand slid from her shoulder toward her throat, and she flinched away instinctively.

"Come now, Anne," he continued smoothly. "We've gotten off on the wrong foot, but I can assure you you'll have no cause to regret becoming my wife. You may have whatever money can buy. Position, houses, jewels... you'll be the envy of women all over Scotland. And who knows," he added, "you may learn to enjoy my company in other ways. I'm sure you'll not force me to repeat another scene like last night."

She continued to stare at him in unblinking silence, hating him for the way he had used her—trembling lest he do so again.

He twisted his hand in her hair, drawing her head forward. "Will you, my dear?" Holding her close, he lowered his mouth to hers and kissed her possessively.

She forced herself to lie still, unresisting at his touch, though her stomach churned sickly and her gorge rose.

After a moment, Percy lifted his head, smiling in approval of her new passivity. "So you've learned something already," he said, releasing her and sitting up. "Were I not so late for a meeting with your father, I'd stay and see what else you've learned." His lips curled into a dark smile above his pointed beard. "I suppose it'll wait. After all, we've plenty of time to get to know each other."

She heard the door close behind him. The sound of his footsteps died away down the hall. Curling herself into a tight, miserable ball, she let anguish sweep over her, submerging every thought.

Lost in her own hell, she did not hear the door open and close or the sound of light footsteps crossing the floor. She started violently when a gentle hand touched her shoulder. "I waited for him to leave, mistress. I thought you'd have need of me," Bess said softly.

Anne dragged herself to a sitting position, drawing the covers across her chest to cover her nakedness. She stared dully at the rumpled blankets, unable to meet Bess's eyes. "I . . . I'd like . . ." she stammered brokenly. Her throat constricted and a wrenching sob strangled her words. She could not speak—she could not even think. Shutting her eyes tightly, she struggled to hold back the tears, but once begun, they were impossible to stop.

"You'll want a bath," Bess whispered in a choked voice. "A bath and some fresh clothing. I'll be right back. Just you sit still, mistress."

Anne nodded, attempting to wipe the fast-falling tears from her cheeks.

Bess touched her arm, sympathetic tears swimming in her luminous green eyes. "I'll order the water heated and be right back. Now don't you move."

True to her word, Bess returned almost immediately to urge Anne out of the bed and into her robe. The girl efficiently stripped the bloodied sheets from the bed and remade it with fresh linens. She picked up Anne's torn garments, folding them neatly and carrying them out with the ruined sheets to remove all traces of struggle from the room before the other servants arrived with the water.

How easily the room could be repaired, Anne thought bitterly. It looked once more as if nothing unusual had happened there. But she would never be the same.

Memories of those hours in Campbell's arms welled inside her, and she began to tremble uncontrollably. She was dirty—so dirty. Dear God, why didn't they hurry with her bath? She moved to the window and leaned against the comforting solidity of the wall, desperately clutching the stone ledge.

Footsteps sounded in the corridor, and Bess flung open the door, scolding the startled servants for their tardiness. Anne did not turn around as the steaming pails were poured into the tub. She did not want anyone else to see the ugly bruise along her jaw where Percy had struck her.

Campbell . . . her hands curled into tight fists. How she hated him! She would see him dead before he used her like that again. And her father . . . her dear father. How he must have hated her to have planned this with Percy. Francis was right.

She closed her eyes against the sudden ache. Oh, Francis . . .

For the first time in many hours she allowed herself to think of him. What a difference a day could make. They had missed happiness by so narrow a margin. Only three more days at the most until his arrival—he was probably on Ranleigh lands even then.

But it was too late. It was over between them—everything was over. She was not the woman Francis had left behind. He would not want her now, and she could not blame him. Not after the night with Campbell.

"Come, mistress. Lean on me. Oh, my dear lady, you'll feel better soon."

Bess's arm went around her, and Anne realized she was shaking. She allowed Bess to help her across the floor and into the tub. The warm water felt good, but there was no easing the hurt inside her. She took the cloth Bess handed her and began to scrub. She scrubbed with soap and water —scrubbed her whole body until her skin was raw and burning—but she could not wash away the memory of Campbell's touch.

She stared in fascinated horror at the purplish bruises on her arms. Time would erase them, but she was marked inwardly in a way that would never change. There was no going back, and the future . . .

Her mind shied away from the thought. It was too grim to consider. There was nothing even to hope for.

She drew a deep breath. Think, she had to think! There was no one to help her—no Francis MacLean to save her. If she were to escape Percy Campbell and her father, she must do it on her own. If she could only make her way north to her uncle, Ian would help her. He would get her onto a ship for England or France.

She glanced at Bess. The girl was hovering anxiously beside her. "I'm done with my bath," she said quietly. "Fetch me a fresh gown. Something with long sleeves," she added, glancing ruefully at the dark markings along one arm.

After her bath, Bess helped Anne dress in an old gown of deepest blue muslin with long concealing sleeves and a high starched ruff. Glenkennon might not like it, but at least the ruff partially concealed the ugly mark along her jaw.

When she was dressed, Bess bade her sit before the mirror. The girl gently brushed the tangles from Anne's hair, pinning up the sides with her pearl-studded combs. The caress of the brush was soothing. Anne closed her eyes, willing her mind to a merciful blankness.

The brush halted abruptly in its passage through her hair. "Oh, mistress, perhaps it's not my place to speak," Bess whispered, "but I think I know how I can get a message to Sir Francis MacLean."

Anne's eyes met Bess's in the mirror. "And why should you wish to do that?"

Bess drew a determined breath. "Perhaps I'm wrong, but I did believe there was something between you." Her fingers tightened on Anne's shoulder. "He'd help us now if he knew."

Anne smiled bitterly and shook her head. Taking the brush into her own hand, she continued the soothing strokes through her hair. "I wonder how many others knew of it, then."

"I only guessed, mistress. No one else is aware of . . ." Bess dropped her eyes, ". . . of anything as yet."

"You were right. There was something once—but Sir Percy ended that last night. I'll not endanger Francis by seeking his help now." She sighed deeply and put down the brush. "I must get out of Ranleigh tonight, Bess. If I can reach my uncle, he'll see me to safety."

Bess knelt beside her chair, gazing at Anne with wide, troubled eyes. "I'll come with you. I'll not let you go alone."

Anne shook her head. "No, Bess. My father would kill you if he discovered us—I've no doubt of that now. But there's nothing worse than what's already happened that they can do to me. I've nothing to lose."

The chapel grew cold and dim with the fall of evening. With one last whispered prayer, Anne rose from the cold stone floor. She moved slowly up the darkening aisle, smiling cynically at the twist of fate that made her thankful, for once, her father was not a pious man. She had hidden there all afternoon, knowing neither her father nor Percy Campbell would stumble upon her.

The day had turned too soon into evening, and she had made few preparations for her escape. She had tried to think of a way to get out of Ranleigh with a horse but could come up with nothing save bribing the guards with the coins Francis had given her. But that was too risky. They might decide to turn her in for an even larger sum from her father.

She would have to settle for the ruse she had used once before and slip out after sundown. The villagers who worked in the castle by day would be leaving then for their homes. Bess had promised to gather food and a suit of men's clothing. With those pitiful provisions, Anne was determined to escape and make her way north.

She slipped furtively across the courtyard in the lengthening shadows. Entering the main door, she darted quickly down the long corridor to a side stairway, hoping to make her room without meeting her father or any of his men. She had almost reached her chamber when her luck ran out, and Edmund Blake stepped from a shadowy doorway to block her path. With a low cry of alarm, Anne jumped back, ready to flee if he reached for her.

Blake glanced over his shoulder, then back to her. "Campbell and your father have been calling for you," he said in a low voice. "They've been drinking this last hour. I suggest you not return to your room."

She blinked at him, unable to believe her ears.

"I've told your maid to await you in the south tower. She's there now with a hot meal." He took her arm, guiding her quickly toward the servants' stair. His hand was hard, more muscular than it appeared. She realized that he'd never before touched her. "It's the second room on the left past the stairs. It's best you go there quickly."

She stared at him in astonishment, still unable to understand his interference on her behalf. Was there a flicker of compassion in his cold, colorless eyes? She turned and hurried up the narrow stairs and along the stale, seldom-used hallway. She had come to a pretty pass indeed if even Edmund Blake felt pity for her, she thought wryly.

Bess was waiting anxiously, a tray of food and wine on a table beside the bed. "Oh, mistress, I've been so worried!" she exclaimed, jumping to her feet at sight of Anne. "Edmund Blake's up to something, but he gave me no choice but to go along."

"It's all right, Bess," Anne said wearily, sinking down upon the edge of the dusty bed. "I don't understand it either, but I'll not be waiting to find out what he's planned."

"I stole some trews and a shirt from one of the stable boys," Bess said, pulling the wad of clothing from beneath the bed. "I've the cloak you told me to bring, and I've sewn the coins and jewels into the lining as you bade me." She held it out to Anne.

"You've done well. Did you find boots near my size?"

"I managed these from the cobbler's shop," Bess said, holding out a pair of small, worn boots for Anne's inspection. "I'm afraid I didn't do so well, though. They've a hole in the bottom. I fear they'd not yet been mended."

Anne threw her arms around the girl and hugged her tightly. "You've done perfectly, Bess," she said, releasing her and stepping back. She shook her head ruefully. "I'm only sorry to set you to such thievery."

"It's no matter." Bess sniffed and lifted eyes shining with unshed tears. "You know I'd do anything to help." She turned away and picked up a woolen cap from the bed. "I brought this, too. I thought we'd pin your hair beneath it."

Anne nodded and sat down on the bed, drawing the tray of food across the bare sacking. She ate and drank what she could force down, knowing she must hurry if she were to escape when the servants left for the village.

After the meal, she dressed silently in the rough, poorly fitting clothing, pulling the breeches tightly about her slim waist and holding them in place with a piece of rope. She pinned up her hair, then pulled the cap down low over her forehead. With the help of a loose shirt, her trim hips might pass for a boy's, but she doubted she could pass close scrutiny in the light of day. Her only hope lay in joining an honest company of travelers and buying their escort north. It was a slim chance—but better than the certainty awaiting her here.

When Anne was ready, Bess snuffed the candle, and they stood together in the darkness of the open doorway. Bess squeezed her hand, and Anne heard the girl sniff tearfully beside her. "Be sure you remember the tale we agreed on, Bess," Anne reminded her. "You must be as surprised as the rest when they find I'm gone." She frowned. "I'm afraid you may be punished for my disobedience."

"Don't you worry, mistress. I'll remember."

With one quick hug of farewell, Anne flung the cloak

over her arm. Stepping into the darkened corridor, she felt for the small dirk she had placed in her belt, then hurried toward the back stairs. Making her way down the narrow spiral to the first floor, she came out between the kitchens and the barracks. She was in a part of the castle now that was not familiar, and she hesitated in an attempt to get her bearings.

Hearing the sound of approaching footsteps, she whisked herself around the corner, peeking out just in time to see two kitchen lackeys heading down the hallway, cloaks and caps over their arms.

With a quick prayer of thanks, Anne followed, crossing the courtyard boldly several yards to their rear. As they approached the gates, she hastened her steps to arrive just behind them. The uninterested guards gave her a cursory glance. She slouched her way through the gates in imitation of the two ahead.

Passing outside, she released her long-held breath in a carefully controlled sigh. She was actually outside the walls. Escape had been as simple as walking through the gate! No one was watching for her; Glenkennon had never dreamed she would disobey him.

She smiled grimly. He had pushed her too far this time. She did not have to endure the unendurable as her mother always had. Even a woman could resist—if she had the stomach for it.

She followed her friends, as she mentally termed the two, only until she heard the sound of the double gates closing noisily behind her. Then she melted silently into the shadows beside the road.

Pausing in the darkness, she took stock of her surroundings. When her absence was discovered, the road and nearby village would be the first places Glenkennon would search. She must make her way around the loch and strike off across the meadow to the wood beyond instead of following the easier path of the road.

She stumbled around the outer wall of Ranleigh to the

darkest shadows on the western side. She noticed thankfully that the moon was naught but a slim, fingernail crescent, and even that fitful light was obscured by the scudding clouds which had moved in with the sunset.

Crouching in the blacker-than-night shadows, she drew a deep breath. The thrill of accomplishment she had felt after getting through the gate disappeared abruptly. The strange night sounds were loud and threatening, and the thought of entering the dark woodlands beyond the loch sent a shiver of fear along her spine. She whipped up her resolve, reminding herself of the reason for her flight. Better the unknown dangers of the woods than another night with Campbell.

She moved forward along the wall, feeling her way hesitantly over the uneven ground. A sprained ankle was the last thing she needed at that point. Squinting into the night, she made out the end of the western wall. She was almost there.

Before she could take another step, a rough hand shot out of the darkness, smothering her startled cry of fear and throwing her to the ground. She caught the flash of a blade just before her body slammed into the hard earth. The blow knocked the breath from her lungs, sending the world spinning around her. Pinned helplessly to the ground, she waited for the sharp thrust of the knife—but the blow didn't come.

A muffled oath sounded. Impatient hands jerked the cap from her head, loosening a strand of hair to trail betrayingly against her shoulder. Still too dazed to struggle, she found herself abruptly gathered into a hauntingly familiar embrace.

"What in God's name are you doing here, lass?" Francis whispered against her ear. "Damn, I could have killed you in the dark, thinking you one of Glenkennon's men!"

"Francis!" she clutched him convulsively, sure she must be dreaming.

"Did I hurt you? Mother of God, I . . ."

She shook her head against his chest, still struggling to get the air back into her lungs.

"God be praised." He lifted her to her feet. "Quick, lass, we must be gone! Someone may have heard." Without waiting for a reply, he drew her along beside him to the edge of the shadows cast by the high stone wall.

"What are you doing here?" he repeated, taking her in his arms as if to assure himself she was truly flesh and blood.

She pushed away, grim reality destroying the fleeting happiness she had felt in his arms. "I had to escape," she said shortly. She glanced over her shoulder into the darkness. "We must go. They may be after me any minute!"

He settled a heavy coil of rope over his left shoulder and slipped his dirk back into his belt. "Come then, lass," he whispered. "You've saved us a full day by being out here to greet me." She could hear the amusement in his voice, yet her own heart weighed even heavier in her chest. After that first rush of relief at finding herself in his arms, she had cursed the luck that had involved him in her escape. If he were brought to harm through her...

She could not finish the thought.

"We'll wait here in the shadows till the moon goes behind a cloud. Then we must run like the very devil across this meadow," he said softly. "Should the moon come out before we reach those far trees, you must drop to the ground. Tuck your head and sit as still as you can." He chuckled softly. "You'll look like one of those rocks scattered in the grass from the castle wall."

She nodded, wondering desperately how she could run over the uneven ground in her poorly fitting boots.

Francis squeezed her hand. "Let's go."

They sprinted down the hill, skirting the edge of the loch and darting across the meadow beyond. Her heart was pounding fit to burst, and her breath came in long, strangled gasps by the time they reached the cover of trees.

Francis was still breathing easily, but he paused, allowing her to collapse onto a log in an effort to catch her breath.

The knifing pain in her side slowly eased. "How . . . how did you know it was me?" she asked, finding her voice.

He laughed low. "I've yet to meet a guard that smelled so sweet, lass. If you wish to pass for a man, you must first get rid of your scented soaps. I recognized the smell at once . . . and you'd no' the feel of a man." He reached for her hand, but she rose nervously and moved away.

He took a step toward her. "Is there aught wrong, love?"

She backed away. "No . . . no. I'm fine now. But we'd best be on our way." She hated herself for the way she was treating him, yet she could not cope with her tangled emotions or the feel of his hands upon her. "I'm afraid my absence may be discovered by now," she added.

There was a long pause. "Aye, lass. We've horses waiting just ahead through these trees."

Refusing to take the hand she knew to be held out to her, Anne moved forward into the darkness. By the time she had stumbled twice and been saved a nasty fall only by dint of Francis's quick hand, she admitted her foolishness.

"You've not the way of walking out here in the dark," he said gently. "Here, take my arm and we'll get on much faster."

She reached for the comforting solidity of his muscular arm, allowing him to draw her along beside him. How he could move so confidently when the ground beneath them was swallowed up in darkness was beyond her ken.

After a short walk, he gave the low, haunting cry of a hunting owl. In a moment, the cry was answered from somewhere ahead. "It's Conall," he explained.

They headed in the direction of the sound. In a few moments a soft voice called, "Over here."

Anne waited nervously in the darkness while Francis stepped forward to speak with his friend. She was aware of them both only as slightly blacker shapes in the blackness all around, but their hushed voices carried easily.

"Our plans will have to be changed," Francis said. "I've brought her with me now."

"How, by all that's holy? You've been gone less than an hour."

"She was outside Ranleigh. I stumbled upon her in the shadows while I was making ready to scale the wall. I almost slit her throat thinking her one of Glenkennon's men."

Conall stepped forward, catching Anne's hand and lifting it to his lips in the darkness. "I'm delighted to have you with us again, lass, but why in heaven's name were you wandering about outside?"

She could feel Francis beside her, waiting tensely for an explanation. "Because tomorrow was to be my wedding day, and I'd no wish to be Percy Campbell's bride," she stated evenly. She was thankful now for the darkness; it hid her shame and the quick tears that started to her eyes.

For one frozen moment, there was silence, then Conall squeezed her fingers. "Desperate measures were obviously in order," he said smoothly. "I'm only glad we happened along. Francis, lad, you've been saying your prayers in Kirk."

"It was because of the stolen gold that Glenkennon pressed you so fast, wasn't it? He had his back to the wall, and you were an easy source of income. Christ's blood!" Francis exploded. "I never reckoned on him moving so fast. But I should have—I should have thought of it!"

He turned to Conall. "Glenkennon will be hot on our heels, so we'd best split up. I'll take Anne and head east to the usual place. You run for Camereigh as fast as your horse can take you. I should see you in a week's time if all goes well. And Conall," he added, "be sure all's in readiness. We'll soon have a fight on our hands, if I'm any judge."

Conall squeezed Anne's hand again, then disappeared into the night, leaving her standing alone in the darkness with Francis. Somewhere nearby a horse snorted and pawed the ground impatiently while the silence stretched uncomfortably between them.

"Did you have anyone to meet you out here, lass?" Francis finally asked. "A horse ... food ... anything to speed you on your way?"

She shook her head, then realized he could not see her in the dark. She cleared her throat uncomfortably. "No. I've the money you gave me sewn into my cloak ... and I had a bit of food, but I lost it when I fell. There was no time to arrange anything more."

"God's body," he swore. "What a close run thing!" He caught her shoulder and drew her against him, brushing a quick kiss against her hair. "I've no horse for you, love, since we'd not planned to take you with us tonight, but I'm sure Leven can carry the two of us easily enough."

Catching her hand, he led her to the impatient animal. "Give me your foot, and we'll be away from here before anyone's the wiser." He boosted her onto Leven's back, then swung up behind her, soothing the restless horse as it sidled nervously beneath the unusual weight.

Anne held herself stiffly in Francis's arms, refusing to relax against him. The feel of his muscular limbs about her shoulders reminded her of Campbell, and she leaned away from him.

What must he have been thinking of her strange behavior? And more to the point, how could she tell him she wished to go to the MacDonnells instead of to Camereigh with him? He'd not let her go easily. Yet she could not tell him the truth. She could not stand to see the love in his eyes turn to disgust. He loathed Percy Campbell almost as much as he hated her father. He could not love a woman who had lain with one of his bitterest enemies, even if it had been against her will.

Besides, Francis was in enough trouble without taking on the added burden of her dishonor. He would be determined to kill Campbell if he discovered the truth. She shivered, knowing Campbell and her father were probably angrily searching Ranleigh for her even then.

"Cold, love?" Francis asked softly against her ear. His lips caressed her cheek, and he moved his arms more closely about her.

Try as she might, she could not sit still beneath his caress. "No, I'm fine," she said, shifting away.

Francis thoughtfully guided Leven toward the familiar territory of Glenkennon's eastern holdings. The hue and cry would soon be up after Anne, and he had no intention of being caught with her and only one tired horse between them. They were making that night for a well-hidden shelter deep within the boundaries of Glenkennon's own land—a place the man would never think to look. He had used it several times in the past few months as a resting place between raids. After the search died down, he and Anne could strike north for Camereigh.

Anne's strange behavior was a puzzle, but he would not press her for answers. She was as tightly wound as a spring waiting to fly out in all directions. He had no wish to set her off until they had put some distance between themselves and Ranleigh, and he could give her his full attention.

But he knew something terrible had forced her into fleeing without thought of provisions or mount. He cursed himself silently for having left her at Ranleigh so long.

CHAPTER TWENTY-THREE

$\mathcal{B}$y morning, the fitful clouds of evening had ranged themselves into a heavy, low-hanging mass that obscured the colorful radiance of sunrise and gave the dawn a sullen cast. The black hopelessness of night gradually lightened until the moor and sky merged into a dismal gray blur around the weary travelers.

Anne closed her eyes and allowed her head to drop listlessly against Francis's shoulder. Sometime during the night, they had left the hills and rocky glens behind and entered a wetter, marshy lowland. The unfamiliar terrain made Anne more uneasy with each passing mile, but she was so tired she scarcely cared what became of her.

As the morning slid away, the ground became more treacherous and the plant and animal life shifted to that which made its home in the bog. Pools of dark, stagnant water shimmered with iridescent rust and orange, and a malodorous black scum grew thickly along the edges of each pool. Thorny brambles grew in profusion on the scattered patches of high ground along with a handful of scrubby, stunted trees. Anne stared at the watery wasteland in dismay, trying to ignore the maddening whine of insects and the stench of rotting vegetation that pervaded the air.

The only cheerful sight was the scattered clumps of wild

marsh marigolds blooming gaily among the thick bracken. As they passed a sunny patch, the rushes beside them thrashed wildly, and a huge frog leaped into the sluggish water beneath Leven's nose.

The startled animal shied violently, half rearing and leaping from the trail into the sticky, sucking mud. Only Francis's strong hand kept Anne in the saddle as the animal sank to his knees. It was several minutes before Francis had him calmed and back onto the narrow ridge of solid ground.

Anne clung to Leven's heavy mane, unable to relax after nearly being tossed into the fetid water. "Francis, are you sure you know where we are?" she asked, breaking the silence that had stretched between them several hours.

"Don't worry, love. I haven't brought you this far to lose you in a bog," Francis replied, his tired voice lifting in amusement. "I've followed this trail often enough, though I'd not advise you to try it alone. The bones of many a foolhardy soul lie in this stinking muck. There are places here where a mounted man can sink from sight."

Anne shivered and clung more tightly to Leven's mane, finding no difficulty in believing Francis's words.

"This whole treacherous expanse is fed by underground springs," he explained. "Even in summer it remains a bog. In winter months it's nigh impassable, though I've crossed it as late as December."

She peered with misgiving at the desolate expanse ahead. "How did you find your way through? There's no trail I can make out."

"Conall was born not far from here. He learned his way about when he was a lad, though few men know the trail."

"But I thought Conall was born at Camereigh."

He shook his head. "Conall's no more a MacLean than you for all he uses the name. His parents were murdered by the English when he was a lad. They'd have finished him off, too, but a clansman dragged him from the burning house, and they fled through this bog. Since the English could not follow, it was assumed the boy perished in the mud."

He fell silent again, as if seeing the picture of a frightened child being dragged through this wasteland. His arm tightened around her. "Since that time, we've used the trail to reach a hideaway known only to a few trusted men. Glenkennon can't follow us here, lass."

"Who holds Conall's land now?" Anne asked, suspecting the answer before Francis spoke.

"Glenkennon."

The ground gradually became firmer beneath Leven's hooves, and the brown water and strange plant life gave way to lush grass and more familiar vegetation. Small, wooded hills rose from the flat expanse of moor, and the stallion pressed forward eagerly, as if realizing his stable was near.

As they topped a sharp rise, Anne gazed down into a narrow glen where a heavy growth of trees followed a winding stream bed. Francis gave Leven his head, and the horse scrambled down the rocky slope, finally halting before a dense thicket of young birch. "We're here, lass," Francis said wearily, swinging down from the saddle.

Anne blinked in dismay. She had expected a shelter of some kind; even a cave in the hills would have been preferable to this place. Francis gestured toward the trees, and she peered into the shadowy grove. A small turf hut stood well back from the clearing, admirably concealed by the thicket. She slid from Leven's back, her legs so cramped and stiff they buckled when she hit the ground.

Francis caught her arm. "Can you stand, lass?"

She clung to the stirrup leather as the blood began to circulate painfully through her numbed extremities. "Of course."

Francis released her and strode to the door, giving a mighty heave to the plank structure to swing it in on its leather hinges. He preceded Anne into the musty gloom, ripping down the tanned animal hide that covered the open space of the single window. His action flooded the room with light and fresh air, but it did little to lift Anne's spirits.

She gazed at her dismal surroundings in consternation. A sturdy plank table stood in the center of the room with two rough, uncomfortable-looking chairs on either side. Along the wall opposite the window stood a smaller oblong table, its roughhewn surface graced by a dusty basin and an empty wooden pail. A squat, wooden chest leaned drunkenly against one wall, the long-abandoned nest of some rodent spilling from behind it.

"It's not such a bad place to hide for a few days once it's aired," Francis said, turning toward her with a smile. "We can..." The smile died abruptly, his features hardening with anger. "Who struck you?"

Anne's fingers flew to the telltale bruise along her jaw. She had forgotten it in her weariness. "No one," she said, faltering at the look of cold fury on his face. "I stumbled on the stairs and struck my head against the wall." She forced herself to smile. "I was lucky to get off with a bruise instead of a broken neck for my clumsiness."

He caught her chin, turning her face to the light and studying the mark narrowly. She wanted to pull away but knew the folly of further angering him.

"Was it Glenkennon?" he asked, barely controlling his wrath. "Did he beat you into agreeing to the wedding?"

She felt his fingers tighten and met his cold gaze nervously. She had never been able to lie to him successfully. "Please, Francis, you're hurting me," she whispered.

He dropped his hand, his eyes holding hers. "Who struck you, lass?" he repeated.

"I told you, I fell. It's as simple as that," she said, moving away from him to inspect the basin and pail with feigned interest. "If you'll bring in some water, I'll see what I can do to clean up the place."

Francis did not move. He stood in the center of the

packed dirt floor watching Anne inspect the contents of the room. She was not going to tell him anything further without a fight. Damn Glenkennon and his cowardly habit of attacking those weaker than himself! The man must have struck her. That ugly bruise was the result of no fall.

"I'm going outside to see to Leven," he said grimly. Snatching up the pail, he ducked through the low doorway without a backward glance.

Francis led the tired stallion around back of the hut to a small lean-to built for the stabling of horses. Unsaddling the big horse, he rubbed him down with a shock of twisted grass, pondering Anne's behavior all the while. She was nervous as a cat, he thought darkly. And strangest of all, she seemed afraid of him. He was used to her rapid changes of temperament, but by God, she had best learn to be honest with him!

He sighed and leaned against Leven's powerful shoulder while the stallion nuzzled playfully at his shirt. There would be time enough between them to get to the bottom of the matter, Francis thought. They would have little to do but talk as they waited out the days in that isolated place. He thought of the way Anne had looked just then with those breeches hugging her slim hips and her shirt unlaced at the throat. He grinned as a flicker of desire quivered through his body despite his weariness. Yes, there would be plenty of time between them.

Francis brought water for Leven from the stream and cut some of the lush grass growing along the bank for the animal's fodder. Having assured himself the horse was well cared for, he rinsed the pail and filled it with fresh burn water for the hut.

When he entered the doorway, Anne was busy cleaning the dust from about the place. He nodded in approval and filled the empty basin with water. "Wash up and we'll eat. I've bannocks and dried meat in that bag. There may even be a bite of cheese, if Conall didn't finish it." He rinsed his hands, then spread the meager fare on the table.

Seating himself in one of the low chairs, Francis watched appreciatively as Anne washed her hands, then splashed water on her face, rinsing away the dust and sweat of travel. Her breasts filled out her boy's shirt in the most eye-catching way, and her narrow waist looked tinier than ever with the rope catching the trews above the enticing roundness of her hips. He smiled to himself, imagining his hand soon following those curves.

Anne shoved back her sleeves and scooped the cold water onto her face again, hoping it would revive her. She needed to keep her wits about her. Francis would be wondering at the change in her behavior, and she had to come up with a plausible tale.

Wiping her wet arms against her shirt, she drew her sleeves down and moved toward the table. She seated herself in the empty chair, ignoring his frowning scrutiny. "What will we do for food once this is gone?" she asked.

"I've snares in the chest there," he said heavily. "After the meal I'll see what can be caught by the burn."

They split the food between them, washing it down with the remainder of the water he had brought in. An awkward silence settled between them, and she sent him a furtive glance. What would he do if she just blurted the truth? Francis knew Campbell; hadn't he warned her about him that day at the loch? He would realize she was not to blame. Perhaps he would even understand.

She stared miserably at her hands. He would understand all right, but no man could ever forgive or forget such an insult. Every time he looked at her, every time he touched her, he would remember what Campbell had done—and he'd never rest until the man was dead.

No, she could not tell him the truth, but she had to tell him something. He deserved to know that she could no longer wed him, that she would not be returning to Camereigh.

She cleared her throat and raised her eyes to his. "I've something to say to you, Francis."

Relief relaxed the taut muscles of his face. "Thank God, lass. You've had me half out of my wits wondering at the change in you."

She took a deep breath and plunged in. "I've decided to go to my uncle at Brise Hall. I've no desire to return to Camereigh with you." She dropped her eyes, toying nervously with the frayed cord about her waist. "I've decided I don't want to marry you after all. You may well be angry, but I've changed my mind."

His eyes narrowed in surprise, but he only folded his arms across his chest and leaned back in his chair. "I see. Then why did you run from Ranleigh if you planned to be Campbell's bride, lass?"

Her eyes flew to his. "What?"

"Do you think you can talk Glenkennon out of the plan when he comes for you?"

"He . . . he won't discover my whereabouts for months," she stammered. "By that time I'll be on my way to England—or maybe France. I hate Scotland," she finished miserably. "I want to go home!"

"Glenkennon will know your position within a fortnight at most. Would you have Ian and his family punished for harboring you?"

She stared at him in consternation. She'd not considered the consequences to the MacDonnells; she had been too busy trying to keep Francis out of the tangle.

He put his elbows on the table and leaned toward her. "You'll return to Camereigh with me as we planned," he said firmly. "I'd not serve Ian such a trick as to drop you at his gates now. Camereigh's a well-fortified stronghold that can hold out indefinitely, but Glenkennon could destroy Brise Hall in an afternoon."

He rose and moved around the table. Catching her arms, he dragged her to her feet. "What is it, Anne? Do you trust me so little you can't tell me the truth?"

His eyes were filled with warmth and understanding; his powerful hands lay gently on her shoulders. Why did he have to look so tender now, she thought unsteadily, now when he was lost to her forever?

He bent his head slowly toward hers, and a sudden longing for the warm comfort of his embrace surged inside her. Just once more, she thought desperately, closing her eyes and lifting her face shyly to his. Just once more to feel his arms about her...

His lips brushed hers, then returned for a long, pleasurable, undemanding kiss. His hands slid along her spine to the small of her back, caressing her weary muscles and drawing her comfortingly against him.

Forgetting all the throbbing pain and worry of the last two days, she melted against him. Her arms crept about his neck, her fingers tangling in his thickly curling hair.

Francis shifted his hold to mold Anne closer against him, all his senses reeling with the feel of her in his arms. He drank in the wild, hot sweetness of her kiss, his body throbbing with a desire he would soon quench. He fumbled with her shirt, his fingers finally rewarded by the feel of the silken flesh of her waist. One hand slid up to cup the outer swell of her breast, but as he touched her, she cried out and jerked away.

"Don't!" she gasped. "Don't touch me!"

"What in God's name!" He stared down at her in mingled surprise and confusion. One minute she was the sensual, willing temptress he longed to possess, and the next she was gazing at him as if she were terrified. "Anne, what is it?"

"I told you, I changed my mind. I don't want to marry you!"

"Damn it, lass!" he exploded. "You're the most changeable woman I've met in my lifetime. Is that the way you kiss a man you've no wish to wed? God's blood, I've put up with this foolishness long enough!"

"I'm not going to Camereigh with you," she choked. "You can't make me marry you."

Her words cut him to the quick. Resting his hands on

his hips, he surveyed her coldly. "You'll ride to Camereigh, Anne, for you've no other choice. But as for a wedding, I won't force you if you're dead set against it. I'll not have a reluctant wife."

His eyes narrowed and he took a step toward her. "But I'll have you, Anne. It's a thing that's been between us from the first, and you want it as much as I, despite your words just now. I'll have you with a wedding or without, lass. The choice is up to you."

Her eyes were large as saucers in the pale oval of her face. As he glared at her, they clouded with frightened tears.

"Sweet Jesus!" he swore, goaded almost beyond bearing. "Anne, for God's sake, you know me better than this!" He caught her trembling form and crushed her against him. "You know I'd not force you, sweetheart," he whispered. "Hush, hush, love. You've nothing to fear."

He held her quivering body, staring over her shoulder in perplexity. "I'll be damned if I know what you want of me, Anne. You blow hot and cold a dozen times a week, but you lie when you say you want no part of me."

Taking her arm gently, he pushed her sleeve back, exposing the ugly bruises that exactly fitted the span of a man's hand. His troubled eyes searched her face. "What of this, Anne? I saw it when you were washing. Does this have anything to do with your change of heart?"

She returned his stare bleakly. "Let me be, Francis," she whispered. "For God's sake, just let me be!"

He drew a deep breath and dropped her arm. "Very well, lass. I'll not press you further about anything. When you're ready to tell me what's troubling you, I'll be here."

Turning wearily, he crossed the floor to the rickety chest, kneeling to search its contents. "I'm going to the burn to see what can be had for dinner. We're like to get hungry if luck's not with me this afternoon."

He drew out two musty blankets and tossed them to her.

"Hang these outside to air. We'll have need of them once the evening chill comes on."

She nodded, still struggling desperately to hold back the choking tears.

"I'll be back before dark, lass. Don't fret," he said softly.

Hugging the blankets miserably to her chest, Anne watched his broad shoulders disappear through the low doorway. What she had done was unforgivable. She had encouraged him to kiss her after declaring she'd no wish to wed him. Small wonder he was angry. Francis must think her the most fickle creature alive!

She sighed heavily and shook her head. She had never been able to control her response to his touch. For a few wonderful moments, he had even made her forget Percy Campbell.

Anne walked out of the hut and flung the blankets over a low-growing birch limb, staring longingly in the direction Francis had taken. He loved her, wanted her. Would it be the same with him as it had been with Campbell?

But Francis would no longer want her if he knew the truth, she reminded herself grimly. No man would. And he must never, never know! She closed her eyes, wondering how she would endure these next few days . . . and nights.

CHAPTER TWENTY-FOUR

$\mathcal{F}$rancis moved slowly along the rushing burn, studying the bracken-choked banks for any sign of game. Hoping to catch one of the large marsh hares so plentiful in the area, he carefully set two snares. Despite his attempt to concentrate on the job at hand, his thoughts turned back to Anne, as he searched his mind for an explanation for her behavior. Not for a minute did he believe her excuse of a change of heart.

He smiled to himself. She had kissed him like the old Anne. He could still feel the warmth of her soft lips, of her arms clinging tightly about his neck. But she had torn herself from his arms when he touched her. His forehead creased in a puzzled frown. There had been genuine fear in her eyes. But what had he done?

He wandered down the stream, finally sinking his net at the foot of a narrow rapid where the clear water eddied into a quiet pool. There would be trout for dinner tonight if his luck there were as good as usual.

With the snares laid and the net carefully placed, there was little to do but wait. Francis leaned back against the rough trunk of a stunted oak, reviewing everything Anne had said, everything she had done since he had stumbled across her last night.

She had been frightened—frightened enough to flee

Ranleigh alone after dark. And she was afraid of him. He saw it in her eyes, in the way she shied away from his touch. And those marks on her face and arm . . .

The realization hit him like a powerful fist ramming into his belly and robbing him of the power of breath. Closing his eyes, he sank to his knees in the grass. "Campbell," he whispered between clenched teeth. "Mother of God, it's Campbell!"

Balling his hands into fists, he pressed them tightly against his closed lids, trying to block out the image of Anne in Campbell's arms. The bitter taste of hatred choked him, and his insides churned with disgust. Anne —his Anne—in that bastard's hands.

It was the only explanation that made sense. He drew a deep breath, fighting the unreasoning rage that consumed him. Campbell had beaten her. That would account for the ugly bruises she carried. And after raping her, he would have been assured a quick wedding. Glenkennon would have raised little outcry; he would have been delighted at the chance to demand more gold in reparation. Between the two of them Anne would have been helpless —reason enough for her foolhardy flight. And it would account for her fear—for her surprising aversion to his touch.

He struck the hard ground with his clenched fist, blaming himself for not murdering Campbell long before. He would kill the bastard now, he promised himself, enjoying the thought of driving his sword through Campbell's stiff body. Never had he felt such a consuming hatred. It sang through his veins and conjured thoughts of various slow methods by which to exact retribution before granting Campbell the deliverance of death.

But what now? Francis rocked back on his heels and stared blindly into the laughing waters of the burn. What could he do for Anne now? His heart ached for her, for the misery and fear she must have been feeling.

She had told him she could not marry him. He groaned

aloud. She must have been frightened half to death, especially after his outburst that afternoon. He was going to have to go back and . . . and what? He had no idea how to comfort her, how to erase the shame and hurt.

He stared helplessly at his fists, still clenched in his lap. He slowly uncurled his fingers and drew a steady breath. Nothing in his past wide experience had prepared him to deal with such a thing. He could not rout Anne's fear with strength or bravery. Oh, he would take care of Campbell; he would silence that sneering mouth forever. But that would not help Anne.

Dragging himself to his feet, Francis noticed for the first time how low the sun had dropped. He checked his net, taking up a large wriggling trout with little satisfaction. Despite his earlier hunger, he could not even think of trying to eat. Moving quickly up the bank, he checked his snares in the fading light. Luck had been with him, for one of the traps held a large brown hare.

He reset the trap, then walked slowly back to the hut, pausing to compose his features before ducking into the sturdy structure. He would not ask Anne any questions, would not push her in any way. She had to tell him the truth in her own time.

Anne glanced up in relief as Francis's broad-shouldered frame blocked the fading light from the narrow doorway. He tossed his catch onto the floor in the corner. "I was lucky," he said lightly. "We can cook enough meat tonight to last into tomorrow. I'll not risk lighting a fire by day. The smoke might be seen for miles."

She nodded, avoiding his searching look. "I gathered wood while you were gone. I was hoping we could have a fire."

He picked up a handful of twigs and dry moss, kneeling to arrange them on a blackened spot in the center of the floor. She watched his strong, capable hands work with the wood and flint. In a matter of moments greedy flames licked hungrily at the tiny branches.

The fire illuminated the darkening room, highlighting Francis's stiff, handsome face. He lifted inquiring blue eyes to Anne's. His quick grin flashed, though it lacked something of its old warmth. "I'll get the trout cleaned up and spitted now. It'll not take long to cook over a hot fire."

While the meat dripped juicily into the crackling flames, Francis brought in several armloads of fragrant marsh grass, dropping them on the floor in one corner of the hut. He lifted one of the blankets from the back of a chair, spreading it smoothly over the pile of grass. "I've slept on this hard-packed dirt many a night, but you'll be needin' something softer." He picked up the other blanket and tossed it down several feet away. "The dirt's good enough for me."

Anne nodded without speaking. He was going to make it easy on her after all.

They both ate hungrily from the delicate roasted flesh of the trout, leaving the hare to cook over the spit for breakfast on the morrow. Francis wished aloud for Donald and his flask of wine, teasing Anne with the memory of that other night when they had eaten over an open fire and she had fallen asleep at his feet.

She smiled, recalling her misery that night—the night that had been the unexpected beginning of her love for Francis MacLean. There had been nothing to fear from him, though she'd not known it at the time. If only they could have gone back . . .

Anne studied Francis's profile. The dancing firelight cast his strong features in relief against the shadows of the room, gilding his raven hair with golden streaks and reflecting from his eyes in dancing lights. A wistful smile curled the corners of his lips, as if he, too, were remembering.

Anne caught her breath at the wave of love and tenderness washing over her, wishing she could tell him what was in her heart. She had hurt him that afternoon, and it was the last thing she wanted. Yet the sooner she was away from Francis, the safer he would be.

Catching herself up sharply before she could succumb to the lure of self-pity, Anne bade Francis a cold good night. She closed her eyes, snuggling into the warmth of her cloak on the fragrant mattress of cut grass. In spite of her misery, she was thankful beyond measure that she was not out in that chill darkness, alone and hungry and wondering if she would ever reach the MacDonnells to the north.

"Anne." The word was a soft whisper beside her. She opened her eyes as Francis knelt and spread his own cloak over her. "Mine's larger, lass, and will easily cover you from head to toe," he explained, tucking the cloth gently about her shoulders. "It'll be cold by morning."

She raised herself on one elbow. "But you'll need it, Francis. Mine will do."

He was so close, she could feel the warmth radiating from his body. An erratic pulse beat revealingly at his throat, and his eyes gleamed down at her from the shadows. "I'm a bit too warm as it is," he said, glancing toward his unwelcoming blanket in the corner. "I'll be fine, lass. Now get to sleep." He touched her hair briefly, then moved away to his place beside the fire.

She gratefully drew his cloak beneath her chin. She doubted she would need its warmth, but the faint smell of sea and heather mingled with his own familiar scent was comforting. Her heavy lids dropped over her eyes again, and exhaustion claimed her.

Francis lay perfectly still, every muscle tense as he tried to place the sound that had awakened him. He rolled over and sat up, his hand caressing the comforting steel of his dirk. He had no idea how long he had slept, but the fire had burned down to a bed of glowing embers, providing little heat or light. Perhaps it was only the snapping coals that had aroused him.

From the corner came a low groan, and Anne mumbled

incoherently in her sleep. He frowned, listening to the torment of her dreams, wondering miserably if he should awaken her or allow her to sleep on uninterrupted.

He rose and added wood to the fire, stirring up the coals with a branch. Wide awake, he watched as Anne moved restlessly in her sleep. Suddenly, her anguished scream rent the night, sending the hair crawling along the back of his neck. He was across the floor in the space of a heartbeat, his hands on her shoulders, shaking her awake.

"Wake up, Anne. It's a dream." He caught her flailing arms and held her against his chest. "It's a dream, Anne," he repeated. "Only a dream. Wake up, sweetheart."

She struggled in his arms, fighting to push him away. "No! Don't ... don't hit me again!"

Francis closed his eyes at her words, drawing her tightly against him. "You're having a nightmare, sweetheart," he whispered against her hair. "I'm here. No one will hurt you now."

She stared at him wildly for a moment, then collapsed, shuddering against his chest. He felt the rise and fall of her breasts against him with her shallow, frightened breathing. His lips brushed her hair and his arms tightened protectively about her. "Nothing can happen to you now. I promise," he whispered reassuringly. "Whatever it was, try to forget it. It was only a dream."

She clung to him desperately, needing the warm comfort of his arms around her—needing even more the reassurance of his understanding. She had to tell him; she could not keep the horror locked inside her any longer. He still believed in her, loved her in spite of everything.

She shook her head against his chest. "No, Francis, no," she choked. "It ... it wasn't a dream." A sob convulsed her body and tears trickled from beneath her tightly closed lids. "Sir Percy ... he ..." She struggled to speak, biting her lip. "He ..." She dissolved against him as racking sobs swept her body.

Francis pressed his face against the cool silk of her hair.

"I know, love, I know what he did. But it's all right," he murmured helplessly. Holding her close, he lived the hurt she felt, defenseless against the pain that bound them together.

He had failed her, he thought darkly, feeling the bitterness of defeat for one of the few times in his life. He should have foreseen the danger. God, why hadn't he taken her away from Ranleigh weeks ago?

He kissed her forehead and her hair, tasting the salt of her tears, as he cradled her in his arms like a frightened child. "It's all right," he kept whispering, stroking her shaking shoulders, massaging the nape of her neck with gentle fingers. "It doesn't matter, love. He'll never touch you again. It's all right."

After many long, heartbreaking minutes, Anne's sobs began to subside, and she finally lay quietly against him. Francis knew—he must have guessed long before—yet he had not turned away from her in disgust. "I'm so s . . . sorry, Francis," she whimpered, struggling for breath. "I'm so very sorry."

He stroked the damp hair back from her face. She stared at him woefully from behind tear-spiked lashes, her look wrenching his heart. "Don't be foolish, love. You've nothing to be sorry for," he breathed.

His mouth traced the delicate line of her cheek to brush gently against her trembling lips. "'Tis Campbell's black soul that'll answer for the deed, though I should have known Glenkennon would offer you little protection."

"Protection?" She laughed bitterly. "Protection? It was my dear father who gave me to the man. My own father, Francis! My own flesh and blood, and he sold me to Campbell to get wages for his soldiers," she choked out. "I knew he never loved me, but I never dreamed he hated me so deeply."

Francis crushed her against him. "Glenkennon isn't your father, Anne," he said softly. "Your father died before you were ever born."

Anne stiffened abruptly and pulled away, staring at him with wide, incredulous eyes. "What did you say?"

"Glenkennon isn't your father, lass. He had your father murdered shortly after Mary MacDonnell's marriage."

She drew a deep, shaky breath. "Tell me."

"Your father was a MacKinnon, lass. The eldest son of the laird of a small clan whose land Glenkennon now holds. We crossed over part of it last night before we came to the bog."

She had stopped crying and sat so still, she might have been carved from stone. "Do you feel up to hearing it, lass?" he asked gently. "'Tis not a pretty story."

At her nod, he frowned, staring into the crackling flames. "When Glenkennon met your mother, he'd just arrived in Scotland and was eager to make a name for himself. He saw her and wanted her. And he was determined to have her, though the lass would have nothing to do with him. She'd fallen in love with Bruce MacKinnon and he with her the first time they'd clapped eyes on each other."

He glanced up. "The MacKinnons weren't a large or powerful clan, but after a time the MacDonnells gave their consent to the match, since they doted on Mary and wanted her happiness above all else. The marriage took place secretly, for by then Glenkennon had his soldiers harassing the MacKinnons.

"When Glenkennon learned of the marriage, he was beside himself with rage. He convinced the commissioners controlling young James that the Catholic MacKinnons headed a conspiracy to rescue Mary Stuart and institute a Catholic state in Scotland. Talk of conspiracy was rife then, and a plot to murder Elizabeth had been uncovered. Before the furor died down, Glenkennon talked the commissioners into issuing a writ of treason."

Francis's voice dropped. "The MacKinnons never had a chance. Glenkennon sent soldiers in the dead of night, and every building down to the lowliest peasant's hut was put to the torch. Men, women, and children were slaughtered without quarter, and only a very few managed to escape the carnage. Old Ranald MacKinnon and his two sons, Bruce and Richard, were slain defending their home, and all in the house perished save Richard's youngest son." He stared down at her. "A servant dragged Conall to safety in the marsh.

"Since the marriage hadn't been made public, Mary was still with her parents at Brise Hall, thus her life—and yours—were spared." He paused, running gentle fingers over Anne's frozen face. "You'd already been conceived, lass, though she'd told no one save her parents and my mother."

The comforting crackling of the fire and the noise of Anne's shallow breathing were the only sounds in the silence. "But how came she to marry Glenkennon?" Anne whispered. "How could she?"

"When Glenkennon learned Mary hadn't been killed, he devised a way to punish the MacDonnells even further," Francis replied grimly. "A few weeks later he kidnapped Mary. He took her to Edinburgh, and from there by ship to England before the MacDonnells could raise the clans. Once at Rosewood, he simply played a waiting game, knowing he held all the cards. By the time you were born, love, Mary was his lawful wife, and Glenkennon held his power over her till her death by threatening harm to you."

Anne sat silent, frozen in disbelief by the unexpected horror of his words. "My mother was forced to wed the man that killed her husband . . . my father," she breathed. "My God, Francis! How did she stand it all those years?"

He drew her into his arms, stroking her hair tenderly. "I don't know, lass. Before God, I don't know."

"Why didn't you tell me this before?"

"I didn't think it wise for you to know the truth while you still lived under Glenkennon's roof."

He was right. She would never have been able to hide

her hatred had she known. "So now I know the truth. Now that it's too late...too late for everything," she added bitterly.

His arms tightened about her. "It's not too late for us, Anne. I've not changed my plans one jot."

She pushed away from him and stared bleakly into the fire. "Percy Campbell ended everything between us."

"Campbell ended nothing but his own foolish life by his deed," Francis replied, "and I'll take care of that soon enough. What happened between you makes no difference in the way I feel, save that I regret not killing the bastard long ago."

"Then you don't understand what he did," she said low. Hot tears of shame began to trickle down her cheeks. "Oh God...," she choked, covering her face with her hands.

He caught her to him, stilling the trembling of her lips with his kiss and warming her shivering form with the heat of his own body. "Hush, love, it doesn't matter," he said softly, drawing her down beside him onto the blanket. He wrapped his arms about her and held her securely against him. "I love you, Anne. Nothing will ever change that."

"B...but you can't, Francis. You can't possibly want me now!"

He lifted the hair back from her face, tracing her lips with gentle fingers. "If that's what you think, you little know the way of it, sweet." He smiled, raining tender kisses on her eyelids and cheeks before moving to take her mouth, gently at first and then with an increasing ardor as her moist lips parted beneath his.

He flicked his tongue across her lips before plunging back inside her mouth to explore the soft recesses within. When she hesitantly touched her tongue to his, he drew it inside his mouth, stroking it in a way that sent warm fingers of sensation curling through her body.

He caressed the sensitive skin at the nape of her neck with one hand, while the other slid slowly along her back, molding her against his hard length in a way that suddenly reminded her of Campbell.

She pushed against him, dragging her mouth from his. "Don't, Francis . . . don't start this. I can't . . . ," she whispered.

His lips silenced her. His hands continued their languorous stroking of her neck and back while his lips lingered over hers, kissing her slowly, expertly, compelling her to open to him again.

Her heart beat unevenly, and her pulses began to hammer in her ears as the same sweet ache that always began with his touch uncurled in the pit of her stomach. She slid one hand against his throat, caressing the rough contours of his face, kneading the corded muscles at the back of his neck. She held her breath as his warm mouth moved to the hollow of her throat, his hands loosening the lacings of her shirt to give him more room.

His fingers brushed against her bare skin. She stiffened, but Francis continued his gentle fondling and the devouring kisses that made her head swim. She closed her eyes, trying hard to concentrate on the reasons she must stop him, but the feel of his mouth on hers was like some heady draught, rapidly seducing her from all reality save the pleasure of his touch.

She slid her hands beneath his shirt, stroking the rippling muscles along his back, trailing her fingers up to toy with the silken hair curling at the nape of his neck. It felt so right, lying there against him. She began to relax again.

His hands moved along her ribs beneath her shirt to cup the outer swell of her breast. His thumb brushed persuasively against one taut nipple, then returned to encircle it with increasing pressure, tearing a low groan of pleasure from her throat. His mouth left hers, trailing downward to meet his hands, his lips taking up where his fingers left off. Grasping her shoulders, he lifted her slightly to tug the linen shirt over her head.

His lips silenced the word of protest she halfheartedly

mumbled, while his fingers sought the sensitive crest of her breast once more. One hand crept downward over her back, drawing her slender hips against the rock hardness of his thighs as his mouth continued its sweet torment.

She was lost, caught up in the spiraling sensations blazing through her, wanting more—needing more. She dug her fingers into his shoulders, drawing him closer. He rolled her onto her back, leaning his weight upon her, pressing her down into the fragrant crushed grass beneath them.

Fumbling with his shirt, he sat up, slipping it over his head and tossing it halfway across the room. His body glowed richly in the firelight, the dark, curling hair shadowing his chest tapering to a thin, intriguing line along his belly. She put out a hand to trace its path, but he caught it, lifting her fingers to his lips, kissing each one before lowering his mouth to hers once more.

His mouth slanted across hers in a wildly consuming kiss, his hands moving to the small of her back, then dropping to her hips to lift her easily across his lap. His fingers stroked the velvety skin of her waist as he untied the rope belt, then struggled with the fastenings of her trews.

Suddenly, the memories of pain and humiliation at Campbell's hands flooded Anne's senses, dissolving all her pleasure at Francis's touch. Unreasoning fear surged through her, and she caught his hands, twisting frantically away from his kiss. "No, Francis, I can't," she gasped tearfully. She struggled to sit up, pushing him away as he reached for her. "I can't . . . I can't stand it again!"

He caught her wrists and held them, pressing her hands against his pounding heart. "Anne, I want you as a man wants the woman he loves," he said earnestly. "I'll not hurt you. I want you to know the pleasure that comes between a man and a woman who care about pleasing each other."

She shook her head, struggling to draw her hands from his grasp. "I already know what it's like."

"No, you don't." Unmoving, he continued to hold her. "Anne, look at me."

She ceased her struggle, slowly lifting her eyes to his.

"Listen to me, sweet. What happens between a man and a woman who love each other is a very different thing from what you've experienced. Did you enjoy Campbell's kiss?"

Her head snapped up indignantly. "Of course not!"

"Did you enjoy his touch, the feel of his arms around you?"

She shook her head, no longer resisting as he drew her chilled body against his own. "Can you tell me now you've not been enjoying my kiss, my touch?" he questioned.

She shook her head again.

"It's different, lass. You'd know that if you stopped to think." His hands slid down her back. "I'll not have you fearful of my touch because of a bastard who took you before me. It doesn't have to be that way." He drew back, his eyes searching her face. "Let me make love to you, Anne. Let me put your fears to rest once and for all."

Her clenched fists uncurled against his chest, her fingers slipping up to caress his face. "I do love you, Francis," she whispered. "I know it will be different... but... I'm afraid."

He brushed her brow with his lips, then touched her quivering mouth lightly before easing her back onto the blanket. He tugged the baggy trews over her slim hips and down her long, shapely legs, catching his breath at the beauty of her bared to his burning gaze.

Anne lay perfectly still against the blanket, her eyes closed, her head turned away from him. He drew a ragged breath, promising himself that he would make up for everything Campbell had done to her, forcing himself to control the clamoring urgings of his own body.

Drawing off his boots and the remainder of his clothing, he eased down beside her and pulled her into his arms.

"You're so very lovely, sweetheart," he whispered, "so lovely..."

He lowered his mouth to hers, his tongue gently parting her closed lips, coaxing her to respond. His mouth molded hers, seducing her to his will as his slow hands stroked her body, spreading a glowing warmth in their wake. He felt her breathing quicken, heard her intake of breath as his fingers worked their pleasurable magic across her body.

He kissed her ear, drawing his tongue along the shell of her earlobe, then moving down to nibble at the hollow of her throat. Slipping lower, his lips found her full, rosy-peaked breast. Drawing the hardened nipple within his mouth, he teased it with the gentle pressure of his lips, making her writhe with the expert teasing of his tongue.

Anne's tortured memories were no match for the physical persuasion of Francis's mouth and hands. She caught his head between her hands, holding him against her, swinging her hips instinctively against his. Her skin burned in contact with his, sending a liquid heat throbbing through her veins and making her quiver with desire.

Francis moved over her with exquisite gentleness, seeking to arouse her passion in every way he knew. He caressed the enticing fullness of her hip, tracing a burning pathway to the soft triangle of hair between her thighs.

She felt his gently probing fingers touching her, arousing her beyond anything she had ever dreamed. She gave a soft, smothered cry, certain every nerve in her body would explode if he did not end this torture soon. She clung to him, tangling her fingers in his hair, returning his inflamed kisses with all the passion she possessed. When he moved between her thighs, she pressed herself against him, knowing only the primitive urge to be a part of him.

Francis gritted his teeth against his need to make a quick end to the torture in his own loins. But he entered her slowly, beginning his rhythmic stroking only when he felt her hips lift to meet his first gentle thrust.

Anne turned beneath him, whimpering at the rising sea

of sensation threatening to burst its dam and wash over her. Nothing mattered, nothing but satisfying the building need he was creating. She dug her fingers into his skin, arching her back as he drove deeper into her, carrying her with him higher and higher until something inside her exploded with a blinding intensity that flung her over the crest of the wave of passion she was riding and whirled her into his shuddering world of pleasure on the other side.

For several minutes Anne lay motionless. As her breathing gradually steadied, she tried to gather her shattered senses. Francis still lay between her thighs. She could feel his heartbeat against her breast, his uneven breathing warm against her throat.

Without speaking, he gathered her in his arms and shifted sideways, easing his weight from her body and drawing her tightly against him. She rested her head in the curve of his shoulder, one arm flung possessively across his chest as a peaceful satisfaction spread through her.

There was nothing else in life that could equal this feeling, she thought in amazement, nothing that could even come close. She snuggled closer, moving her fingers inquisitively along the hard muscles around his ribs, exploring the contrast of the smooth texture of his skin against the rough mat of hair covering his broad chest.

Francis gave a low chuckle. "Are you ready again so soon, love? Oddsfish, you'll be the death of me." He trapped her errant fingers between his hands, lifting them to his lips to press a slow, delicious kiss against her palm.

Anne laughed delightedly, pleased with herself, her lover, the whole, wide world at that moment. "I never dreamed it would be like this," she said softly, smiling into the friendly darkness.

"I know." His hands slid over the velvety soft contours of her hip. "You've fought me tooth and nail every step of the way. But I've known this had to happen almost from the beginning."

She twisted her fingers in the hair on his chest. "But you were so hard on that first journey to Camereigh. You can't tell me you were in love with me then."

"Love had little to do with it at that point in the game," he said with a throaty chuckle. "Let's just say you were beginning to get under my skin by the time we made Camereigh." He wrapped his arms about her, crushing her tightly against him and breathing in the fragrance of her hair.

She sighed deeply as his fingers stroked the back of her head. "You made my heart do somersaults even then," she confessed. "And I wanted you to kiss me long before you did."

"But I'm such a shy lad," Francis mourned. He tangled his legs with hers, shifting his body so that Anne was suddenly beneath him. "I suppose we'd best be makin' up for lost time," he breathed, moving his hands in a way that was anything but shy.

CHAPTER TWENTY-FIVE

$\mathscr{A}$nne awoke to the lilting song of birds outside the window. Though the hut still held the cool dimness of early morning, she knew instinctively that it was late. Rolling over drowsily, she sought the warmth of Francis's body, but the place beside her was empty and cold.

She opened her eyes and sat up, clutching the blanket about her naked shoulders. Francis was gone, but he had left a single yellow flower floating gaily in the wash basin. He was somewhere close about.

Stretching slowly, Anne leaned back against the wall. What a difference a few hours could make. A day earlier, everything had seemed hopeless. She had been sure Francis wouldn't want her—that his pride would revolt at taking Campbell's leavings. Yet he had taken her to him, loving her wholly and without restraint, giving of himself so completely, he had toppled the walls she had erected between them.

And she had made him happy, she thought wonderingly, recalling the warm laughter in his voice and his tender touch as they had lain together, flushed and content in the aftermath of their lovemaking. He had taken her up from the depths of hell to a heaven she'd never imagined, and she knew she had given him happiness in return.

An invisible weight lifted from her shoulders. Her life

was beginning anew. Her childhood had been haunted by her father's rejection, and she had seen herself as unworthy—undeserving of being loved. The realization that she owed no allegiance to the man she had mistakenly called Father so many years—a man she had learned to hate—poured over her inner hurts like a healing balm.

Her eyes dropped to the blanket, and she traced a flaw in its weave. Francis had known how to ease the hurts and heal the memories. She blushed at the thought of the passion he had aroused in her, recollecting those last incredible moments when all rational thought was swept away before their hunger for each other.

Brisk footsteps suddenly sounded outside. The door swung inward, and Francis ducked through the cramped entranceway. Her heart skipped a beat as his dazzling smile lit the room.

He placed a bucket of fresh water on the chest, then straightened, crossing his arms and leaning his shoulders against the door facing. His appraising look traveled slowly from her disheveled hair to her naked shoulders, bringing a flush of embarrassment to her cheeks. "Good morning, love," he said with a lazy smile.

She drew the blanket more tightly about her shoulders, unaccountably tongue-tied after their passion in the night.

"You might at least give me a smile, lass," he teased. "'Tis expected the morning after."

She felt her face redden again, but she smiled in answer to his broad grin. "I'm afraid I don't yet know what's expected. But give me time and I'll learn."

He moved toward her, stopping to remove the hide covering from the window, sending sunlight and fresh air to flood the room. "I covered the window to keep the sun from waking you," he explained, dropping to his knees beside her. "I thought it the least I could do after keeping you awake most of the night."

"I don't think you heard me complaining, m'lord—then or now."

Francis leaned forward and kissed her, his warm lips moving over hers ever so gently as his strong fingers stroked the tangle of hair back from her face. She closed her eyes, reveling in the tenderness of his touch, his gentleness more reassuring than all the passion of the night before.

"I love you, Anne MacKinnon... and I want you for my wife as soon as may be," he murmured, cupping her face between his hands while his eyes caressed her face.

She returned his look silently, all her fears for him suddenly returning. Hadn't he told her weeks before that Glenkennon might use her to hurt him? Because of his love for her, Francis would be vulnerable, and between the two of them Glenkennon and Campbell might yet destroy him. She tore her eyes from his, wishing she could be light and self-assured, hoping her words would not stumble.

"You've no need to wed me, Francis. I don't expect it because of last night." She raised her chin, forcing herself to look at him evenly. "I've no regrets."

He released her and rocked back on his heels, struggling to control his amusement. "I'm glad of it, lass. I'd like your conscience clear tonight."

At her startled expression, he gave up the struggle, and his rich laugh echoed through the room. "God's foot, lass! Are you telling me you'll not have me? I never thought I'd have to drag my wife kicking and screaming before the Kirk."

He rolled his eyes toward the ceiling. "I've a confession to make: I lied to you yesterday. I'll have you to wife reluctant or no'. I've spent too much time and energy pursuing you to let you go now."

"You know what I mean, Francis." She dropped her eyes, her fingers nervously smoothing the blanket between them. "What will you do when Campbell talks of me... when he flaunts that night, as you know he will?"

His hand captured her fingers. "He'll never have the chance," he said abruptly.

At the sudden change in his voice, she glanced up. The laughter had fled his face, and his blue eyes were dark and hard as a frozen mountain tarn. "Campbell won't live out the fortnight, nor will any other who slanders you."

"But that's just what I don't want, Francis!" she said desperately. "I don't want you to fight him. That's why I hated to tell you." Her fingers clutched his. "Promise me you'll not go after him, Francis. Promise me!"

"I can't promise you that, lass, but I promise we'll talk of it later." He caught her face gently between his hands, forcing her to look at him.

She was acutely aware of the feel of each separate finger against her skin, of the way the tiny lines crinkled the brown skin at the corners of his eyes. She had never loved him more. Lifting her hand, she traced his hard mouth with trembling fingers. "I won't have you shamed because of me, Francis," she whispered. "I'll not wed you."

He shook his head impatiently. "You bear no shame for what happened, Anne. You were raped by a man who took you by virtue of his greater strength. God save us, it's a common enough happening! There are many women in Scotland and elsewhere who've been used against their will—and I fear the practice will continue as long as law is a matter of whoever's strongest."

She swallowed heavily, forcing herself to voice the last sickening fear that held her back. "But what if I'm with child?" she whispered, unable to look at him as she said the words.

"The child will be mine," he replied without hesitation. "You've no need to fear I'd turn you away because of that."

She closed her eyes and drew a deep breath. Francis had recognized her fear before she had given it voice.

His hands dropped to her shoulders and his words grew teasing again. "It's rare for a lass to be caught with a bairn on her first try. I'm thinkin' we'd best give you more practice."

Her eyes flew to his, which were trained on the curve of

her breast where the blanket had slipped a few inches. He brushed a knuckle across the exposed fullness, and she clutched the blanket tighter. "Hadn't you better see to Leven?" she murmured.

"I took care of him while you slept away the morning."

"What about your snares? We'll be hungry by dinner time."

"I've taken care of all my chores and have naught to do till evening but see to your pleasure," he said with a lazy grin. He bent toward her, nuzzling the delicate lobe of her ear. "Besides, I'm hungry now . . ."

"Francis, it's day!" she gasped, feeling timid and uncomfortable at the thought of making love in the glaring light.

He slid the blanket from her shoulders. She attempted to cover herself, but he caught her wrists, holding them firmly at her sides. The blanket dropped to her waist, and she blushed to the roots of her hair beneath the heat of his gaze.

"'Tis a sin to cover such beauty, lass," he whispered thickly. Leaning forward, he bent her back onto the tangle of twisted blankets and fragrant grass and kissed her until she forgot the daylight.

The days in the secret glen passed so quickly, Anne could scarcely credit the proof of her senses when each one ended. She and Francis swam together in the icy waters of the sun-dappled pool, and he taught her to fish using such makeshift implements that they both collapsed in hilarity when she actually landed a shimmering, silver trout. He taught her to use a dirk and the secret of slipping through the forest as quietly as a deer, though she knew she could never hope to emulate his skills.

She grew to welcome the coming of the velvet night when they made love beneath the stars with the cool winds caressing their heated bodies. When the weather was inclement, they drowsed together beside the fire, lying contentedly in each other's arms as they listened to the rain drip from the trees outside.

With a cheerful disregard for the discomfort of her living conditions, Anne wished the days might go on forever. The monotony of their diet and the lack of a change of clothing were a small price to pay for her happiness, for Francis was hers, body and soul. She loved the open, unguarded expression on his face, the tenderness of his hands, the way his man's body responded to her naked form.

She learned to please him in a hundred little ways, repeatedly marveling at the pleasure they brought each other. She no longer felt any hesitancy when he reached for her—just an eagerness rivaling his own, which set the flames dancing in the depths of his eyes.

In her heart she knew he would never again be hers so completely. She longed to keep him there, away from Camereigh, from duty, from the world which waited outside the protective circle of the bog to destroy them. But she knew the world would not be kept waiting forever.

It was a dreary evening of wind and wet, the icy rain reminding Francis and Anne that autumn was not far away. They had eaten a hearty dinner and made love beside the fire, finally falling asleep to the muffled sound of rain on the roof.

Francis slept lightly, as he always did, but shortly after midnight the sound of a horse whinnying in the distance set his senses on the alert. Every nerve strained as he listened for further sounds, but nothing could be heard save the steady drip of rain and the mournful sighing of the wind through the trees.

Anne lay soft and warm in his arms, sleeping deeply after their play a few hours earlier. Unable to resist the temptation, he ran his lips along the creamy expanse of her throat, breathing in her sweet scent once more before awakening her.

"Wake up, love," he whispered. "I fear we may have company." At his words she was instantly awake. She clung to him a moment, then rose and began slipping into her clothing without a sound.

Francis dressed hurriedly in his shirt and breeks, placing his dirk in his belt and picking up his sword. "I think I heard a horse, but I can't be sure," he explained, tugging on his boots. "I'd best see to it, though. You stay here and be quiet unless you hear anything unusual. If you do, slip out the window and hide in the thicket along the burn." He drew her into his arms and kissed her lightly, then slipped out the door into the night.

The sound of the rain muffled all noise of his passage as Francis moved quickly between the trees. The cold rain fell unheeded against his face, sliding down the rugged planes of his cheek to run wetly into the corners of his mouth. So attuned were his instincts to raiding in the dark wet of a Highland night, that he first felt, rather than saw, the shadowy figure crouched beside a tiny, spitting fire.

Holding his sword at the ready, he circled behind the man, moving cautiously between the ghostly, skeleton-white trunks of the shivering birches. He paused within ten feet of the intruder. "Have you a strong desire to get your throat slit, man, or have your wits simply been addled by too much whiskey?" he demanded.

Lowering his sword, Francis moved boldly into the stranger's line of vision. "I've never known you to be so careless, Donald. You should know better than to come up on me unannounced in the dark."

Donald gazed at him unmoved. "Frankly lad, I've some knowledge of your nature. I'm no' such a fool as to come upon you and the lass in the middle of the night, and me unexpected as I am. I've no wish to embarrass myself," he stated dryly.

Francis grinned and squatted down beside his friend. "I take it there's no trouble at Camereigh or you'd not be sitting out here so calmly, delicate sensibilities or no'."

"Nay, lad, there's no trouble, but it's been close on a fortnight and we'd seen naught of you." He studied Francis narrowly. "At the very least I expected you to be uncommon tired of rabbit and trout and much in need of a wee dram of spirits."

Francis rubbed his wet cheek in amazement. "Has it been that long? I've not kept track of the time."

"And is that the way of it now, lad?" Donald asked with a low chuckle. "Shall I leave you with the food and spirits and be on my way?"

Francis reached for the flask Donald raised and took a long pull of the fiery whiskey. It was a well-aged brew, and he savored the mellow warmth of the blend as he shook his head.

"No. We'd best be on our way on the morrow." He squinted into the mizzling rain. "I can see you'd the wit to bring a spare mount. Thanks be to God for that."

"Aye. Conall told me the girl had no horse." Donald paused, then cleared his throat uneasily. "How is the lass?"

"She's fine . . . now," Francis said, taking another drink. "Glenkennon attempted to force a marriage on her and Campbell was only too eager to act the bridegroom." He stared at the flask with brooding eyes. "It's my own fault," he said heavily. "I should never have left her with that devil so long."

Scowling darkly, Donald reached for the flask and took a drink. "When do we ride for Dunbarton?"

"As soon as I get Anne safely to Camereigh and you and Conall discover me a minister." Francis slapped Donald on the shoulder, a boyish smile lightening the gravity of his face. "Would you care to attend a wedding, man?"

"God help the poor lassie an she be forced to wed the likes of you. A lass like her coulda done much better, I'm thinkin'."

"More talk like that and I will send you away," Francis said with a laugh. "Come on, man, bring your food and whiskey, and let's get out of this damned rain!"

They sheltered the horses as best they could before entering the hut. Inside, there was no sign of Anne, and Francis gazed about in surprise. While Donald knelt to blow up the dying coals, he opened the door and called her name into the darkness.

After a tense moment, Anne appeared, her face and hair running wet with rain, her clothes plastered revealingly to the contours of her body. She clasped a wicked-looking dirk tightly in one shivering hand and gazed at him questioningly.

"It's only Donald, lass, come with food and spirits and a mind to keep me from mistreating you. Come inside and dry off. What in heaven's name are you doing out in the rain?"

She cast a welcoming grin at Donald before pushing past Francis into the center of the room. "I'd no wish to be caught inside if we'd been discovered," she stated calmly. "I'd prefer a cold, hungry spell in the woods any day to an evening spent with Glenkennon and his men. Besides," she continued, giving him an impudent grin, "I thought you might need some help."

She slid the dirk back into her belt with the air of one prepared to use it, smiling at Donald's incredulous expression. He must have been amazed at the changes in her, she thought wryly. Gone was the shy, teary-eyed young lady of the rustling skirts and blushing countenance. A different woman stood before him.

Francis threw back his head and laughed at his friend's shocked face. Catching up a blanket, he tossed it around Anne's shoulders. "What think you of my lass now, Donald?" he asked, turning to the man. "She's a bit of an outlaw, I'm afraid, but she might be just the thing for a good-for-nothing reiver like myself. What say you to adopting another MacLean?"

"I'm for it, lad, if you think she can be managed," Donald said with a smile. He patted a spot on the dirt floor beside him. "Here child, sit yourself down and dry out, else you'll catch your death before we get you back to Camereigh."

She squatted beside him, settling herself cross legged before the blazing fire. "Donald, I always run into you when I'm wet, cold, and dirty," she stated in an amused voice. "Have you any magic in your bag for me this time?"

"No magic, lass, but perhaps a clean shirt and some food and wine will go a ways to makin' you feel more the thing." He rummaged through his pack, finally holding up a flask triumphantly. "I brought Camereigh's best for you." His eyes slid over her teasingly. "Unless you'd prefer a stronger brew now."

"It'll take more than wet and cold to make me appreciate that vile stuff," she declared, making a face at Francis as he nursed the whiskey Donald passed.

She accepted the wine along with a goodly portion of delicious crusty bread, edging back into the shadows while she watched the two men talk.

Francis was glad to see his friend, she thought with a twinge of jealousy. He must have missed the companionship of his men. He was leaning forward slightly, his face alive with excitement as he shot Donald eager questions about Camereigh. Their talk was the foreign tongue of men—words of strategy, clan levies, and armaments figured largely in the conversation.

A dull ache began in the pit of her stomach, chilling her heart like the cold wet outside had chilled her shivering body. She was losing him . . . losing him to a world where she could never follow.

She rose dispiritedly and made her way to the pile of blankets where they had so recently made love. Turning away from the men, she closed her eyes, scolding herself miserably for her foolishness.

Hadn't she warned herself this wouldn't last? Francis would never belong to her, or to anyone, she reminded herself firmly. He would never be content to sit idly beside his hearth, counting his herds and planning his harvests.

Like the wind in a high gale, life with him would be wild and stormy, and she would be swept along on whatever course he determined. He was a man she could never possess, though he possessed her heart and soul.

"Did we put you to sleep with our talk, sweet?" Francis called. He moved across the floor to her side, kneeling to tuck the blanket beneath her chin.

"No. Donald's wine just made me sleepy." She could not see his expression in the shadows, yet she knew he was smiling. It was amazing how she no longer needed to see him to know what he was thinking. The touch of his hand, a change in the rugged timbre of his voice were enough.

He bent and brushed her lips with his own. "Then sleep well, for tomorrow we ride for Camereigh." His hand caressed her forehead, lingering along her cheek. "I'm sorry to be leaving so soon, lass," he whispered. "Donald will never know how unwelcome he is."

His fingers traced the smile on her face. "I promise we'll have more time together later," he added quietly. "Just the two of us."

She smiled to herself in the darkness, warm and alive again because of his words. So Francis was not anxious to return either. She fell asleep to the soothing sound of rain dripping from the trees and the low-voiced conversation of the two men.

CHAPTER TWENTY-SIX

$\mathscr{T}$he fiery dawn was just unfurling its brave banner across the heavens as the travelers left the shadowy glen. Anne paused on the rocky slope, turning for one last glimpse of the dark birch thicket and the dancing silver burn winding like a ribbon through the whispering shadows. She had been happy there, though she had known the magic could not last.

She struggled to shake off the strange foreboding that had settled over her at thought of leaving the glen. A hundred dangers waited outside, not the least among them Glenkennon and Percy Campbell. Would they snatch away her new life before it was even begun?

She had known little security in her nineteen years, and past experience had not taught her to trust any kind fate to see to the ordering of her life. Yet with Francis, anything seemed possible. With him she was ready to fight for the second chance at happiness that life so unexpectedly offered.

The journey to Camereigh was a long one, the riders traveling back trails and steep, seldom-used passes through the line of jagged mountains rearing about them. At night they camped near glassy blue lochs hidden away in the curve of the hills where nothing moved but the wind, and the only sound was the lonely cry of an occasional bird.

They saw no sign of Glenkennon's men, a circumstance Donald explained with a sly grin. "The search is concentrated west near the coast," he said. "The lass has been sighted there once or twice, so I've heard."

By the afternoon of the fourth day the soaring stone towers of Camereigh came into view. Reining in her mount, Anne stared in amazement. Scores of men and horses milled in confusion on the meadow below the castle, the unfamiliar plaids and pleated kilts of a half-dozen clans making a dazzling splash of color against the vivid green of the grass and the brooding gray of stone walls.

At sight of the MacLean laird, the piper struck up an air, the plaintive wail sending a chill along Anne's spine. The men pressed forward eagerly. "A MacLean," they shouted, in the age-old cry of Francis's clan.

Following Francis, Anne turned into the throng. A rough veteran jogged along on foot beside her mare. He threw her a wink and shouted hoarsely, "A MacKinnon."

Another voice took up his words and then another, until the cry echoed deafeningly from several hundred throats. Francis leaned toward her. "I can see Conall's hand in this. The men were waitin' for the sight of you."

She gazed dubiously at the men, smiling and jostling each other as they crowded closer to see her. They shouted the rallying cry of her clan, a treasonous cry forbidden a score of years. Suddenly her heart skipped a beat. She was not one of the hated English—she was a MacKinnon!

The wild skirl of the pipes echoed through her blood, sending it racing hotly along her veins. She rose in her stirrups, jerking the hat from her head and waving it exuberantly at the surging tide of fighting men around them.

The roar of approval was deafening. "A MacKinnon . . . a MacLean! A MacKinnon . . . a MacLean," they chanted as the three threaded their way into Camereigh's narrow gates.

Once inside the courtyard, Francis caught Anne from her horse, swinging her about in a dizzying circle. He set her on her feet and gave her a hearty kiss, much to the shouted approval of his men. Breathless and laughing, she pushed away and gazed around her.

Conall vaulted lightly down the stairs. "How did you like your welcome, lass?"

She laughed up at him. "It's one I'll not forget... cousin."

His face split into a wide, delighted grin. "'Tis pleased I am to welcome you into the family... though it's a different connection I'd be seeking with so comely a lass." He gave Francis a wink. "When you find yourself outdone with this lad, you've but to send me word. I'll be happy to show you the ways of a true gentleman."

"Why, I thank you sir," she returned. "I'll remember your words, but I find I've not yet a complaint to make."

"And that's a kinder answer than any you deserve, Conall MacKinnon," Francis put in. "Though we may stand condemned for this day's treason, at least I'll no' be havin' to claim your red head as one of my MacLeans. 'Tis a thought that's dear to me indeed."

"And have you three frightened the pur child to death with yer rough talk?"

Anne swung toward the door at the sound of Kate's dour voice, pleased beyond measure at the sight of the smile transforming the woman's sturdy countenance. "Welcome back, Anne MacKinnon," Kate said softly.

"Thank you, Kate. It's good to be back."

In her usual brusque manner, Kate took charge of the situation at once. "You'll be comin' along with me now. I've a hot bath steamin' upstairs and some fresh...," she cast a disparaging glance at Anne, "...and more seemly clothing laid out."

She hustled Anne inside. "You'll be havin' yer same room. Oh, and I saved the gowns we'd made for you. 'Twas not beyond reason we'd have you back again, I was thinkin'."

The three men watched as the women disappeared.

Conall put a hand on Francis's arm. "I've ale drawn inside. You can wash the dust from your throat while I give you an account of what's gone forward here."

"I recognized Glengarry's men and near three score MacPhearsons. Is Robbie arrived?"

"Aye, the MacPhearson's here, but he rode out this morning with Sir Allan MacGregor," Conall replied. They entered the hall, and he poured three tankards of ale. "Walter MacLeod and his men are camped two miles from here and Euan Grant with his clansmen at Cairndonagh. Oh, and Colen's sent word. He's organizing the northern clans and will be here in a few days." He took a deep drink, gazing at Francis mischievously. "'Tis such a gathering as hasn't been seen in many a year... and I've been hard pressed to give an excuse for your continued absence, lad."

Francis smiled ruefully. "I didn't mean to leave it in your hands so long, Conall, but all's in order. Now if I can discover a man of the Kirk, all will be done." He frowned. "I'd have Anne well married before Glenkennon arrives. We could prove Bruce MacKinnon as her sire, but I fear she'd be made Glenkennon's ward should he lay hands on her."

"I'm ahead of you there, Francis," Conall put in with a grin. "Anticipating the need, I've nosed out a churchman and sent riders. He should be here in another day or two. After all, I must see to my cousin's welfare now."

Francis laughed and shook his head. "God's foot, Conall! How will I survive with you for a kinsman?"

"Very well, God willing."

"When do we ride for Dunbarton, Francis?" Donald asked bluntly.

Francis sobered at once, the laughter dying from his eyes. "The day after my wedding." He put down his empty tankard. "Conall, I'll have you see to things a few more days. Donald and I must ride to Dunbarton. We've a score to settle with Campbell."

Conall emptied his tankard and set it carefully on the table beside the others. "Well, you'll not find the bastard this side of hell." His eyes lifted to Francis's face, meeting his friend's questioning stare evenly. "Someone's been before you with a debt to settle."

"What?"

"Charles Randall picked a fight with the dog and slew him in Campbell's own hall. Word reached us here two days ago." Conall dropped his eyes discreetly. "No one's certain the nature of the quarrel. Some say 'twas cards, others that a lady was involved." Steady gray eyes lifted to smoldering blue ones. "I, for one, favor the cards—'tis well known the man cheated like a knave."

"Damn that hot-tempered fool! He couldn't leave it to me . . ." Francis drew a deep breath, clenching one fist against the table. "Aye, 'twas most likely the cards," he said heavily after a moment. He glanced up. "Was Charles hurt?"

"Not seriously in any event. He rode back to Ranleigh and kicked up the devil's own rumpus with the earl."

A mocking smile twisted Francis's lips. "It sounds as if Glenkennon's empire is crumbling around him—Anne gone, Charles in open rebellion, Campbell dead. Faith, the man must be beside himself. What I wouldn't give to see his face!"

"You'll see it soon enough," Donald reminded him. "And though young Charles cheated you of a grudge match, Ian for one will be glad his nephew has a bit of proper feeling to his credit."

"Aye, the lad's a game one," Francis remarked. "Ian has no need to blush for the boy."

Anne did not see Francis again until dinner brought them together that evening. As servants passed the steaming platters of food, he drew her to stand beside him, casually announcing their plans to wed. The resulting shouts of approval were deafening, and so many toasts had to be acknowledged, Anne feared she would be drunk before she could manage any dinner.

The meal passed with an ease she had dared not hope for, the men treating her with a gentle gallantry that made her comfortable at once. No one mentioned her relationship to Glenkennon; she wondered if Francis had forbidden it. Conall and the handsome young MacPhearson laird fought good-naturedly over the right to pour her wine, while from across the table the older Walter Mac-Leod entertained her with stories of her father and the MacKinnon clan.

Excusing herself after the meal, she left the men to talk more comfortably of weapons and war. Francis promised to come to her, but to her impatient heart it seemed hours before his step sounded in the corridor.

"Sweet Jesu, I thought I'd never get away!" Francis said, striding impatiently through the doorway. He drew her into his arms and kissed her at once, his hands sliding down her back to mold her against him.

His kiss sent her head spinning, and the feel of his arms drew the breath from her lungs. It had been days since they had been alone together. Her fingers curled tightly against the rigid muscles of his shoulders; her lips moved eagerly against his own.

All too soon the kiss ended, leaving her shaken and wanting more. Ducking her head against Francis's chest, Anne marveled at her feelings. What had come over her these last few days? It seemed Francis had but to touch her and the very bones of her body turned to water. She knew too well the heights to which he could take her now, and she stepped away from him quickly before she could be further bewitched by his touch.

"I'd at least a couple of reasons for wanting to see you tonight, lass," Francis teased, "but now I can think of but one. I'm loath to be parted from you another night—I'll have Kate move your things into my room now."

Her eyes flew to his. "No, Francis, please . . . not before these lords."

He raised one dark eyebrow in surprise. "I'm not much of one for patience, lass, and I'm loath to exhaust what little I have awaiting a minister. Nor will I play a ridiculous game slipping back and forth from your room in my own house. I'm no' such a hypocrite," he added coolly.

"But Francis, it's just a night or two at most." She colored slightly. "It's . . . it's difficult for me, too, but you must see how it is. Those men, your friends, treated me tonight with all the respect due a lady. God knows I've little enough honor left, but I'd not have them turn my name into that of a whore."

Francis shifted uncomfortably before her steady gaze. She was right. God knew she was right, though his body ached for the physical aspects of her love. He'd never been one to worry over much about the rigid doctrines of the Kirk—he'd even been openly contemptuous of some of the dour, canting Presbyterian ministers who stopped at Camereigh. Yet he could not openly flaunt Anne as his mistress before these lairds.

Closing his eyes, he took a deep breath. "Very well. Remain here till the minister speaks over us—but God grant he rides a fast horse!"

Anne smiled. "Thank you, Francis. It'll not be long, I'll warrant."

Francis moved to the empty fireplace, staring broodingly at the cold ashes behind the grate. "There was something else I wanted to tell you, lass," he said, frowning. "Campbell will not trouble us further. He's dead."

"Thank God!" she whispered fervently. Her mind flew back to the last time she had seen Campbell, when he had left her with a sneering promise to return. He'd never touch her again . . . never! "How did it happen?"

"Your brother slew him in a fight before several witnesses—apparently before he could say aught of you, lass.

No one knows the cause of the quarrel, but Charles put it about Campbell was cheating him at cards."

Anne's fingers clutched the bedcurtains anxiously. "Was Charles hurt?"

"No." He glanced up. "The lad must have learned the truth somehow."

"Bess would have told him if she had the chance. I only hope she didn't endanger herself by revealing what she knew."

Francis clenched his fist along the carved stone mantel. "I wish Charles hadn't been so quick with his sword. I've lived these last days for the thought of sending Campbell to hell!"

Anne rose and moved to his side, placing a hand on his sleeve. "Well, I'm glad it's over. I was afraid, Francis; I was so afraid they'd destroy you. I even wondered if Glenkennon had planned the whole thing to trick you out of Camereigh."

He covered her hand with his, bending to press a kiss against her forehead. "You'll not be rid of me so easily, lass."

Straightening, he glanced at the door with a heavy sigh. "I suppose I'd best be gone now if you don't wish me to remain the night." He smiled slightly, touching her cheek with his hand. "Try to get some sleep, lass. Kate'll have you up with the dawn to see to our guests. From what Conall tells me, we've more people than space."

He let himself out into the hallway, quickly traversing the distance to his room. It had been nigh on to a week since he had made love to Anne, and the hot throbbing of his blood reminded him all too sharply of his need. He glared at his great empty bed, loathing the sudden confinement of his chamber. He was too restless for sleep. With a muttered oath, he spun on his heel and strode out the door, jerking it shut with a satisfying slam that echoed down the corridor.

Hurrying down the central stair, he moved past the entrance to the hall with long deliberate strides. Conall and Robbie MacPhearson were still drinking and dicing at a table beside the door. He swept by without a word.

Seeing Francis stride by, Conall sprang up in alarm. "What's to do?" he called.

"Nothing!" Francis snapped back.

"God's foot! Where are you going in such a pelter then?" Conall called, following him down the corridor.

"For a dip in the sea . . . if it's anything to you."

Conall blinked at him in stunned surprise, then doubled up with laughter as understanding dawned.

Swearing furiously, Francis strode out the door and across the courtyard, Conall's raucous laughter following him into the night. He moved quickly out the gates and through the sleeping camp outside, damning his friend and all women everywhere.

By morning Francis's good humor was largely restored, and he rose and breakfasted before dawn on a haunch of venison and a loaf of crusty bread from the night before. There was much to be done, but first he would talk to Conall. There was one matter still troubling his peace.

He found his friend asleep in his bedchamber. "Roll out lad, I've need of you," he called, entering the room.

Conall groaned and pulled the pillow over his head. "Softly, Francis, for God's sake. Must you shout fit to wake the dead?"

Francis chuckled. "Don't tell me you tried to best Robbie with the dice last night. He can drink any man under the table. All you'll get is a sore head and an empty purse for your trouble."

Conall's muffled groan sounded from beneath the pillow. "My thanks for the warning. You're a few hours late."

Francis moved to the wash basin and picked up the pitcher. Returning to Conall's bedside, he jerked the pillow from his grasp and trickled the cold water into his face.

"The devil take you, Francis!" Conall spluttered, sitting up with a gasp. "You'll pay for that!"

Francis tossed his friend a towel, then settled himself on the bed. "Do you want the rest of this over your head? Now sit up, lad, and listen. I must be off to the MacGregor camp on the hour, but I'll speak with you first."

Conall stared at him, suddenly alert. "Is anything amiss?"

Francis shook his head. "No more than usual. There's something troubling me, though, and I'd have your word on it before I ride out."

Conall towelled his face and leaned back, waiting.

"We both know Glenkennon's a canny devil, and he realizes we've men enough to make a fight," Francis began. "I've no doubt we'll make a good showing if Glenkennon fights fair. Trouble is, he's never been known to. He might as easily have hired assassins in the wood as not."

The two exchanged troubled glances. "If anything should happen to me, I want your word you'll get Anne to France. Once she's there, we've friends who'll protect her."

Conall began to protest, but Francis cut him short. "I've sent men to ready a ship. It'll be waiting on Dornoch Firth at that spit of beach we've used before. Swear to me now, you'll take her and ride like the devil for Dornoch the moment you see things turn for the worse."

"Let Donald take her to France," Conall said, leaning forward. "If Glenkennon brings you down, he'll not live out the day, though I crawl back from hell to see him dead!"

"Donald's a bit too old for my lass, don't you think?" Francis asked, his lips quirking into a smile his eyes did not share. "I'm asking you to do it. Would you refuse me, Conall? You know as well as I Anne would be better dead than to fall into Glenkennon's hands now. It's a thought that keeps me awake nights."

Conall sighed heavily. "God rot the man! If that's what

you want, I'll swear it. I've followed your orders too long now to say nay to anything you ask."

Francis smiled and rose to his feet. "I'd not ask this particular favor of anyone but you, lad," he said softly. "I'll have Donald put together a heavy purse and some provisions to be kept in readiness. You'll be able to ride at a moment's notice."

The two gazed at each other solemnly, then Conall's cocky grin materialized. He leaned back, grasping the pillow to his naked chest. "I believe you're getting cold feet at the idea of a wedding and would seek any way out," he teased.

"Not a chance! And I'll find you such a wench to lead you a pretty dance once this turn up with Glenkennon is done."

Anne leaned her cheek against the cool window glass in the empty parlor, wondering if she would see Francis before evening. He had been gone by the time Kate awakened her, and she had been so busy since, she did not even know if he had been back to Camereigh.

A weary sigh escaped her. She thought she knew the ways of running a large household, but Kate was amazing. All morning, Anne had watched in awe as Kate directed the army of servants about the endless tasks at Camereigh. No job was too large or too small for Kate's investigation. She even checked the supply of grouse and red deer the morning shooters brought in, helping cook decide what supplies must be pulled from their own larders to augment the fresh meat. The stores had to be husbanded carefully to see the Macleans through the coming siege and the winter that would come hard on its heels.

Already there was more of a nip in the morning air, though the warm sun of midday drove all thoughts of winter from the mind. Autumn in the Highlands would be brief—a glorious riot of color blazing red across the moors and gleaming every shade of gold in the forests of sheltered glens. Those achingly beautiful images would be painted again and again across the hills and in the shivering waters of the mountain tarns until the harsh winds of winter sent the last quaking leaf to its death on the frozen ground.

But what would winter's icy breath bring for Anne? These next few weeks would mark a turning point in the lives of all at Camereigh. Glenkennon would come, and Francis and Conall would go out to fight him—of that much she was certain. She pressed her hands against her eyes, wishing she could see the future.

Francis had warned her they might have to flee, even if the tide of battle were with them. The MacLeans would face the wrath of Jamie Stuart for daring to lift arms against his authority in Scotland. Francis could be declared a traitor and forced to leave Camereigh forever. But they would be together, she reminded herself. She'd never allow him to send her away again.

The noise and bustle of an arriving party of horsemen drew her attention to the courtyard. Perhaps it was the Camerons! Francis had said they'd be there any day. She searched excitedly among the arrivals for Janet, longing for the companionship of Francis's sister.

Her eager search was poorly rewarded. As she studied the little band, the hood of one woman's light traveling cloak fell back, revealing the exquisite profile of Elizabeth Macintyre.

Anne groaned aloud. Of all the people she least wanted to see! Turning, she flew to the stairs, calling for Kate. The woman appeared, huffing and puffing as she rounded the corner from the direction of the kitchens.

"The Macintyres have arrived!" Anne stated breathlessly, her heart pounding unaccountably in her throat.

"Well, is that any cause to be shriekin' about the castle, child? I thought Lord Randall hisself to be at our door from the sound of ye."

"But Elizabeth is with them," Anne said, gripping the wooden railing of the stairs.

"Seein' as how the lass is Sir Alsdair's daughter and him one with us, 'twas to be expected," Kate said with a penetrating look at Anne. "Certainly you knew she'd be stayin' here until the trouble's over."

Anne gazed sheepishly at her hands. "I suppose I didn't think. Of course, she should be here."

There was a flicker of understanding in the look Kate directed at her. "Sir Francis not bein' at home and none other fitted to act hostess, 'tis your place to do the honors of the house. Pull yourself up, child, and welcome our guests."

"She'll be furious," Anne stated with a wry smile, deciding Kate understood the situation very well.

"Aye, there's like to be fireworks afore the day's over," Kate said with a twinkle in her gray eyes. "But I've never seen a MacKinnon who'd run from a fight. Now come down, lass. I'll be behind you."

Anne hurried down the stairs, reaching the door just as it was thrown open by servants from the hall. As the travelers entered, Anne found herself face to face with an astonished Elizabeth.

"You!" the woman hissed softly, her brilliant hazel eyes narrowing at sight of her rival. "What does a Randall at Camereigh in these times?"

Anne's cheeks flamed with brilliant spots of color. She longed to tell Elizabeth exactly why she was there, but Kate stepped between them.

"I'll just take your wraps now. We've food and drink in the hall and Mistress Anne will be seein' to your comfort," Kate said, giving Anne a long look.

Recovering both her poise and her manners in the same instant, Anne made herself known to Elizabeth's mother and invited the group into the hall. Lady Macintyre was a frail, faded image of her daughter. It was easy to see where the girl got her looks. It was also easy to see where the petulant beauty got her disposition, Anne discovered, as Lady Macintyre disdainfully declined the offer of refreshments and insisted on being shown her room at once.

By the time Anne had seen the women to their chambers, Elizabeth had recovered from her surprise. "I'm sure you understand my astonishment at seeing you, Mistress Randall," she said with a throaty laugh. "Does Francis think to stop Glenkennon again by using you . . ." She gazed at Anne slyly, ". . . or are you making yourself useful in other ways?"

"I'm trying to help in whatever way I can," Anne remarked. "Poor Kate has her hands full seeing to things with Camereigh in such an uproar."

"You know what I mean," Elizabeth said sharply. "Let's end this pretense. What are you doing here?"

Anne met Elizabeth's look evenly. "I'm here because Francis and I are to be wed, Elizabeth. You may make what you will of that."

Elizabeth's pale face went red with fury. "I don't believe it! It's me he wants. He's shown me every time he had the chance."

"Perhaps he has . . . but it's me he asked." Anne moved toward the door, eager to be away from the look of hatred on the woman's face.

"I'd not be so sure if I were you," Elizabeth said, her confident voice stopping Anne just as she reached for the door. "A man may change his mind . . . even on the eve of his wedding."

Anne turned. "Don't fool yourself, Elizabeth. You don't know Francis as well as you think." She drew the door shut behind her with a prayer that her words were true.

CHAPTER TWENTY-SEVEN

*A*nne didn't believe Elizabeth's words for a minute. No, she assured herself, the haughty beauty didn't trouble her at all. She stared into the mirror, anxiously surveying her reflection. The new gown of deep green satin Kate had hemmed that morning fit her trim figure becomingly, and she had washed her hair earlier, then brushed it till it gleamed. Now the shining mass hung down her shoulders with no adornment but a simple black ribbon. The style might not be fashionable, but Francis preferred it that way.

With one last reassuring glance in the smoky glass, she hurried down the hall to the laird's room where Francis had asked her to meet him before dinner. As she opened the door, he rose to his feet, a smile lighting his dark face. "Ah, lass, I've just had welcome news. The minister should reach us by midday... what say you to becoming Lady MacLean on the morrow?"

She blinked in surprise. The next day her wedding day? "Oh, Francis, tomorrow would be wonderful!" she exclaimed, stepping into his ready embrace. She felt his arms tighten about her and his lips brush her hair. The tiny knot in the pit of her stomach dissolved. There was nothing to fear from Elizabeth. She had been a fool to let the woman's words cause her a moment's disquiet. "I only wish we could wait for Janet and the MacDonnells," she said, drawing away from him. "Do you think they'll be here in time?"

"I hope so, lass, but we dare not wait. Glenkennon and his men marched north out of Ranleigh yesterday afternoon."

His words shattered her happiness, sending her contentment splintering about her like fragments of broken glass. Glenkennon was on the march.

"He's coming here . . . now?"

"Well, he'll not be here tomorrow, lass," Francis said lightly. "It'll take five to six days with an army any size. He's in no mind to push his men to exhaustion and have them fall panting at our feet. He'll take his time and hope to arrive with men fresh and eager to fight."

"So he's coming. I'd hoped . . ." She broke off, unable to finish the sentence.

"You knew this day would come, Anne," Francis said softly. "This fight's been brewing a good twenty years. Don't fear, love. We're ready. And tomorrow you'll be my wife," he added, touching her cheek gently. "Of that much I'm certain . . . though afterward it'll be as God wills."

"He can't will the victory to anyone as evil as Glenkennon," she whispered.

Francis laughed. "I'd no' presume to speak for Him, but I've arranged to see you taken care of no matter the outcome."

She stared up at him in consternation. "Francis, don't you dare even think of sending me away! You'll think Glenkennon's wrath that of a child compared to mine if you try anything so foolish as you did last spring!"

"I'll not send you away," he replied. He caught her throat with gentle hands, pressing his thumb against her throbbing pulse. "I've no life apart from you," he whispered, taking her lips in a long kiss.

After a moment, he raised his head, his eyes holding hers reassuringly. "Don't fear, lass," he repeated. "With all the Highlands roused against him, Glenkennon doesn't stand a chance. He's lost, Anne. He doesn't know it yet, but he's lost."

His gaze suddenly shifted from her face, traveling slowly over her to take in the significance of the new dress. The deep blue of his eyes went warm with knowing laughter. "If I'm not mistaken, lass, that's a new gown. You and Kate have been busy, it seems." Taking her hand, he spun her around before him. "But I'd best keep you away from Robbie at dinner tonight . . . the MacPhearson's ever had an eye for green."

He took her arm, and they walked together down the stairs and into the crowded hall. Seating her beside him at the laird's table, he gave the hovering servants a quick nod for the meal to begin. All about Anne the conversation was of the coming English, the men laughing and making bets upon what hour Glenkennon's men would turn tail and run. It seemed that she alone in all that large company failed to view the coming battle with any degree of eagerness; she alone dreaded the hour when Glenkennon and his men would appear outside the gates.

When the meal was over, Francis rose to his feet and calmly began explaining the events set in motion by that message from Ranleigh. Under cover of sunset, all the sheep and all but a few of Camereigh's cattle were being driven deep into the mountains.

The last of the harvest had been gathered, a tribute to Francis's planning, when as far back as spring he had insisted on an early planting. The gamble had paid off. The late frosts hadn't come, and the storehouses were swollen with the most plentiful harvest Camereigh had ever seen. What little remained in the fields would be systematically destroyed. Francis had already given the order to burn the fields and storehouses of his crofters. His people were busy firing their lands even then.

The forests and moorland surrounding Camereigh would be hunted to exhaustion, so no red deer or grouse or even any lowly hares might be found to feed Glenkennon's men.

His army would be forced to keep up a long and expensive supply train through the hostile mountains where trained raiders already waited in readiness to harry the train and keep supplies from reaching their destination.

As Francis ended his recital, a breathless silence held the room. Laughing, confident faces had gone serious at his words. Reaching down, he clasped Anne's hand, drawing her to her feet beside him. "And I've word a man of the Kirk, Charles Dorton by name, will reach us tomorrow. Since none of you," he gazed pointedly at Robbie MacPhearson, "have been able to convince my lass of the folly of becoming my wife, you're invited to my wedding tomorrow afternoon." A deafening round of cheers went up and the serious moment passed as Francis had meant it to.

Nearly an hour later, Francis and Anne broke away from their well wishers. Francis accompanied her upstairs, but Anne was too restless at thought of Glenkennon's coming for sleep. "Could we walk a while tonight?" she asked softly.

Francis chuckled. "Does the idea of threading your way through close on six hundred unruly clansmen appeal to you, lass?" He grinned down at her. "Now I think on it, I did promise you another walk on the beach some months back."

She smiled, remembering the warm feel of sand between her toes and the crystal image she held of his naked body outlined against the backdrop of crashing seas. "That's a promise I'll hold you to."

He leaned his arm against the door, bending toward her. "A walk on the beach is out of the question tonight, but mayhap a turn on the battlements will answer, lass."

She nodded. "I've a need to feel the wind."

They climbed the twisting narrow stairs of the eastern tower, finally stepping out onto the battlements to the surprise of the men patrolling there. The perpetual sea breeze immediately made itself felt, billowing Anne's skirts against her legs and sweeping her hair across her face.

Though the wind was steady from the sea, they could smell the acrid odor of smoke rising from the burning crofts to the east. The night sky glowed a hideous crimson, and the occasional flicker of dancing flames could be seen in the distance.

"Is there danger it will spread?" Anne asked, gazing in horrified fascination as the eerie colors shifted across the dark heavens.

Francis's grip on her arm tightened so convulsively, she winced. "No," he said harshly. "The danger is that not enough will burn. Christ's blood! That it should come to this!"

She pressed her cheek against his shoulder, realizing how it hurt him to watch his lands burn. His arm went around her and they stood beside the wall silently drawing strength from each other as the sentries noiselessly paced out their watch.

When they returned to her chamber, Francis poured two glasses of wine. "To our wedding day," he said solemnly, lifting his glass toward her, "and to all the tomorrows we'll share, lass."

She nodded, wondering at his words. Francis was no different from any other man. Only a keen wit and a stronger sword arm than most had enabled him to triumph over his enemies. No magic protected him. Base treachery or sheer strength of numbers might still bring him low.

She took the glass he held out, swallowing the wine quickly in the hope it would ease the tightness in her throat. Might their hours together already be numbered . . . and how many had she foolishly wasted?

Her fingers tightened about the stem of her glass and she tossed off its contents in one long draught. Placing a hand upon the brown velvet of Francis's doublet, she leaned toward him, her eyes dark and burning with urgency. "Stay with me tonight."

Francis set his glass down in haste, its contents spilling over the side, staining the lace tablecloth a bright, spreading red. His only answer was to catch her to him in a deep, compelling kiss.

Anne and Francis were married the next afternoon before as many friends as could be squeezed into the hall. Much to Anne's disappointment, neither the Camerons nor the MacDonnells had arrived, but Francis would not hear of waiting longer.

Despite the expected siege, the kitchens of Camereigh turned out such a feast as overwhelmed Anne's imagination, and the wine and ale hauled from the cellars seemed enough to drown them all. With the cheerful music of the pipes and the laughter and bawdy jesting of their guests, it was easy to forget the future in determined merrymaking of the present.

The evening quickly spun itself out, and Anne made ready to leave the hall, honoring Lady MacPhearson and two MacGregor women with a request to attend her. She entered Francis's candlelit bedchamber, grateful for the quiet of the room after the noisy din of the crowded hall. Kate had readied the chamber, lighting perfumed tapers and turning back the sheets on the great bed.

"Here, lass," Kate said, stepping forward out of the shadows. She held out a gown of finest lawn, so sheer it seemed made of clinging cobwebs instead of cloth and thread. "I've been busy at it since you came back to us," she said, more gently than Anne had ever heard her speak. "I'd not have you wed without a proper covering to come to your husband in. 'Twould be bad luck."

Anne caught the gown against her, running her fingers along the carefully sewn lace trim of the bodice. Every stitch had been set with care and love. She bent to kiss Kate's weathered cheek, tears sparkling in her eyes. "Thank you, Kate. It's beautiful," she whispered, blinking rapidly. "God knows we need no bad luck now."

Kate suffered one quick hug, then turned away. "You'd best be into it and wastin' no time," she remarked, her voice returning to its usual gruff tone. "The lads below are no' so into the cups, they'll be long in followin' ye."

With Lady MacGregor's help, Anne slipped out of the gold silk dress she had worn for her wedding day. Stepping carefully into the gown, she watched as Kate hung the dress away, remembering the other evening she had worn it, when Francis had first kissed her. So much had happened since then...

Kate suddenly put a finger to her lips. "Listen! They be comin'."

The rough laughter of half-drunken men sounded down the hallway, the off-key notes of a ribald song raised above the din. As they listened, the noise grew louder, the footsteps finally halting outside the door.

All at once, Anne's courage deserted her. She rose and fled behind the velvet curtains of Francis's great bed, shivering a little with a sudden, ridiculous nervousness. The door swung open and the room was filled to bursting with laughing, shouting men. Francis was half dragged, half carried into the room and dropped, unceremoniously, on the floor.

"Lass, you must show yourself if we're to have a moment's peace," Francis called, laughing.

Anne drew aside the curtains and leaned out, thankful the side of the bed remained in shadow. Blushing furiously, she slid her bare feet over the side and rose gracefully to stand before them. The loud talk ebbed to a murmur. Then a low voice muttered from the back of the room, "Damn the shadows, lads—what we need is more light!"

"There'll be no more candles lit here," Kate said, bustling forward. "I'll not have you great fools goggling at the child." She gave Conall a push toward the door. "Out with you; can you no' see you're not needed here?"

Francis put an arm around Kate's shoulder, drawing her against him and dropping a kiss onto her graying head.

"Kate's right. Out, everyone, or I'll take my sword to you. No, Robbie, you've had your look. Now be gone!" Enlisting Conall's aid, Francis hustled everyone from the room, locking the door firmly behind the last departing guest.

Slowly he turned to Anne, light and shadow playing over his rugged countenance like the brush of an artist. "You may come all the way out now, Lady MacLean," he commanded softly. "I'd like to see if marriage makes a difference in a lass."

Anne stepped from the shadows, the lovely gown a gossamer shimmer that did little to hide the beauty of the body beneath. "As you see, m'lord, I'm not dressed to receive guests." She heard Francis's sharp intake of breath, watching with quickened heartbeat as his eyes slid slowly over her.

"Kate made the gown," she volunteered when he made no effort to speak.

"Kate's determined to help provide Camereigh with an heir."

Her own blood began to burn with the heat of his perusal. "Then you like it," she said, turning in a slow circle.

"Aye, though the garment has little to do with what I like."

She stood before him, unmoving, while his right hand began a slow journey down the back of her neck and along her spine, caressing the soft swell of one hip then moving up along her side, passing lightly over her breast to cup her chin. A slow trembling began deep inside her at his touch, and waves of increasing warmth rippled from the path of his exploring fingers.

With one curiously shaky hand, she began unlacing his shirt, finally tugging it from his shoulders and dropping it to the floor. Stepping closer, she laid her face against the warm flesh of his chest, marveling at the swift, steady beat of his heart beneath her cheek. The beat quickened as her hands dropped to the lacings of his breeches. Her fingers brushed against the taut muscles of his thighs, quickly sending his breeches to join the rest of his fine garments on the floor.

With a groan, Francis gathered her into his arms, his mouth moving over hers with an urgency that sent her senses cartwheeling against restraint. Her lips parted eagerly for the bold stroking of his tongue, her entire body responding to the feel of him against her. Her arms dropped from his shoulders to the rippling muscles of his back then lower to caress the soft skin of his buttocks, drawing him against her in an attempt to hurry the fulfillment of the urgent need she was beginning to feel.

But Francis was in no mood to hurry. The unexpected tryst the previous night had taken the edge off his hunger, and he meant to enjoy his wedding night to the fullest of every pleasurable second. He moved against her, teasing her with the promise of his body, his mouth dropping to the hollow of her throat, while his hands ranged with expert thoroughness over every sensitive curve.

The sheer cloth of the gown was no hindrance. He pressed her against him, his obvious desire quickening hers, his fingers expertly teasing the hardened nipples thrusting impatiently against the confining lace of her gown.

He stepped back unexpectedly. "Not so fast, lass," he murmured, holding her away from him. Releasing her shoulders, he moved across the room to pour two glasses of wine from the crystal decanter on the sidetable.

Anne stared at him in disbelief, her own senses clamoring for fulfillment. "Francis . . . what are you doing?"

Without a trace of self-consciousness, he turned, holding out a brimming glass. "I'm having wine, love. Won't you join me?"

His eyes gleamed at her in amusement over the rim of his glass. Moving forward suspiciously, she took the glass.

"Shall we sit a while, Lady MacLean?" he inquired, taking her arm and drawing her with him toward a chair.

In spite of her amazement, Anne couldn't restrain a giggle. The sight of Francis in all his naked splendor behaving as if he were coolly entertaining guests in the parlor was too much for her.

He sank into a chair beside the fireplace, pulling her onto his lap and settling her against his chest. His fingers stole up her back beneath her hair, massaging the stiffness from the muscles of her neck. Pushing away the golden mass, his lips traced the route of his fingers, then lifted to find her eager mouth.

Her warm lips parted beneath his, luring him into her. She tried to shift sideways, but his arm tightened about her waist to hold her motionless. His right hand slipped beneath her gown, stroking upward in long, slow movements along her thigh while she steeled herself against the shivering pleasure of his fingers. "I'm not sure what you're up to, m'lord, but I tell you I like it," she whispered against his ear.

He gave a throaty chuckle, shifting her in his arms so she reclined, half facing him. "I'm enjoying my wedding night, sweet Anne," he replied. "As my father told me years ago, 'Making love's like the brewing of whiskey—the longer it takes, the finer the blend.'"

She could see the tiny pinpoints of light dancing in his eyes as he bent his head to kiss her again. She buried her fingers in his hair, clinging passionately to him as he brought her to the edge of reason with his skillful hands and teasing mouth.

Finally he, too, had had enough of that exquisite torture. Slipping his hands beneath her knees, he scooped her up into his arms, striding quickly across the room to deposit her on her knees in his great bed.

With an impatient movement of his hands, he had the gown from her. Seizing her wrist, he drew her down beside him, measuring his powerful length against her aching body. He threaded his fingers through her hair, his mouth seeking hers hungrily as he shifted her beneath him, finally unleashing the passion he had held in check while bringing hers to a peak to match his own.

In the aftermath of lovemaking, they lay together, limbs entwined, a pleasurable languor ebbing through their bodies. Anne felt the reassuring thud of his heart against her breast and the even rise and fall of his chest with his breathing. For a moment she thought he slept, then he shifted out of her arms and got up.

She rose on one elbow, watching him move about the room extinguishing the candles. The light of the dying fire danced across his bronze body and caught the deep scarlet of the velvet bed curtains, making them glow like spilled blood. She shook her head at the thought; she would allow no dark imaginings tonight.

Returning to the bed, he slipped beneath the sheets, drawing her into the curve of his shoulder. "Faith, if I'd known making love to a wife to be so pleasurable, I'd have taken up the practice long ago."

"Poor man," Anne mourned with mock sympathy. "What a miserable time you've had with naught but mistresses to keep you company. Such a burden you've borne all these years." She shook her head. "And such a cheerful face you've managed to put on it, too. I'm sure no one suspected your unhappiness."

"Aye," he said dolefully. "No one knows the misery of a man without a wife. Why, I didn't even realize it myself till now."

"Your misery is legend, Francis MacLean," she retorted, flouncing out of his arms.

He laughed and drew her down beside him. "You're not jealous of my past, are you, love?" he questioned softly. "I promise there's no reason to be."

The words of Elizabeth Macintyre echoed through her mind. Had he ever lain with her? Touched her with his knowing hands?

The flicker of jealousy died a quick death. For whatever reason, Francis had chosen her for his wife. His past did not matter any more than hers, and she needed no reassurance other than his word.

Sighing happily, she relaxed against him. "No, my love . . . only of our future."

But at Ranleigh, the future was a thing of dread, the present scarcely to be endured. Bess cowered in one ill-smelling corner of her cell. The darkness about her was a palpable thing, a damp, malevolent blanket of despair effectively smothering every spark of hope. She wondered desperately how long it would take her to go mad in the unrelenting blackness of the dungeons far below the castle walls.

Something rustled in the vermin-ridden straw nearby, and she stumbled a few steps away. Rats! Dear God, she had always hated the things! Now she could not see them; she could only hear their high-pitched cries and the scrabble of their tiny claws across the stone floor of her cell.

She put a hand over her mouth to hold in the scream building inside her. She knew that if she lost her hold on herself, if she screamed just once, she would not stop. She would go on and on, like the poor wretch she had heard days earlier. The screaming had continued for hours—then it had ended as abruptly as it had begun.

She took a deep breath to calm herself. Charles Randall would help her; he had promised she would come to no harm for aiding his sister. He had left Ranleigh immediately after she told him about Campbell, but surely he would be returning soon. The young lord was not one to give his word lightly, even to a serving maid. He would come, she promised herself; he had to.

And what of her dear mistress—where was she? Had she truly escaped Glenkennon and Sir Percy? The thought steadied her. If her stubborn silence had bought her lady a few days lead, it was well worth it. She would tell Lord Glenkennon nothing, even though the bastard left her there forever.

From far away, she heard the slamming of an iron door. The tramp of several pairs of booted feet sounded heavily in the corridor outside, pausing before her cell. Her heart began to pound with excitement. Charles Randall—he hadn't forgotten!

The door creaked open and a blazing pine torch was thrust into her cell, momentarily blinding her. "Here's the wench now, Godfrey," a harsh voice remarked.

A rough hand grasped her arm, sending her to her knees. "My lord Glenkennon's done with waitin', girl. He'll have the answers he wants, or you'll be wishin' fer death long before I grant it."

"But I know nothing save what I've told him!" she gasped, blinking up at a dark, bearded man in the blinding glare of the torch. "I can't give him any answers unless I make them up!"

"Then say yer prayers if you be knowin' any," he said with an ugly laugh. Jerking her to her feet, he flung her ahead of him out the narrow door of the cell. "I'll take her from here, Thomas," he said over his shoulder. "And I doubt you'll be seein' the wench again. She doesn't look enough to stand up to much."

Bess darted a quick glance down the shadowy hallway, wondering if she dared make a break from the man. If Charles had not returned, this man would surely kill her!

As if reading her thoughts, the tall soldier grabbed her arm. "Don't even think it, girl! I've not the patience fer a tussle tonight," he snarled. "Now come along. My lord's awaitin' upstairs."

Bess followed the man up the steep, spiraling dungeon stairs, her heart hammering so loudly in her ears she could scarcely think. What could she say; what story could she give Glenkennon that he would not immediately know for a lie?

They traveled a maze of dark, intersecting hallways, climbing several more sets of stairs until the soldier stopped short, so unexpectedly she stumbled into his broad back. Taking a key from his belt, he unlocked a wooden door and thrust it open. The cool rush of the night wind touched her face with the fresh scent of dewy grass and damp heather. Above her head a thousand stars glimmered across the dark heavens, winking in and out of the racing clouds.

"Come, lass," the man said low. "We've a scant half hour before a guard'll be posted on this side of the wall. I've rope here to see us over the battlements and two good mounts waiting just beyond the loch. Have you the stomach for it?"

Bess stared at him in amazement. "But aren't you Glenkennon's man?"

He shook his head. "Only for such time as was necessary."

"Then y . . . you're not going to k . . . kill me?" she stammered, still trying to gather her scattered wits.

His teeth flashed white against the dark of his bushy beard. "I'm no' the man to mistreat so comely a lass," he whispered. "Besides, I've my orders. Your mistress has need of you at Camereigh, lass. Now let's away before these bastards discover the trick."

CHAPTER TWENTY-EIGHT

$\mathcal{T}$he following day dawned with a bustle of activity no one could have predicted. Anne hurried down the corridor, intent on finding Kate. The MacDonnells had finally arrived, but one of the maids had foolishly given the room set aside for Anne's uncle to Euan Grant and there was no space left in the comfortable east wing save the rooms prepared for the Camerons. Rearranging guests would be a great deal of trouble, but Anne was determined her uncle would not sleep in the far north barracks.

Rounding the corner before the stairway, she paused in surprise at sight of a boy some eight or ten years of age halfway to the first landing. Seeing her, another lad, several years senior to the first, halted on the bottom step. "Your pardon, mistress, I don't believe we've met. I'm sure I'd have remembered," he remarked, staring up at her with a disturbingly familiar smile.

Before Anne could speak, there was a commotion in the hallway, and Francis walked in with a tall, auburn-haired man. Taking in the situation at a glance, Francis strode to the foot of the stairs, an unholy gleam of mischief shining in his eyes. "Come down, lass, and meet the gentlemen I exchanged you for last spring. My nephews, Will, here and Evan." He nodded up the stairs. "And this is Jamie Cameron. Gentlemen, may I present Anne MacKinnon MacLean, late of Ranleigh... now my wife."

There was a moment of stunned silence. Will's handsome face stained a dark, angry red, and Evan stared up at her, blue eyes round as saucers. Anne gazed at them in dismay. This was not the way she had hoped to be introduced to the Camerons.

"Francis, how could you?" Janet demanded, suddenly sailing around the corner with Kate trailing in her wake. "To be wed without waiting for your own sister! I'll never forgive you," she scolded, brushing past him and heading up the stairs toward Anne.

Anne started down the steps, and the two met and embraced halfway. "Anne, this is wonderful! Now I have a sister." Janet threw her grinning brother an exasperated glare. "Francis, you know I've waited years to see you wed. Could you not have waited one more day?"

Francis leaned an elbow on the carved newel post. "I thought it best to get the thing accomplished before Lord Robert joined us for the ceremony. But I'd be happy to do it over if you like."

Jamie Cameron moved to the foot of the stairs and sent Anne an engaging smile. "Come down, lass, so I can give you a proper welcome to the family."

Anne studied his face uncertainly, searching for any sign of hostility. She had dreaded this meeting with the Cameron men, knowing they had reason for hating Glenkennon.

As she descended the last few stairs, Jamie smiled encouragingly and reached up to take her arm. "So you're the lass that's caused all this uproar," he teased. "Forgive the inspection, but I'd a lively curiosity to meet the woman our Francis couldn't live without. Welcome to the family, indeed!"

The words and the look that went with them gave Anne a warm feeling of acceptance. "I'm sure, 'twas the other way around, sir," she said with a shy smile.

Young Evan presented himself then, bowing formally over her hand as an older man would do, but shooting questions at her with the honest straightforwardness of childhood. Only Will remained aloof. In the excitement of getting acquainted, no one noticed him edging away from the group.

Feeling the draw of his gaze, Anne turned, catching the animosity that blazed in his eyes before he looked away. She took a hesitant step toward him. "William, I'm pleased to meet you at last. Francis has spoken of you and Evan so often I feel I know you."

"Well, I've no claim to knowing you, but I've had the pleasure of meeting your father." He eyed her contemptuously. "I can't believe Francis has been so taken in."

"Will! Keep a civil tongue in your head, boy!" Francis snapped.

"Well, it's true! She's Glenkennon's daughter, and if the rest of you have forgotten our stay with the earl, I haven't. I'd sooner see you dead than married to one of his blood!" Will snarled.

Francis scowled and started toward him, but Anne caught his arm. "Francis, don't! I understand how he feels. I expected it from all your family."

She turned to the boy. "You've bitter memories of the man you call my father, Will, but they can be nothing compared to my own. You were in his power only a few weeks, but I've lived with it all my life." She returned his glare with a steady look. "You can tell me nothing of his cruelty. I know it far better than you."

The boy's eyes shifted uncertainly before her searching look. For a moment, no one spoke, then Anne turned to Kate as though nothing unusual had occurred. "Kate, would you show the Camerons to the rooms we've readied? I'm sure they'd like to get settled this afternoon." Her gaze swept the group. "If you'll excuse me now, I must find space for my uncle."

Giving Janet a warning look, Anne gathered up her

skirts and moved down the corridor. She had expected this—oh, yes, she had expected this and much worse treatment from Francis's friends and family. But she would show them, she vowed. She would show them she was nothing like Glenkennon.

A short time later, Janet Cameron found Anne busy in one of the upstairs bedchambers. Drawing the door closed behind her, she moved quickly across the floor. "Oh, Anne . . . I'm so sorry about what happened!"

Anne shook her head. "Hush, Janet. 'Tis nothing to me."

Janet studied Anne's face. "Yes, it is," she said softly. Taking Anne's arm, she led her toward a pair of chairs flanking the fireplace. "Sit with me, Anne. I'd like to explain something," she said, settling into a chair.

"Will's worshiped Francis ever since he was old enough to tumble about and pull himself up by my brother's boot tops," she began slowly. "Seeing Francis give his love and loyalty to any woman would have been hard for the boy, but in normal times, he'd have had a chance to get used to the idea. This was just so sudden, so unexpected, he's had no time to adjust."

"And Francis has betrayed him by falling in love with his enemy," Anne remarked bitterly.

Janet nodded. "That beating he took, those weeks in a dungeon cell changed him. He's not yet a man with a man's understanding, but he's learned a man's hate." She clasped her hands together anxiously. "It's so difficult to stand by and watch him struggle with it, Anne. It's Francis he's always turned to, even when he couldn't talk to Jamie or me . . . yet now he feels betrayed. I know he'll understand once everything's been explained . . . once he's had time to think."

"I hope so. I've no wish to cause a rift between Francis and his family," Anne replied. Her troubled eyes lifted to Janet's face. "And how do you and Jamie feel about our marriage?" she asked, holding her breath.

"Very pleased," Janet said promptly. "I've no doubt you're the woman to make my brother happy. After you left here last spring, the change in him was incredible. I worried about him so. It was as if nothing mattered to him anymore."

Anne dropped her eyes, staring into the fire. It was a time she could not yet bring herself to discuss. The pain was still too close beneath the surface, the scars not yet healed. "The summer was a difficult time," she said.

Janet chuckled unexpectedly. "Of course, I'd an inkling what Francis intended when he arrived at our gates and demanded my mother's necklace. Those rubies have been worn by the bride of every MacLean laird for generations. I was but keeping them till Francis found himself a wife."

"And I actually threatened to sell them," Anne gasped, looking up. "Francis was so impossible at first, and I was so angry, I—"

She broke off, staring at Janet in horror.

Janet began to laugh. "Oh, Anne, I can't wait to hear everything! I know you must see to your uncle now, but first thing in the morning, you and I are going to have a long talk."

The next day's dawn made a poor showing, muffled as it was by dark, rolling clouds, which swept along before a cold, driving wind out of the northwest. Rain slashed against the leaded windows, its driving beat the only sound in the laird's room save the crackling of the flames in the great fireplace.

Francis drummed his fingers restlessly upon the arm of his chair, longing to ride out into the teeth of the storm. He was tired of the press of people about him and the endless frustration of waiting for Glenkennon. Just this morning, he'd had word that the earl's army was still three day's march to the south. It was reported that the men were moving slowly, and morale was not good. Two deserters had been shot at a river crossing, their bodies hung from the gnarled limbs of a stunted oak to serve a grim warning to others of like mind. "Damn," Francis muttered. He was ready to have the thing done!

An insistent knock brought his head up with a jerk. Christ, couldn't a man have a moment alone in his own house? "Come in," he snapped, scowling at the offending portal.

The door swung open, and William Cameron stepped over the threshold. "I've been looking all over for you," he said stiffly. "I'd have speech with you, sir."

"You've found me. Say your piece, if you must."

Will moved to stand before the desk, his lips pressed into a stubborn line. "You've not spoken to me since yesterday, sir. Your displeasure is obvious." He took a deep breath. "This is your house—I've no desire to remain if you wish me to leave."

Francis leaned against the chair back, his dark face impassive as he studied his nephew. The boy was obviously struggling to maintain his dignity. "Leave? No, I don't wish you to leave. We'll need every able-bodied fighting man these next few days." He picked up a pen and toyed with it a moment. "I didn't speak to you last night because Anne didn't wish it. She was afraid I'd rip the insolent tongue from your head if you provoked me again." His piercing eyes lifted to Will's closed face. "I didn't give you the thrashing you deserved yesterday only because she would have been distressed."

Will's blue eyes flashed fire and his fists clenched tightly against his thighs. "My father's already given me a tongue-lashing. You've no right!"

"I've every right," Francis rejoined coldly. "As you pointed out, this is my house."

Will drew a deep breath. "I didn't come here to fight with you." He moved to the window and stared miserably out into the rain-drenched courtyard. "I don't remember ever being at outs with you, Francis. I . . . I don't care for it."

"Nor do I."

Will shot a sideways glance at him, then returned to his study of the courtyard. "You must . . . care for her a great deal," he said in a tight voice. "I never thought to see the day you'd turn your back on your family and imperil your clan because you were besotted with a pretty face."

"Is that what you think I've done?"

Will whirled to face him. "Can't you see this is all one of Glenkennon's plots? He gambled on you becoming enamored enough of the girl to bring her into your confidence. Don't you find it strange he dangled her under your nose here for weeks? That he let you into Ranleigh with such ease, then out again without mishap? Francis, she could be betraying us even now! God's blood, she's his daughter!"

The pen snapped between Francis's fingers, and he threw it away disgustedly. Rising from his seat, he leaned toward Will, his cold, blue eyes speaking his anger. "If you were any other man, you'd be facing a length of steel now, lad."

Will stiffened, but his gaze didn't waver. "I know that, sir, but it had to be said. And I'll have you know I'm not the only one at Camereigh asking questions about your bride."

Francis's heavy brows rose contemptuously. "Who else here calls my wife an enemy?"

"There are others," Will stated vaguely.

"I said who, boy? Has the MacPhearson complained to you? Has Euan Grant whispered this ugly tale in your ear in confidence?" he scoffed.

Will turned and stared disconsolately out the streaming window. "No, sir."

"Then let me tell you what I think, Will. You've been listening to the lies of a jealous woman," Francis said quietly. "Elizabeth Macintyre has been spreading those tales since she arrived at Camereigh. No one else has listened, recognizing her words for what they are. But I'm sure she's pleased to have discovered a way to hurt me through you. That's what she wants, you know."

He paused, but Will did not turn around. He sighed heavily. "Anne is not Glenkennon's daughter, Will. She was born of the legal union of Bruce MacKinnon and Mary MacDonnell. Until a few days ago, none knew the story save Conall, Ian, Donald and myself. You may apply to any of them for the particulars since you think me too 'besotted' to know the truth."

"If you say it's true, I'll believe it," Will murmured without turning around. "I've no need to ask the others."

Francis nodded in satisfaction. "Even if Anne were a Randall, I'd not question her loyalties, Will. The easy time Conall and I had inside Ranleigh was not so untroubled as you believe. Anne risked a great deal to warn me when my life was in danger. She's always thought of my safety and happiness before her own. There are many reasons I could give for my belief in her," he added, "but frankly, lad, it's none of your business. Glenkennon's used her as a pawn in his struggle for power. If you knew all, you'd realize she's more reason to hate the man than you and I together."

The room was silent save for the slow patter of raindrops from the rapidly dwindling storm. "I suppose I've been a fool," Will said hollowly. "But Mistress Macintyre was so convincing. She made me believe she was afraid for you, and . . . and I was, too." He turned sheepishly to Francis. "And I was ready to believe anything against a Randall."

Francis rose and moved to Will's side. "There's not a man alive who's not believed the lies of a beautiful woman, Will. Let it be a lesson to you, lad." He shook his head and sighed. "It's partly my fault for allowing her venom to flow unchecked. I've refrained from doing what's necessary out of respect for poor Alsdair, but the time's come to end the woman's vicious lies."

Will gazed up at him in surprise. "Can you do that, sir?"

Francis tousled the boy's hair affectionately, but his voice was grim. "Aye, I can do it."

Anne clutched the heavy ledgers to her chest as she hurried down the hallway. Donald had given her the books to take to Francis when he had brought the welcome news. Glenkennon was experiencing such bad luck it would be days yet before he could reach Camereigh. Her mind leaped ahead. Perhaps the trouble was so severe that he would be forced to turn back. The snows of winter would soon be upon them, making campaigning impossible. Then it would be spring before he could mount another assault, and anything could happen by spring.

Rounding the corner, she ran straight into William Cameron, their collision scattering the ledgers to the floor in all directions.

Will steadied her and stepped back, clearing his throat uncomfortably. "I . . . I beg your pardon, m'lady. I trust you're not hurt."

"Not at all," Anne said, recovering herself. "I'm justly served for paying no attention to my direction."

Will bent and began gathering the books without meeting her eyes. "These are heavy. Could I carry them for you?"

Anne smiled at his stiff, self-conscious manner. "No. I thank you for the offer, but I'm only going as far as the library. Donald asked me to take them to Francis."

He placed the books in her arms. "You'll find him in the laird's room then, not the library." His eyes lifted to hers, and he smiled ruefully. "And I believe you'll find him in a better mood than that of last night." For a moment he looked as if he wished to say more, then with a graceful bow he was gone down the hall.

Anne stared at his retreating back, wondering what his courtesy betokened. Francis had been hurt by the rift with his nephew, she knew, though he had refused to discuss it with her. Janet had assured her the boy would come around. She hoped he had.

Upon reaching the laird's room, she turned the latch and went in. At the sound, Francis glanced up, a welcoming smile smoothing the worried furrows from his brow. He rose and took the ledgers from her.

"Donald had to ride to Cairndonagh. He asked me to bring you these," she explained. Her eyes lifted to his hopefully. "Francis, is it true? Donald said Glenkennon's men have turned against him, and that they're still days from here. Do you think they'll have to turn back?"

He brushed a kiss against her brow. "I doubt that, love, but it's no secret that the more trouble they have, the better for us." He drew up a chair for her, then lounged back onto the desk. "Tell me what you've been about this morning."

"I've had a long visit with Janet," Anne said, sitting down. "She insisted on knowing all about our courtship." She chuckled and shook her head. "I'm so glad she's pleased with our marriage. I've never had a sister before, and I've missed having a woman to talk to since Mother died. There's been no one save Bess." She stared down at her fingers unhappily, twisting them together in her lap. "And I don't even know what became of her after I left Ranleigh."

"Well, you might ask her that when she arrives," Francis said, grinning.

She stared up at him in surprise. "What?"

"If all's gone according to plan, she should be on her way here by now. My people have kept an eye on the lass. They'd orders to snatch her away at the first opportunity."

"Oh, Francis, you've no idea how worried I've been about her!"

He raised one dark eyebrow. "Don't I, though? You've mentioned her at least a dozen times a day since we returned."

She threw him a grateful look. "I didn't mean to trouble

you with it. I know you've many important matters on your mind."

He shook his head. "The lass helped you through a difficult time. I'd not leave her friendless to weather Glenkennon's wrath."

Anne rose and walked to the window, throwing it open to allow the cool, damp air to rush inside. So Bess was safe; she might even be somewhere nearby.

Anne gazed up at the sky. It had stopped raining, but the heavy mists still swirled about the castle battlements, obscuring them from sight.

She leaned her elbows upon the casement, inhaling the damp smell of wet moorland and heather, suddenly longing to be outside in the wind. "Couldn't we ride out this morning?" she asked, glancing back at Francis. "Not far . . . just down the beach and back. I've not been outside the walls since we arrived, and once the English come it could be months before we have the chance again. Surely there'd be no danger with Glenkennon so far away."

Francis smiled indulgently. "Aye, I'll take you for a ride, lass. It's what I've been wantin' all morning myself. Go change. I'll call for the horses."

Anne hurried across the floor, pausing to glance back at him as she reached the door. "By the way, I saw Will this morning."

"Oh? And how was the lad?"

"Friendly enough, though a trifle stiff." She stared at Francis suspiciously. "Did you speak with him, Francis?"

"Aye, though not in the way you fear," he replied. "The boy came to me earlier. He's not a bad lad, Anne—he just didn't understand. I set him straight quickly enough." He grinned. "Now hurry if you wish to ride. It's like to rain again, and I'll not have you drenched."

Stepping into the courtyard fifteen minutes later, Anne was surprised to see several heavily armed clansmen mounted and waiting beside Francis. She glanced at him questioningly. "Must we ride with an army?"

"Aye, love, but only a small one," Francis returned. "Glenkennon and his men may be miles away, but I've given orders no one rides out with less than a half-dozen men. We'll go for our ride, but we'll go armed and ready."

Conall led a dainty dappled gray mare to Anne's side. "Is my cousin protesting our company, Francis?" He scowled at her in mock severity. "What an ungrateful wench you are."

She laughed and allowed him to boost her into the saddle. "I'd never protest company, Conall. Rather, I hate to be a plague upon you!"

"No Highlander considers it a plague to ride with a comely lass, cousin." Conall winked broadly and moved away as Francis nudged Leven over beside her.

"How do you like the mare?"

Anne stroked the animal's satiny neck. "Well enough, I suppose, though I do miss Cassie. I hope she's been cared for."

"One of my men exercises her daily, but she's growing fat on the best hay in Glenkennon's stable. Don't fret lass; I plan to have her back."

She stared at him, amazed, then broke into helpless laughter. "Oh, Francis, is it Gawain? He seemed marvelous good with horses for a Lowlander."

Francis merely smiled mysteriously and shrugged his shoulders, giving Leven his head toward the open gateway. Anne put her heels to the mare, following Francis's lead out the narrow gate onto the wet, spongy turf of the meadow.

Crossing the open space, the riders entered the drenched woodland where shivering raindrops hung on every leaf. In spite of the damp, threatening weather, the band was in a mood of high glee, Conall and Francis swapping insults and Donald interjecting a wry comment now and again.

Upon reaching the narrow stretch of beach, the party halted, watching in awe as the breakers rolled in from the sea, twice as large and powerful as usual. Shells and pieces of wood littered the sand along with a number of large stones that had been flung up along the tide mark, mute evidence of the force at work beneath the waves. Anne longed to dismount and inspect each treasure at length, but she knew time did not allow it.

All too soon Francis ordered their return. The clouds had lowered and the mists were sweeping in again, heavy with the threat of rain. Shivering, Anne drew her cloak more snugly about her as the party made its way across the open moor south of Camereigh.

"Riders ahead, m'lord," one of the men sang out.

Anne glanced up in surprise. Had someone come after them? She watched curiously as horsemen began to emerge from the misty border of birchwood ahead. A cold breath of wind swept over them, whipping the manes and tails of their mounts and lifting the trailing fog from about the riders ahead.

Jerking her mare to a halt, Anne stared in disbelief. The man sitting his horse squarely in their trail was none other than Glenkennon.

CHAPTER TWENTY-NINE

$\mathcal{F}$or a moment, time stood still on that lonely windswept hillside outside of Camereigh. Nothing moved save the wind, which caressed Anne's face and breathed across the rippling grasses like a thing alive. All was silence—even the strident sea birds that usually filled the skies above Camereigh were strangely absent. Beside her, Conall broke the stillness with a furious expletive, but Anne could not drag her eyes from the hateful apparition materializing from the swirling mist ahead.

"Shall we make a push to get round them?" Donald asked softly.

"No." Francis shifted in the saddle, tightening his reins. "From his position Glenkennon can cut us off easily enough. We'd be forced back against the sea if we tried to run."

"There are eight of them and six of us. Let's take them," Conall urged.

Francis's eyes slid to Anne. "I think not, Conall." He returned to his study of Glenkennon. "The earl is signaling for speech with us. Let's oblige him, shall we?" He glanced at Anne. "Are you with us, lass?"

She nodded. "I'd like the chance to tell my dear stepfather what I think of him."

Francis gave her a look of approval and set his horse

forward at a slow walk, one hand resting motionless on his thigh in close proximity to both pistol and sword hilt. He rode seemingly at ease, his dark face impassive, betraying none of the thoughts which must have been whirling in his head.

Anne began to pray, silently—desperately. Not Glenkennon—not now. He should still have been miles away for God's sake! If only she had a pistol, a knife, anything!

When scarcely a dozen yards separated the two parties, Francis signaled a halt. Glenkennon walked his mount forward to meet them. His cold gaze turned to surprise when it reached Anne. "I wasn't aware you'd chosen to add a second charge of kidnapping to the list of your other crimes, MacLean. Not that it matters," he added. "One charge of treason is enough to have you drawn and quartered like the black traitor you are."

"Only if James agrees. Or have you dispensed with the need to request his majesty's permission?" Francis asked dryly.

Glenkennon's thin lips curled upward in a malicious grin. "I have full sanction to destroy you, along with the rest of this nest of traitors. But if I needed further cause, you've given it to me. No man will fault me for rescuing my daughter from the clutches of an outlaw."

Francis raised a questioning eyebrow. "Can it be you've not heard the happy news, m'lord? Several days past, Anne MacKinnon formally wed Francis MacLean before the eyes of the Kirk and several hundred witnesses. The bride's cousin gave permission for the wedding. You see, her stepfather wasn't invited. I'm afraid this is one marriage you won't be able to keep a secret, Randall."

If Glenkennon was surprised, he covered it quickly with a look of pitying amusement. "Anne, my dear, you were a fool to run to him. I suppose he's given you some trumped up tale, but I assure you it's false. You're my daughter and your place is at Ranleigh until I say otherwise."

Anne glared at him, swallowing back the hot words tha

sprang to her lips. She had best hold her tongue, lest she make matters worse for Francis.

"What? Nothing to say?" Glenkennon shook his head. "I suppose an annulment of this misbegotten marriage is out of the question now, but you'll make a lovely widow. Black is such a becoming shade to women of your complexion."

"Did it become my mother?" Anne asked with biting scorn. "Did she wear black after you murdered my father?" She met his gaze evenly. "I shall wear crimson when they lay you away—crimson, a glorious shade of rejoicing!"

"Such spirit," Glenkennon said with a cold smile. "I'm afraid poor Percy deplored it almost as much as I. And what of you, MacLean?" he asked, turning to Francis. "Were you surprised when you took your virgin bride to your bed? Did she come willingly . . . or were you forced to use a bit of persuasion?"

Conall's hand grasped the curving butt of his pistol, but Francis halted him with a glance. "What do you want, Randall?" he asked, coolly ignoring the earl's goading.

"Why, your death, MacLean. I make no secret of it."

"And how do you propose to accomplish it?" Francis inquired in a hard voice.

"Oh, there are many ways, but I've decided on taking the pleasure personally."

Francis looked pointedly over the hillside behind Glenkennon. "I see no force of men backing up your brave talk."

"I've no doubt you know to a certainty how many men I have and exactly what their position is. But you see, now I've no need of them," Glenkennon said with a triumphant smile. "I've but to raise my finger and there will be seven pistols trained on your lovely wife. Unless you wish her death, you'll meet me now . . . alone."

"I'm happy to oblige you," Francis replied curtly. "You can have no objection to my sending the lady from the field. I'll not have her watch."

"None at all," Glenkennon replied affably. "However, if anyone comes over that hill from the direction of Camereigh, I shall give my men orders to shoot you and as many of your men as possible . . ." he smiled mirthlessly, "before they shoot us." He turned to Anne. "I shall come for you later, my dear. We've much to discuss." With a mocking bow in her direction, Glenkennon turned his horse and rode back to his men.

Anne watched him ride away with a feeling of despair. He had some trick up his sleeve, she was sure. She turned. "Francis, you can't—"

"There's no time for it, lass," he said, abruptly cutting her off. Swinging down from Leven's broad back, he lifted her from her mount. He grasped her shoulders, his eyes boring into hers. "Listen to me, Anne. I'm sending Conall back to Camereigh with you. Go with him and obey his every word, even if you don't understand. Time may be of the utmost importance. If he says move, you move! Understand?"

She shook her head. "I'll not go anywhere without you, Francis. Besides, you need Conall here. Glenkennon won't fight fair! Don't you know that by now?"

His hands tightened on her arms and he shook her in exasperation. "There's no time to explain it, Anne, but you must go! Trust me . . . I'll join you as soon as possible."

Donald stepped forward. "Go now, lass," he said curtly. "Every moment you're here puts the lad in more danger. He'll fight the better knowin' you're safe."

Anne stared at Donald, knowing his words were true. Glenkennon would use her to destroy Francis if he got the chance. "You're right," she whispered around the growing lump in her throat. "I . . . I'll go if you say I must, Francis."

He caught her chin, tilting her face toward him. "Don't fret, lass. I'll join you at Camereigh shortly." His hands dropped to her shoulders and he drew her roughly into his arms. "I love you, Anne MacLean," he whispered. "No matter what happens, remember that." He bent his head his mouth slanting across hers as if he sought to possess all of her in the brief moment left them.

She clung to him desperately. Dear God, what if he never held her so again?

Francis released her and stepped back. "Conall, I'll put her on Leven. Make sure the devil doesn't break her neck." Catching her about the waist, he lifted her onto the stallion's back. "Nothing Glenkennon has can catch Lancer or this brute. Take them if need be...and God speed."

Conall nodded grimly. "Look to your back, my friend."

Anne clutched the reins Francis thrust into her hands. He lifted her hand, wordlessly pressing her fingers to his lips. Releasing her, he stepped away. "Get her out of here, Conall," he said harshly, bringing his hand down hard upon the stallion's powerful satiny hindquarters.

The horses were away like a shot across the hillside. They had almost reached the crest of the hill when the first clash of steel rang out in the eerie silence. Anne sawed violently on the reins, swinging the plunging stallion about. She watched in horrifed fascination as Francis and Glenkennon came together with a lunge that sent the harsh sound of grating steel echoing across the moor again.

With an oath, Conall grabbed the reins from her hands, drawing her mount along with his as they sped toward Camereigh. They thundered into the gates to the surprise of the men on watch. Conall flung himself from his horse and immediately began barking out orders.

Sliding from her mount, Anne stumbled toward the door, unable to forget that terrifying glimpse of savagery on the hillside. The image of Francis lying dead at Glenkennon's feet filled her mind. The earl had been sure of himself, oh, so sure! Dear God, what devilish plot had he hatched now?

She scarcely noticed Conall as he grabbed her arm and forced her up the stairs. Tripping clumsily, she grazed her knee, the pain suddenly focusing her attention on the present.

Conall lifted her to her feet, dragging her up the last few steps. "Get into the trews and shirt you wore here, Anne," he bit out. "Tell Kate she's to bring me the bag she's packed. She'll know what I mean. Hurry now!"

His curt words struck through her. "I'm not going anywhere, Conall! Don't you know Glenkennon's planned some trick?" She grasped his arm desperately. "I'd think you, of all people, would stand by Francis now!"

"Christ, Anne! Do you think I want to leave?" He ran his hands through his hair distractedly. "I'd be back there now if I'd not promised to see you safe to France. Don't you understand?" he asked, gazing at her purposefully. "If Glenkennon gets his hands on you, everything Francis has done will be for naught."

"You can't mean to leave now! You can't think that Francis won't . . . won't . . ."

She choked on the words, the hot tears held in check so long suddenly springing to her eyes.

With a groan, Conall drew her into his arms and they clung to each other in frightened misery. "No . . . no I don't," he whispered. "And Donald will see Glenkennon plays no tricks. Francis'll probably come riding into Camereigh by the time you've changed, and he'll have nothing but a laugh for the fear he's caused us."

Anne could not answer. The hollow ache in her throat had spread to her chest, cutting off her breath.

"Now run, change . . . and be quick, cousin," Conall murmured. "I'll be waiting in the courtyard."

She nodded, feeling the harsh rub of his shirt against her damp cheek. "I'll hurry," she whispered.

It took only a moment to make the change. Hurrying downstairs, Anne raced across the courtyard where a small crowd was gathering before the open gates. At sight of her, Janet started forward, putting an arm around her and drawing her close.

Anne squinted across the soggy meadow into the misty treeline. "Shouldn't they be returning by now?"

"Aye. But they'd have fought like ten demons," Conall said grimly.

Anne strained her eyes for any hint of movement across the meadow. Francis would defeat Glenkennon. He had to—it couldn't end like this, she thought fiercely. Dear God, please let him come back to her! Nothing else mattered if only he were alive!

Something moved in the misty bank of trees. She took a step forward, attempting to see. Beside her Conall groaned and caught her shoulder as Donald rode slowly into the open leading her gray mare. A body was slung across the saddle, the laird's cloak wrapped carefully around it. "Dear God . . . no," she whispered, flinging off Conall's hand and stumbling forward. "No, please no."

Lifting tear-filled eyes from her mare's grim burden, she watched the remaining clansmen follow Donald from the wood. She blinked once, twice, trying desperately to clear her vision. One unusually tall, dark clansman raised his sword weakly, waving it in a sign of victory.

There was a triumphant shout from the guards on the wall above. With a cry, Anne began to run. Out the gates and down the hill toward the riders she flew, tears streaming unchecked down her face.

Francis spurred his horse forward, jerking it to a halt as he drew even with Anne. He slid from the saddle, leaving the reins to trail along the ground as the animal bounded toward Camereigh.

She had a hasty glimpse of a torn, bloodstained shirt, then she was caught up in a crushing embrace that swept her from the ground. For a moment she knew no more. She returned Francis's fiery kiss with a fine disregard for Donald and the grinning clansmen who rode slowly past them.

"You're hurt," she said when Francis finally released her. She pushed away and gazed at him in dismay. His shirt was

rent in a dozen places, the fine white linen a disreputable
combination of blood, sweat, and dirt. A makeshift bandage of torn cloth covered his left shoulder, but dark red
blood oozed sluggishly through the pad. He reached for her
again. "For God's sake, Francis, stop it!" she snapped.
"You'll bleed to death if we don't get you inside!"

"It's no' so bad as it looks, love. Above half of it is
Glenkennon's," he said with a wry smile. "I've nothing but
a few scratches, and this," he said, indicating his shoulder.
He brushed a tear from her cheek with a gentle finger.
"You didn't think you'd seen the last of me, did you, lass?
I've told you before—I'm no' so easy to be rid of."

She could not return his smile, not when his life's blood
still spilled from his body. She took his arm and together
they started toward the gates.

Francis kept his right arm around her, holding her firmly
by his side as his family and clansmen swarmed around
them. He was leaning against her heavily now. He must
have been more sorely hurt than he would admit, she
thought fearfully. "Conall! Donald! Help me get him inside before he bleeds to death!"

Francis winced as Conall caught his arm. "Gently lad,"
Donald murmured. "He took a nasty thrust."

They started toward the hall, but Francis hesitated,
glancing back over his shoulder. "Walter."

The young clansman holding Anne's gray mare came to
attention.

"Get the earl's body inside. Tell Kate he's to be laid out
in the chapel as befits his rank. And send a rider after
Charles Dorton. We'll need a churchman to speak over
him."

Donald spat disgustedly on the cobbles. "If you ask me,
the man doesna deserve it." His eyes moved slowly around
the group. "His lordship had a suit of linked steel beneath
his jack. No doubt, he thought Francis couldna touch
him."

A low growl of anger rumbled from the men. Anne

stared at Glenkennon's body in disgust. He lay so still, his blood trickling down the mare's leg to puddle in the grooves between the cobbles. She could scarcely believe that he no longer had the power to harm her, that she and those she loved were beyond his reach for ever. It could so easily have been Francis. Her hold tightened on Francis's arm.

"Leave it be, Donald," Francis said wearily. "It's over now."

With Conall's help, Anne got Francis installed as comfortably as possible on the settle in the private hall. She quickly removed what was left of his shirt, while Donald and Janet fetched bandages and salves. Setting to work at once, she washed the blood from his wounds, giddy with relief none were as deep as she had feared.

When Donald returned, he knelt beside Francis, gingerly removing the blood-soaked rags he had hastily bound against Francis's shoulder. As the cloth came away, Anne barely stifled a gasp. Glenkennon's sword had laid the flesh open to the bone. She bit her lip. It was a bad wound. What if the bleeding could not be staunched?

As if reading her thoughts, Francis glanced up and smiled thinly. "'Twas meant for my heart, lass. Be thankful Randall's aim was off." He winced and drew his breath in sharply while Donald packed the wound tightly to stop the fresh bleeding. He recovered himself as the wave of racking pain subsided. "Where's Ian?" he asked, twisting his head in an attempt to see around Donald.

Ian stepped forward. "Here, Francis."

"Are your MacDonnells armed and ready to march?"

"Aye, and hot to avenge Glenkennon's trickery!"

"As you see, this shoulder may tie me by the heels a few days," Francis said, leaning forward. "Take Robbie and his men and as many MacLeods and Grants as can march on the moment and move south to scatter Glenkennon's troops."

"Jamie." He turned to his brother-in-law. "You bring the

Camerons and the MacGregors up a league or so to the
rear in support. And mind, I want no fighting unless it's
forced on you. To now, no one's raised steel against the
crown save myself, and I'd as soon keep it that way. Glenkennon's men should scatter and make a run for it at first
sight of your force, but you never know," he added grimly.
"There's no telling what fool is leading them now. They
might decide to turn and make a fight of it."

He leaned against the settle back and closed his eyes,
lines of pain and weariness etched deeply about his mouth.
Anne slipped a pillow beneath his arm, wishing she could
do something more to give him ease.

The room cleared quickly as men hurried to do the
chief's bidding. Francis tried to settle his shoulder more
comfortably, but nothing seemed to lessen its fiery ache.
He glanced at William Cameron, still hovering nearby.
"Pour me a drink, Will. This shoulder's plaguing me like
the devil."

Will nodded, hurrying to pour a stiff whiskey from the
side-table.

Francis accepted the glass gratefully, draining it in two
long draughts that quickly dulled the throbbing pain in his
arm. Sagging back against the pillows, he closed his eyes,
letting a numbing weariness take over.

"How'd you do it, sir?" Will asked softly.

A grim smile twisted Francis's lips. "You mean Glenkennon?"

"Aye."

Francis opened his eyes. "I learned quick enough I
couldn't pierce steel, so I had to bide my time, waiting for
a chance at his head or heart. I thought my time was up,
Will—he almost had me more times than I care to remember. God's blood, but the man was a swordsman!"

There was a long pause as he stared into his empty glass.
"I let him swing at my shoulder," he said at last. "With his
sword buried in me, we were close enough I could get my
blade through the arm hole of his mail. I must have

pierced his heart, for he was dead by the time I got him to the ground."

"And what of his men?"

"One drew a pistol, but Donald was watching for the like," Francis replied. "He winged the fool and the rest scattered for the woods like frightened rabbits."

"Mother of God, I wish I'd been there!"

"You could have had my place for the asking," Francis said dryly.

Anne's blood ran cold at the story. Glenkennon had come so close to triumph. "That's enough talking now, Francis," she said, putting a hand on his forehead to stroke the tangled curls back from his brow. "You must rest."

He caught her hand and pressed his lips against her wrist. "And you should change, madam wife," he responded, looking her up and down. "You've enough of my blood covering you to make me wonder I've any left."

She glanced down at her bloodstained clothing and nodded in agreement. "Will, can you sit with him, while I go upstairs to change? Mind you don't let him get up."

"I'd like to see this runt keep me down if I choose to get up."

Will grinned at her. "Don't worry. I can manage."

Anne bent and kissed Francis's brow, then turned and went out the door toward the stair. Relaxing with a satisfied smile, Francis closed his eyes.

For several minutes silence reigned in the room. Then the stillness was broken abruptly by a woman's high-pitched scream and the noise of shattering glass from above.

For a split second the two men stared at each other in amazement. Then Francis was up and across the room, grabbing up his freshly cleaned sword. He took the stairs two at a time, Will following close on his heels. Kicking open the door to his chamber, he flung himself into the room, sword at the ready.

The sight across the floor checked him on the threshold. On the far side of the room, Anne stood motionless amid the wreckage of an overturned table and the shattered decanter and glasses that had stood upon it. Behind her stood Edmund Blake, calmly clasping a knife to her throat.

CHAPTER THIRTY

$\mathscr{A}$nne fought down the urge to scream again as Francis lurched into the room. He swayed, then leaned weakly against the door facing for support. Above the sound of her own breathing, she heard the noise of running feet below. Help was on the way! She strained against Blake's hold, but the man was surprisingly strong. She couldn't break his grip.

"Francis! Thank God it's you," Blake breathed, lowering his blade.

"What's the meaning of this, Edmund?" Francis snapped, gesturing toward them with his sword.

Blake loosened his grip. Taking advantage of his slack hold, Anne flung herself out of his arms and across the floor to Francis's side. Without her as a hostage, the MacLeans could easily handle Blake.

"I'd no wish to frighten the girl," Blake began apologetically, "but she screamed when she saw me, and I knew your men would be on me in a trice. I'd no desire to be run through by some fool of a clansman who'd not think to ask questions till after he'd put a hole in my chest."

Francis nodded curtly, then turned to Anne. "I'm sorry you've been frightened, lass. It's all right—Edmund Blake is a friend."

"Francis, no! Have you forgotten I heard him planning

your death?" She clutched his arm. "I don't know how he's tricked you, but he's no friend to us!"

By this time a dozen angry clansmen had gathered in the corridor, weapons in hand. Francis shifted so all could see him. "There's naught amiss, lads . . . just a misunderstanding. We've played Glenkennon for a fool. Edmund's been my informant at Ranleigh for years." He turned to Will. "Take these men downstairs and see if you can calm things down."

Will glanced hesitantly from Blake to his uncle. "I'll stay with you," he said stubbornly.

Francis shook his head. "I'll call if I need you. Now be gone. I've private matters to talk over with Edmund."

Will nodded doubtfully. Ignoring Anne's imploring look, he closed the door softly behind him. Worried Macleans clustered around him at once. "Find Donald and Conall," he ordered. "They may know more of this. Naill, you and Murray remain by the door. If you hear anything unusual, break it in!"

Inside the spacious bedchamber, Francis moved across the floor, carefully avoiding the scattered fragments of broken glass. He held out his right hand. "It's good to see you, Edmund, though you chose a hell of a way to announce yourself into my household."

Edmund clasped Francis's hand firmly. "Young Bruce managed to smuggle me inside. Once within I found it easy enough to make my way to your door. I thought it best to await you here, thinking no one would see me." He lifted one pale eyebrow. "I should have known you'd have someone sharing your chamber by now."

Francis glanced at Anne. She had not moved from her place beside the wall. "Anne and I were married three days ago," he said quietly. "I'm sorry you missed the celebration."

"So am I." Blake studied Anne with the unnerving gaze she remembered. "From the looks of the child, she still thinks I mean to harm you." He chuckled mirthlessly. "I doubt even you can convince her I'm not the devil himself come up from hell."

Francis did not smile. "I don't envy you those years in Glenkennon's service," he said. Turning to Anne he held out his hand. "Come here, lass. You must meet another of your kinsmen. James Edmund MacKinnon—the man you've known as Edmund Blake."

Anne stared at Blake in surprise. "No, Francis," she said, shaking her head, "this is a trick. Blake's been with Glenkennon for years! I remember his name from my childhood when Glenkennon spoke of Ranleigh." She moved to stand protectively beside Francis. "Sir, do you deny you schemed with my fa... with Glenkennon to murder Francis?"

"No, child, I don't deny it," Blake stated in his composed voice. "I schemed with Glenkennon to murder your husband on several occasions, but I made sure Francis knew the plots as well." His crooked smile twisted his face. "That evening we three met at the loch, you'd stumbled upon a meeting between us."

She stared at him silently, remembering that evening clearly enough. Could it be that Francis had gone there to meet him?

Francis put an arm about her. "It's true, Anne. Edmund kept me informed of everything at Ranleigh. Through him I knew Glenkennon's plans as soon as he made them. How do you think I slipped in and out of Ranleigh so easily? I know no witchcraft." His gaze shifted back to Blake. "I owe Edmund my life many times over."

Anne studied Blake's pale, expressionless face. Suddenly, the pieces of the puzzle shifted into place—things Francis had hinted at, Blake's own behavior when he had kept her away from Percy that last evening at Ranleigh. It seemed incredible, but it had to be true.

"You must forgive me," she said, meeting the man's penetrating gaze evenly. "I've been used to thinking you the enemy so long, it will take time before I'm comfortable with you in this light. I'd not wish you to think me ungrateful . . . especially after all your help."

He smiled. It was the same twisted smile that had used to make her go cold with dread, yet now it spread to his eyes, warming their wintry bleakness. "I understand your feelings, madam. Few would be so truthful. I often wished to tell you you'd a friend at Ranleigh, but I knew it'd not be wise. You'd not have believed me, and besides . . . it amused Glenkennon to see your fear. He trusted me the more because all others despised me."

There was no hint of self-pity in his voice, yet his words touched her as nothing else might have. She had feared him, as had everyone else at Ranleigh. He had borne loneliness all these years in order to destroy Glenkennon. "You're a MacKinnon?" she asked uncertainly.

"Aye. I was naught but a lad in my teens when Glenkennon murdered your father. Save for a lucky chance that had me in France at the time, I, too, would have met my death." He gazed at Francis. "I've waited a long time to see Glenkennon meet his end, but thanks to you, it's happened." Scowling, he touched the bandage on Francis's shoulder. "We'd best get you to a chair—you're bleeding."

Francis glanced down at the fresh red stain, but shrugged Edmund's hand away impatiently. "It's only begun after that dash up the stairs. It'll cease if I sit quietly."

"Francis, for God's sake, sit down!" Anne exclaimed. "You've lost so much blood already you can scarcely stand." She sent Edmund a look of entreaty. "Help me make him rest, sir. The two of you can talk as well sitting down, I should think."

Francis grinned. "We'll have no peace if we don't do as she says, Edmund. Come, I've glasses and whiskey down the hall and much to say to you."

Anne saw Francis established comfortably in the laird's room before reluctantly leaving the two men to their conversation. Though she accepted Edmund's story, she could not shake off a nagging fear when she thought of him alone with her weakened husband. She would find Conall; surely he'd know if the man could be trusted.

"Tell me, Edmund, why was Randall at Camereigh this morning with his army still several days' march to the south?" Francis asked, settling wearily into a chair.

"Hoping for an encounter with you. He was running out of money and time, and his troops were rebellious and growing worse by the hour. Glenkennon knew he'd never hold them for a siege, especially after learning you'd burned off your lands and there'd be no forage for men or animals."

Francis nodded. "I thought that might give them pause."

"Some of his troops had fought Highlanders before," Edmund continued. He blinked at Francis impassively. "You'd not believe the tales of savagery that were rampant among the men."

"Exaggerated by yourself no doubt," Francis said with a chuckle.

"Actually I denied them most vehemently, as I recall."

"Making the men all the more certain of their truth."

Edmund shrugged. "For the first time in his life, Glenkennon found he couldn't terrify his men into obedience. He was beside himself with rage, knowing he hadn't the gold to mount another expedition of the like. I added fuel to the fire with news a move was afoot at court to recall him from Scotland."

"And was there?" Francis asked, leaning forward eagerly.

"Not that I know of," Edmund replied with his twisted smile, "though I know our beggar king was growing tired of Glenkennon's requests for money. Jamie'll cajole little more gold from his suspicious English subjects to pour willy-nilly into Scotland."

He sipped his whiskey thoughtfully. "Glenkennon's determination to see you dead had become an obsession. It led him to act unwisely, thus he played into our hands. He hoped to lure you out of Camereigh and destroy you himself, thinking once he'd removed you, the clans would be demoralized and his men could easily hack them to pieces." Edmund's cold, lashless eyes met Francis's gaze unblinkingly. "He didn't count on you gaining the upper hand. Glenkennon thought himself indestructible. It was his greatest weakness."

Silence pervaded the room for several long moments. Francis emptied his glass and set it down on the table. "What think you of my chances for avoiding a hangman's noose now, Edmund?"

"How fast are your horses, lad?"

Francis leaned back with a grim smile. "That bad, eh? Well, my horses are fast enough to leave the English in a cloud of dust, and I've a ship waiting to carry me to friends in France should it become necessary."

"I'd keep them ready," Edmund said seriously. "England must view this affair as a challenge to her right to control us. After all, Glenkennon was the acknowledged voice of the crown here. Any attack on him is an attack upon England. However, it's not hopeless. James's English nobles have been clamoring for the constant unrest here to be ended, though they've not wished to advance a shilling toward it."

Edmund placed his palms together, studying his long white fingers thoughtfully. "And it would be an excellent opportunity for Jamie to repudiate Glenkennon's debts." He glanced up. "I've my suspicions Douglas was sent to Ranleigh to nose out what he could of Glenkennon's dealings with the Scots. I made it my business to watch him. I even allowed him to stumble on information suggesting the earl's agents stirred up unrest for the sole purpose of having him called in to put it down. Naturally, it was then his duty to seize the lands of the families involved."

"Douglas didn't like Glenkennon," Francis said softly.

"No. It wouldn't surprise me to learn you've a friend at court."

"I pray God he's successful," Francis said with a heavy sigh. "I've no regrets myself, but I'd hate to drag Anne into an outlaw's existence."

Edmund nodded and cleared his throat uneasily. "I deeply regret what happened to her at Ranleigh, Francis. It was all over and done before I'd an inkling of what Glenkennon planned. Believe me, I'd have risked all to stop it if I'd known."

Francis shook his head. "It was my own fault, Edmund. I should have had her out of there weeks before."

"None of us could have foreseen what that devil would do," Edmund returned. "The world thought her his daughter. I erred greatly in thinking that protection enough."

"Aye, but the two responsible are dead, and in time Anne will forget." Francis smiled slightly. "I've reason to think the lass happy enough with the present state of affairs."

Edmund chuckled. "Yes, save for me. I'm not entirely sure . . ." He broke off as Conall poked his head through the door.

"Edmund, you cold-blooded bastard! You know I'm glad to see you, but couldn't you think of some entrance save holding the lady of the house at knife point?" He chuckled and advanced farther into the room. "You've set the whole house by the ears, and Donald and I have had the devil's own time calming things down."

"Not being blessed with your engaging address, cousin, I did what was necessary to avert disaster," Edmund replied impassively.

"Well, I don't mean to interrupt, but I feel it wise for Francis to show himself below." He grinned at Francis. "Your people are getting more anxious by the moment."

"We're done," Francis said, rising. He turned and glanced down at Edmund. "One more question before I explain you to my household, Edmund. Was young Randall with his father's men?"

"No. He's still in the south searching for his sister."

"God's wound! You mean he doesn't know she's safe here?"

"I didn't dare inform the lad before things were settled with Glenkennon. I'm not sure Charles will look on her marriage with favor."

"He must be told of his father's death and Anne's marriage," Francis said bluntly. "See to it."

Some days later, Anne was sitting with Janet in the parlor when a door downstairs slammed and running feet sounded on the steps. Anne glanced up from her needlework and met Janet's questioning look. Rising, she moved to the parlor window and gazed down into the courtyard. Two sweating horses were being led toward the stables, while the men below stood in small groups, talking excitedly.

She turned to Janet. "Do you suppose it's news from England?"

"It's scarcely been a week since Glenkennon was buried," Janet returned calmly. "I doubt Jamie Stuart could have acted so quickly."

"I . . . I think I'll go downstairs," Anne murmured, trying to match Janet's calm tone.

Janet nodded and returned to her sewing.

Anne gathered up her skirts and hurried down the stairs, her heart beating heavily in her chest. She knew it was too soon for news, yet with every rider that entered Camereigh's gates, she feared—and hoped—word would come.

Francis had tried to reconcile her to the possibility that the news would not be good, yet she prayed fiercely he would be pardoned. For herself, she cared not where or how they lived, but she wondered how a man who lived and breathed for his clan might live apart from them and be happy.

When she entered the hall, Francis looked up from the circle of men about him. "Is there news?" she asked, holding his gaze.

"Aye, but not what you think. Your brother'll be with us on the hour."

"Is he alone?"

"He rides with a dozen men," Edmund MacKinnon put in, taking her arm and leading her to a chair. He poured a glass of wine and placed it in her hand. She sent him a grateful smile. She had quickly grown accustomed to Edmund's presence, even to the point of wondering why she had thought him such a sinister creature at Ranleigh. He was unusual looking, to be sure, but he was possessed of a mind that could untangle any problem. And Francis admired him; that was enough for her.

"Do you think he's coming to see me?"

"We've no way of knowing what's on the lad's mind," Francis returned. "I've just struck down his father, Anne. He may be coming here to avenge Glenkennon."

She gripped her glass tightly. Would the nightmare never end? The vengeance and killing just begat more killing. "You won't fight him will you, Francis? Your shoulder's just starting to mend."

"I've no desire to cross swords with Charles, but we must see what the lad intends."

They hadn't long to wait. Charles's party of horsemen clattered through the gates while MacLean clansmen emerged from all sides of the quadrangle, hands hovering near their weapons.

Anne watched as Charles dismounted and pushed his way through the circle of MacLeans. His eyes found hers, and his pace quickened. "Anne . . . Anne, thank God!" he exclaimed, grasping her by the shoulders. "I've been half out of my mind with worry! Are you safe?" He jerked her into his arms in a rough embrace. "Are you truly well?"

She smiled up into his anxious face. "Yes, I'm fine, Charles. I'm sorry you've been worried."

He held her an arm's breadth away, still studying her intently. "I've been combing every inch of the coast, imagining you in every possible danger. Ever since Bess told me about—" He broke off abruptly, drawing her into his arms again.

She pressed her cheek against his shoulder, closing her eyes. "It's all right, Charles. You've made everything all right," she whispered.

"And what of Bess?" he asked after a moment. "While I was gone, she disappeared from Ranleigh and I could find nary a trace of her."

Anne pushed away and glanced back at her husband. "Francis had her brought here. We were afraid of what might happen to her."

Charles swung to face Francis, keeping one arm protectively about Anne. "Is it true you've wed my sister, Mac-Lean?" he asked, his eyes going hard.

"Aye. We were married a fortnight ago."

He glanced at Anne. "If you were forced into this, it won't stand."

"No, Charles, it was nothing like that. Francis and I have wished to be married for months," she said, taking his arm. "Please come inside. I've much to tell you."

Charles followed them stiffly into the hall, gazing from Anne to Francis in growing consternation. "God's love, woman! Can you be happy knowing your husband killed our father?"

"Glenkennon was not my father," Anne said at once. Quietly but firmly, she recounted the story of their mother and the tragic MacKinnon clan, finally describing Glenkennon's plots against Francis and his last ill-fated attempt to destroy the MacLean chief.

Charles heard her out in unmoving silence. When she reached the end of her recital, he rose wordlessly, walking to the table to pour a tankard of ale. "He was an evil man . . . I suppose I've known it a long time now," he whispered, his throat working convulsively.

He took a long swallow of ale, staring blindly at the table. "But God, it's hard to admit of a man whose blood runs in your own veins! I kept trying to make excuses for him, even after I learned what he did to you, Anne. I went after Campbell, telling myself Father didn't realize the man Percy was. I blamed everything on Campbell..."

He glanced up in sudden outrage. "And do you know what Campbell did? He laughed! He actually boasted about the deal he'd struck with Father!" Charles swallowed hard. "About what he'd done to you."

Turning, he smashed his clenched fist onto the table. "God, I wish Campbell were alive again, so I'd have the pleasure of running him through once more!" He leaned forward, closing his eyes. "And Father... I should have left his house long ago."

"Was anyone with you when you fought Campbell, lad?" Francis asked curtly.

Charles shook his head. "We were alone when I challenged him, though his servants came running fast enough when he started squawking like a damned capon. Christ's mercy, the coward didn't deserve to die by the sword! I'd have hanged him from the beams in his own hall if I hadn't needed to shut his mouth before he spilled his filthy tale to half the world."

Anne rose and went to his side. "It doesn't matter anymore, Charles," she said placing a hand on his arm. She stared up into his tired gray eyes, suddenly realizing her words were true; the pain was gone. She smiled at Charles wonderingly. "It doesn't matter at all," she repeated softly.

Charles gazed at her silently. "I suppose we're only half brother and sister," he whispered. "Do you hate me, Anne ... do you hate me for being part of him?"

Her hand tightened on his arm. "You were never part of him, Charles. And as far as I'm concerned, you're my brother—the brother I'll always love."

Francis moved to join them at the table. "I'm in your debt, Randall. Campbell was my responsibility."

Gray eyes lifted to blue uncertainly. "You know I came here to meet you for Father," he admitted slowly. "But now..." He shook his head, his words trailing off.

"Aye, lad. I'd a hunch you'd think your honor demanded it," Francis said. His eyes narrowed thoughtfully. "No man can decide for you, but to my mind there's been enough blood shed a'ready."

Charles nodded. "And what honor can a Randall claim, after all?" he asked bitterly.

"A man must make his own honor—or disgrace," Francis replied. He caught Charles's shoulder bracingly. "You're tired, lad. Rest the night with us. Your sister would be thankful of your company."

Francis's eyes reassured Anne across the room. "I'll see to the lodging of your men and animals now and engage for the good behavior of my MacLeans. Kate will bring you food."

Charles watched the intimate smile Anne exchanged with the tall MacLean chief, feeling the cold clutch of loneliness about his heart. By the look of things his half sister had a husband who pleased her, but what had he save a shameful legacy of murder and deceit? MacLean was an honorable man; deep down Charles always had known that. But merciful God, what was he?

Charles slept poorly, and morning found him as troubled as when he had gone to bed. He had no intention of challenging Francis. He should by rights have been begging the man's pardon instead. And now that he knew the story of the MacKinnons, the sight of Edmund and Conall shamed him past bearing. It was their land he called his own— land they had been hounded from by his father.

During breakfast he announced his intention of riding for Ranleigh. Anne begged him to stay, but he was adamant. "Don't fret over me," he said at the sight of her worried look. "I've a desire to see England again. Scotland's not such a pleasant place for me now." He smiled slightly. "I won't be gone long, though. I'll send you word when I return, Anne."

Francis sent for the horses to be brought around, and the little group trailed forlornly into the courtyard.

Charles swung onto his fretting bay. "Take care of my sister, MacLean," he said, directing a hard look at Francis.

"Aye, with pleasure, lad," Francis returned. "You may not choose to take advantage of the offer, but you're welcome at Camereigh any time."

Charles stared down at him. "My thanks, MacLean." Transferring his reins into his left hand, he carefully extended his right toward Francis. "As you said, it's time for the bloodshed to be ended. Here's my hand, if you're not ashamed to take it."

Francis stepped forward and grasped Charles's hand firmly. "Godspeed, lad. Come back to us soon."

Anne sat alone on the sun-warmed beach. Autumn was upon the land. The chill rains fell more often, and heavy mists appeared each morning and sometimes lingered throughout the day. There had already been one hard frost, but the warmth of the sun that day belied the proximity to the season of snow.

Anne watched in drowsy contentment as gentle waves rolled up the narrow crescent of sand, greedily gobbling up what they could of the loose grains only to redeposit them upon the coast with each new movement of the waters. She removed her shoes and stockings, enjoying the feel of warm sand sliding between her toes and the radiant glow of the sun's powerful rays upon her upturned face. Life was so sweet, she thought dreamily. She no longer feared she might bear Campbell's child, for her time had come upon her soon after Charles's visit.

She drew up her knees, leaning her chin upon her arms, staring out over the tranquil expanse of glittering blue water. If only the news from England would be good . . .

Without warning, an osprey descended from the clear arc of blue above, scarcely breaking the surface of the water as it swooped with blinding speed upon its unwary prey. Clutching a gleaming fish in its curved talons, the great bird flapped triumphantly away.

Anne shifted uncomfortably, her contentment in the day's beauty suddenly fled. Could the wrath of King James descend unexpectedly from England with equally devastating results? Would soldiers come upon them in the dead of night as they had her father twenty years earlier?

Why had there been no news, she wondered fearfully. It had been a month since Glenkennon's death, ample time for action, yet still they knew nothing of how the matter was viewed at court. Francis remained outwardly calm, telling her the long silence was a good sign, but she knew he was worried. She often awoke in the night to find his place beside her in the great bed empty. Upon arising, she would find him standing motionless beside the window, gazing silently out into the night.

The crunch of boots upon sand brought her back to the present. She turned. Francis stood a half-dozen paces behind her, his leather jack thrown open to the warmth of the day, his raven-black hair tossing fitfully in the wind.

He stared at her a moment without speaking. "I've news from England, lass," he said at last. "A messenger just arrived with letters."

His face was a mask, telling her nothing. She scrambled to her feet, her anxious eyes never leaving his.

"It's good," he added hastily at her expression. "So damnably good I can scarce believe it!"

With a strangled cry, she flung herself across the sand into his arms. He swung her about, then set her down, keeping one arm about her.

"I've a letter from Nigel Douglas here," he said, lifting the paper, "writ with the full knowledge of the king. I'm to be pardoned," he went on slowly. "And not only that . . . Camereigh's to be created a barony."

"A barony!" she gasped. "And we thought we might be fleeing for our lives. Oh, Francis . . ."

He nodded. "Douglas must be a golden-tongued devil to have so neatly turned the situation to my benefit! Edmund was right. Douglas was sent here to investigate Glenkennon's handling of his duties. What he found made it obvious the earl was unfit to administer the king's justice. The Randalls have been stripped of their lands in England and must pay a heavy fine to the crown for Glenkennon's traitorous dealings."

"But . . . Glenkennon's dead," Anne said haltingly.

Francis frowned and gazed darkly out to sea. "Charles is a Randall. The lad won't succeed to his father's earldom, but he'll retain his property here in Scotland save Ranleigh and the lands immediately surrounding it."

At her stricken look, he drew her into his arms. "From what I understand, the lad preferred Scotland to England anyway. And he'll be close enough he can visit us often."

She buried her face against his shoulder, wondering at the swift pain his words had brought. Life was never perfect. It seemed with each pleasure there must be pain to balance the measure. "Yes, of course, but it isn't fair, Francis. Charles was so proud to be a Randall!" She closed her eyes, letting the comfort of his encircling arms bring her ease.

"Douglas writes that a new man will be appointed any day now to succeed to Glenkennon's duties at Ranleigh," Francis said, changing the subject. "The two under consideration are fair men and should be well respected here, as he says, 'in spite of being good Englishmen.'"

He brushed his lips against her hair. "We owe Nigel Douglas a great deal, I'm afraid," he murmured softly. "I hate to think how matters might have gone without his intervention. He writes he'll be returning to Scotland to help govern in the interval until James's new representative arrives. He's even looking into the old MacKinnon case. He writes that the whole thing stinks to heaven of Glenkennon's greed."

Placing a finger beneath her chin, he tilted it until she gazed up into his puzzled eyes. "Was the man in love with you, sweet?" he asked, half laughing and half serious. "I swear I know of no other reason to make him busy himself so on behalf of our families."

"Of course not," she responded with a slight smile, "though he was a friend I held dear those bleak days at Ranleigh."

"Just how dear?" Francis questioned politely, raising one intimidating eyebrow. His powerful hands moved down to embrace her waist, drawing her unresisting body close against his own. "Have I any cause for jealousy?"

Without answering, Anne slid her fingers caressingly over his broad chest to the back of his neck where the thick hair curled softly against the leather of his jack. She drew his dark head down to hers, whispering something in his ear that made him throw back his head in delight, his white teeth flashing against the bronze of his face as his rich laugh floated out across the tiny bay.

"And it is for me also, Anne MacKinnon MacLean... and will be for all time," Francis said softly, the amused expression on his face fading into tenderness while the sound of his laugh echoed from the towering granite cliffs behind them. His mouth lowered to hers in a message as ageless as the windswept rocks around them, while far above the unconquerable Highland winds whispered laughingly across the meadows of Camereigh.

Highland Passion

Anne stepped from the shadows, the lovely gown a gossamer shimmer that did little to hide the beauty of the body beneath. "As you see, m'lord, I'm not dressed to receive guests." She heard Francis's sharp intake of breath, watching with quickened heartbeat as his eyes slid slowly over her.

"Kate made the gown," she volunteered when he made no effort to speak.

"Kate is determined to help provide Camereigh with an heir," he replied softly.

Her blood began to burn with the heat of his perusal. "Then you like it," she said, walking slowly toward him.

Francis did not reply. Instead, his hand reached out and began a slow journey down the back of her neck and along her spine. She could see tiny pinpoints of light dancing in his eyes as he pulled her close and bent his head to kiss her. She buried her fingers in his hair, clinging passionately to him as he brought her to the edge of reason, hoping this moment would go on and on until the end of time. . . .